RUTHLESS EMBRACE

His brows snapped down and she quaked internally at the anger that flashed in his brilliant blue eyes.

"Have ye no more sense than to follow him? Ye are forever throwing yourself full fling into things ye don't understand."

She stiffened, irritatingly aware he was right, which only added fuel to her flaring temper. "Someone must keep track of those ridiculous pistols."

He drew an exasperated breath.

"Didn't ye realize it was a potentially dangerous situation? I'd rather ye were just a bit afraid."

"You'd know if I were. *I* don't hide beind a mask of stupid indifference."

That stung him, she saw. Before she had time to recover, to make the apology that sprang to her lips, he dragged her ruthlessly into his arms.

His mouth pressed firmly down on hers, not in anger, but with an evocative pressure that turned her bones to water and left her clinging to him, lost in a welter of desire she barely understood . . .

A Tempting Miss

JANICE BENNETT

ZEBRA BOOKS
KENSINGTON PUBLISHING CORP.

ZEBRA BOOKS

are published by

Kensington Publishing Corp.
475 Park Avenue South
New York, NY 10016

First printing: December, 1989

Printed in the United States of America

For Adriana—
for starting it all

Chapter 1

Stillness engulfed the drawing room of Halliford House in Cavendish Square. Eyes closed, Miss Augusta Carstairs faced the polished mahogany mantel above the blazing fireplace, mustering her forces. Abruptly she spun about, setting her dusky ringlets flying around her waist, and held out her hands, beseeching.

"Kiss me! Take me in your arms if that is your will!"

The only response to this dramatic utterance was a most unflattering giggle.

Miss Carstairs dropped her pose and fixed her fifteen-year-old sister with a baleful glare. "That was a *very* emotional moment, Lizzie. It's not supposed to be funny."

"I can't help it." Miss Elizabeth Carstairs tugged a false beard of a brilliant shade of carrot red from her chin and rubbed her fingers around her itching mouth. "It tickles."

"*Do* be careful, Lizzie, you'll ruin it!" In a cloud of sprigged muslin, Miss Sophronia Lansdon sprang up from the settee where she had been watching the rehearsal. Her mousy fluff of curls bounced about her plain face as she took charge of the maltreated whiskers. "There, I shall have to brush them now."

"Why do we have to use them in the first place?" Lizzie shoved at the dislodged strands of her brown hair in a halfhearted attempt to tuck them back into place.

"But they make you look *so* distinguished, Lizzie." Augusta schooled her countenance into a soulful expression, but her huge blue-gray eyes sparkled with mischief at her sister's disgusted face.

"Yes, they do," Sophronia assured her in all sincerity. She stroked the preposterously colored beard into a semblance of order and tried to return it to Lizzie's chin.

Lizzie made a sound perilously close to a snort and wrinkled her freckled nose as she ducked out of the way. "They look ridiculous. Besides, I'm not even going to be *in* the silly play."

"As a matter of fact, you are." Augusta smiled brightly at her horrified sister. "Monty has cried off."

"What? When you have so little time? That really is the outside of enough! Though I can't say I blame him, I suppose," Lizzie added judiciously. "No one in his right mind would want to play this role—or wear that thing."

"I still cannot believe Captain Montclyff could serve us such a backhanded turn." Regretful, Sophronia laid aside the maligned beard.

"Oh, can't you?" Augusta sank down onto a delicate Sheraton chair. "There is no telling what Monty might do. He is the most disobliging man. I have no idea what could have induced him to agree to be in my plays in the first place."

"Do you suppose he quit because he made such a cake of himself in the last one?" Lizzie regarded her sister with an air of too innocent curiosity.

"He—he didn't make a cake of himself—precisely," Sophronia protested. "He only forgot most of his lines."

"*And* had to have me repeat them for him." Augusta picked up the script from the low table beside her, glanced over the frequently rewritten lines, and knew the craven wish she had never thought up the idea of giving these plays in the first place. It was for such a worthy cause, though. She would do it again—and again—if it were a hundredfold as much work. The fact that the performances provided a delightful, exciting escape from her everyday, *un*romantic routine was of only secondary importance.

Resolutely, she turned back to her sister. "You must see we need you, Lizzie. We have only four days. Do you not want to help?"

"No," came her blunt response.

Augusta directed a look of severe reproach at her. "Our sole purpose is to raise money for the orphans from that dreadful war. You *cannot* be so hard-hearted. Or have you forgotten, after only three years, what it is like to lose your father in

8

battle?" To her consternation, ready tears threatened, which she blinked back. *She* hadn't forgotten—neither their father nor the dire consequences of being totally without financial support.

"I remember very well." Lizzie folded her arms in front of her and thrust out her stubborn chin. "But I think you might have thought up this idea earlier. If you'd performed one of your silly productions for Napoleon, I'll bet he'd have retired to Elba right then and there. That would have saved countless lives."

A sigh escaped Augusta. "She's right, Sophie. This play *is* awful, even with all the changes we've made."

Sophronia plopped down again on the sofa, clasped her hands in her comfortable lap and shook her head in resignation. "Do you think the others will mind if we alter a few more lines?"

"I don't know. Lieutenant Kettering actually *liked* that last scene," Augusta said dryly. "He told me—" She broke off, not liking to remember the fulsome compliments that accompanied his remarks. She didn't want his attentions—or those of any of the other gentlemen who paid her ardent court. She was cursed with a contrary heart, and she knew it. It wasn't reasonable, after two years—including one brilliant London season—to long for a certain 42nd Highland Regiment major, who appeared so dashing in his kilted uniform yet looked so disapprovingly upon the romantic fantasies of a sixteen-year-old damsel.

"Lieutenant Kettering wouldn't like that scene if he had to be in it." Lizzie's words recalled Augusta from her melancholy thoughts, back to the argument at hand. "And you'd think Lord Wentworth would be ashamed to be directing this play. You can't tell me he approves of that nonsense you just spouted!"

"He agreed to the changes, remember," Sophronia said.

"Well, he'll have to find another hero," Lizzie informed them. "I said I'd help with rehearsals, but I refuse to stand up in front of a room full of people and tell my own sister that 'the glittering stars in the velvet sky pale before the whatever of her eyes.'"

"Glory." Augusta and Sophronia supplied the missing word together.

Augusta drew a long ringlet over her shoulder and twisted the glossy dark strands about her fingers. "It's only for one performance," she tried. "Perhaps we can turn it into a farce. I'd only need to change a few words here and there. Would you not enjoy making a mockery of these ridiculous lines, Lizzie?"

"No." The syllable was uncompromising.

"But Lizzie—"

"I will not wear that beard."

Augusta sighed, recognizing her sister's unmovable stubbornness. "Very well. But until I can find someone with a kind heart and pity in his soul who can *sympathize* with the poor victims of the war"—she fixed her sister with a stern eye—"you will have to fill in."

Lizzie made no further protest, so Augusta rose to collect pen and ink to make what improvements she could.

"It's a pity Lord Wentworth is so serious about the play." Sophronia watched Augusta dip the quill and scratch out several words.

"I was lucky he agreed to help. He is making a much better job of directing us than your brother did on the last one. And he cares as deeply about providing for the orphans and widows as I do." Augusta lined through "billowing tresses" and instead likened the play's heroine's hair to "a midnight waterfall of silk," and felt a touch of satisfaction as Lizzie groaned.

"It does become somewhat monotonous, though, to hear him go on about how anything the military does is horrid. But I suppose all diplomats are like that." Sophronia frowned as Augusta crossed through the next several words, then nodded in agreement with the changes. "The war went on for far too long," she added. "It is such a relief now that Bonaparte is settled on Elba."

Augusta laid the pen aside. "There, Sophie, do you think you could manage a fit of the vapors at the end of the second act?"

"If she doesn't, the audience will." Lizzie plopped down on a chair before the crackling hearth and twitched the script out of Augusta's hand to glance through it. "Lord, you don't think Wentworth will agree to direct a farce, do you? He's been so vocal of late about 'unseemly levity in the military.'"

Augusta smiled, but it slipped awry. "You even missed his

little discourse at the rehearsal last night. He kept going on about the need for more stringent discipline among the officers. I believe he wishes they had all been sent to America so they would have some fighting to keep them occupied. He was calling for court-martials for even the most trifling offenses."

"It is ridiculous!" Sophronia's hazel eyes flashed. "After all they have suffered on the Peninsula, and now with this new war in America. It—it is only natural they should be a little wild!"

"Of course it is. When I think how many of them were wounded—" Augusta broke off, dismayed by the pain a memory could bring. She hadn't even seen Major Edward MacKennoch since he'd been shot; not, in fact, since that terrible day he'd come to say good-bye to her family. . . .

"Lord Wentworth has the weight of the Diplomatic Service behind him, which gives him the ear of some very highly placed officials." Again, Lizzie's words recalled Augusta's drifting thoughts.

"They will ruin the lives of any number of young gentlemen, all because of—of high spirits!" Sophronia exclaimed.

Lizzie fixed her with a considering eye. "Has your brother been up to some bobbery again?"

"No! He—" Sophronia shook her head, but tears filled her eyes. "Excuse me, I—" She sprang to her feet and hurried from the room.

Augusta exchanged a speaking glance with her sister and followed.

Sophronia stood in the marble-tiled hall, her fingers gripping the edge of a marqueterie pier table that rested against the paneled wall. Her shoulders trembled. Augusta walked quietly up behind her and laid a gentle hand on her friend's arm.

"Come up to my room." Without waiting for a response, she took Sophronia firmly by the elbow and led her along the richly decorated passage to the curved mahogany staircase. Two flights of steps brought them to her bedchamber on the second floor, overlooking the front of the house and the little garden with its wrought-iron railing at the center of the square. It was all so safe, so respectable—so totally unromantic. She closed the door behind them and turned to Sophronia.

"Tell me."

Sophronia sniffed, gave her a quick, watery smile, and groped in her reticule for an embroidered handkerchief. She dabbed at her eyes and resolutely blew her long straight nose. "It—it is Perry." The words came out muffled by the fine lawn.

"I thought as much." Augusta sank down on the silken rose coverlet on her bed and patted the place next to her, invitingly. "What has your brother done now?"

"You make it sound as if he were forever getting into scrapes!" Sophronia glared at her.

"Well, you must admit, he is always ripe for any lark, and he does take the most outrageous starts."

A wan smile flitted across Sophronia's woebegone features and she sat down beside her friend. "Cork-brained notions, Lizzie calls them."

"What is it this time?"

Sophronia drew a shaky breath. "He—he hasn't told me, but I fear he has been gaming again."

"All gentlemen do. It's expected of them." Augusta spoke with all the assurance of a reigning Incomparable with one extremely successful London season behind her.

"Perry has grown wilder of late." Sophronia crumpled the handkerchief and stared unseeingly at the resulting mass of wrinkles. "If you saw him in an unguarded moment . . ." She broke off, as if seeking the right words to express her worry. "He has become defiant. Mamma hasn't the least notion how to handle him. She just says that Pappa was always hey-go-mad, too, and that Perry will settle down in time. But I'm so afraid he'll get into trouble before then." She looked up, a worried frown creasing her brow. "You know what Lord Wentworth says about discipline. If Perry is caught out in any—any indiscretion, he might well face a court-martial, and that would end his career."

Augusta bit her full bottom lip. "Is he in trouble? I—I *could* speak to Halliford."

Sophronia shook her head. "Not at the moment—at least, I don't think he is. But I live in dread of his doing something rash. Oh, if you knew what it was to worry so about a brother! But you have Adrian."

"True, Adrian is too busy studying to get himself into a fix

12

these days," Augusta agreed, not without considerable pride.

"And you have someone to take care of you," Sophronia went on.

That drove the momentary smile from her lips. "My sister's husband." Her voice sounded dry, even to herself.

Sophronia opened her hazel eyes wide. "But he's a duke! Halliford," she breathed. "You are so lucky, Augusta. He can solve any problem for you."

"Not quite every one." Her lips twisted into a sad smile. "But he is certainly useful—and very willing to help." She dismissed the subject of her important and influential brother-in-law. There were some situations that the power of the Halliford title and fortune couldn't magically vanquish. Not even the capable duke could undo the damage done by a silly chit of a girl when in the throes of her first, unrequited infatuation. A young lady of sixteen, no matter how romantic her disposition, should possess more decorum than to try to induce a gentleman to kiss her.

Augusta shook off the bitter memory. Scarcely a day seemed to go by that she wasn't haunted by that last encounter with Major Edward MacKennoch, and suffer anew a wave of mortification. That single episode had gone a long way toward maturing her. But it hadn't killed her dreams.

"Perry just needs a steadying influence," Augusta asserted, to give her thoughts a different direction.

Sophronia nodded. "I know. I'm sorry. I—I'd better be leaving. Will you be going to the Brockdales' tonight?"

Augusta shook her head. "Helena is not feeling quite the thing. We thought we would dine early and spend a restful evening at home for a change."

"You could come with us. Mamma is always happy to include you, you know that." Sophronia regarded her hopefully.

Augusta thanked her, but declined. She saw her friend downstairs, then went back to the Gold Saloon, empty now except for the forlorn red beard lying on top of the prop trunk in the corner. Lizzie had made good her escape.

Frowning, unable to shake off her unsettling concern for Sophronia and her brother Perry, Augusta made her way up to the first floor. At least, Perry enjoyed himself. Men had all the fun. They could get into scrapes and kick up a dust, and people

13

merely laughed. But just let a young female yearn for adventure and she would be branded a shocking hoyden, perhaps even fast, and be denied vouchers to Almack's.

The door to the sunny room at the front of the house dubbed the "ladies' sitting room" stood slightly ajar and Augusta peeped inside. In a padded wing-back chair drawn up before the crackling fire sat Helena, Duchess of Halliford. One hand held an embroidery frame and the other plied a needle with care in and out of the fine lawn of a christening gown. Demetrius, their extremely fat black cat, sprawled in her lap, dozing peacefully.

Helena looked up and a smile crossed her pale face as Augusta pushed the door wider. "Are you done already, Gussie? How was the rehearsal?"

In spite of herself, Augusta smiled. "Awful. We just can't get through that one scene without either laughing or arguing." She sank down on the Aubusson carpet at her sister's feet. "When is Halliford due back?"

"Is something amiss?" Helena's wide gray eyes flew to her sister's face in dismay. "Of course Halliford will help, he always does, but—"

"No, dearest." Augusta squeezed her hand. "Everything's fine."

"Am I being a goose?" Helena managed a smile. "It just seems there is always some scrape or calamity for him to deal with."

"The last three years have been lively, haven't they?" Augusta tickled Demetrius's stomach, and the cat stretched, then curled up again. "Enterprising, I think Halliford called us." She looked up at her sister fondly. "Will nothing ever convince you that he *enjoys* the—the somewhat unusual incidents Lizzie, Adrian and I have—er—perpetrated?"

Helena shook her head. "I do wish he were home. The house seems dreadfully empty when he's away, doesn't it?"

"Not for much longer." Augusta's grin turned impish.

Helena sighed ruefully and ran a hand along her increasing girth, causing the cat to protest. "Sometimes I think there might be twins."

Augusta's heart lifted at the prospect. "A little Halliford and a little Helena. It would be of all things the most delightful! And so—so *special,* to have two, who would look almost exactly

14

alike." She sank her head on the padded arm of the chair and gazed into the fire while her sister returned to her embroidery.

Helena had all the luck, Augusta decided. Rescued from abject poverty by a wealthy duke in the most romantic manner—what young lady could desire more? But a duchess's sister had no need for a knight on a milky white charger to rescue her from dreadful persecutions. Her life was one of luxuries, that was her problem. Beautiful dresses, ton parties, all the pin money she could desire. What she needed were a few of the requisite tribulations for a true heroine! Then perhaps her romantic dreams could come true.

She longed to live out a fairy tale of her own. She created such wonderful, idyllic dreams, full of delightful adventures. But then her handsome make-believe prince took on the features of a certain Scottish major, who told her to quit being so foolish, and her fanciful imaginings evaporated.

Augusta stood abruptly, unable to remain still. She dropped a kiss on her sister's forehead, then returned to the Gold Saloon. Lizzie would come back soon and they would have to go over that ridiculous scene again. She sat on the sofa near the fire, leafed through the script, but didn't really see it.

Her thoughts displayed a distressing tendency to dwell on Major Edward MacKennoch, but she forced them to concentrate instead on Helena. Not all was perfect for her sister—at least, not at the moment. Helena tried to conceal her illness over this long-desired pregnancy, but she couldn't fool Augusta.

Nor had she missed her sister's concern for her lively family causing her husband any more trouble. The duchess might be the sweetest creature in nature, but she suffered from an extreme sense of guilt at foisting her entire family onto the duke.

Augusta sighed again. Helena deserved to be happy and free from family worries. She had suffered enough, trying to care for her parentless brother and sisters before the duke came into their lives as if sent by a fairy godmother. And now, with a baby at last on the way, she mustn't be upset!

The door opened, and she looked up. Not Lizzie but the ever-correct Willis. "Yes?"

The butler bowed with just the correct degree of deference due his mistress's sister. "Captain Montclyff has called, Miss

15

Augusta." He stepped aside to permit the visitor to enter.

"Oh, has he," Augusta muttered, and rose for a confrontation. She did not take kindly to one of the main characters walking out on her play this close to the performance.

"My dear Miss Carstairs." Captain Goeffrey Montclyff, imposing in the gold-laced blue coat of the Tenth Royal Hussars, strode forward and captured her hands. "Lovelier than ever, if that is possible." He gazed down at her diminutive form, an unnerving, smoldering light flickering in the dark eyes that showed beneath an unruly shock of sandy brown hair.

"And quite vexed with you, Monty." Completely unmoved by his brooding, Byronic pose, she pulled free of his clinging clasp. "What on earth do you mean by withdrawing on us at the last moment?"

"Not at the last moment, my adorable Augusta. Any of the others can take on the role. But it's really too much to expect me to endure an audience every time I'm permitted to whisper words of love in your ears."

"Isn't that 'shell-like ears'?" she asked, never one to miss a quote.

He laughed softly, though his amusement did not reach his eyes. He closed the space between them and tried to slip an arm about her slender waist. "You must know that I adore you."

She dodged neatly. "I know it is fashionable to pretend to," she countered. Another quick step and she had an arm chair between them.

"You need not be shy or missish with me." He came closer and she backed off again.

"I believe you would do best to address yourself to Halliford." She collided with the settee and warily edged behind it.

"I thought we could approach him together." Still, he pursued.

"There is no need to approach him at all." She spoke as gently as possible, hoping to soften the blow.

His brow snapped down, and Augusta's gentle heart hardened. Not blighted love but blighted ambition showed clearly in his face. Her expected dowry, provided from the abundant coffers of the Halliford fortune, brought her more

16

offers than did her standing as last season's Incomparable. Mercenary rather than romantic dreams motivated too many gentlemen. Her temper flared.

She strode straight past him and pulled the bell rope, then turned to face him. "I am sorry to disappoint you. Willis will show you out."

"I am not a man to be dismissed so lightly." He stood his ground, his manner confident. His dark eyes rested on her in an unsettling mixture of avarice and desire. "You might do well to reconsider."

She shook her head. "I think not."

A scowl settled over his sardonic face as he strolled up to her. It sent a shiver through her. Instinctively, she stepped back.

"Yes, a fluttery little bird," he murmured. "You are quite right to be afraid. I will not be denied what I want. Remember that."

"In this case, I fear you must." She managed to keep her voice calm.

"Must I?" He didn't move, but suddenly he seemed to loom over her, threatening and dangerous. "Must I, indeed? It's not wise to cross me, you know. You will regret it, my dear. Mark my words, you *will* regret it."

The door opened and Augusta spun about in relief to see Willis standing on the threshold. Behind him, an under-housemaid peeped in, her eyes round and avid. Captain Montclyff laughed unpleasantly, made Augusta an elegant leg, and strode from the room.

Augusta sank down in the nearest chair. Had he just threatened her? What would Halliford—but she couldn't keep running to him with her troubles. It was time she found her own protector, her own capable husband. If only she could find a gentleman who was dashing, whose deep laugh would send thrills of delight through her, who would vanquish the fortune hunters and sweep her off her feet and away to his beautiful castle. . . .

She looked toward the fireplace, disturbed, needing to divert her mind. The script lay on a cabriolet table and she picked it up. That should occupy her fully. She wanted this play to be better than the last, to earn more money for their

17

cause. And she still had that ridiculous "kiss me" scene to re-hearse with the reluctant Lizzie.

The well-sprung curricle bounced as the off wheel struck an uneven cobblestone, but Major Edward MacKennoch barely noticed. He sat in withdrawn silence beside the duke of Halliford as the latter drove his difficult pair to an inch through the bustling traffic of the London streets. The laudanum was wearing off, he noted. His left knee ached, less from the ball that had been lodged there than from the rough-and-ready methods of removing both it and the resulting bone fragments. At least he had kept his leg—and his life. That made him luckier than many of his regiment, his doctor told him repeatedly. Major MacKennoch retained his doubts.

The chill February breeze ruffled the straight fair hair that protruded from beneath his shallow beaver. He made no move to pull his great coat closer about him. At least the discomfort of cold provided some feeling, some sensation of still being alive. He wasn't sure he deserved to be; he had failed to protect the regimental colors of the Black Watch. But now he had been offered the chance to redeem himself—if he was to believe the improbable interview he had just sustained with the Secretary of War.

"It's a considerable task." Halliford spoke at last.

"Aye." Major MacKennoch stared straight ahead.

Halliford cast him a measuring glance. "Lord Bathurst would not have assigned it to you if he did not feel you were able to handle it."

"Aye," the major repeated, his voice hard. "He did not say on what grounds his suspicions were based. Do ye know, Your Grace?"

Halliford shook his head. "He didn't tell me that. But if he's right"—and his voice took on a grim note—"it must be stopped."

"Selling military secrets to the French." Only the softest hint of a Scottish burr touched the major's words. "I would have thought someone in the Horse Guards would be better suited to discovering the truth."

Halliford cast him a quick glance before returning his attention to his horses. "Such an investigation would hardly

18

be secret. You have sold out—no one will suspect your interest. And posing as my secretary will provide you with a reasonable excuse to be asking questions around the War Office."

"Do ye mind having me thrust upon ye, Your Grace?" His mask of imperturbable calm firmly in place, Edward Mac-Kennoch turned to regard his temporary employer.

"Actually, I'm in need of a secretary. Bathurst knew that, which is why he asked for my help." Halliford grinned and an unexpected boyish charm transformed his harsh features. "I fear you will have to serve to some extent in that capacity to maintain the fiction. But your duties for me will be light— mostly reminding me of appointments and reading over my speeches before I give them to the House. That will leave you free to work on your assignment for Lord Bathurst."

"I will do my best to fill the position to your satisfaction, Your Grace."

"Then you can begin by dropping that damned formality. Is your leg paining you?" Halliford drew in the mettlesome pair and turned onto Oxford Street.

"Nay," the major lied. He kept his eyes focused somewhere between the off-horse's ears. He had been chosen for this assignment because of his very unsuitability. Well, why shouldn't people talk freely before him? A lame ex-42nd Highland Regiment major didn't exactly pose a threatening appearance to anyone.

"There is one duty I would be very grateful if you would take on immediately for me." Halliford slowed the pair to allow a carter's wagon to maneuver into traffic. "Do you remember my sister-in-law Augusta?"

Edward stiffened. Miss Augusta Carstairs. He remembered her all right, though it had been over two years since he had last laid eyes on her. A delicate beauty and outrageous flirt, even at the tender age of sixteen. She had made sport of him, knowing him far beneath her touch. He did not look forward to renewing the acquaintance.

"Have you heard of the project she instigated? Her group of volunteers performs short plays for the ton, about two a month, and charge an exorbitant fee for the tickets and refreshments. The proceeds go to aid war orphans and widows."

19

Halliford paused and the major realized some comment was expected from him. "Commendable."

"Augusta has a tendency to rewrite the scenes, though," Halliford explained. "And she likes to involve me in the process. That will now fall under your province."

Major MacKennoch almost thanked him for this dire warning, but stopped himself in time.

They turned onto Holles Street, then a block later onto Cavendish Square. Halliford drew the curricle up before a large mansion and his tiger jumped down and ran to the horses' heads.

Edward MacKennoch stood, gripped his cane, and carefully climbed down to the street. His square jaw jutted out and his piercing blue eyes took on a steely glint. Pain was a weakness. A MacKennoch never gave in to it—nor even admitted it existed. Leaning on the walking stick as little as possible, he joined Halliford on the flagway.

The front door flew wide and Willis, flanked by two footmen resplendent in the blue and silver Halliford livery, hurried down the steps. Under the butler's supervision, the lads quickly unstrapped Halliford's portmanteau and Edward's valise from the back of the curricle and carried the baggage into the house. Major MacKennoch stood back for Halliford to precede him, and they entered the elegantly appointed hall.

Halliford handed his curly beaver to Willis, who laid it with loving hands on the occasional table, then turned to help the duke remove his multi-caped driving coat. The major tossed his own hat aside and eased the thick fabric of his olive drab Benjamin off his stiff shoulders. Damn old wounds. They always returned to haunt him in cold, damp weather.

"Is Her Grace at home?" Halliford looked about the hall, as if hoping to see her.

"In the ladies' sitting room, Your Grace."

Halliford hesitated only a moment. "Go into the Gold Saloon, Major. I'll be down in a moment. I want to see how she goes on." Without waiting for a response, he almost bounded up the stairs.

Willis took Major MacKennoch's coat and handed it to the footman who had appeared from the nether regions. "In here, sir, if you please." He led the way across the tiled hall to a room that ran along the far side of the house. He bowed slightly, opened the door, then stood back to permit Edward MacKennoch to enter.

The major had barely a moment to take in the quiet luxury of his surroundings. His gaze riveted on the dainty figure in clouds of peach figured muslin who faced the fireplace opposite him, her back toward the door. Matching peach ribands caught her glossy dark ringlets up to the crown of her head, then permitted them to cascade down her back to below her slender waist.

He caught his breath as she spun about to face him, her eyes closed tightly. Lord, the chit was more beautiful than ever! That delicate oval face, the fringe of dark lashes, that impossibly perfect translucent complexion—something stirred within him, which he forced down.

"Kiss me. Take me in your arms if that is your will!" Eyes still closed, she held out her arms to him, beseeching, alluring, offering a promise too enticing to be refused.

Damn the chit and her flirtatious tricks! He thought he had made his feelings known the last time they'd met. His temper flared, momentarily overthrowing his habitual control. It might all be a bluff on her part, but he'd make her think twice before taunting him again.

He reached her in three unsteady steps, dragged her ruthlessly into his arms, and did her bidding. Her soft lips felt like velvet beneath his, and for the briefest moment he permitted himself to savor the experience.

She stiffened in his arms and pulled back. Huge blue-gray eyes filled with shock stared up into his and horror robbed her expressive countenance of its delicate color. With a strangled cry, she jerked free and ran from the room.

The major stared after her, his square jaw set in grim determination. In future, she'd behave; he'd seen to that. Damn her for making it necessary! And damn her for making him angry enough to give in to an unreasoned impulse.

He drew a deep, steadying breath. Losing his temper was an almost unprecedented experience. And in this case, a risky one. It might very well cost him his position in this household—and jeopardize his assignment.

Suddenly, his lips curved upward into a long-absent smile. That kiss had been worth it.

Chapter 2

Augusta slammed her bedchamber door behind her and sank onto the edge of her bed, every inch of her slender body trembling. Edward MacKennoch! Dear God, of all men, of all the things she could have been doing . . . *Where had he come from?* Complete chaos prevented her brain from functioning properly, but one thought came through, remorselessly clear. She had made a complete fool of herself *again* and redoubled his old disgust of her.

She fell back against the pillows, too distressed to consider her wrinkled gown or mussed hair. Even if she went to him and apologized, explaining about the play, the damage had been done. He had thought her flighty and shallow before. Now he would be convinced of it. Why, oh *why*, had she simply assumed it was Lizzie coming into the room and spoken those ridiculous words?

It was all Major MacKennoch's fault! A *gentleman* would have known she wasn't issuing open invitations to anyone who might wander in. He should have apologized for disturbing her, she could have explained about the scene, then everything would have been all right. But no, he behaved in the most abominable, insufferable manner and took shocking advantage of the situation! That she had extended to him a similar invitation in all sincerity when last they'd met over two years before, she tried hard not to remember.

She hugged herself, shivering. What a mess she had made of things! Again. She could only hope his visit would be fleeting, that he would leave as soon as he paid his respects to Helena, and she could try to put him out of her wistful thoughts once more. She went to the cheval glass mirror, straightened the damage to her appearance, and set off in search of Lizzie, that font of all household knowledge.

She was not disappointed. As she reached her sister's room, Lizzie came striding down the hall with her swinging, carefree step, obviously big with news. She must have been in the servants' hall again, for she carried a selection of fresh fruit on a tray. Her ability to cull snacks—and information on any subject—never ceased to amaze Augusta.

"Halliford is home," Lizzie told her. "And you'll never guess who he has brought with him."

Augusta rather thought she could, but kept her own counsel. For once, she forbore to lecture her sister on the impropriety of gossiping with the servants. "Tell me."

Lizzie led the way into her room and bounced down on the bed. "Major MacKennoch is his new secretary."

Augusta sat abruptly in the nearest chair, her knees not up to the task of supporting her. "His—do you mean he—Major MacKennoch—will be staying? *Here?*"

Lizzie nodded, apparently not noticing the anguish in her sister's voice. She selected a large red apple and crunched into it. "I must say, he looks grimmer than I remember. And that dreadful scar! Think we can cheer him up?"

Augusta closed her eyes and tried to prevent the shudder that ran through her. "I doubt Major MacKennoch would appreciate the attempt."

"Well, it would be for his own good. He's all closed up. Do you remember ever hearing him laugh?"

Augusta shook her head. What she remembered she was not about to share with her pragmatic and most unromantically minded sister. Lizzie would never understand her attraction—nor how she ever could have come to make such a complete fool of herself.

Lizzie took another generous bite. "Maybe he'll help us with the play. Do you think he'd like to wear the orange whiskers?"

And be the recipient of that "kiss me" line? Contemplation of that thought left Augusta feeling distinctly ill. "I don't think you should ask." She stood and went to the door.

"True." Lizzie giggled. "Could you imagine his face if a lady

23

ever begged him to kiss her?"

Augusta fled the room.

Major Edward MacKennoch sat across the massive cherry wood desk from Halliford in that worthy's bookroom, taking rapid notes in his precise copperplate. A formidable stack of papers lay before him. He finished recording his comment, then looked up at the duke, waiting.

Halliford leaned back in his chair. "Those are all the details Bathurst gave me before he called you in. Do you have any questions?" His unwavering regard remained fixed on the major.

Major MacKennoch glanced over the pages of closely written ideas and instructions he had just jotted down for himself. Everything seemed fairly straightforward. "Nay, Your Grace. Except—"

"Yes?"

"Do ye have any current business that might reasonably take me to the Horse Guards?"

Halliford's brow lowered in a thoughtful frown. "We'll have to think of something. On what topic can I give a speech where we would need information from them?"

"Dissatisfaction with this war in America?" the major suggested. "There was a great deal of talk on the ship that brought me back—and none of it complimentary."

Halliford nodded. "That might get them talking. And mention the Congress of Vienna to your acquaintances and see what response you get."

Major MacKennoch rose stiffly to his feet. "Shall I begin at once?"

"No. That might look suspicious. Settle in first. You already have quite a job just going through those." The duke gestured to the papers that rested on the corner of the desk. "Have you unpacked your things yet? Then why don't you? I won't be needing your help with anything until this evening."

The major bowed, then went out into the corridor. It was short, with only four doors opening onto it, and it led directly to the entry hall. Another, even shorter, corridor led off from there at an angle—toward the dining room and the basement kitchens. A wide, curving mahogany staircase that won his instant admiration led upward.

He climbed carefully, leaning on the banister and his cane, and paused to orient himself on the first floor. Several drawing rooms occupied one side of the house. The breakfast parlor stood opposite the landing. Through the open door, he glimpsed a sideboard laid with cups, saucers, and a teapot. Even cold, he could use some of that right now.

The tea proved to be lukewarm, but very satisfying. He poured a second cup, and balancing it on its delicate china saucer to take with him, he started for his room on the next floor.

And down the stairs toward him came a vision in a rose merino riding habit. A close-fitting hat covered the top of her dark brown hair, in which hints of mahogany glinted, and a plume curled against her delicately flushed cheek. Miss Augusta Carstairs hesitated on the landing, and her luminous blue-gray eyes opened wide in dismay. For all the world, she reminded him of a terrified fawn, frozen in its tracks the moment before it bolted.

Augusta felt the blood drain from her cheeks. She had avoided him all afternoon by remaining in her room. She should have known the moment she ventured forth—even to escape the house by riding in the park—she would run into him. She drew an unsteady breath and tried to regard him objectively. It wasn't possible.

The neat, no-nonsense cut of his coat of blue superfine and the military precision of his neckcloth suited him—though not nearly as well as had the kilted uniform he wore the last time they'd met. Red highlights glinted in the almost straight blond hair that waved back from his high forehead and just touched the collar of his shirt. Her gaze brushed across the deep scar that slashed his left cheek from the corner of his eye to the edge of his mouth, and the pain he must have known tore at her heart. His face was an expressionless mask, like a statue, devoid of human emotion and feeling.

But that was not the way he had been only hours earlier. Color returned to her cheeks in a rush. Firmly quelling her internal trembling, she forced her own expression into one of haughty disdain and took an unsteady step toward him. "Good afternoon, Major."

His mouth tightened and his piercing blue eyes held hers.

25

What little remained of her poise evaporated on the spot.

"Miss Carstairs." He spoke stiffly. With the briefest of nods, he moved past her, and leaning on his stick, he limped up the stairs.

She stared after him for a moment, then resolutely turned away and entered the sunny breakfast parlor he had just exited.

At the sideboard, she poured herself the last quarter-cup of cool tea, and found she no longer felt any desire for the late nuncheon she had sought. She stared moodily out the window and sipped the remainder of the strong liquid.

Edward MacKennoch. How she had dreamed of seeing him again. But not like this! In her mind, they always met at a country ball on a balmy summer's eve. She wore her most becoming gown and the Halliford sapphires—though she knew Helena would never permit her to wear colored gems in reality. That made no difference in dreams, though. The major always stopped just over the threshold of the ballroom, for he saw her immediately; he had eyes for no one else. His reserve dropped away from him. He strode directly to her side and drew her away from her admirers and into his arms for a waltz. He gazed down at her with undisguised worship in his eyes and she laughed easily and said exactly the right things to captivate him. . . .

A sigh shuddered through her. She was eighteen—too old to indulge in such ridiculous romantic fantasies. But oh! it was so much more fun than dull reality.

Why, though, she wondered savagely, must it be Major Edward MacKennoch, the most unromantically inclined gentleman of her acquaintance, who reduced her to a stammering heap just by his presence? He was handsome, in a rugged sort of way, though without his regimental kilt he lacked a certain measure of dash. Since coming to London, she had met any number of gentlemen whose romantic good looks and classic perfection of feature should have turned her head. But not one of them set off this uncomfortable turmoil within her.

The second footman tapped on the door with the information that her horse had been brought around and awaited her out front. She shoved aside her cup and hurried down. A good long ride was what she needed, something to clear her thinking. She could also use Lizzie's matter-of-fact bluntness and humor to jolly her out of her depression, but that young lady possessed a disconcerting habit of asking all-too-perceptive questions.

A chill wind whipped the skirts of her habit about her ankles as she emerged onto the street. February was much too early to be in town. She could only be glad so many others had also come ahead of the Season. The Congress in Vienna, as far away as it might be, kept the diplomats and members of Parliament busy in London.

She greeted Cuthbert, the large roan purchased for her by Halliford, and fed him the roll appropriated from the sideboard in the parlor. The groom held cupped hands to assist her into the stirrup, and in a moment she settled onto the quiet gelding's saddle. The lad then swung onto the back of his own chestnut, and as Augusta urged Cuthbert forward, he fell in just behind. The roan, long inured to the hazards of London traffic, plodded peacefully along the familiar route.

The park, much to her relief, appeared nearly empty; the icy nip of winter kept all but the most restless of the Fashionables indoors. After allowing Cuthbert to trot for one circuit, in which she encountered only two other riders, she urged the mellow beast into a controlled canter. A rousing gallop would do her more good, she reflected ruefully, but that was not something permitted in the park, even when thin of company. Another of life's staid, unromantic, commonplace rules.

As she began her third circuit, she heard her name called and turned to see Sophronia Lansdon mounted on her gray mare, and accompanied by her brother, Lieutenant Peregrine Lansdon. Perry, Augusta noted, looked even nattier than usual in a regimental coat of such undeniably elegant tailoring that she could only wonder at the staggering bill to his snyder it must represent. She reined in and waited for them.

Two things became abundantly clear as the couple neared: Sophronia was not happy; and Perry, despite the cocky nonchalance of his manner, was frightened. Augusta shoved her own problems to the back of her mind and managed a bright smile of greeting for her friends.

"How pleasant to see you." Sophronia took her hand in a warm grasp as if they had not seen one another only hours before.

"Chilly out, ain't it?" Perry Lansdon hunched his shoulders

as if seeking warmth in his coat. "Ridiculous weather to go riding in the park."

"Now, Perry—" Sophronia cast an uneasy glance at her brother.

"You're certainly looking smart today," Augusta broke in. "New tailor?"

Perry preened, but the haunted look in his eyes belied his pride. "Schultz."

"I didn't think it looked like Scott." Augusta nodded knowledgeably and was rewarded by a weak grin from Perry. "Are you not busy with your regiment this afternoon?"

Perry snorted. "Lord, there's nothing to do! Just morning duty, and we can get free from even that for rehearsals. I wish I might have joined in time to go to America—at least then I might have seen some action. That would have been something like! Even going with the Army of Occupation to the Low Countries would be better than this. It's devilish flat here."

"Augusta, you talk to him!" Sophronia exclaimed.

"Button up, Sophie." Perry glowered at his sister.

"He won't listen to me."

"Who could blame me? Lord, no one wants a pack of sisters forever plaguing the life out of one!"

"What's the matter?" Though Augusta thought she could guess. "Watiers?"

He flushed to the roots of his wavy brown hair. "What's Sophie been telling you?"

"Nothing." Augusta caught the docile Cuthbert's head as his nose strayed into a patch of new weeds at the side of the path. He came away chewing contentedly.

Perry threw a fulminating glance in his sister's direction. "Bunch of tattle-mongering females!"

"It's only natural that we worry—"

Sophronia made a deprecating gesture but he ignored her and rounded on Augusta. "What business is it of yours if I choose to have a flutter now and then?"

"None whatsoever. Have the cards been against you?" Her tone held only amused understanding.

He tried to grin, but it was a pathetic attempt. "Devilish," he admitted. "And the ivories, too. But I'll come about, never you fear. Not one to steer my barque off Point Non-Plus."

"Halliford says one can never win when one needs to."

28

A hollow laugh escaped Perry. "Lord, he's in the right of it. But that's not a problem he's ever faced, I'll wager."

"Only when he plays with Lizzie and she holds him to ten counters. Are you scorched?"

He glanced up at her, startled by her bluntness. "Oh, nothing to keep me awake at night or anything like that. I'll be flush again in no time. I have no end of nacky notions, just you wait and see."

Augusta glanced at Sophronia's frowning face. Perry's denial of being in the basket sounded just a shade too casual. "What 'nacky notions' in particular?"

"You're as bad as Sophie! Just never you mind. Maybe I'll borrow Roddy's lucky pistols. After all, they worked for that damnable fellow Montclyff so I don't see why they shouldn't work for me."

"What on earth do you mean?" Augusta glanced at Sophronia for a clue, but her friend shook her head in bewilderment.

"Now, you're not to go telling tales, you hear?" Perry fixed the two ladies with a compelling eye. "Mum's the word."

"About what?" Augusta demanded.

"Roddy. He's got a pair of dueling pistols, beautiful things, made by Manton, and set with a couple of blood red rubies."

Augusta shivered. "How—how appropriate."

Perry grinned with real enthusiasm for the first time. "Thing is, you see, it's rumored that no one who's used 'em has ever missed."

"Perry!" She fixed him with a stern eye. "You're not going to—"

He laughed, repressed excitement glinting in his eyes, banishing his earlier distress. "No, I'm not taking to the High Toby with 'em. But they're *lucky.*"

"In what way? And what has this to do with Captain Montclyff?"

"Oh, he borrowed 'em one night when Roddy was about three parts disguised. Didn't use 'em, precisely, just stuck one of 'em in his pocket before he went to a certain little gaming hell, just in case."

Augusta didn't ask in case of what. Based on her brief and not altogether pleasant acquaintance with Captain Geoffrey Montclyff, she decided she would rather not know.

"And he won," Perry went on, his enthusiasm growing. "So he kept the thing and went again the next night. And do you know what?"

"He won again?" Augusta regarded him in concern. A three-year acquaintanceship with Lieutenant Peregrine Lansdon left her with a pretty fair understanding of his somewhat erratic thought processes. "So you plan to borrow them, too? What does Lord Roderick think about that?"

Perry hunched a shoulder. "If he doesn't know, he can't mind, can he?"

"Perry!" Sophronia stared at him, dismayed. "You wouldn't—"

"*Borrow* them, I said. Dash it, you make it sound like I meant to steal the damned things!"

"Perry!" Sophronia protested, shocked by his language.

Perry flushed. "Don't get into such a flap about it, Sophie. And mind you keep your tongue. Don't know why I'm telling you all this, for I never knew such a young rattle-pate as you."

"As if I would! You know very well it was Dolly who always told when we got up to any mischief."

"Why don't you just *ask* Lord Roderick if you can borrow them?" Augusta suggested, neatly interrupting an argument she knew from experience could go on for a very long while.

Perry stared. "What cork-brained notions you females take into your cock-lofts. *Ask* Roddy?"

"Well, why not?"

"He doesn't think we know the things exist!"

"He—" Augusta stared at him, bemused. "Why ever not?"

"Thinks the source of all his luck is a deep dark secret. Lord, he'd have fits if he found out we knew!"

"Then how could you . . ."

"Talks when he's in his cups. Brags about 'em, then forgets he's said a word."

"It—it doesn't sound precisely honorable," Sophronia asserted.

Perry glared at her with all the youthful injury of his nineteen years. "I wasn't asking you. Lord, I never thought *you'd* come crab over me! Here is my one chance to bring myself about. You ought to be glad!"

"But Perry, if you're caught—"

"I'll make dashed sure I'm not, you can count on that! To

30

listen to you, you'd think a fellow never engaged on a lark before!" He looked from one to the other of the ladies, his enthusiasm fading beneath a wild, haunted look. "You have no idea to what desperate measures a fellow may be driven, have you? Well, I'll bring myself about, just see if I don't." His voice rose as his repressed fears threatened to get the better of him. "If I can just get one of those pistols away from Roddy . . ." He broke off, swung his horse about, and dug in his heels. The animal bolted forward.

Sophronia caught her reins to prevent her own mount from following. Augusta's placid roan cropped another mouthful of grass and raised its languid head to watch the departure.

"You—you don't think he'll get himself into trouble, do you?" Sophronia turned to Augusta in concern.

"It's probably just wild talk. He wouldn't really do anything wrong, you know that."

Sophronia remained silent for a moment too long. "N—no, he wouldn't. It's just that he thinks the most dreadful things to be the veriest jokes. He is too impetuous and—and prime for any lark, as he puts it. And no matter what he says, I *know* he needs money."

Augusta kept her uneasy reflections to herself. As one, she and Sophronia turned their mounts and continued their circuit about the park. Augusta's groom, who had stayed well back and out of earshot while they talked, rode up behind them. A lone curricle followed the carriage drive, and only a few riders approached along the tan bark. The Season might have started months early, but the Fashionable Promenade would wait for warmer afternoons.

The dreariness of the gray sky drepressed Augusta's spirits, yet she was loath to return to the warmth and comfort of Halliford House. Major Edward MacKennoch would be there—and with her luck, she'd run straight into him. She rode in silence for another two rounds with Sophronia at her side while her mind dwelled on this cruel twist of fate that placed them under the same roof. But that got her nowhere except chilled to the bone.

By the time they reached the gate on their next round, Augusta had come to a decision. Sophronia, who shivered in her saddle, made no objections to returning home. They left the park, then proceeded through the streets to the townhouse

31

rented for the season by Mrs. Lansdon in Half Moon Street. Augusta said good-bye to her friend, then returned to Cavendish Square under the escort of her groom.

They drew up before Halliford House, and Augusta hesitated only long enough to muster her retreating forces. She was no hen-hearted creature to cower in her own home. She would face Major MacKennoch at once and explain what had happened that morning. Then, provided she could make him do anything other than look down his aquiline nose at her as if she were a particularly unpleasant sort of insect, they might contrive to rub along tolerably well in the future. It was a pity, though, they had to share a house.

Squaring her shoulders, she marched up the front steps. Willis opened the door and bowed her inside. She stripped off her riding gloves, dropped them on the table, and plunged right in before her courage deserted her. "Where is Major MacKennoch?"

"In His Grace's study, Miss Augusta."

She thanked him and made her purposeful way toward the back of the house. If Halliford were there, she would feel the most frightful fool—not to mention having the wind taken out of her sails. She could never do her explaining in the duke's presence. It would be bad enough facing the major.

At the door, she knew a momentary qualm. Resolutely, before she lost her nerve, she tapped lightly, and the deep voice that issued the curt order to enter did not belong to her brother-in-law. Reassured on that head, she entered.

Major MacKennoch sat behind the great desk, a folder containing numerous closely written sheets open before him. He looked up from his reading and a touch of steel glinted in the depths of his blue eyes. The next moment a shutter seemed to close over his face. He came to his feet with the help of his cane.

"Am I disturbing you, Major MacKennoch?" She sounded breathless and she knew it, and despised herself for that weakness. Unconsciously, she straightened up to her full height and wished she could appear as outwardly calm as the reserved Scot.

"What may I do for ye, Miss Carstairs?" His cool voice gave away no trace of his mood.

She found herself wondering how many of his subalterns he

32

terrified. Probably all of them. She schooled her features into a semblance of his detached mask, and hoped it hid her nervousness. "I wish to explain about this morning."

His fingers tightened briefly on the curved top of the stick he still gripped. "I believe the less said about that nonsense, the better."

The burr in his voice sounded stronger than before, causing an unfamiliar and not altogether unpleasant reaction in her stomach. "It *was* nonsense," she agreed, finding her voice with unaccustomed difficulty.

Had she come to taunt him? He hadn't thought her capable of such callousness—only romantic foolishness. His brow lowered a fraction and the steel in his eyes turned to ice. "So we are agreed, Miss Carstairs."

She stiffened but forged on. "You are—and were—suffering under a misapprehension. I had no desire for you to kiss me."

"Ye have a very odd manner of making your wishes known, then, Miss Carstairs. The last time we met—"

Color flamed in her cheeks, lending fire to an already beautiful countenance. "It would be best if that time were forgotten, Major."

He inclined his head. "As ye wish." He kept his voice level. Her invitation had been meant for someone else. Irrationally, it hurt to think he had been only one of a possible long line of gentlemen she begged to kiss her over the years. A MacKennoch, he reminded himself, should not be wounded by a silly little flirt, no matter how lovely her eyes or deceptively sweet her expression. It wasn't reasonable.

Her expressive eyes widened in horror as if she'd read his thoughts. "It wasn't! I mean—" She broke off, her face a picture of confusion. "I am not in the habit of—of making such provocative suggestions. I was rehearsing for a play."

A play. Of course. The melodrama of her request *belonged* in some amateur dramatic production. And Halliford had warned him.

Her remarkable eyes glinted with nervous tears. "Oh, what a muddle I have made of this all! I am *so* sorry, Major MacKennoch. It—it was the most dreadful circumstance, your walking in like that."

"Aye, it was." He had himself back under control. In all

33

honesty, he wished it hadn't happened. The memory of her soft lips beneath his returned to haunt him. He could not help but wonder if they would still taste as sweet if he repeated his offense.

She managed a shaky smile, as one not altogether convinced they had reached an understanding. "I—I am sorry to have disturbed you." She hesitated, then hurred from the room.

He slumped back down into his chair, Halliford's speech momentarily forgotten. Emptiness settled inside him. She *had* disturbed him, there could be no denying that fact. *Damn* her for it—though it wasn't her fault. And damn himself, too, into the bargain, for wanting her to come back, just so he could gaze at her. A MacKennoch was not a man to be so bewitched.

A flightly, insincere, romantically inclined little chit had no place in his life. He had more important things to consider, like the security of his country! So why did he permit her to disrupt his calm, ordered thoughts? He picked up the papers and resumed his reading with a determination that defied interruption. He would not again give her the opportunity to unsettle him.

Chapter 3

Augusta climbed the stairs slowly, trailing a finger along the polished banister. Major MacKennoch seemed to have accepted her apology and her explanation. That *should* remove her embarrassment when next they met. Yet it wouldn't remove the fluttering she felt in the pit of her stomach or the longing that swept over her that he might kiss her again. Unfortunately, that was not something he was likely to do.

She reached her room, rang for her abigail, and began removing her boots. She had to go on living in the same house with the man. Perhaps he would now acknowledge that she had grown up, that she was no longer the silly romantic little fool he had called her two years before. Perhaps he would even come to like her. . . .

A brief reflection on the cool, emotionless Major Mac-Kennoch erased the growing image of his going farther, of his perhaps paying her ardent court. Another man, maybe. But *not* Major MacKennoch. Was that what she wanted from him? If so, she would be doomed to disappointment.

When her maid arrived, Augusta put off her habit and donned a round gown of pale blue muslin. The maid combed out her hair, then braided it and wound it in a crown about her head. Augusta peered anxiously into the mirror. The style made her look older, she decided, pleased. She even *felt* less flighty. Major MacKennoch would find little about her appearance to criticize. Her satisfaction evaporated as she realized she did this for the sole purpose of making a good impression on *him*. Disturbed and more than a little depressed, she went in search of Helena.

The ladies' sitting room, where her sister was usually to be found at this time of the afternoon, was empty. Nor was Helena in either the conservatory or music room. Worried, Augusta ran back up the stairs to the second floor, and tapped lightly on the duchess's bedchamber. Her Grace's abigail opened the door, gestured for Augusta to be silent, and admitted her into the room.

Helena lay on the great bed, surrounded by three huge cats: Odysseus, the gray and white; Penelope, the long-haired white and gray; and the black Demetrius. The duchess's fine-boned hands rested on fur, and a steady, rhythmic purr was the only noise. But as Augusta advanced into the room, her sister's eyes fluttered open.

"Gussie?" She started to rise on one elbow, but Augusta hurried forward and pushed her gently back. "Oh, this is absurd! As if I were ever ill a day in my life, before this."

"And you probably never will be again, dearest. Now, don't move. I just wanted to check on you." She scooped up Penelope, who had just stretched and showed every sign of redisposing herself across Helena's stomach.

"Will you be holding a rehearsal in the Gold Saloon this evening?" Helena stroked Demetrius to a purring frenzy.

"No, Lieutenant Kettering and Lord Roderick Ingersoll have had their duty rosters switched and couldn't get free. We are to meet in the morning—if you are certain it will not disturb you."

"No, of course not. I thought I might come down to watch for a bit."

"Now, that *would* make you ill." Only partially reassured, Augusta left her sister to rest and made her way downstairs to continue addressing the cards announcing their play to the newest arrivals in town.

The evening passed quietly. Major MacKennoch joined the family at table, made polite conversation with each of them— even Augusta—but did not once relax his rigid control or drop the polite mask that hid any emotions or thoughts. Augusta felt as if he had erected a wall around himself to close everyone out.

As soon as the meal ended, he excused himself and made his way to Halliford's study to resume his indoctrination into the duke's affairs. Augusta stared after his departing figure, frowning. Her fascination with him made absolutely no sense. He was *not* romantic. He was cool, reserved, and utterly and completely disinterested in her.

And that was just as well. Even if he were disposed to like her—which she did not think at all probable—he was not the husband for her. She needed a gentleman who could bring her independence from Halliford, who could free Helena from responsibilities to her family. Not for a moment could she contemplate marriage with a dependent of the duke. So why did that knowledge not set her at ease in his presence? Soon after the tea tray was brought in, Augusta excused herself and went to bed.

Late the following morning, the first member of her little troupe arrived and her thoughts took a more productive turn. Lord Wentworth looked about the empty saloon, and a mock frown settled over his normally jovial features.

"My dear Miss Carstairs, have they deserted us?" He settled his ample form into an overstuffed chair and smiled benignly on her.

"I don't think we should despair quite yet." She put down the pen with which she had been addressing more cards and crossed to a pedestal table on which stood several decanters, glasses, and a plate heaped with biscuits. "Would you care for some Madeira?"

Wentworth waved the offer aside. Instead, he picked up the script that lay near at hand and leafed through it. "What's this? More changes?" He chuckled suddenly. "My dear, this is priceless. A farce?"

Augusta let out a sigh of relief. "We were afraid you might not quite like the alterations."

Lord Wentworth shook his head, but his smile faded. "Rum business about Montclyff not standing buff, though. Kettering or young Lansdon will have to take on the part."

"That will probably be best," Augusta agreed. "Perhaps Perry—"

She broke off as Willis bowed in another arrival. Lieutenant Jack Kettering, resplendent in scarlet regimentals of the Seventh Foot, paused just over the threshold and tugged at one end of his remarkable black mustachios. A warm smile lit his eyes as his gaze came to rest on her. He strode forward, possessed himself of her hand, and raised her fingers to his lips for a lingering kiss.

"Kettering, there you are, my boy." Wentworth waved the script in an affable manner. "You'll take on the part of Percival, won't you? I'll have to fill in for your role myself, I suppose."

"I shall be honored. How could anyone resist the opportunity to play the hero to Miss Carstairs—if only in the realm of make-believe?" He pressed her hand ardently.

The door opened and she turned to see Major MacKennoch standing on the threshold, his expressionless eyes resting on her. She drew her hand away from Lieutenant Kettering, embarrassed, desperately not wanting the major to think she flirted. Warm color touched her cheeks, but she braved it through. "May I help you, Major?"

"His Grace has requested that I render ye any assistance ye might need with your rehearsal." He spoke stiffly, as one discharging an unpleasant duty.

It left her frustrated; she might as well have held her peace yesterday, for all the good her explanations had done. She raised a delicately arched eyebrow. "Did he warn you this would fall under your province?"

"Aye."

"And yet you accepted the position." She spoke in wondering tones. "One can only marvel at your bravery."

"Nay, Miss Carstairs. I have seen action on many fronts."

Amusement—she would swear it was really amusement!—lit his eyes. Her heart gave a double beat, then settled as a warm glow rushed through her. "I can only hope they were not as horrendous as this will be."

"Miss Carstairs!" Lord Wentworth spoke with mock reproof. "What an opinion you will give him of our little production."

Thus recalled to the presence of the other two people in the room, Augusta introduced Major MacKennoch. He bowed, then turned back to her.

"Is there any way I can be of assistance?"

Yes, she thought. Smile. But his voice now held only polite inquiry. She shook her head. "No. Unless you would care to stay and watch?"

"Nay, I will return to His Grace's study." He took his leave, bearing all the air of one who had successfully completed a difficult assignment.

She glared after him. For one moment, she'd thought he might unbend. Before she could come up with more than two choice names to call the exasperating major, the door opened once more. Sophronia and Perry, accompanied by Lord Roderick Ingersoll, entered. Augusta's already disturbed thoughts took another, and even more unpleasant, turn at sight of the latter's face.

Lord Roderick's normally amiable and vacuous countenance bore a haunted expression. His large, brown eyes were opened wide, and he cast darting glances at the other members of the assembled troupe. Even his dress appeared less precise than usual and his cravat, normally the envy of his acquaintances, had been knotted in a haphazard manner. No care had been expended on his curling reddish-brown locks, and they tumbled in riotous disorder that normally would have sent him in anguished pursuit of his brushes.

Nor did Perry look his usual natty self. While never aspiring to the sartorial heights achieved by Lord Roderick, Perry took great pains over his appearance. This morning, he seemed to have dragged on a uniform without the assistance of his batman and without first assuring himself that it had been properly pressed. The fact that the boots of both young men showed fingerprints and traces of dust spoke volumes for the distressed states of their minds.

Perry greeted the assembled company with false brightness. But as he cast a furtive, uneasy glance about the room, he met Augusta's searching gaze. He looked quickly away, faint color tingeing his abnormally pale complexion.

What, she wondered, had occurred to frighten him so? And Lord Roderick as well. She could only hope Perry hadn't indeed put his plan into action and "borrowed" Roddy's pistols without his permission. Something, though, had badly unsettled the both of them.

Lizzie, the orange beard dangling in her hand, strolled in, followed by the huge gray and white Odysseus. Arming herself with several biscuits from the plate, she plopped down in a comfortable chair near the fire to watch. The cat settled in her lap and proceeded to take a thorough bath.

"Well, well, shall we begin?" Lord Wentworth looked about the unenthusiastic troupe. "Come now, we must read through

39

the new lines. Lord Roderick and Miss Lansdon? We will begin with your scene, I believe. Lord Roderick?" he repeated, prodding that young gentleman, who sat staring unseeingly off into space.

Roddy started, then took his place. Sophronia joined him and, adopting without much success the uneducated accents of a serving wench, read her part. Lord Roderick missed his cue, Lord Wentworth prompted him, and Roddy stammered an apology.

Augusta watched in concern. A quickness of mind had never been one of Roddy's strong points, but this went far beyond his usual vagueness. So far, he had put forth considerable effort for their little productions. This time, Lord Wentworth, using supreme patience, was forced to lead him through the scene, line by line.

She glanced across to where Perry sat hunched in his chair, watching Lord Roderick in frowning silence. Almost, she thought, he might have come from a battle. She had seen much that same look of horror on the war-weary faces returning from the Peninsula. Deep lines etched about his eyes that never wavered from his friend. Probably it could all be attributed to the aftereffects of a too-convivial evening with a few choice spirits, but Perry's wild declarations of the day before flooded back to her mind. Had he embarked upon one of his "nacky notions"—only to have it turn against him?

A slight tug at her hair distracted her and she turned to see her sister holding one of her long blue ribands. Lizzie rolled her eyes in mock despair at Roddy's acting, threw Augusta an impish grin, and proceeded to dangle the purloined satin temptingly before Odysseus. While Roddy continued to stumble over words that refused to stay in his memory, she encouraged the cat to pounce.

Lord Wentworth cast her an indulgent, though somewhat disapproving, glance, then returned his attention to his players. "You are not listening to me," he complained. "I expect you to exert a little effort. Remember our cause."

Lieutenant Kettering, lounging in a chair, smiled, bantering with the elder man with the ease developed through close association over the plays. "A little of that much-needed military discipline you are always talking about could be used here."

Lord Wentworth directed a quelling glance at him. "Well, why shouldn't I support discipline? Look at the crazy antics the officers have been getting up to for the past few months. Gaming, fisticuffs—I'm surprised I haven't heard of any duels!"

Perry flushed. "What a fuss is being made over a few high spirits! The Army of Occupation has all the luck, being in Brussels where things are at least *happening*. What can anyone expect of the officers left behind?"

"Wild to a fault," Wentworth maintained. His tone held a hint of steel at odd variance to his jovial countenance. "Drinking heavily, squabbling at the drop of a hat—next I suppose you'll take to killing each other to relieve your boredom."

Perry blanched and a blue tinge crept about his mouth.

"And thieving," Lord Roderick stuck in. His countenance took on a florid hue. "Thought officers were supposed to be gentlemen, but I've seen some very improper behavior."

"Don't be a fool." Perry glared at him. "Nothing untoward is going on, at least nothing not to be expected of officers after years of hard campaigning."

"What you need is another war to whip everything back into shape." Lord Wentworth's voice dripped sarcasm.

"What a horrid thing to think about. Our troops aren't even back from America yet." Augusta shivered. The tension that vibrated in the room made her uncomfortable.

Wentworth laughed, though it sounded oddly tight. "They should leave more of these matters in the hands of the Diplomatic Service. Everyone in the War Office is too rackety by half. Young Peregrine here may speak of the fun going on in Brussels and Vienna, but it will only be successful if left to our people, not you military men. Don't know why they have Wellington at the Congress at all. Not a job for him."

Kettering leaned forward, a slight smile just playing about his lips. He, alone of the company, did not seem on edge. "I believe the duke is playing a very important role, nevertheless."

"Nowhere nearly as important as the diplomats, my boy. If we'd taken control when Napoleon first seized power nearly twenty years ago, things would have gone very differently, very differently indeed."

"Yes, they'd have been much more boring," Kettering stuck

41

in, playing devil's advocate. He threw a provocative glance at Perry, but that young gentleman remained silent, not rising to the obvious opening.

The rehearsal resumed and did not stop again until after one o'clock. Perry and Lord Roderick left quickly to report to their commanding officers, though, as Lieutenant Kettering assured the concerned Sophronia, they could probably have remained longer with impunity. Their captain was one of the play's more ardent supporters.

"Well, my dear." Lord Wentworth took Augusta's hand in parting. "We have three more days. I don't think our performance will be all that terrible."

Lizzie snorted. "For you or your audience?"

Lieutenant Kettering, who had paused in the doorway, smiled. He waited until the others took their leave, then bowed low over Augusta's hand. "Will you do me the honor of driving in the park with me this afternoon?"

"I'm sorry. Perhaps another time? You will be on leave this coming week, will you not?"

"For the next ten days."

She nodded. "Today I want to make certain my sister takes the air, so Lizzie and I will be driving with her."

She disentangled her hand from his and wondered why his handsome dark good looks didn't stir her heart. She was glad of the excuse not to accompany him! He was entertaining, a wit, and his appearance in his scarlet regimentals sent many a maiden sighing, but Augusta, despite her romantic yearnings, could not discover within herself the slightest tendre for him.

That, she reflected ruefully as she saw Lieutenant Kettering to the door, she reserved for Major Edward MacKennoch. She returned to the Gold Saloon and began repacking the few props they had used into the heavy trunk that stood in the corner. Wistful thoughts about the major got her nowhere.

A sigh escaped her and she sank down on the floor, the ginger whiskers in her hands. Would he like the play? A vague dream formed in her mind of his being impressed by her histrionic abilities, but it died aborning. He would far more likely disapprove—particularly of the "kiss me" scene.

"Was the rehearsal successful?" The major's deep voice sounded behind her, as expressionless as ever.

She almost jumped, for she hadn't heard him enter; she must

have left the door ajar. "Not overly." A delicate flush crept into her cheeks and she kept her face averted from the gaze she was certain would miss nothing. She shoved the whiskers into the trunk. "I thought our second production would go more smoothly than the first, but it is quite the opposite. You can have no idea how mortified we all are."

He came up behind her and set a large horse pistol in the rough wooden box that housed it. Augusta took it from him quickly and placed it on top of the beard. She felt tingly, breathless, and dreadfully nervous. He created complete chaos in her.

"Will there be another play after this one?" He sounded so calm, betraying none of her agitation.

Obviously, she did not have the same effect on him that he did on her. The thought was lowering. But it also made it easier to think. She nodded. "And another, and another after that, I hope. The first did so very well for our cause."

She started to rise, and he offered her his hand. Tentatively she took it, and her internal trembling started all over again at the strength of his clasp. He pulled her easily to her feet, as if he were not hampered in the least by his injured leg or having to keep his own balance with a cane.

"And it *is* fun, despite our complaining." She rushed into speech.

He released her and closed the heavy lid. "How are your preparations for the performance? Do ye need me to do anything for ye?"

She wished she could believe the offer came from his own interest in her affairs rather than on Halliford's orders. She shook her head. "On Thursday—the day of the event—we will, of course, but everything else is under control. Right now I have only the refreshments to order."

Shyly, she looked up into his face, but his calm mask defied her to read his sentiments. Her gaze came to rest on the scar that slashed across his cheek, and her tender heart twisted. She hadn't a doubt he'd disguised the pain he felt, even from the doctors who tended him. It didn't seem right—or natural—to hold emotion so tightly reined in.

Abruptly he stepped back. "Ye will send for me if ye have need." He strode quickly from the room.

Augusta stared after him, her thoughts still on that terrible

43

scar. How she wished she might have been the one to nurse him back to health. She would have cared for him, eased his suffering; and she would have seen that cold, withdrawn shell fade and love grow in its place in those icy blue eyes.

She cut off the daydream. He had been right two years ago. She *was* a romantic fool.

Depressed, she concentrated on the refreshments that had to be ordered for the performance, and soon lost herself in making detailed lists. She could not let Helena be disturbed by this or any other matter concerning the play. She had imposed on her dreadfully already, using the large double drawing rooms at Halliford House for their theater.

She read over the list of pastries to be ordered from the confectioners, then set it with the list for the other refreshments. Pausing in the hall only long enough to order the carriage brought round for her visit to the caterers, she ran upstairs to change her gown and put on her bonnet.

She came back down half an hour later dressed in a carriage gown of amber muslin and a merino pelisse in a warm shade of brown. On the landing she came to a halt. Major MacKennoch stood in the hall below beside Halliford, not as tall as the duke but every bit as impressive a figure. An officer whom she didn't recognize faced them.

Major MacKennoch heard her slippered step on the carpeted stair and turned to look up at her. Well, he thought, perhaps it was no wonder men behaved so foolishly over her. She was a beauty. She probably had no idea of the damage she caused.

She hesitated as if sensing their tension. The officer hastily excused himself and ducked out the front door. The major could hardly blame him. If he knew Miss Carstairs at all, the next twenty minutes—if not the next few days—were likely to be extremely unpleasant.

Halliford strode up to the foot of the stair and his sister-in-law came down the last few steps. Tentatively, she placed her fingers on his offered arm. Her gaze traveled from his concerned eyes to the major's face. She looked quickly away from him.

"What is it?" Her voice quavered ever so slightly.

And damnably attractive it was, too, the major reflected. Did she cultivate those airs to enslave the unwary? He could only be glad he was not of their number. He would never face an

44

opponent over pistols in the cold gray dawn for the sake of her eyes—no matter how lovely they might appear.

Now, they clouded with worry as she turned back to Halliford. The duke gave a reassuring pat to her hand, which still rested on his arm, and led her down the hall toward the back of the house, to his book room. The major followed.

Once inside, Halliford pressed her gently into a seat. The major took one look at her pale face, poured a brandy from the decanter on the side table, and handed it to her. They were about to be treated to a fit of the vapors, he supposed. He should probably pour himself a shot.

She stared at the amber liquid in the cut crystal glass in consternation, then looked back up into his face. His gaze rested on her, expressionless, hiding his dread of the hysterics to which he had few doubts she would shortly succumb.

Halliford cleared his throat. "I wish to speak to you about Captain Geoffrey Montclyff."

Bright color flooded Miss Carstairs's cheeks. "He has not approached you, has he? Oh, I told him there was no need!"

So the little flirt had been playing fast and loose with that gentleman's heart. More fool he, to become entangled in a web of her delicate and tantalizing weaving.

Halliford exchanged a glance with the major. "He won't be approaching anyone, anymore," Halliford said.

"What do you mean?" She turned to Major MacKennoch, her confusion patent.

"He's been shot." The major kept his voice level. He had an uneasy suspicion they should have hartshorn or smelling salts or some other such nonsense on hand.

"He's been . . ." Her voice trailed off. Her fingers clenched about the delicate stem of the glass and she stared at it as if she'd forgotten she held it. She took a long sip and swallowed, shuddering as the unaccustomed brandy burned down her throat.

"I'm sorry we have to break this to you, Gussie." Halliford watched her closely in concern. "I gather you were not partial to him, after all?"

"On—on the contrary, I—" She shivered. "He is the most dreadful man. I turned down his offer yesterday morning." She looked up, gathering her senses. "You said he was shot? Killed?"

Halliford nodded. "A duel, it seems."

"A duel!"

The major watched her closely. Was that remorse? He had expected her reaction to be dramatic, all for show. But her restraint spoke far more eloquently.

"Augusta?" Halliford laid a gentle hand on her shoulder.

She blinked, then shook her head. "I—I'm all right. He was angry when he left yesterday—but he must have known already of this meeting before offering for me." Surely, affairs of honor took time to arrange! And she had turned him down, refused his offer. What mood must that have induced in him when he faced his opponent in the chill dawn?

"There will be some measure of scandal, I fear," Halliford's deep voice warned her.

"A scandal?" She looked up, surprised. "Why?"

"The duel seems to have been surrounded with unusual circumstances."

"In what way? Whom did he meet?"

"That is one of the circumstances. His body was found at Paddington Green, just lying there. The other participants had left."

"Left? But—" she broke off, appalled. Her gaze encountered the major's frown and she looked hurriedly away. "What usually happens?"

Halliford's lip twitched slightly. "*Usually* the doctor or his seconds would convey the body back to the victim's home."

Augusta closed her eyes. She hadn't liked Monty, but still . . . "That is the *least* they could have done," she whispered. "How could someone just *leave* him?" She stared at her hands for a moment, then rallied. "You—you spoke of a scandal?"

"The authorities have no idea with whom he fought. There is bound to be an investigation and no end of questions. And I greatly fear his determined courtship of you will be examined rather closely."

Augusta drew a deep breath and let it out slowly. *More* trouble for Halliford . . .

"It might be wise," her brother-in-law went on, "if you were to retire to the Castle for a while. There is bound to be a certain amount of unpleasant talk about your honor being defended. There will always be a few people who would be glad to see the

46

Incomparable brought down a peg."

Augusta leaned back, closing her eyes. Montclyff dead—and in a duel. But not over her honor—though who would believe that once the tattlemongers shredded her character? The thought revolted her—and Helena would be devastated. They could leave now, this day, and avoid it all. They could slip quietly away to Yorkshire, and when they returned to London, some new scandal would have taken over. But Helena was so very unwell, and she would never allow Augusta to travel such a great distance without her chaperonage.

She opened her eyes. "I'm not so craven. To run is foolish, for it would only confirm the gossip."

Halliford's grip tightened on her shoulder and he nodded his approval. "That's the girl. We'll see this through."

A knock fell on the study door and Halliford called "Come in" over his shoulder. Helena hesitated on the threshold, her soft gray eyes wide in concern.

"What has happened?" She looked at each of them in turn, then hurried forward to kneel at her sister's side. "Gussie, are you all right?"

Halliford lifted his wife to her feet and kept one arm about her waist. Tenderly he kissed her forehead. "Nothing is the matter, my love, that need concern you. An officer has been shot in a foolish duel."

"But Augusta?" She threw an anxious glance at her sister.

"I knew him, that is all, dearest." Gamely, Augusta rose to the occasion. "He was the most disagreeable man, I assure you." Shaking off her own reaction, she stood. To her relief, her knees supported her. "Halliford is quite right, you know. It need not concern you in the least. He merely had been making me the object of his odious attentions."

"The scandal . . ." Helena looked back up at her husband, aghast for her sister's sake.

"No one will dare breath a word about Augusta."

Not a trace of doubt sounded in the duke's voice, but Augusta knew it to be a bluff. The mantel of Halliford's protection might surround her, but the Beau Monde could never resist such a choice on dit concerning a member of his family. The duke led Helena from the room, his arm firmly about her. Augusta sank back down in the chair.

She had done it again—distressed her sister and placed an

47

unwelcome burden on Halliford. It would take the duke's influence to silence tongues. She had imposed on him once more. No, the sooner she got herself safely married to some respectable and boring gentleman, the better it would be.

She looked up and saw Major MacKennoch still standing before her. She handed him her glass without finishing it.

"Are ye all right, Miss Carstairs?" No trace of emotion—or interest—sounded in his voice.

She tried a wan smile, but it faded before the steely, accusing glint in his eyes. He blamed her for Montclyff's death, probably thinking the captain just another victim of her flirtations. So much for her hopes of developing at least a friendship with him. And that knowledge felt like ice in her stomach.

Chapter 4

The shock of Captain Geoffrey Montclyff's death quickly gave way to inevitable questions in Augusta's mind. She lay on her bed, disdaining the offers of laudanum drops, hartshorn, composers, and even the vinaigrette that her maid seemed to feel necessary to support any young lady of quality through a crisis. All she wanted was solitude—and a few answers.

Why had Monty fought a duel? What had it been over—and whom had it been with? No matter how hard she tried, she could not rid her mind of the fact that she had rejected his offer the morning before his death.

Did that—and she—have anything to do with that dreadful meeting at Paddington Green? It couldn't! she assured herself, feeling ill at the possibility. The idea was ridiculous!

Yet her thoughts flew to Lieutenant Jack Kettering, who made no secret of the fact he considered himself the most devoted of her court. Would he have felt obligated to defend her in such a horrible manner if Monty's evil tongue had been at work on her? No, it was preposterous! Surely, if Lieutenant Kettering had killed his man at dawn, he could never have appeared so calm and teasing at their rehearsal later in the morning.

She huddled into the shawl draped about her shoulders by her persistent abigail. There had been someone—no, two people—who had not been at ease at the rehearsal. But the prospect of either Peregrine Lansdon or Lord Roderick Ingersoll fighting a duel was ludicrous. No, Monty knew any number of people—and his cutting tongue had undoubtedly won him more than his share of enemies.

49

This got her nowhere! Resolutely, she cast off the shawl and stood up. She still had her errands to the caterer and confectioner to run. She strode down the hall to Helena's room and knocked softly on the door. Dorson, Her Grace's abigail, opened the door and informed her that the duchess slept. Satisfied, Augusta went in search of Lizzie to accompany her on her visits. If anyone could provide the ultimate decisions on refreshments, it would be a sprightly fifteen-year-old with a healthy appetite.

Augusta delayed only long enough to dash off a brief message to the Willoughbys, crying off from attending their dinner party that night. Even though she had not particularly liked Captain Montclyff, she could not remain unmoved by his death. Nor did she feel up to facing the inevitable whispers and comments of polite society so soon.

She gave the note into the hands of the second footman, then called to Lizzie to stop dangling ribands in front of the playful Demetrius and join her. She led the way out to the waiting landaulet, only to draw up short on the front porch. Major MacKennoch stood beside the carriage, deep in conversation with the driver. His single-caped coat of olive drab indicated that he, too, intended to go out.

The major looked up, his expression coolly assessing, but he made no move to leave. An unpleasant certainty took root in Augusta's mind.

Lizzie, feeling none of Augusta's constraint, ran lightly down the steps. "Are you going with us?" she demanded in her forthright fashion.

"Aye." His impenetrable gaze rested on her for a moment, then moved on to Augusta.

Sensing the challenge that lurked in his blue eyes, she followed her sister. "An escort? Or do you have errands of your own?"

"It is His Grace's wish that I accompany ye." He waved the footman aside and himself opened the carriage door and let down the step.

Lizzie clambered in, but Augusta hesitated on the flagway. "There is absolutely no need."

The major raised a haughty eyebrow. "No need for His Grace's secretary to obey his wishes?" He kept his voice low so that only she heard his words, but there could be no mistaking

50

the coldness that lurked in his tone.

"Forgive me." She stopped with one foot on the step and her hand resting on the door frame of the landaulet. "I never meant to slight your dedication to duty. That is something you would never shirk. But I am also certain that if Halliford knew how distasteful it was to you in this case, he would not force you to—to bear-lead me."

His lip twitched in self-derision, though he merely inclined his head in acknowledgment. She entered the carriage and he followed, balancing with care on his cane as he eased himself into the facing seat.

Good God, he wasn't reduced to bear-leading females yet— was he? He still had one very important task to perform for Lord Bathurst. And he would also do his best to serve Halliford, when the two duties did not conflict.

At the moment, that meant bear-leading this female. His presence would prevent anyone from accosting her and asking intrusive and impertinent questions about Captain Montclyff. That he would like to ask her a few of his own, he tried to dismiss from his mind. Her relationship with that disreputable gentleman was no concern of his. He forced himself to stifle unwelcome speculation on the subject.

He stretched his stiff leg into a less uncomfortable position. Miss Carstairs's expressive countenance instantly registered concern, and she reached for the cushion that lay on the seat between her and Miss Elizabeth. His quick scowl stopped her, and she flushed. Quite prettily, too, he noted with an unwelcome pang.

"I have no need of it." He spoke the words stiffly. Nor did he need her help or concern, or anything else she chose to offer. Did she think him incapacitated? He was not one to hide behind any woman's petticoats. He might have lost his usefulness to his country as a soldier, but he was still a man, and in possession of his pride.

"Forgive me." Her lovely blue-gray eyes clouded and she dropped the offending cushion as if it had become distasteful to her. "I am accustomed to Richard. He simply would have laughed and thrown it back at me."

Lord Richard Chatham would, the major reflected. The loss of his leg hardly seemed to bother Halliford's brother at all, now that he was married and a father. And that young gentleman was possessed of far less reserve than a disabled Scotsman.

They reached their first destination in New Bond Street and Lizzie bounded down to the flagway. Augusta rose, but stayed in the carriage. "Do you mean to remain in Halliford's employ for long?" she asked bluntly.

The question surprised him; surely she did not guess that his position only served as cover for his real assignment. His brow creased as he automatically closed out intrusion on his innermost thoughts, and he threw up his familiar barriers of defense. "My poor Miss Carstairs. Ye must be anxious to be rid of my presence."

"Not as anxious as you must be to be rid of mine," she said with a rueful candidness that would have done Lizzie credit.

"I would not say that."

"No, a gentleman *couldn't,* could he?" Her smile held a touch of wistfulness. She followed her sister, who waited a few feet away with ill-disguised impatience.

The major's frown deepened. With a sense of surprise, he realized he sympathized with her. She must deeply regret their previous meetings. And he couldn't blame her for that. He regretted them, too. The memory of her lips, soft as rose petals beneath his own, flickered across his mind, only to be thrust aside at once. She had seriously disrupted his calm, something that no female had ever succeeded in doing before. He didn't like the sensation.

He positioned his stick and descended to the street with care. They entered the confectioner's and he stood at the back of the shop while she conducted her business with her sister's assistance. He had hurt her with his rejection of her help, and that also surprised him—and disturbed him more than it should. It seemed the little Carstairs possessed a heart, albeit an impulsive one that undoubtedly ruled her very pretty head—with less than felicitous results. Still, he could not but admit she had received the tidings of Captain Montclyff's death with surprising fortitude—and commendable remorse.

They returned to the carriage for the three-block ride to the caterer's. Augusta sank back against the squabs and cast a darkling glance at the major. He gazed out onto the busy street and an expression of pain, of unbearable sadness, flickered across his countenance for the briefest moment, then vanished

52

under his taut control. Her tender heart ached for him.

What, she wondered, went on behind the usually closed mask of his expressionless face, in the mind he kept shielded from the world? He obviously possessed emotions like other men. Why could he not permit them to show? Only in rare, unguarded moments did he betray himself. She would give a great deal to see him animated, to see a spark of warmth or friendship in those cold blue eyes.

They completed their errands in near silence. Upon their return to Halliford House, Augusta thanked the major for his escort, then hurried away before he could make it abundantly clear that only unpleasant duty had bound him to her side for the afternoon. She made her way to her room, where she put off her bonnet, then went to check on Helena.

She found her sister seated in her accustomed chair before the crackling fireplace in the sitting room, all three cats sleeping peacefully on the floor at her feet. As she opened the door, Halliford leaned over Helena, their faces very close. The duke smoothed back his wife's soft brown hair from her forehead and kissed her gently. Augusta started to draw back, but he saw her and straightened up.

"I find I must return to the Castle for a few days." His clipped tone betrayed his displeasure at this turn of events.

"Cannot Major MacKennoch go in your stead?" Augusta exclaimed, dismayed.

He shook his head. "He hasn't been with me long enough to handle this on his own."

Augusta looked to Helena, trying to gain a clue as to what her sister might prefer. "We could all go," she suggested. "The town is so dreadfully thin of company, it hardly matters. Indeed, I would very much like to return to the country."

The slight scuffing of a boot on the carpeted hall sounded behind her and Augusta turned and found herself looking up into the cold, disapproving eyes of Major MacKennoch. His jaw tightened as he gazed down at her and to her fury his upper lip flickered into a curl. Chagrin and anger fought within her and the latter won.

"It will be quicker if I go alone." Halliford spoke lightly, his tone reassuring. "I should not be gone above a fortnight. I doubt you'll have time to miss me."

"You may be sure we will take care of Helena." Augusta

53

withdrew from the room, closed the door firmly behind her, and rounded on the major, who remained impassively where he stood.

Things could not continue as they were; to live with the major's thinly veiled dislike would be intolerable. She would have it out with him now, once and for all. "Will you spare me a moment?" With difficulty, she kept from snapping the words.

He inclined his head. "I am sorry to disoblige ye. I must speak to His Grace before he leaves."

"This won't take long. I can understand—under the circumstances—" She broke off as warm color heated her face. She did not permit herself to lower her gaze. "You have every reason to hold a low opinion of me, based on the last time we met two years ago. But I am not a foolish sixteen any longer. Can you not contrive to put that incident out of your mind?"

"Ye are mistaken. I have forgotten it." His careful control betrayed itself by the pronounced burr in his otherwise emotionless voice.

"Yet still you make no secret of not approving of me." She wouldn't—couldn't!—let him see how that hurt. "Why are you angry with me right now?"

Something—disappointment?—flickered in his eyes, only to be banished the next moment. "It is Her Grace I'm thinking of. Can ye not do the same?"

"What do you mean?" She stared at him, bewildered more by that unidentifiable emotion than by his words.

"Did ye change your mind? Could ye not face the gossip about your involvement with Captain Montclyff, after all?"

Augusta gasped. "It is no such thing!"

"The duchess is obviously too unwell to travel, yet here ye are, so afraid to face possible scandal and recriminations that ye are willing to sacrifice your own sister."

"How dare you say that!" Her hands clenched in indignation. "I was not in the least *involved* with him, and I *was* thinking of Helena. I thought she might rather go with Halliford, and exchange the noisy racket of London for the serenity of Yorkshire."

"Her Grace has already chosen to remain," Major Mac-Kennoch informed her shortly. "Will ye excuse me?" Without another word, he moved past her, knocked, and entered the sitting room.

Augusta glared at the door as it closed behind him, fury struggling with her injured feelings. She didn't know if he believed her or not, and that distressed her. Not, of course, that *his* opinion mattered. She just didn't care to have anyone think ill of her.

Halliford departed within the hour, bent on making the journey to Yorkshire as quickly as possible. Augusta stood with Helena and Lizzie at the door until his curricle rounded the corner, carrying the duke out of sight. Helena sighed deeply, then managed a shaky laugh as Augusta solicitously helped her back indoors.

"I am not an invalid, merely increasing!" Still, and despite her words, she looked wan and unhappy.

How terrible it must be to love someone that much, Augusta reflected. But still, her own heart yearned for such a commitment. She thrust that thought aside. Despite her romantic daydreams, it did not seem to be for her. Since no gentleman other than the impossible major roused any tender emotions within her, the marriage which she would undoubtedly soon make would be one of convenience, based on mutual regard and not passion.

Over Helena's protests, Augusta helped her up the stairs and obliged her to lie down on her bed with two of the cats to bear her company. She would have the duchess's dinner sent up, she promised. And her own and Lizzie's as well, so they could dine together. That way, Augusta reflected as she made her way downstairs to relay this request to Willis, she would not have to sit down at table that night with the major.

By the following evening, Helena felt much improved and anxious to escape the house and the suffocating solicitude of her abigail. They had been invited to an informal hop by Mrs. Lansdon, and Helena announced her intention of attending. They dined early, and Helena chatted brightly at the table. Augusta aided her to the best of her ability, though she found Major MacKennoch's silence as disconcerting as ever.

She welcomed with profound relief Willis's announcement that the barouche had arrived. Major MacKennoch accompanied them outside, handed the duchess into the carriage, then turned to Augusta. He maintained his hold on her hand, preventing her from sitting.

Augusta met his intent gaze with a touch of defiance. "You need have no fears," she informed him tartly. "I will not let her tire herself." She pulled free and the major closed the door.

The drive took less than twenty minutes. Lights glittering in the windows of the Lansdon townhouse in Half Moon Street greeted them as they pulled up in front. A footman hurried out to let down the steps.

The rooms, though not crowded, were comfortably filled. The season might not yet have properly begun, but any number of politically inclined gentlemen and their families remained in town, waiting for any news from the Congress taking place in Vienna. Such an opportunity was not to be lost by the parent of a large family of daughters.

As they entered the first drawing room, conversation ceased among the knots of people standing closest to the door. It began again the next moment, too bright, too artificial. *She* had been under discussion, Augusta realized. Her dainty chin jutted out in defiance, and fixing a brilliant smile to her lips and taking Helena's arm, she swept inside.

Mrs. Lansdon, ethereal in a robe of lavender gauze, fluttered up to welcome them, all smiles and sighs for their condescension in paying her humble home a visit. "And there is a particular friend of yours come this evening," she declared. Taking the duchess's arm, she led her solicitously to a chair where she might be comfortable. "Now where—ah, speaking with Lord Wentworth."

A tall, fair-haired gentleman towered over that jovial peer. His dress, from the elegant cut of his dark blue coat to the exquisite folds of his pristine neckcloth, bespoke the Corinthian. He looked up at his hostess's words and a cynical smile lit his bold blue eyes as they rested on Augusta. Thirty-four years of active—and frequently riotous—living lined his face with character. Few maidens encountered the dashing Mr. Frederick Ashfield without losing their hearts.

Augusta was not of their number. "Frederick is here," she told Helena stiffly.

"Is he?" Her sister looked up, hopeful.

"I'll bring him to you."

Augusta started toward him, but Mr. Frederick Ashfield excused himself to Lord Wentworth and met her halfway across the room. He took Augusta's hand, his eyes dancing

56

with amusement at the coolness of her expression. He bowed deeply before her. "How charming to see you."

"Indeed. We had no idea you were in town."

"I have only just arrived." They neared Helena and Mr. Ashfield's smile warmed. "My dear duchess. How do you go on? I'm surprised Halliford has let you out of the house without his protection."

Helena smiled as he claimed her hand. "He has had to return to the Castle for a few days. Come tell me how you go on."

He took the seat beside her, and Augusta, satisfied that he could be trusted to care for her sister, strolled off in search of Sophronia. Mr. Frederick Ashfield might be Halliford's oldest friend, but Augusta never felt quite comfortable with him. There had been some problem or fight, involving Helena, before her marriage. The new duchess had avoided Mr. Ashfield at first, but her embarrassment or constraint had worn off and she now welcomed his friendship. Augusta wished she could do the same.

She smiled slightly at her own lingering foolishness. In the back of her mind, she had cast Frederick Ashfield in the role of ogre in her sister's fairy-tale romance. Apparently she was loath to give him another, less villainous, part. She would have to make the effort.

Her usual court did not gather about her this night, she noted. She refused to let it bother her. She spotted Sophronia and waved, but as she moved to the girl's side, a stir occurred by the door. Perry Lansdon sauntered in, flanked by Lord Roderick and a well-set-up officer just above average height whom Augusta didn't recognize. His close-cropped dark hair waved back from his forehead—except for one lock that fell artlessly toward his eyes.

Augusta glanced briefly at the classically handsome features, then returned her attention to Perry. Deep shadows accented that young gentleman's eyes, standing out in sharp contrast to the unnatural pallor of his complexion. His manner was subdued, almost withdrawn, despite the jollying of his companions.

Roddy laughed loudly at something the other officer said and took an unsteady step into the room. In his cups, Augusta noted in dismay, then her eyes narrowed. Roddy might be vague, but his ton was excellent. He was never one to show himself at an evening party three parts disguised. Nor, for that matter, had she ever before seen him more than slightly up in the world.

Mrs. Lansdon drifted up to her son and presented a cheek for his salute. She greeted the other two officers, then directed Perry toward his sister. Ever one to do his duty, he approached her with his two friends in tow.

"H'lo, Sophie, h'lo, Augusta." Lord Roderick grinned at them fatuously.

Perry ignored him. "Captain Vincent Trent. M'sister, Sophronia. And Miss Augusta Carstairs," he added in a perfunctory manner.

Augusta smiled and acknowledged the introduction. Captain Trent bowed to her, then turned to Sophronia. He took the girl's hand, smiled down into her hazel eyes, and Augusta saw her friend melt beneath his devastating smile. He bowed and strolled off, leaving Sophronia to gaze after him with what Lizzie would have referred to as a besotted expression on her face.

Another gentleman came forward and Augusta found herself led off to exchange pleasantries with his aging parent. While she reported to this formidable matron on the financial success of their first play to benefit the war orphans and widows, she looked about the room, searching for her sister.

In relief, she caught a glimpse of her through the open doors that led into the card room. Helena was playing with Mr. Ashfield—probably piquet, an occupation that would keep them both content for some time. Augusta turned back to her companion, only to have her attention caught once more, this time by Sophronia.

The girl strolled into the card room, looking about as if searching for someone. Apparently disappointed, she came back out. But the next moment she found her quarry and her wistful gaze rested on the scarlet-coated back of Captain Vincent Trent, who conversed with a strikingly beautiful blonde.

Augusta sighed for her friend's obvious longing. The matron at her side raised an eyebrow in surprise at her distraction, and Augusta hurriedly embarked on a lively description of the current play. Gather supporters, she reminded herself. The more tickets she could induce the members of the ton to purchase, the more money she would raise for her cause.

It might have been a trick of the angle at which she saw Captain Trent, but when Perry and Lord Roderick entered the card room a few minutes later, she could have sworn he repositioned himself as if to keep them in view. She fell silent, allowing her elderly companion to animadvert upon the many plays she had seen over a span of some fifty and more years.

Captain Trent remained where he was, ostensibly fascinating the lovely young lady who hung on his every word. But when Perry hunched a shoulder and left the card room with Roddy again trailing at his heels, Captain Trent moved once more. Perry and Roddy made their way to the drawing room, where a refreshment table had been set out, and Captain Trent shifted his position a third time.

Try as she might, Augusta could think of no reason why that gentleman should be watching Perry and Lord Roderick. He had come with them, after all. On impulse, she excused herself to the matron, but before she could reach the refreshment table, Sophronia joined her. Augusta caught a last glimpse of Perry tossing off a glass of champagne punch and casting nervous glances around before Sophronia claimed her attention.

"I *hate* parties, Augusta." She raised woebegone eyes to her friend's face.

Augusta stared at her in dismay. "You cannot mean that."

"I do! I—I just don't *take*." She tucked her hand through Augusta's arm and led her off. "Perhaps I should retire to the country for the rest of the season."

"Sophie!" Augusta tried to laugh, but the bleak unhappiness of her friend's tone startled her. Captain Vincent Trent's lack of interest must have hurt her deeply. Augusta wished savagely that Perry had not brought that gentleman to the party.

"It is the most sensible course to follow," Sophronia averred. "Since I am not likely to receive any eligible offers, I ought to step aside. That way Mamma can save money now so that Julia can be presented next season." She tried hard not to sniff, but failed.

Augusta squeezed her hand. "That is just foolishness, and so you know when you are not feeling low. Julia is only sixteen. She can wait another two years—though I doubt there will be any need."

59

Sophronia threw Augusta a grateful, albeit disbelieving, smile. "That is something you need not worry about, at least. I expect you have already received any number of offers."

"You mean the Halliford fortune has." Augusta's voice hardened. "You should consider yourself lucky. When a gentleman enjoys your company, you may be certain he is not calculating the potential size of your dowry."

Sophronia stared at her in startled dismay. "Oh, no, Augusta! You—you're beautiful! I—" She broke off as the string quartet hired for the evening struck up the opening chords of a country dance in the next drawing room. "Oh, dear! Mama will be wanting me." She excused herself and hurried off to find her parent.

The door opened for a late arrival, and the butler ushered in Lieutenant Jack Kettering. He greeted his hostess and Sophronia Lansdon with profuse apologies for his tardiness, attributing it to a lame leader which had left him stranded a good ten miles outside London. Mrs. Lansdon, who always had a soft spot for a personable young officer, waved aside his excuses and urged him to seek out convivial company. Lieutenant Kettering assured her that he would and headed directly toward Augusta, who stood close by.

"Good evening, Lieutenant." He, at least, had not deserted her because of gossip! Augusta comtemplated the dark, dashing good looks of the officer who raised her fingers lingeringly to his lips, and experienced not the least stirrings in her contrary heart.

"You look unusually solemn tonight."

The glowing look in his deep brown eyes as they rested on her left her in no doubt as to his sentiments. She swallowed hard and managed a shaky smile. "I am only concerned for my sister."

"She appears to be in good hands." He nodded toward the card room, where Frederick Ashfield hovered over the duchess, offering her a glass of lemonade.

Satisfied that her sister had not yet tired, Augusta allowed Lieutenant Kettering to lead her into the dance. No one in their set actually moved away, she noted, but the looks that were cast at her were rife with speculation and more than one young lady whispered behind her fan to her partner. Augusta clenched her teeth and smiled. She would just continue as if nothing were amiss until the ill-mannered gossips realized, from her total lack of concern, that there could not be one shred of truth in any of it.

The whispering would distress Helena, though. Augusta's thoughts drifted from the music. She really needed an eligible husband, someone to lend her the air of propriety that her romantic disposition lacked. The callow youths who normally flocked to her side would not serve the purpose—nor had she any desire to be tied to any of them.

Lieutenant Jack Kettering took her hand as he led her in a stately promenade. He was no callow youth, nor did he bore her. She could do far worse than marry him, she supposed. He came from an old and respectable family. He might not be wealthy, but he had a considerable competence as well as his pay, and she knew him to have expectations. He was dashing, romantic, and very modish, always *point de vice,* the *dernier cri,* without aping the dandy set. And he openly worshiped at her feet.

He peered anxiously at his shoulder, craning his neck to catch a glimpse of his collar. "Have my shirt points wilted?" he whispered in exaggerated concern.

That brought an honest smile to her lips. "They are in perfect order—as you well know."

He sighed in relief, then bowed to her as required by the movements of the dance. "You were looking at me as if my cravat were rumpled. And that I *knew* to be absurd." He raised a comic eyebrow, inviting her to share his mild joke.

She did. It was kind of him to try to divert her; he could not help but have heard the gossip. He amused her, though he didn't touch her heart. With a sinking sensation, she recognized that only one gentleman did. Major Edward MacKennoch's piercing blue eyes haunted her, fascinated her. Firmly, she thrust his intrusive presence from her mind.

It refused to be banished, and instead lingered throughout the dance. She could almost imagine it was he who partnered her instead of Lieutenant Kettering. He would wear his kilt, and those icy eyes would become as warm as a summer sky. She continued through the steps, lost in her dream of a solid, fair-haired gentleman who smiled, even laughed, who had no need for a mask of aloofness. They would waltz, not in a crowded drawing room but on a moonlit terrace, and his arm would

61

tighten about her possessively, and . . .

The music ended and she came crashing back to reality. Jack
Kettering stood opposite her, not Edward MacKennoch. The
major couldn't waltz with his bad leg—and he didn't even like
her.

Disturbed by her shocking lack of practicality, she excused
herself to Lieutenant Kettering and moved away, seeking
solitude. Familiarity with the Lansdon household stood her in
good stead, and she slipped down the hall to the conservatory,
which had been closed up for the evening. What she needed
was a quarter of an hour of silence to give herself a firm
lecture.

She took a seat on the far side of the room, on a bench
shielded from the door by an assortment of potted plants. She
had to give serious thought to marriage, to leave her sister in
her much deserved peace and provide herself with a measure of
freedom. With a husband, she would not be as vulnerable to
vile gossip.

If only she could contemplate Jack Kettering! He was
everything she ought to love in a man—he was extremely
handsome and possessed of a well-developed flare for the
romantic. Dark, brooding, with that air of hopeless devotion—
what more could a female desire?

Yet irrationally, her wayward heart yearned for the fair,
craggy ruggedness of Major Edward MacKennoch. He didn't
even come close to the image of the brooding poet made
popular among the young ladies by Lord Byron. Depressed,
Augusta sank her chin into her cupped hands, her elbows
resting on her knees.

The door across from her was pushed wide and she shrank
lower on the bench, hoping not to be seen. The last thing she
wanted was to be disturbed. Someone came in—no, two
people, she realized. They spoke with voices lowered so that
she barely heard their deep tones. Chair legs scraped on the tile
floor as they seated themselves, and a sigh escaped Augusta.
She had no desire to be trapped in here, an unwilling
eavesdropper to a private conversation.

But as she started to rise, a few scattered words reached her.
"Troop movements" she heard, quite clearly. Then "Wellington," followed by "Elba" and the whole phrase "well enough
planned so that nothing can go wrong this time."

Wrong? Her interest perked up. Halliford and Major MacKennoch would be interested in anything new concerning Bonaparte. But still, she had no right to listen. She had better make her presence known.

". . . ingenious new method to pass the information, which should . . ." The words trailed off into a mumble.

"You will be well paid, as usual," came across clearly.

Augusta barely had time to wonder why, before the answer reached her.

"Napoleon will be suitably grateful, you may be sure."

Chapter 5

Augusta started to straighten up, then ducked down again. Did she just hear what she thought she did? *Could* this be a discussion concerned with *helping* Napoleon? The thought left her weak with shock.

The next moment, though, she forced her ridiculously romantic imagination back under control. The whole thing was preposterous. Those men couldn't possibly be discussing the passing of military secrets to the French to aid Bonaparte!

"It will not be hard," the one man continued, his words so soft she could barely hear. "All will be chaos in Brussels."

The other voice murmured something, which she couldn't quite catch, then the first man spoke again. "No, but you will make an admirable new assistant. Your regiment will be posted there within two weeks. We had best not meet like this again until we are both there."

The scraping of chairs reached Augusta once more as the men rose. Booted footsteps sounded crossing the marble floor, and the next moment the door opened, then closed. Silence filled the conservatory, and Augusta let out the breath she had held.

She remained where she was until to her disgust she realized she trembled. Common sense took over. There was no need to cower there, afraid to be seen—the men had left! And more importantly, the whole thing was nothing but a pack of moonshine. Napoleon was safely ensconced on Elba.

That helped steady her. Those two men must have been discussing something quite different, quite harmless. Her imagination had run away with her—again. And let *that* be a lesson to her not to read so many lurid novels and take part in melodramas. She was beginning to behave like one of the foolish heroines, who were forever succumbing to fainting spells and the vapors over the merest trifles.

It was time and past she overcame her overly romantic tendencies. What, after all, had really just occurred? One voice she had barely heard at all. The other spoke so low, she could not have recognized it even if she were intimately acquainted with the speaker. And that, she told herself firmly, was what made it all seem so suspicious and mysterious. She must have filled in missing words and misinterpreted the few she heard. She was, in short, no better than a silly peagoose. Still, she could not be easy.

On impulse, she jumped up, hurried to the door, and peeked out. There was no point in acting any more of a fool than she already had. She would simply see who it had been, then an innocent explanation for the peculiar bits she overheard would present itself.

Only one man, an officer in scarlet regimentals, stood in the hall, loitering, as if he waited for a timely moment to reenter the crowded drawing rooms. He might be delaying so that he would not be seen to enter with his confederate. That thought stirred up her suspicions again. He turned, casually, and from her vantage point behind the door she recognized Captain Vincent Trent.

She blinked. Captain Vincent Trent? Now, that settled the matter, surely. A friend of Perry Lansdon's was hardly likely to be involved in a treasonable plot to sell military secrets to Napoleon! More likely, he had escaped the crush for a breath of fresh air. Her fears became more preposterous by the moment. If Captain Trent were doing anything in the hall, it would be keeping an eye on Perry and Lord Roderick, as he had been doing earlier.

She froze. Perry Lansdon and Lord Roderick Ingersoll? No, that possibility was even more ludicrous than thinking the captain might be involved! She had made a dangerous mystery out of bits and pieces of a harmless conversation—as in the game she used to enjoy, where one child whispered a sentence to another, and it became more garbled with each repetition. She had heard only fragments.

But what if something *were* going on? That possibility had to

65

be considered. She bit her lip as she tried to decide what to do. She ought to tell someone—but who?

She waited for several minutes after Captain Trent returned to the drawing rooms, then followed. Helena sat on a sofa beside a matron of comfortable proportions, laughing at something her companion said to her. She would be all right for a little while longer, Augusta decided.

She strolled forward, still uncertain, only to be intercepted by a young officer bent on claiming the next dance. As no other ideas presented themselves to her, Augusta allowed herself to be led into a set that formed for a reel.

While she went through the motions, somehow keeping in time with the music, she considered her best course. It took only a moment for her to dismiss her first impulse, which was to run to her sister as she had always done in the past. She could not disturb Helena.

But what about Frederick Ashfield? She glanced back toward Helena and saw that gentleman standing once more at the duchess's side, his quizzing glass leveled at a rather pretty young lady dancing near by. He would not be a good confidante, she decided. He was nothing more than the amusing rattle Halliford had once called him.

She sighed then smiled at her partner, who regarded her in concern. For the remainder of the dance she tried to focus her attention on him, much to his delight, but as soon as the music ended, she made her excuses and slipped away.

She looked around, studying her fellow guests. Several cast glances in her direction, and murmured to each other behind fans or shielding hands. Warm color flooded her cheeks, and her jaw clenched. So much gossip about her, and all because a gentleman who'd paid her court had been killed in a duel! It wasn't even as if she had ever been seen to encourage him.

Had the duel been over her? It made her ill, just thinking of the possibility. She wished she knew what they said—or rather, she didn't, for she had no interest in common, vulgar talk.

She turned away, determined not to provide society's cats with more fuel for their scandalized whisperings and on dits by showing she cared. But it did disturb her—and for more reasons than one. Who would listen seriously to her tales of possible treason when sly innuendoes about her raced through the ton? It would be thought nothing but a ploy on her part to provide the polite world with something new about which to chatter.

If only Halliford had not departed into Yorkshire at this particular moment. She could always turn to him—even though it upset Helena. Suddenly, she felt very much alone.

Jack Kettering strolled up, claimed her for a second dance, and led her back to the floor. Several more couples joined them, forming a set. Augusta glanced quickly around and spotted Sophronia, partnered by Captain Trent, in the next group. Augusta's eyes narrowed as they rested on him.

"Don't let the ridiculous gossip bother you," Lieutenant Kettering said softly. "Tomorrow there will be something new to occupy society's tongues." He followed the direction of her gaze. "Or is there something else worrying you?"

"Are you particularly acquainted with Captain Trent?" she ventured.

"I have not the honor." He bowed to her as the dance began. "Are you?"

"I only met him tonight." She frowned. "Still, he does appear to be the gentleman."

"High praise," he murmured. "I could hope you might speak more warmly of me."

Surprised, Augusta's gaze flew to his ardent expression. But the young lady behind her in the line came forward, and Augusta was forced to leave her partner. The next few minutes passed in a daze while her thoughts whirled in a new direction.

Unless she was very much mistaken, Lieutenant Jack Kettering was attempting to fit her interest. But with a sinking heart, she knew she wouldn't encourage him. If she chose, she could make a far more splendid match with one of the dull peers or self-centered Corinthians who deigned to admire the Incomparable. The sad truth was that she didn't want any of her suitors to drop the handkerchief. In spite of her determined practicality, a deep-rooted idealism within her wanted more than a comfortable marriage.

"You are much too solemn this evening." Kettering took her gloved hand and directed her in a stately circle about himself. "What may I do to bring the stars back into your eyes?"

She managed an almost convincing laugh. "Help me rewrite

67

the play so that I do not dread the performance."

He shook his head in mock sorrow. "I should have guessed it would be a feat beyond my poor ability. Could I not, perhaps, fetch the moon for you? That would be easier by far."

They continued a lighthearted banter concerning the play until the cotillion ended. The musicians rose for a brief interval, and Lieutenant Kettering led Augusta through the knots of conversing guests until they reached Sophronia.

The girl looked up, her face glowing, and a trembling smile parted her lips. No pale little dab of a creature any longer, Augusta noted with a surge of delight that evaporated the next moment. Sophronia blossomed under Vincent Trent's attentions—and Augusta could not trust him.

Lieutenant Kettering offered to fetch refreshments and Captain Trent excused himself. Sophronia's blush deepened as he bowed over her hand, and a sigh of pure ecstasy escaped her when he strolled off.

"Is he not the most delightful of men?" she breathed.

Loud voices, coming from the direction of the card room, interrupted Augusta's noncommittal answer. She and Sophronia exchanged a startled look and hurried, along with a number of others, to discover what had occurred. To their dismay, a small group stood about Perry and Lord Roderick, who apparently had just begun a hand of piquet. Neither appeared to have a head clear enough to cope with the intricacies of the game.

"Hundred pound points, I say!" Perry cried.

"No, really now," Lord Roderick protested.

"You told me to name a stake." Perry leaned heavily on the table and peered bleary-eyed at his opponent.

"Within reason, man, within reason!" Roddy shook his head, thickly. "This is your mother's house, remember, not some hell."

Perry snorted. "Then put up your precious ruby pistols as stake, since they've lost their luck."

Roddy made hushing gestures, but to no avail. Perry rose to his feet, deeper color darkening his already flushed countenance. But before he could speak, Captain Trent strode forward, pushing through the spectators, drawing the attention of both combatants. With a single sweep of his arm, he cleared the cards from the table, gathering them into an untidy heap.

"Enough!" His voice sounded thick, as if he'd been imbibing heavily. "Want to cast the ivories."

Augusta stared at him in surprise. Only a few minutes ago, Captain Vincent Trent had been as sober as she. That he put on an act, she could not doubt. But why?

Lord Roderick, his brow clouded, threw him a scathing glance and turned back to Perry. "You leave my pistols out of this! Remember, I could say a thing or two about your activities of late, if I were one to talk." He seemed pleased to have gotten this out without slurring his words too badly.

Perry almost turned purple. "Could say a thing or two, m'self."

They faced each other, tense, badly muddled, but Captain Trent again intervened. As if he saw nothing amiss, he hooked an arm around each of them and hauled them, protesting, past the interested onlookers and into the hall. With an exaggerated sweeping bow to Mrs. Lansdon, he ushered his two companions out of the house.

"Should we stop them?" Alarmed, Sophronia stared at the door that the footman shut behind the three gentlemen. "Perry is in no state to go gaming."

Augusta shook her head. "Captain Trent is very much in possession of his senses. I don't believe they will wind up in any hell this night." But she did wonder what the captain's motive might be. Altruism? She didn't think so—not after the way he had been watching Perry and Roddy.

"Convivial evening?" Kettering, glasses of punch in his hands, emerged from the throng that remained about the card room door.

"Is it?" Augusta tried to match his casual smile, but failed.

Sophronia raised stricken eyes to his face. "It was unforgivable of Perry to behave so at Mamma's party."

Kettering laughed easily. "I am sure no one objected. Young gentlemen are often somewhat wild."

Sophronia nodded, unconvinced.

A footman came up to her, bowed slightly, and murmured something about refreshments. With a word of excuse, Sophronia hurried away with him.

Augusta watched her go. Just how wild *would* a young officer of Perry's erratic stamp become?

"Your lemonade?" Kettering held out a glass, his concerned

gaze resting on her face.

She thanked him absently, took it, and stood in silence at his side while she sipped the beverage. Her uneasy gaze kept returning to the door, while her active mind sought answers.

Frederick Ashfield strolled up, nodded to Kettering, then turned to Augusta. "Contemplating something momentous?"

She shook her head and managed a brittle smile.

"I am glad." He offered his arm, and common politeness demanded that she take it. He led her off, out of hearing of her former partner. "Should I apologize for interfering, I wonder? No, I do not think I shall. Really, my dear, the besotted expression on his face whenever he gazes at you! He behaves like a moonling!"

Augusta stiffened. "He behaves as a gentleman."

"Does he? Really, you quite relieve my mind. Our friend Kettering has somewhat of a reputation. I could not reconcile it with my conscience if I did not make a push to save you if I thought you considered anything so reckless as an alliance with him."

She tried to withdraw her hand, but he held her firmly. "I am not a fool," she informed him tartly. "Your only fear is that I might embarrass Halliford. You may be very certain I shall do nothing of the sort."

"I am relieved to hear it," Mr. Ashfield drawled. "By the by, Helena is looking very unwell. I came in search of you just to drop a hint in your ear."

Her irritation forgotten in a moment, Augusta thanked him and headed directly to tell her sister that she was tired and wished to return home. Helena received the tidings with relief, and ordered the barouche at once. In less than fifteen minutes, the duchess entered the carriage and sank back against the squabs, closing her eyes in exhaustion.

Silence filled the night, broken only by the steady clopping of the horses' shod hooves on the cobbled pavement. Augusta closed her eyes also, but her thoughts raced on at full speed. She had tried, very hard, to dismiss that peculiar conversation she had overheard from her mind. But she had not succeeded.

And now the obvious course of action occurred to her. There was one person who would surely know what—if anything—should be done.

As Willis bowed them into the entry hall at Halliford House,

Augusta peered down the left corridor toward the back of the house. To her relief, she caught a glimpse of a light burning in the duke's study. Major MacKennoch was still awake.

She removed her wrap, but before she could hand it to the waiting footman, the major emerged from the back room. He strode quickly toward them, his brow lowered in a frown.

"Is everything all right, Your Grace?" His worried eyes studied Helena's tired face. "Ye are early."

"Oh, it was *I* who was tired," Augusta assured him blithely. "Helena is doing wonderfully. But it is time she went upstairs."

"I am not helpless." Helena regarded her sister in fond exasperation. She started across the hall to where their candles stood on a low table beside an oil lamp.

Augusta touched Major MacKennoch's sleeve, and he looked down at her in surprise. "I wish to speak with you," she whispered.

He darted a piercing glance at her from beneath his reddish brows, then gave her an almost imperceptible nod. He headed back to the study, leaving Augusta to help Helena up the mahogany staircase.

Lizzie, wrapped in a warm dressing gown of blue velvet, joined them on the second landing. Her bright, inquisitive gaze took in the strained expression on both her sisters' faces and she nodded wisely.

"Was the evening a crashing bore? Honestly, dancing!" Her tone held nothing but loathing. "What a paltry party." She trailed Helena and Augusta up the last flight.

In the duchess's chamber, Augusta rang for her abigail, then helped her sister to undress while Lizzie flopped down on the bed.

"Edward beat me at jackstraws," that young lady announced presently, sounding rather pleased.

"Did he?" Augusta stared at her blankly. The cold, proper Major MacKennoch, playing at jackstraws with Lizzie? And allowing her to call him Edward? It didn't seem possible.

As soon as the maid Dorson appeared, Lizzie, yawning, took herself off to bed. Augusta hurried back to the book room, where she found the major going over a handful of closely written pages and making neat notes in their margins.

He looked up, his face expressionless as he laid aside his

71

work. "What may I do for ye?"

She took the chair opposite him and stared at her hands for a long minute. "I hope there is no need to do anything—except, perhaps, to tell me I am concerned over nothing."

"I will do my poor best."

She caught the dry note of amusement in his voice and shot him a suspicious glance. His features remained solemn. Her gaze drifted from his face to his broad shoulders. His coat did not fit as exquisitely as did Halliford's, but this more casual style suited his ruggedness. He was independent, a loner—and just being in his commanding presence gave her a sense of confidence, as if he had already taken her problems into his infinitely capable hands.

Encouraged, she repeated what she had heard—admitting completely that it was all nothing but bits and scraps of a low-voiced conversation. When she finished, she gazed up at him, wondering what he would say.

"Are ye certain of the words, or could ye have been mistaken?" No trace of emotion colored his tone. As usual, he betrayed nothing of his thoughts.

"I cannot be positive of anything."

He took a slow, deep breath, considering. "It could very well be no more than your overactive imagination."

Her lips tightened, though she nodded. "That, and the—the strain and upset of Captain Montclyff's death."

Something flickered in his eyes, like a spark springing to life, but to her growing irritation he merely nodded.

He lowered his gaze, deliberately veiling his sudden stirring of exasperation. Here he had spent a fruitless morning at the Horse Guards asking subtle questions, and the little Carstairs had stumbled across what he sought by accident! The situation would be laughable if it weren't so frustrating.

Or so potentially dangerous. One—no two—of the guests at Mrs. Lansdon's home were apparently involved in a treasonous undertaking, and one about which Lord Bathurst had been unable to gain any clear information.

He tented his fingertips and regarded the young lady before him. Foreboding filled him at the eagerness in her eyes. She would be only too ready to plunge into what she undoubtedly considered a romantic adventure. She had no idea at all what hell this assignment could be. He must allay her suspicions and prevent her, no matter what, from becoming involved.

"Ye are quite right." He kept his voice level. "Ye are indulging your delight in romantic flights of fantasy beyond permission." He watched her closely, trying to gauge by her response how deeply she believed in her story. "I can only hope ye did not burden Her Grace with such a ridiculous farrago of nonsense."

A flash of hurt crossed Augusta's expressive countenance, and he felt as if he had struck an innocent kitten. Chagrin dulled her usually luminous blue-gray eyes. Such very large eyes, he noted. His response—to both her injured expression and her eyes—took him aback.

In a moment, she straightened up and those magnificent eyes flashed. "You think I imagined the whole thing!"

"Nay." He spoke with deliberation. She had told him the truth, of that he was certain. The only thing that surprised him was that she had waited to tell someone responsible rather than blurting out her tale to one of the hey-go-mad young officers who must dog her footsteps. Or that she hadn't sprung up from her hiding place and confronted the two men on the spot. She was too impulsive—and that, in a situation like this, could prove deadly.

"What *do* you think?" She regarded him in uncertainty.

He drew a deep breath, and knew it was time to lie. "I believe ye heard an innocent discussion."

Her lips tightened. "And I made up the rest because I'm flighty and undependable and—and a peagoose!"

"It is hardly my position to—"

"To insult me?" she broke in. "Let me inform you, Major MacKennoch, that I find your attitude unchivalrous and insulting in the extreme! The very least you could do would be to admit there was the slightest chance I *had* overheard something. I may by no means be positive myself, but—"

"Then I can be very certain ye heard very little, indeed," he broke in, cutting off her tirade. Her bosom heaved with her anger and he forced his gaze away.

She rose to her feet, then addressed him at her most dignified. "I simply request that you give the matter some consideration instead of dismissing it out of hand because you heard it from *me*." Only the trembling of her shoulders betrayed her emotion.

She made a magnificent picture. The major lowered his gaze and studied the quill he still held. He couldn't let on to her about his assignment. She was just foolish and romantic enough to decide to help him, and to go rushing headlong into danger. And that he could not allow—he owed it to Halliford, he told himself, though he found, somewhat disturbingly, that he would protect this vibrant, beautiful creature for her own sake.

That thought alarmed him. Did he have so little sense as to fall under her spell? That was something no sane, ineligible man could afford to do.

He raised his gaze, found the anger gone from her expression, and something inside of him melted. She stood before him, confused, vulnerable, yet proud and brave. She *had* matured since he saw her last, and not just physically. Both concern and intelligence shone from those lovely eyes. She behaved with great presence of mind. She had presented her story in a reasonable manner, completely devoid of drama or histrionics—but that was beside the point at the moment.

She squared her shoulders. "I hoped you would at least have the common courtesy to take my fears seriously. You seemed the best person to know what to do. Since I was wrong, I must apologize for troubling you. Good night, Major." She turned stiffly and headed toward the door.

Prompted by some urge he couldn't identify, he yielded. "Wait."

She looked back, her expression rife with suspicion. He came around the corner of the desk and stopped before her, looking down into her enchanting face.

"If ye really heard what ye think ye did, there is a very good chance ye could be hurt—and badly—if ye are not careful. I don't want that." That much, at least, was safe to say.

The glow that warmed her eyes was more reward than he had ever contemplated. Uncertain, he extended one hand toward her, then drew it back before she could respond. Abruptly, he returned to the desk, extinguished the candles, then ushered her out of the room.

Without speaking, he closed the door and escorted her to the hall, where their tapers awaited them. He lit hers from the lamp, then his own, and stood back to permit her to precede him up the curving stair.

At the second floor, where their paths separated, she turned to him. "What will you do about it?"

"Nothing." He kept his voice steady and hoped she would not guess he lied.

Bright color suffused her cheeks and her eyes sparkled in the wavering light of the flames. "You didn't take me seriously at all, did you? I am not the flighty little idiot you obviously think me!"

She spun about on her heel and marched off with surprising dignity for such a dainty little figure. She reached her room, opened the door, and slammed it behind her without a backward glance.

She rang for her maid, then flounced down on her silken coverlet. How dare he hold such a low opinion of her intelligence? It was enough to make her want to throw things at him—or better, to determine the truth of the matter herself! She was not about to give up tamely, as did he. What should she do next? And who should she tell—if anybody?

Her abigail entered and helped her out of her evening gown. While Augusta sat before the mirror, staring at the reflection of her maid brushing out her gleaming hair, she tried to keep her thoughts off Major MacKennoch, then abandoned the unequal fight.

His injuries had healed, she was sure—at least his physical ones. His knee had improved in just the few days he had been at Halliford House. He must be ready for some form of action again. Yet when she offered him a challenge, he said he would do nothing!

So that gleam she had surprised in his eyes must have been fleeting, before he decided the whole story was no more than a ridiculous flight of fantasy. He was unchivalrous and insulting beyond words, and she was glad she had told him so. How infamous of him not to believe her! That she hadn't been certain herself, she now ignored.

But her fury with him brought her no closer to answering the question of what she should do now. Nothing, like the major? Should she pretend she had never heard anything? She had been so certain he would know what to do, that she could turn the matter over to his capable hands! But he had let her down.

She still fumed the following morning as she sat in the

breakfast parlor, glaring at her tea and toast. She had half a mind to tell Lizzie about that perplexing conversation, just to hear her blunt opinion. But knowing Lizzie, given one hint of a mystery and she would take to playing Bow Street Runner and follow Captain Vincent Trent around everywhere he went. That thought brought a smile to her lips.

It faded the next moment. The door into the parlor opened and Edward MacKennoch stepped over the threshold. His frown set deep creases in his brow, giving him an unpleasant resemblance to Halliford at his angriest. She looked at him and felt her heart sink to the bottom of her stomach.

"There are four officers here to see ye." His voice, unlike his countenance, betrayed nothing.

"Four? About the play?" She touched her lips with her napkin and stood. "Could not Willis have told me?"

He remained where he was, blocking her way. "They are not here about any play."

"Then—"

He towered over her, solid, severe—like an iceberg. "They have come to ask ye questions concerning the death of Captain Montclyff."

Augusta actually felt the blood draining from her cheeks, leaving her clammy. "I—I will come at once."

Still, he didn't move. "Ye should not see them alone."

"No, but—" She shook her head. "It cannot be helped. It would distress Helena too much to be present."

"If ye would like, I will go with ye."

"Oh, would you?" Relief flooded through her. He might not approve of her, but he could be counted on to protect Halliford's interests—and in this case, that would include her. "Thank you," she breathed.

The officers awaited them in the Gold Saloon. Augusta entered hesitantly, glad of the major's solid presence just behind her. He escorted her to a seat, turned to the men who had stood at her entrance, and neatly assumed charge.

"I am Major MacKennoch, His Grace of Halliford's secretary. What may we do for ye?" His tone held just the right blend of haughtiness and composure.

The senior officer, a captain, stepped forward. "We are sorry to have to disturb Miss Carstairs, and will try not to distress her unduly. But the situation regarding Captain

76

Montclyff is not quite what we imagined at first."

"What—?" Augusta stared at him, perplexed.

The major's hand clasped her shoulder, silencing her, and she subsided. "In what way?" he asked, his imperturbable calm soothing her.

The officer cleared his throat. "At first, it was assumed that the captain met his death in an unfortunate duel. Such things are not unheard of, though they are strongly disapproved of. But we have been unable to discover any trace of his unknown opponent—or any seconds. Nor has a doctor come forward."

The man cast an uneasy glance at Augusta, then addressed himself to the major again. "Captain Montclyff sustained two wounds. One, just grazing his arm, was quite trifling. The second pierced his heart."

Augusta swallowed hard, forcing back a sensation of nausea. Major MacKennoch's grip tightened on her shoulder in a reassuring gesture.

"What are ye implying?"

"Two wounds on one man in a duel are impossible." The officer met his steady gaze. "Captain Montclyff was murdered."

Chapter 6

"Murdered?" Augusta whispered the word, her eyes widening in shock. "But . . ."

Major MacKennoch intervened once more, stilling her with the tightening grip of his fingers on her shoulder. "What steps have ye taken?"

"Very little information has come to light, sir." The officer shifted under the major's penetrating gaze. "No overheard quarrels, no threats against him, nothing that could even have led to the duel. And as I said, no other party, no seconds, and no doctor. It was set up to look like a duel, and would have been accepted as such, only the killer needed two shots to do away with his man."

Augusta leaned back in her chair, feeling ill. She hadn't liked Montclyff, but *murder* . . .

"If Miss Carstairs will answer a few questions?" The officer's voice broke through the fog that seemed to surround her.

She looked up, numb, and nodded.

"Did he call to see you on the day before his death?"

"Yes." From the manner in which the officer regarded her, she realized she had made no sound. She cleared her throat and tried again. "Yes."

"What was his purpose?"

She hesitated, glanced up at the major, and found him watching her every bit as intently as did the officer. She looked down at her hands. "He had been working with us on one of the short, rather silly plays we have been presenting to benefit the war orphans and widows. He had withdrawn from his role

78

the day before."

"Did he come to explain?" The officer's voice sounded deceptively gentle.

Augusta's cheeks felt warm, then clammy. "In a manner of speaking. He—he came to offer for me."

A fair-haired lieutenant who had remained silent until now murmured something to one of his companions, who nodded. Their senior remained outwardly calm, but a sudden gleam lit his eyes.

"And you said—?" He almost purred the words.

"I—I stopped him as soon as I realized his intent."

"I see." The officer drew several papers from a folder tucked under his arm and consulted his notes. "And how would you describe his mood when he left?"

"He was not pleased." In spite of herself, a rueful note crept into her voice.

"Not pleased," the officer repeated. "Might he have been angry?"

Augusta nodded, wishing the men would leave. Major MacKennoch remained beside her, detached, cool, listening, yet reassuring just by his presence. Still, she felt isolated.

"Very angry?" the officer pursued. "Would you care to tell me what he said?"

Augusta looked up into his closed face and felt her uneasiness grow, though she did not understand why. "I don't think I remember. It wasn't pleasant."

"Is this necessary?" the major broke in. "Have ye not distressed her enough?"

"I am sorry, Major. It is very necessary. Might he have threatened you, Miss Carstairs?"

Warm color stole into her cheeks. "He—he spoke a great deal of nonsense. I'm afraid I don't really remember."

"Did he not say that you would live to regret refusing his offer?"

Augusta concentrated on her hands, which lay clasped in her lap. "He had a very unpleasant way about him," she said with real feeling.

"Perhaps I should inform you, Miss Carstairs, that I have taken a statement from one of the maids, describing the threats he shouted at you and the manner in which he slammed out of the house."

79

Augusta blinked. "I don't think I'd have described it that way. Captain Montclyff is—was—not one to shout." She shivered, suddenly chilled. "He became cold and very precise when he was angry."

"And he was angry, Miss Carstairs?" The gentleness of the question invited confidences, promised sympathy and understanding.

She nodded again, though she had not been deceived. "He hated to be crossed."

"Is there anything else you would care to tell us?"

Augusta glanced up at Major MacKennoch and found his gaze resting on her, his eyes narrowed. "I'm not hiding anything," she snapped at him. "It just wasn't the sort of interview that is pleasant to dwell on. He was angry and disagreeable, but I wouldn't have said any more so than usual. I did not like him, and I believe it very possible that his cutting tongue won him many enemies, but I don't know of anyone who—who would want to murder him."

"Do you not, Miss Carstairs? Not even to assure that your honor was defended?"

"My—" She stared at him, her eyes opening wide.

"A suitor, unless he had the honor of being engaged to Miss Carstairs, is hardly likely to murder a man she had rejected." The major fixed the officer with a stern eye. "Only a lady's father, brother, or guardian is like to take such drastic measures. And since her father is dead and her brother is presently up at Oxford, that leaves only her guardian. Are ye perhaps implying that His Grace, the duke of Halliford, committed a foul murder and staged some cowardly duel to cover his crime?"

Considerably abashed, the officer denied any such intent. He shoved his notes into his folder and handed them to one of his subalterns. He straightened up, attempting to recover the ground he had lost. "Are you fixed at Halliford House for the present in case we need to ask you anything else?"

"Miss Carstairs will be pleased to help in any way she can." Major MacKennoch stepped forward, effectively placing himself in front of Augusta and shielding her from further contact with her inquisitors. "Ye have only to inform either His Grace or myself."

The officer met his gaze squarely in a test of wills. After a moment, his eyes slid down. "Thank you, sir." He allowed Major MacKennoch to escort his party to the door.

Augusta remained in her chair, staring into the fire. When the black Demetrius meandered into the room and insinuated himself into her lap, she barely noticed. She merely stroked the thick, velvety fur, and found a measure of relief for her unsettled mind in this peaceful occupation. She did not even look up when the door to the Gold Saloon was pushed wide once more.

Major MacKennoch strode in and stopped just before her.

"Murdered," she said without looking up. "I can scarcely believe it."

"Can you not? Captain Montclyff does not sound as if he were a pleasant gentleman."

A wan smile twitched her lips and her hands tightened on the purring cat. "He wasn't. Did they tell you anything else?" She raised her gaze to his stern face.

Major MacKennoch shook his head. "They are being—shall we say somewhat circumspect?—about it."

Augusta drew a deep breath. "I felt as if they believed *I* had murdered him myself."

"Nay." Something flickered in his eyes that might almost have been amusement. His expression softened, as if a thaw had set in and warmed the ice that habitually ran through his veins. Augusta suddenly felt weak for a very different reason.

The major reached into his pocket, drew out a chased silver snuffbox, and helped himself to a pinch. "I doubt they believe ye actually pulled the trigger. Ye must remember, though, how those officers will be thinking." He fingered the box, apparently examining the powdered contents. "Perhaps ye were afraid of what Captain Montclyff might do to make ye regret your rejection of him. There is more than one foolish young gudgeon who might be inspired—at your instigation—to defend your honor."

"You have such a delightful way of phrasing things."

His clear blue eyes lit with sudden humor. "My apologies. Ardent young gentlemen, I should say."

"You should, indeed." Her brow creased as she frowned. "But you told the officers it wasn't likely that any of them would."

"True. They will think it anyway, of course."

81

She shook her head. "It doesn't make sense. What could Captain Montclyff have done—or been about to do—that could hurt me badly enough that I might have wanted him killed?"

Major MacKennoch snapped his box closed and returned it to the depths of his pocket. "I have no idea," he said shortly. "More likely they suspect one of your suitors of being jealous. It would be best if this matter were cleared up. Try to think. It is very possible ye are aware of more than ye realize. Ye were part of the same group, working together on the plays. I've noticed the easy terms upon which ye all stand with one another. Ye knew many of the people he knew."

"But—none of them are murderers! Captain Montclyff knew any number of people! What about his regiment?"

The major strode over to the fireplace and stared down at the crackling logs. "I wish ye were not involved in this!" Anger filled his voice.

"Do you think *I* enjoy it? You make it sound as if it were all my fault!"

He turned to look at her over his shoulder, a curious, accusing light in his piercing eyes. "I suppose ye did not cast out lures to him."

"I did not!" Indignant, she sprang to her feet. "I did nothing to encourage Monty to pursue me in the—the most odious manner."

"Did ye not?" he mused. "No, I suppose your flirtatious ways are just a part of ye that ye cannot help."

"You are insulting, Major."

"I am trying to do my job, Miss Carstairs, which is to protect His Grace's interests." A touch of exasperation crept into his voice.

"Then you need not concern yourself with me."

"I fear the duchess might feel differently." His tone held nothing but apology.

She gritted her teeth. "You may be very sure I shall not let Helena be disturbed. Or Halliford." Turning on her heel, she left the room.

As she reached the hall, Lizzie bounced down the stairs, a half-eaten roll in one hand and the white and gray Penelope curled comfortably in her other arm. Sight of her cheerful, prosaic sister went a long way to soothing Augusta's shattered nerves. Major MacKennoch was insufferable.

"What's put you all on end?" Lizzie took a large bite from the roll. "Are the others here?"

"Others?" Augusta stared at her blankly.

"The rehearsal," Lizzie explained with great patience, as if to a child. "It's gone on ten o'clock."

"Oh." With an effort, Augusta rallied. "I had completely forgotten it. I wondered what you were doing out of bed already."

Lizzie blinked wide, humorous gray eyes at her. "Having breakfast, of course." She finished the roll in another bite, shifted the unprotesting cat into a more comfortable position, and headed for the Gold Saloon.

Augusta followed her into the room used for rehearsal as a knock fell on the front door. Major MacKennoch, she was glad to see, had already left.

They had barely settled themselves when Willis showed in Sophronia and Perry, neither looking overly happy. Sophronia managed a wan smile in response to their greetings and sank down in a chair beside the fire that burned merrily against the late February chill. Her worried gaze rested on her brother.

Augusta turned to regard him as well, and noted at once his natty appearance. She raised an appreciative eyebrow. "No one else can look quite so à la modality in uniform."

"The neckcloth," Perry assured her. He displayed his elaborate creation with an air of pride, as if nothing more momentous occupied his mind. But dark circles under his eyes and an unusual pallor beneath his tan betrayed him.

Sophronia interrupted her brother's preening. "We saw several officers leaving. Did they come about the play?"

Augusta's smile faded. "No. About Captain Montclyff."

Perry looked up from his examination of his coat sleeve. "What the devil did they want?"

She stared at him, surprised at the sharpness of his tone. "They believe Captain Montclyff was murdered."

"But a duel—" Perry broke off, his hazel eyes wide, giving him a very youthful and vulnerable appearance.

"There were two bullets," Augusta explained. "One grazed his arm, the other—the other killed him."

"Two—" Perry looked about the room, spotted a decanter of Madeira on a side table, and crossed over to it. He poured

83

himself a liberal glass and swallowed it in one gulp. He poured a second, then turned to face Augusta. "*Two* bullets did you say?"

She nodded. "The officers believed that the duel was merely a pretense, arranged after the murder to—to disguise the circumstances."

"Oh, my God." Perry sank onto a chair and stared at the glass. He took an unsteady sip. "Murder. But it—" A shaky laugh escaped him. "Lord, I suppose we should have guessed Monty would end up that way. Dashed unpleasant fellow." He stood and paced restlessly to the fire. "Well, shall we get on with the rehearsal?" He strode over to the trunk that held their assemblage of props and ruthlessly dragged them out.

Major MacKennoch, seated in Halliford's study, set down his quill and frowned. He had left the copy of the *London Times* in the Gold Saloon. He had better retrieve it before it would mean breaking in on the rehearsal.

As he approached, he saw that the door stood slightly ajar. That probably meant they wouldn't mind an interruption, so he pushed it farther, took two steps into the room, then paused. A scene was about to begin.

Miss Carstairs stood before the fireplace, staring into the flames. Lieutenant Lansdon, resplendent in a pair of the most shocking ginger whiskers he had ever beheld, stood just behind her. Miss Lansdon and Miss Lizzie sat together on the couch, watching critically.

"I cannot be denied any longer," Perry announced in most unenthusiastic accents.

"A moment longer," Lizzie corrected.

Augusta spun around, hands extended, eyes closed. "Kiss me. Take me in your arms if that is your will!"

"No, dash it! I mean, I'm not really supposed to, am I?" Perry protested.

The major winced. How could he ever have responded to such an obvious theatrical line? And the worst of it was that he wanted to again.

"You don't actually have to kiss her," Lizzie assured Perry. "But you should at least put your hands on her shoulders."

Augusta sighed and opened her eyes. "Can we never get

through this ridiculous scene without—" She broke off and stared in consternation at the major, who remained near the doorway.

"Excuse me." He came forward. "I believe I left the newspaper in here."

"Of course." She eyed him warily. "It's on the table behind you."

He picked it up, then turned back to her. She hadn't moved at all but still watched him with that guarded expression. The temptation proved irresistible. "Ye play that scene remarkably well."

"Too well." Her tone sounded rueful, but she maintained her composure to admiration.

"Why don't you help us?" Lizzie suggested. "Perry is hopeless. You could wear the whiskers instead."

A quavering began within him that escaped in a deep chuckle. It surprised him. "I am certain Miss Carstairs can find a far more suitable hero to play opposite her."

"None with your ready responses," she said dryly.

He inclined his head in acknowledgment of her point, only to be struck by an unsettling realization. Miss Carstairs had indeed grown up; she was no longer the silly little chit he had encountered two years ago. And for some unfathomable reason, his opinion seemed to matter to her. He found that oddly touching.

He steadied himself. An attachment to a lady of quality was a weakness, something which a MacKennoch never betrayed. His father had drilled that tenet deeply into him. A MacKennoch was strong. An association with a certain order of female could be permissible, as was a marriage of convenience—when such an alliance would further his career. An affair of the heart was foolishness. And a MacKennoch was never a fool.

He met her gaze and knew the impulse to indulge, just this once, in a bit of foolishness.

"Please forgive my intrusion." Discretion being the better part of valor, it occurred to him that a strategic retreat was in order.

"You are most welcome to stay—if you can bear to watch this scene." An irrepressible smile just touched her lips.

He returned it before he could stop himself. Lord, those

mischievous, twinkling eyes. Her flirtatious tricks had given way to something far more dangerous—open, engaging manners and an innate sweetness of disposition. She could break hearts without even trying. But his would not be permitted to become one of them.

"Why don't you stay?" Sophronia chimed in.

"We could use a new audience," Lizzie added. "Penelope here has fallen asleep."

Edward MacKennoch hesitated, sorely tempted, though he knew it would not be wise. His refusal was cut off as the door opened once more and Willis bowed in Lord Wentworth.

His lordship made a leg to the ladies and nodded a greeting to the major. Then his gaze drifted to Perry and the ridiculous whiskers and he shuddered. "No!" He pronounced the single syllable with loathing. "They do not blend well with your scarlet coat."

Lizzie nodded. "I told him so."

"Well, I suppose it cannot be helped at the moment. Let's see how it goes on." Lord Wentworth took a seat, folded his arms across the generous expanse of his waistcoat, and waited.

Perry and Augusta began the scene once more. Edward strolled to the back of the room, but did not leave. Instead, he propped his shoulder against the wall and watched. In a very few moments, he found himself seriously hard pressed not to laugh. The sensation seemed alien to him; he had not experienced it for a very long time, he realized in bemusement. But the scene was really awful, despite Miss Carstairs's creditable job of acting. Lieutenant Peregrine Lansdon, though, waving a ridiculously large horse pistol, was so artificial it became hilarious.

They finished, and Lord Wentworth nodded. "Playing it for a farce, I see. Well, well, I don't suppose there's any other way for it. But we must change a few of the lines."

Perry groaned and Augusta sat down with a sigh. "But we must give it tomorrow night!" she protested.

Lord Wentworth, already poring over the pages of the script, nodded absently. He didn't even look up when the door opened once more and Lord Roderick and Lieutenant Jack Kettering strolled in together.

"What, more changes?" Kettering regarded Lord Wentworth in mock horror.

"Not again!" Roddy glared at him, affronted. "No, really, it's too much to expect of a fellow."

"Well, it does need something." Augusta rose to offer the new arrivals refreshments.

"Like abandoning?" Lizzie met her sister's rebuking gaze with one of limpid innocence.

"We will be done with it tomorrow night." Sophronia soothed the irritated Lord Roderick. "Next time, let us get a less—"

"Less ridiculous one." Lizzie finished the sentence for her in a spirit of misguided helpfulness.

Lord Wentworth silenced them, showed the corrected page to Augusta and Perry, and told them to try it again. They did, and Lizzie shook her head in disgust.

"Perhaps it was better the other way," Sophronia suggested.

"Which isn't saying much," Lizzie added brightly.

Roddy nodded. "Change it back."

"Well, we've got to settle on something." Jack Kettering regarded the little troupe in amusement. "If we don't, we'll each be performing a different version tomorrow night."

"That might help it." Everyone ignored Lizzie's comment, so she subsided for the moment.

"I've managed to learn one set of lines," Perry said, and ignored Lizzie's hoot of disbelief. "Let's stick to those."

"I still think Perry and Lieutenant Kettering should exchange roles. I thought Kettering was to take over as hero." Lizzie looked around for support, but found none.

Kettering frowned. "I prefer what I'm doing. But there is still one scene . . ."

"As long as I'm not in it." Perry folded his arms in an uncompromising manner.

Roddy looked uneasy. "Well, it's Augusta's production, of course, but I'd rather you don't go playing around with any of my lines."

"No." Lord Wentworth gave him a dry smile. "That wouldn't be a good idea."

The rehearsal resumed. Major MacKennoch, abandoning all pretenses, took a seat on a long sofa and settled down to enjoy himself. About halfway through the scene, Willis admitted an officer who appeared vaguely familiar to Edward. The newcomer cast an appraising glance at the actors, then strolled over and joined the major. He frowned slightly in an effort of recognition.

"Captain Trent, isn't it?" Edward MacKennoch extended his hand. "We last met at Badajos, I believe."

Vincent Trent's brow cleared. "Major MacKennoch. You've sold out."

"Injuries," he said shortly. "Have ye come to be entertained?"

"Not exactly." The captain hestitated, but clearly still regarded the major as a senior officer, despite his putting off his uniform. "This business of Captain Montclyff has interested me. I pulled a few strings and have gotten myself put in charge of the investigation."

"Have ye, now." The major drew himself up to his full height and looked down his aquiline nose at the shorter, more stockily built captain, who took the seat beside him. "Miss Carstairs has already been questioned—and distressed unduly, I might add."

"No, I haven't come to harass her." Captain Trent hurried into speech. His gaze transferred to the performers, then drifted to Lord Wentworth, who kept his intent regard focused on the little troupe.

The major eyed Captain Trent, assessing him. He had heard good reports of him in the Peninsula, but had not known him very well personally. A Corinthian, he decided, with a will of iron showing through the thinnest velvet glove. Not a man many would care to cross. If it came to a battle of wills between them, though, he did not doubt that he would himself come off the victor.

He nodded slowly, satisfied. He could not decide whether or not he liked the captain, but he knew himself to be in control. He definitely did not like the way the man's gaze rested on Miss Carstairs. Was it in admiration of her undeniable beauty—or in suspicion? And if so, suspicion of what?

That question disturbed the major. But if Captain Trent thought he was going to hound Miss Carstairs, he would come up against more than he had reckoned with. Edward might have retired from active duty owing to physical injuries, but he knew how to protect his own—or rather, his employer's—interests.

At last, Lord Wentworth gave the final scenes his approval.

"We will gather at seven tomorrow night," he informed his players. "Is everything prepared?" He turned to Augusta.

"Yes. We will set the stage first thing in the morning."

Sophronia cast a wistful glance in the direction of Captain Trent, whose entrance had not escaped her. He did not look at her, so she turned to locate her brother. Together, they took their leave.

One by one, the others departed. Lizzie slipped out with them, leaving Major MacKennoch in the empty room, facing Augusta.

He rose from the sofa, but did not head for the door. Something about the way she just stood there looking at him, so very vulnerable, touched him. A man could lose himself in those luminous eyes. He forced his gaze away.

On the occasional table near him, he spotted one of the massive horse pistols that had been used as props. He picked it up, weighing it in his hands, then brought it to her.

"Perry is so careless." She did not meet his gaze. The telltale flush of a lingering embarrassment touched her cheeks.

"At least it's not loaded."

She shook her head, smiling suddenly. "No one would dare! Perry is the most dreadful shot. I have no idea how he has survived in the army."

The major went to the prop trunk and lifted the heavy lid. An array of unusual objects, from elaborate stage jewelry to a well-worn saddle, met his startled eyes. He sifted through the motley assortment of items and finally drew out a rather beautiful cherry wood pistol case.

"Let me put that away." He opened the box, but it was not empty as he had expected. Inside rested an exquisite pair of dueling pistols traced with gold along the barrels. A large, blood red ruby nestled in the stock of each gun.

Then his gaze moved to the deep red velvet lining and his eyes narrowed. The color appeared uneven, splotchy, as if badly stained. A faint but all too familiar odor reached him. His stomach lurched at the memories of battle and searing pain it conjured up; he fought it back. A cold certainty gripped him and he touched one of the crusted purplish patches.

It was damp. His finger come away stained with traces of brownish red. Blood.

And it must have been spilled very recently.

Chapter 7

"Is something the matter?" Augusta walked up behind Major MacKennoch and peered over his shoulder.

He drew his handkerchief from his pocket and wiped off his finger with care. His gaze rested on the brownish red streaks on the muslin square as he forced himself to consider other possibilities. It couldn't be water spilled on an old stain, though. That would produce a darker, muddier color, not this diluted red. This looked more as if someone had tried to wash out fresh blood.

He crumpled the handkerchief before Augusta could see the telltale marks. The last thing he wanted was for her to jump to unwarranted conclusions—as possibly he did. But he had seen enough blood in his time to know this stain, even diluted as it was with water, must be less than a week old.

Thoughtfully, he drew one of the gleaming pistols out of the case. "Rather pretty props you're using. Either those rubies are real, or they're remarkably fine paste copies."

"But I've never seen them before. They're—Oh!" She broke off, staring at them in consternation. "I wonder if they're Lord Roderick's! Perry said something about rubies. These must be his lucky pistols."

The major turned to look at her over his shoulder. "But what are they doing here—in a prop trunk?"

Augusta shook her head. "It certainly seems odd, doesn't it?" Then her eyes widened in dismay. "Perry said something about borrowing them without—without asking. Do you suppose he plans to return them this way? Or that he is playing a joke on Lord Roderick?"

Major MacKennoch made no reply. Once more, he ran a finger over a stained portion of the velvet. Crusty flakes of dried blood broke loose. Only that one patch was damp. With care, he weighed the pistol in his hand, testing the balance, then laid it back in the case. He picked up its mate, raising it as if he were taking aim. His brow snapped down. "This one is loaded."

"Loaded?" The word caught in Augusta's throat. "But— that is dangerous! Especially the way we have been playing about with the horse pistols!"

The major nodded, his expression grim. His gaze returned to the bloodstained lining of the case. "I wonder how long that has been there." He touched the damp patch again, then scrutinized the stain on his fingertip. "And I wonder why one is loaded and the other—" He broke off and subjected the other gun to a careful examination. "The other hasn't been cleaned since it was fired."

"You cannot mean . . ." Augusta's voice trailed off. She stared at the major with horror in her eyes. "Do you think these are the pistols used to shoot Monty?" The words came out in a hushed whisper.

"The officers said the guns weren't left at the Green." He hefted the empty pistol, studying the intricate tracery of gold filigree that wove along the barrel. "These are certainly distinctive. They would lead directly to their owner." He spoke slowly, weighing the merits of a theory to himself.

Augusta sat down abruptly. "No!"

Major MacKennoch turned to look at her, surprised at how much emphasis she managed to place in that one syllable.

"Monty was hit by two shots. But one of these guns is still loaded." She clenched her hands together, regarding him in unwavering earnestness. "That *must* mean these cannot have been used."

"Well, if Captain Montclyff held one, it wouldn't necessarily have been fired, would it?"

"Then where did the second shot come from? No, this is impossible. If Perry had them—"

"Yes?" He rose from where he had started to bend over the trunk and turned to face her.

"It's impossible. Perry can't hit anything! And there would have to be another pistol somewhere!" She stared down at her hands, then looked up into Edward's inscrutable face. "What should we do? Tell those officers?"

Edward picked up the second pistol and looked from one to the other, a deep crease in his brow. "I think not," he said slowly. "I believe we will do best to leave them alone for the moment." He rocked back on his heels, considering. "Captain Trent appears to me to be a gentleman too prone to acting without due consideration. Yes, I believe we will wait."

"Captain Trent! Oh, no, we mustn't tell him! He—" Augusta broke off.

"He what?" Gently, the major prompted her.

Augusta shook her head. "I didn't mention it to you before because it seemed so absurd. But that—that nonsense I overheard the other night—I believe Captain Trent to have been one of the two men."

"The devil ye do." Edward stared at her, hard. "Why?"

"When I left the conservatory, he was in the hall, just waiting, as if he were giving someone time to enter the drawing room alone so they would not be seen going in together."

The crease in Edward's brow deepened. "Ye didn't see anyone else?"

She shook her head.

"But ye had been listening. Could not he have been, as well?"

"It's possible. That's why I didn't tell you. But I keep thinking about it, and I simply cannot conceive how he could have hidden himself if he'd been in the hall when the men left the conservatory. Nor could he have heard anything. I only did because I was in the room. And he watches people." An involuntary shiver swept through her.

"What do ye mean he watches people? Who?" Edward returned the pistols to their case, but he kept his gaze on her worried face.

"Perry, Miss Lansdon, Lord Roderick, even others, for all I know. Earlier that evening, I thought he was following Perry and Roddy."

"First he may be involved in treasonous activity, and now he 'pulls strings' to be placed in charge of this investigation." The major stared hard at the open cherry wood case he held. "Interesting. Very interesting."

"Do you think he is involved in Monty's murder?" Augusta

barely breathed the question.

Her tone of hushed excitement brought a real smile to his lips. "I don't know. But don't ye go making any accusations!" he ordered.

"As if I would! You seem to have a very low opinion of my discretion."

"No." His voice gentled. "But ye do tend toward impulsiveness."

Delicate color tinged her cheeks a very becoming pink. It wasn't reasonable for a taciturn Scot to notice how that brought out the mahogany highlights in her thickly curling dark hair. But he did, and found it too much to his liking.

Abruptly, he picked up the loaded pistol and carried it to a table, where he set about removing the ball and powder with care. This done, he returned it to the case, which he closed with a snap. He restored it to its place near the bottom of the prop trunk. Augusta tossed a short velvet cloak over the top, then lowered the lid.

Edward raised a questioning eyebrow. "Is everything the way it should be?"

"Yes. What do we do now?"

"Since this is all nothing but conjecture, there isn't much we can do."

"Nothing?"

He smiled at her dismayed expression. "I am every bit as curious as ye are about this, but what would ye recommend? Running to the authorities—Captain Trent, perhaps?—and telling him that the pistols which may or may not have been used to murder Captain Montclyff have turned up in what amounts to your possession?"

Her face fell. "But we aren't certain—"

"Precisely. We are not certain. So we must wait—and watch."

"It doesn't sound like much."

"What do ye want to do, go dashing off on some romantic adventure?"

Her lips twitched into a wry smile. "At least the pistols should be safe enough there." She cast one last, worried glance at the prop trunk, then allowed the major to escort her from the room.

Captain Vincent Trent. She was more than willing to suspect

93

him of being involved in something. But what? Captain Geoffrey Montclyff's murder? The sale of military secrets? Both? And Sophronia, the sweet, silly creature she was, had formed an undeniable tendre for him. Augusta could only hope her friend had not fallen for a villain.

Willis, flanked by the second and third footmen, awaited her in the hall to set up the "theater," and her worried thoughts found a new avenue. The imminent approach of the play took precedence over all other matters. A great deal of preparation lay ahead.

The major followed them to the two drawing rooms that had to be thrown together, and observed the beginnings of chaos. Before it could get out of hand, he intervened. "Can I be of assistance?"

Augusta regarded him doubtfully. "Do you really wish to become involved in this?"

"It was His Grace's express wish." A slight smile played about the corners of his mouth.

Augusta found it delightful. It transformed his whole face, making him no less rugged but infinitely more approachable. She averted her eyes with difficulty. "I want to disrupt the household as little as possible."

He nodded. "Then if our good Willis will show me how things were arranged for the last production, I will take over that chore and allow him to return to his own duties."

This being more than agreeable to the butler, the preparations went far more smoothly than might have been expected. Augusta watched with mingled awe and satisfaction as Major MacKennoch, with all the efficiency of an experienced officer, directed the two footmen in the arrangement of both the stage and the seating for the large audience they hoped to attract.

Helena, wandering onto the scene a short time later, stared about in admiration. "So much activity," she murmured. "So many things to be done." She rounded on Augusta, who strolled in from the small saloon that would be laid out for refreshments. "Have you heard from the caterers or should we warn Cook?"

Augusta took her sister firmly by the arm. "I am not going to permit you to take charge. No, don't argue with me. For once you are going to do as you are told and just sit still and watch."

94

"But I—"

Augusta marched her to a sofa that now stood against a side wall. "Quit trying to put up a brave front. I have a very capable assistant in Major MacKennoch."

By the time the cast began assembling the following night, everything was in readiness. Only a bad case of nerves at performing before an audience assailed Augusta. Nor, she realized as she greeted the others, was she alone with that problem. Lord Wentworth wandered around the makeshift stage, frantic, loudly bewailing the lapse of forethought that had led him to agree to become director of so unprepossessing a production. The others were little better.

"Where are the props?" Sophronia looked accusingly from one to the other of the troupe, as if she thought someone had hidden them deliberately to provoke her.

"Here." Major MacKennoch moved away from the trunk on which he'd been half sitting.

Perry managed an almost convincing laugh. "Do stop pacing, Kettering. You have probably been more composed before going into battle."

Kettering flushed. "At least then I had confidence."

"We're not facing a firing squad," Augusta rallied them. "Try to be as bad as possible, it will make it all the funnier."

Lizzie, who had strolled in with Frederick Ashfield to watch preparations, smiled brightly. "Yes, perhaps people can be induced to donate money on the condition that you don't give any more plays."

Augusta directed an injured glance at her.

"Just so." Mr. Ashfield strolled over to the prop box, raised the heavy lid, and glanced interestedly inside.

Sophronia looked up from trying to straighten the filmy shawl she needed for the first act. "Are the guests here already?"

"No need to panic just yet." Frederick Ashfield turned a smile of frank enjoyment on her. "I only came in to wish you all luck."

Helena entered, the pallor of her complexion enhanced by the dark green of her gown. She looked at the distraught troupe and an uncertain smile wavered on her lips. "Is everything ready?"

Frederick Ashfield gestured to Lizzie. "Take her upstairs

and convince her to lie down until the performance," he murmured as the girl joined him. Lizzie nodded and did so at once, over Helena's halfhearted protests.

"Thank you." Augusta watched her sisters leave the room. "I have been trying to get her to rest all day, but she will worry so. Oh, I wish I had found somewhere else to hold our plays! I never should have suggested Halliford House."

"The opportunity to visit a ducal home has probably been the cause of more ticket sales than all the other factors put together," Mr. Ashfield pointed out dryly.

Augusta sighed, for it was probably true. Although only the elite of society would attend, invitations to Halliford House were not that common. Few would miss the opportunity to enter these illustrious portals.

Lord Roderick, delayed by his duties, put in a belated appearance. Recalled to a sense of the advancing hour, the actors separated to put on their makeup and costumes in the upstairs rooms allotted to them. Major MacKennoch left his position near the prop box and with his limping stride approached Augusta.

"Why don't ye ask young Lansdon if he knows how the pistols got there?" he murmured. He made his way past her to the curtain and began to make unnecessary adjustments.

She nodded and hurried after that young gentleman, intercepting him as he reached the stairs. "Perry? Do you have a moment?" She drew him down the hall to Halliford's book room.

He cast her an uneasy look. "What do you want, Augusta? I've got to get into my costume." His closed expression did not promise much in the way of confidences.

She tried anyway, and asked her question without preamble. "How did Lord Roderick's ruby pistols come to be in the prop box?"

He turned white, then a purplish hue flushed his countenance. "I don't know what you're talking about! How should I know where his dashed pistols are?"

Her eyes narrowed. "But weren't you going to borrow them?"

"No! I never laid a finger on the dashed things! Give them back to Roddy and be done with it!" He pulled away and pushed out the door.

And in the hall stood Captain Vincent Trent. His comprehensive gaze took in both of them, and Augusta didn't doubt for a moment he had overheard everything they said. A slight smile just touched his lips. He nodded to them, then strolled back toward the main hall and the drawing rooms, where the first of the guests had already gathered.

What a shattering way to begin the evening. Augusta slowly mounted the stairs. Had Captain Trent put the pistols in the trunk to see if she—or one of the others—recognized them as the weapons used in the duel? But then how had he gotten hold of them? Unless—could he have placed them there so that *she* would look guilty? What better way to protect himself than to be in charge of the investigation!

She had no idea how she managed to get into her costume, but somehow the cast assembled, Major MacKennoch drew back the curtain, and the performance commenced. The next hour, which began as little more than torment, improved as they made their initial mistakes and the world did not come to an end. The laughter from the audience, some of it at the right moments, raised their spirits, and the final curtain was drawn to enthusiastic applause.

Augusta sank back against the prop trunk, met Major MacKennoch's smiling eyes, and breathed a sigh of relief. "We did it!"

Jack Kettering made a sweeping bow before her. "And all due to your brilliant performance."

She waved that aside. "We *all* did quite well. I am exceedingly proud of us. But right now I want to get out of my costume."

She started toward the door, but it opened and in came Lizzie, again accompanied by Frederick Ashfield. Augusta looked from one to the other. "Well? How was it?"

Mr. Ashfield leaned against the door jamb in a negligent manner. "I don't think it will be necessary for the *entire* cast to go into the country until society finds something new to laugh about," he pronounced judiciously.

"You really carried it off rather well," Lizzie agreed. "In spite of Perry's beard falling off when he was supposed to be kissing you."

Augusta giggled in nervous reaction. "I nearly went into whoops when Roddy picked up the horse pistol and demanded

97

what on earth he was supposed to do with it."

"Well, if his intended victim hadn't had to reach out, grab it, and point it at herself, it wouldn't have been so bad." Frederick Ashfield shook his head. "My compliments, Miss Lansdon. That was very quick thinking."

Major MacKennoch came forward. "Our compliments to ye all. Miss Lizzie? May I assist ye with the refreshment tables?"

The players made their various ways to the rooms where they could change their clothes and remove makeup. Augusta hesitated a moment, her uncertain gaze on the prop trunk, then she shrugged. Had the major been concerned, he would not have left the backstage area. Besides, she was exhausted. She headed for the stairs after the others.

At the first landing, she found Jack Kettering waiting for her. The others, she noted in dismay, had already disappeared. He followed her up the last half-flight, but when they reached the hall, he moved in front of her, blocking her way.

He drew a deep breath and clasped her hand. "I cannot wait another moment, I must speak."

She stared at him, surprised. "What about? Surely not the next play!"

"No. For once, I am in earnest." He drew her fingers to his lips. "My beautiful Augusta, I have loved you from the moment I first set eyes on you. I want nothing more than to lay my heart at your dainty feet."

That line would have sounded superb in their recent farce, but Augusta refrained from pointing that out. "This is hardly the time—" She shook her head, not wanting to encourage him. "The play has been such a strain."

He dropped to one knee, grasped the hem of her muslin skirt, and raised it ardently to his lips in an almost theatrical gesture. "You need have no fear, I will not press you. Indeed, it would be most improper of me to do so," he added, with a sublime indifference to the impropriety of his current actions. "I dare not approach Halliford for his permission—yet. I am naught but a lowly lieutenant, hopelessly unworthy of you. But I shall prove myself, never doubt it." He rose, claimed her hand once more, and pressed a passionate kiss onto her palm. Before she could recover, he turned abruptly on his heel and walked off.

Augusta stared after him, embarrassed even though there had been no one nearby to witness the little scene. She should have been prepared for such a declaration—but she hadn't been. She had grown so accustomed to his air of hopeless worship, it had not seriously occurred to her he might one day bring himself up to scratch. Somehow, it had all seemed nothing more than an act. But apparently his heart might be deeply involved after all.

But hers was not. At least he hadn't pressed her—for that she could be grateful. And he wouldn't approach Halliford, so the duke would not be put to the trouble of turning him down for her.

She made her way up the next flight of steps and hurried to her own room. To her relief, she found her maid awaiting her, and in less than twenty minutes she returned to the guests. Everyone, she noted in relief, seemed to be having a pleasant time. She strolled from room to room, receiving laughing congratulations and thanking people for coming. All went smoothly.

In the drawing room, where the stage had been hastily dismantled, she spotted Helena sitting quietly in a corner, conversing with Mrs. Lansdon. At least the duchess left the role of hostess to Lizzie, who accomplished it with a flair, ably aided by Frederick Ashfield. Augusta smiled, appreciating that gentleman's worth for perhaps the first time.

She started across to join Helena, only to come up short as she caught a glimpse of someone out of the corner of her eye— Captain Vincent Trent changing his position so he could watch her! Her ready temper flared. What on earth did he think she might do? Sell some military secrets under his very nose, or perhaps murder someone in her sister's drawing room? This was the grossest piece of impertinence, and she was not about to let him get away with it.

She would see that his watching stopped! If he were not simply trying to make her nervous, if he were actually innocent in this dreadful business and had the effrontery to believe *her* to be somehow involved—well, she would lead him a merry dance, and no mistaking that! If she could induce him to confront her—possibly even accuse her of treason or conspiring to commit a murder—in front of the major, that gentleman would send the captain about his business in short order. Major MacKennoch would rise to her defense, like a knight on the field of combat, and charge in to protect his lady in distress. . . .

She bit her lip, her ever-fertile imagination going to work as she quickly scanned the crowded room for ideas. Major MacKennoch stood by the door, conversing with several officers. He was within reach—when she needed him. Her gaze moved on and settled on the prop box, which stood in the corner with its lid open.

Casually—so casually as to draw Captain Trent's instant attention to herself—she strolled over to the trunk. With exaggerated stealth, she slipped one hand behind her and began groping inside. When she found a heavy pistol case, she turned and opened it—and stared into a box empty except for the horse pistols.

She searched rapidly through the contents of the trunk, but the cherry wood case with the ruby-mounted pistols was missing. Bemused, she gazed down at the box she had laid aside. She had herself put the horse pistol away after the play, and seen the other box there. That could have been no more than three-quarters of an hour ago!

Uneven footsteps came up behind her and she spun about to see Major MacKennoch approaching through the knots of people. Flat disapproval replaced the almost relaxed camaraderie that had marked his expression earlier.

"If I might have a word with ye for a moment?" His voice betrayed his displeasure. Without waiting for her reply, he took her arm and escorted her from the drawing room. Not one more word did he vouchsafe until they reached Halliford's book room. He shut the door behind them and rounded on her, steel once more glinting in his icy blue eyes. "Perhaps ye would care to explain why ye are behaving in so peculiar a manner."

She felt cold all over, but forced herself to ignore his anger. "The ruby pistols are missing! Did you take them?"

"Of course not. And I don't want ye interfering in that. Nor did ye answer me." He was not about to be diverted. "Why were ye acting so strangely?"

She shrugged, beginning to feel ashamed of herself. "Captain Trent was going to so much effort to watch me, I thought his efforts ought to be rewarded."

"Of all the foolish, ill-judged starts!" Deep creases formed in his brow. "Have ye no concept whatsoever what a dangerous

100

game this might be? Trent is not a man to be trifled with. Ye are like to get yourself into serious trouble!" He glared at her, but she kept her head high, refusing to cower. "And ye know that would distress the duchess," he added as a clincher.

Her chin sank and began to quaver, though she tried to control it. To her dismay, she wasn't sure which upset her more—his thinking her foolish or the prospect of upsetting Helena. And she *had* been foolish. She had let her temper—and daydreams—run away with her.

But she wasn't about to admit it! With an effort, she faced him squarely. "The only way to ensure Helena's peace is to settle this problem. She certainly would not be pleased if she knew I were considered a suspect in a murder!" Her eyes sparkled as she warmed to the theme. "We need to know what Montclyff did on his last day, after proposing to me in such an odious manner. How can I go about finding out?"

"Don't get involved any more than ye already are. The matter is being attended to by Captain Trent."

"I don't trust him." Augusta thrust out her chin in defiance. "What if he is guilty?"

"Why should he be?" Edward countered.

That gave her pause. "I don't know."

"Ye are too impulsive."

"You've mentioned that before."

An involuntary chuckle escaped him. "Ye are also—" He broke off, as if recollecting himself.

"A peagoose? Featherhead? Pluck to the backbone?" She made the suggestions in a spirit of pure helpfulness. "Really, if you are going to ring a peal over me, it will be all holiday with you if you let considerations of vocabulary get in your way."

"I see ye do not have that problem." He spoke with some asperity, though he could not disguise the twinkle in his eyes.

She shook her head. "It is far better than being some simpering miss, forever succumbing to palpitations and distempered freaks."

"Aye." He gave up the unequal struggle against his amusement and his rich chuckle sounded once more.

She liked the sound, so deep and comfortable. In fact, she liked Edward MacKennoch. That realization surprised her. She had been infatuated with him before; now it was different.

His gaze rested on her and his smile faded. "Ye'd best be

getting back."

"Are you not coming?" She tried not to feel disappointed, but still she did.

He shook his head. "I have some thinking to do. As ye said, the ruby-mounted pistols are missing."

She would have liked to stay and discuss the matter with him, but he opened the door and held it pointedly for her. She went out, but could not resist making a face at him. As the heavy oak panel closed behind her, she thought she again heard that delightful chuckle.

She went slowly down the corridor, lost in a happy replaying of their encounter. She *liked* him when he unbent like that. He could be fun. And she wondered if he fully realized that fact yet, himself.

As she neared the main hall, she heard someone coming heavily down the staircase. Roddy's head and shoulders came into view the next moment, and to her surprise he cast an uneasy glance about. He behaved every bit as surreptitiously as she had tried to act only a little while before.

She drew back around the corner where he could not see her, and waited. The door to the Gold Saloon opened and Perry came out just as Roddy reached the bottom step. For one long, pregnant moment they stared at each other.

"Is it—?" Perry regarded his friend in anxiety.

Roddy nodded. "Yes. Lord, we shouldn't have tried to get rid of it." He cast an uneasy glance about, then strode to the front door and let himself unceremoniously out.

Augusta looked after him, startled. There had been a very large, squarish bulge beneath his unbuttoned coat. Just the sort of bulge a pistol case might make.

Chapter 8

What were Perry and Roddy talking about? Getting rid of
the pistols? Or the bloodstains? Augusta stared at the closed
door, bewildered.

Frederick Ashfield came out of the saloon and Perry, casting
him a quick glance, darted across the hall and into one of the
crowded drawing rooms. Augusta came slowly forward,
frowning.

"Ah, there you are." Mr. Ashfield saw her. "Helena was
asking where you might be." He stood aside, gesturing for her
to enter the room he'd just left.

"Thank you." There was no hope for it; she would have to
go through the motions of the polite hostess, assisting Lizzie,
until the guests took their leave. Then perhaps she could seek
out Edward MacKennoch again and tell him of the latest
development in the unconventional movements of a certain
pair of exquisite dueling pistols. It pleased her, to have
discovered something he did not know.

Almost two hours passed before the front door finally closed
behind the last lingering members of the audience. Lizzie
yawned cavernously. "I never thought they would leave." She
looked about the wreckage of the drawing room, with the
numerous chairs pushed every which way, and shook her head.

"Go up to bed." Augusta gave her a gentle push, then linked
her arm through Helena's and guided her weary elder sister
toward the staircase. But as soon a she handed the duchess
over to the care of her capable abigail, she hurried back down.

Major MacKennoch stood in the back hall, a candle in his
hand, the book room behind him dark. He glanced up as

Augusta made her purposeful way toward him, and a resigned expression settled over his face.

"Now what have ye been up to?"

"Me?" Augusta regarded him with exaggerated innocence. "It is Lord Roderick, this time."

His eyes narrowed. "Is it now." He ushered her back into the room and rekindled the recently snuffed candelabrum that stood on the desk. He set his candle down beside it and turned back to her, folded his arms across his chest, and waited.

"I believe I know what became of the ruby pistols." That ought to impress him, she thought.

His brow creased. "What the devil have ye been about now?"

"Not me." The exasperation that crept into his tone wounded her—particularly after the friendliness of their earlier conversation. "I told you—Lord Roderick. He and Perry are behaving in the oddest manner, and when Roddy left, there was a great bulge beneath his coat, about the shape of the pistol box."

"Did he see ye?" He snapped the question at her.

"No. I don't think Perry saw me either."

He drew a deep breath. "Is it not possible for ye to stay out of things beyond your abilities?" The Scottish burr sounded more pronounced in his voice. No amusement remained.

Her eyes widened. "You knew!" she accused him.

"Aye. I saw Lord Roderick take them. He seemed overly concerned with the inside of the case."

"Why didn't you tell me?"

"I wanted to consider first who might have placed the pistols in the prop trunk—and why—and also why Lord Roderick removed them in so stealthy a manner when they are his."

Augusta regarded him, hurt. "I want to know the answers to those questions, too! I do not like being excluded."

"It was time for thought, not impulsive action."

"That is unkind. I have done nothing untoward!"

He raised a cynical eyebrow.

She flushed. "I don't like strange goings-on and I don't like being suspected in this hateful manner. I will not permit Helena to be disturbed or upset, and I intend to do anything I must to make sure she isn't. And if that means finding out for myself if something terrible is going on, then I shall. And I shall not permit you to interfere!"

His annoyance melted beneath a sudden and irresistible smile. "Such spirit. And ye are not but a wee lass."

She swallowed, finding her mouth strangely dry. "Perhaps I have grown up at last."

Their gazes met and held, and stillness surrounded them. Warmth lurked in the depths of his fascinating eyes, setting a responsive flush coursing through her veins. It proved as disconcerting as it was potent. She looked away first.

"Why—why do you suppose Captain Montclyff was murdered?" She rushed into speech.

"Nay, lass. I have no idea. I did not know the man."

Unsettled by the lurking amusement in his deep voice, she gave a shaky laugh. "Perhaps he was involved in what I overheard the other night—the sale of military secrets."

"Why do ye say that?" His tone remained smooth, but a sharpness now entered it. "Do ye have reason to suspect he might have been?"

"No." She shook her head. "That horrid conversation has been on my mind, that is all. And Monty was just the odious sort of person whom one *wants* to have been guilty of something."

"Well, in this case he was the victim, not the murderer."

"I—I know." Augusta hugged herself. "But I keep remembering what that man in the conservatory said, about a new assistant. Why? What if Monty had been his old one?"

Major MacKennoch leaned back against the mantel and gazed down at the dying embers in the hearth. "We are not even sure if what ye overheard had sinister overtones at all, or if it was quite innocent."

"Do you think I was wrong?" She asked the question point-blank.

It was his turn to hesitate. "I don't know."

His tone sounded guarded, as if he did not tell her the whole. She shot a suspicious glance at him. "Don't you?"

"I have heard something about the sale of military secrets before," he admitted. "But if there is anything to it, ye must not be in any way involved."

"Helena would not like it," Augusta agreed, though not without regret.

"Not to mention the potential danger to ye." His lips

twitched into an extremely attractive grin.

She cocked her head to one side. "I don't see why anything should happen to me."

"Aside from Halliford wringing both our necks if I let ye get into trouble by searching for answers." His grin broadened.

She should have known his smile would be devastating. The deep scar across his cheek only added to the effect. Even his eyes twinkled down at her, a window on his enjoyment. She found it exceedingly difficult to breathe.

"I have several acquaintances in the Horse Guards," he said, breaking the spell. "I believe I shall call on them tomorrow and make some discrete inquiries."

Her heart swelled. "You *do* believe me!"

He nodded. "I thought it best not to let ye know before, for fear ye would jump in without thinking, trying to get to the bottom of it. But since that is what ye are doing anyway, perhaps it is best ye should know."

She straightened her slight shoulders and fixed him with an accusing eye. He offered a friendship for the sole purpose of keeping her out of trouble! His disarming smile flashed again, as if he guessed her thoughts, and her anger evaporated. No, it was more than that; their friendship was real. And that certainty made her glow all over.

"It *still* might all be nothing," she pointed out.

"Very true. With Napoleon safely on Elba, I would have thought that the problem was past." He fell silent, staring off into the distance, but Augusta did not feel closed out. "Yes, he said at last. "I will pay another visit to the Horse Guards. And"—he turned to her—"I will tell ye what—if anything—I learn."

He relit his candle, extinguished the flames in the candelabrum, and held the door for her. Augusta hesitated. "Is there something else?" he asked.

She bit her lip and nodded, a mischievous twinkle in her eye. "Why do you not wear your kilt?"

He froze. "I have put off my uniform." His words were cold, ending the discussion.

She persevered. "But can you not wear the tartan of your own clan?"

He drew a deep breath. A bleak expression flickered across his face before his impenetrable mask settled once more into place. "I have sold out."

"But you are no less a Scotsman." Without giving him time to think up a rebuttal, she left the room.

It had to be that silly matter of the regimental colors. He had received his knee injury while defending them—and he had failed, according to Halliford, and their banner had been captured. Apparently, a Scotsman took that more to heart than did the British soldiers.

Perhaps one day he would forgive himself and don his kilt once more. She tried to picture it as she got ready for bed. It would be a proud and romantic moment, following some indescribably brave deed. He would redeem himself in his own eyes and she would be there to share his joy. What role she would play, precisely, she glossed over; that didn't matter. But afterward, he would go to his room, take his kilt down from the back of his clothes cupboard or wherever it was he stored it out of his sight, and put it on. And then . . . But here her imagination backed off.

Before she would have ended this delightful daydream with his sweeping her into his arms and kissing her. She shied from that thought at the moment. Edward had become a real person to her, not the object of her idealized fantasies. She no longer knew what she wanted from him.

This new uncertainty remained with her the following morning as she ran lightly down the stairs bent on her early morning ride in the Park. As she reached the hall, she drew up short, then proceeded more slowly as she saw who awaited her—Major MacKennoch, dressed in buckskins, gleaming topboots, and a coat of olive green superfine that set off the reddish glints in his unruly blond locks. A military precision marked the neat folds of his neckcloth.

Augusta stared, transfixed, as his solid, muscular figure strode toward her with only the slightest limp. Why had she never realized how *very* masculine he could be? He could prove a dangerous pitfall for a romantic young lady—provided she overlooked his *un*romantic streak. At the moment, that seemed all too easy.

She forced her gaze from shoulders that appeared very broad—perfectly so. "Do you ride this morning?" Her voice sounded only slightly breathless.

"If ye would not mind the company. I find I think better in

the open air than I do in a closed room."

Warm color rushed to her cheeks and she walked ahead quickly to hide her reaction. In the street, he dismissed her groom and himself tossed her up into Cuthbert's saddle. He mounted stiffly, but once on his horse's back, his injuries did not seem to bother him. They started forward in a companionable silence, through the back streets that would lead them to Hyde Park.

"What do we really have?" Major MacKennoch spoke at last. "Captain Montclyff is murdered for some unknown reason. Someone—or several people—may or may not be selling military secrets. And Lord Roderick's ruby pistols keep appearing and disappearing. Are we dealing with three separate problems?"

Augusta could not help smiling at his unexpectedly humorous tone. "Only imagine the mess we could get ourselves into if we try to interweave them! It's obvious, of course. Monty was murdered with the ruby pistols because he interfered in the sale of military secrets! What could be simpler?"

"Well," he grinned, "when ye put it that way—" He broke off. "Is that not Miss Lansdon?"

Augusta looked up as a hackney passed near them, headed in the opposite direction. Inside, she could see the unmistakable profile of Sophronia. The girl almost cowered in a corner, huddled in a muffling cloak, hazel eyes wide and miserable.

"Why yes, it is. But in a hackney? And she looks so unhappy!" Without stopping to consider possible consequences, Augusta turned Cuthbert after the carriage.

With an audible sigh, Major MacKennoch followed, muttering under his breath.

Augusta threw him a suspicious look. "Did you say something?"

"I?" Edward regarded her through impossibly innocent blue eyes.

"Something about jumping in and not thinking?" Augusta pursued.

"Would I have cause?" He brought his horse up along side of her.

She caught a mischievous gleam in his eyes and her pulse quickened, pleasantly so. "I want to make sure she is all right."

The hackney turned a corner and Augusta urged her mount onward. Ahead of them, the carriage disappeared down a side street. They continued in that direction for some time, then turned once more. They were no longer in a fashionable quarter of town, Augusta noted, and was disturbingly glad for the major's calm, solid presence at her side.

"This is no place for ye." Major MacKennoch no longer sounded amused.

"Nor Sophronia." Augusta threw him a worried glance. "She may need our help."

"I would feel better if ye turned back. I'll go on alone."

"No!" Augusta rounded on him. "I will not—"

"Ye are attracting a deal of attention. This is not a usual haunt for fashionable ladies," he informed her dryly.

Augusta looked about, uneasy, unable to deny the truth of his words. "Sophie should not be here either," she repeated. "And she is quite alone."

"That is no one's fault but her own." This time, he merely sounded goaded.

Resolutely, Augusta kept going. Two blocks later, the hackney drew to a halt. Sophronia jumped down and said something to the jarvey, who nodded and prepared to wait. The girl cast a frightened glance down the narrow street, but did not seem to see them among the carts and wagons. She hurried across and into a shop. And under her arm, she carried a very distinctive and all too familiar box.

Augusta caught her breath.

"Ye will wait here." Edward's order brooked no disobedience. He swung carefully to the cobbled paving, handed his reins to her, and strolled casually toward the shop, his limp almost unnoticeable. He passed the line of grimy windows, directing no more than the most casual of glances at them, and continued.

After passing three more shops, all equally as disreputable in appearance, he crossed the street and returned to Augusta. He reclaimed his reins and swung up into his saddle. A deep frown marred his brow.

"It would appear to be a pawn shop," he explained.

"And the ruby-mounted pistols?" The significance of the case had not escaped Augusta.

He nodded. "In vulgar parlance, she has just put them up

the spout."

"But how did Sophronia get them from Lord Roderick—and why? And why pawn them?" She regarded him, bewildered, as if she expected him to provide a reasonable answer.

The major shook his head. "Either for money, or to hide them." He only answered the last of her questions. "But at any rate, I cannot like ye being involved in something that appears more complex by the minute."

They rode on before Sophronia could come out of the shop and catch them watching her. The park forgotten, they returned to Halliford House in silence. None of this made sense, Augusta repeated to herself. She only hoped it didn't matter as much as she feared it might.

The business of Sophronia and the ruby-mounted pistols continued to trouble Augusta the rest of the afternoon. As she dressed for a card party that evening, her thoughts remained far from her appearance, much to the dismay of her abigail.

Augusta's first inclination, to confront Sophronia with what they had seen, she banished. She could not force her friend's confidence, and she had a strong suspicion that Perry lay behind the girl's strange actions. Perry, and his never ending run of ill-luck at cards and dice.

Helena, looking better for the first time in weeks, accompanied Augusta to the Richardsons' townhouse in Clarges Street. Within minutes of arriving at the party, Augusta had the satisfaction of seeing her sister borne off into a quiet corner to play whist with Frederick Ashfield, Lady Mallory, and Mrs. Cadogan. Augusta started off in search of a piquet partner, only to be pounced on almost at once by Lord Wentworth.

"A triumph last night!" He beamed on her. "An absolute triumph."

"Well, it came off better than I had expected," Augusta admitted, smiling at his enthusiasm.

"A triumph," he repeated firmly. "You must be very proud of your effort. Tell me, have you started to plan our next production?"

"Not yet. Does this mean you will be willing to take part again?" She found she looked forward to the prospect, for he made a capable director.

"Of a certainty. I have discovered a new play, the most

delightful short farce, written by an officer! Will you read it?"

"I shall be delighted." Augusta was warmed by his enthusiasm. "Only think of the many people we aided last night. And our next production will help even more."

"Do you think you might have a part for me?" A deep, masculine voice sounded right behind her.

Startled, Augusta spun about and looked up into Vincent Trent's face. She swallowed hard.

Lord Wentworth beamed at him. "We shall be honored to add you to Miss Carstairs's humble troupe. Won't we, my dear?" Jovial as ever, Lord Wentworth clapped Trent on the shoulder.

Augusta eyed the captain with distrust. "I would not have suspected you went in for amateur dramatics."

"But to help such a worthy cause? All of the ton talks of your endeavors, Miss Carstairs. I can only be surprised that more members of society have not begged to take part." He smiled at her, but it held little warmth.

Lord Wentworth laughed. "As long as they make handsome donations, that is all we ask."

"You will inform me of the first rehearsal?" Trent pursued. "I would hate to miss it."

"Tomorrow?" Lord Wentworth glanced at Augusta for confirmation. "You see, I am all eagerness to begin."

"Perhaps the day after?" Augusta suggested. "Can you send the script over in the morning?"

This agreed to, Wentworth took his leave of her, promising to inform as many of her previous troupe as he could find of the arrangements.

Trent turned to her, a satisfied smile playing about the corners of his mouth. "This should prove a most delightful experience, Miss Carstairs. Tell me, did Captain Montclyff enjoy his role? Or did he—"

"Surely you can ask your questions of the others, Captain?" She directed a false smile at him and walked away.

Their hostess, Mrs. Richardson, bore down on her and paired her with an inarticulate young officer for a game of piquet. By the time they had declared points, sequences, and sets, and the first three cards were led, Augusta knew herself to be the superior player. She concentrated on drawing out her companion who, undone by such condescension on the part of

111

the Incomparable, was quickly reduced to a stammering heap.

She was rescued from his incoherent conversation two hands later, when Jack Kettering strolled over and leaned a hand on the back of her chair. When the cards were gathered, politeness demanded that the young officer offer his place, which Kettering immediately accepted. He took the cards and shuffled.

"Do you know, everytime I see you of late we seem to be discussing a play." His smile should have warmed her. "What a pleasant change this is."

She accepted the cards he dealt her. "But it will not last for long." She selected three for discard and placed them facedown at her side. "Lord Wentworth has found a new play and is sending it to me tomorrow. I hope we can begin rehearsals by the following afternoon—if enough members of our troupe are free to come."

He rolled his eyes in exaggerated dismay and watched as she made her selection from the stock. They fell silent as they sorted their cards.

"A point of five?" she asked.

He conceded. "Why do you look so worried?" he said suddenly.

She looked up to see him watching her intently. "I haven't a sequence worth speaking about," she sighed. He laughed and returned his attention to his cards.

Her gaze rested on Kettering's serious expression as he concentrated on his hand. He loved her—she couldn't doubt that, not after his declaration of the night before. And he possessed such dashing good looks. Yet not for one moment could she consider becoming his wife.

For all his unromantic ways, she felt far more comfortable with Edward MacKennoch. She trusted him, she realized. She felt so secure when he was at her side. Her gaze rested on Lieutenant Kettering's face, but it was Major MacKennoch's stern features she saw.

They played the last trick, and not much to Augusta's surprise, Kettering was the winner. Her thoughts were far from the game. He shuffled, but before he could deal, Frederick Ashfield joined them.

He nodded to Kettering, then turned to Augusta. "Helena is asking for you." He held her chair as she rose, then led her off.

"Do you know," he said in all affability as they strolled to the next room, "Lieutenant Kettering's reputation as a rake almost equals my own."

Augusta could not help laughing. "Shocking," she said, trying to sound severe.

"That's what I thought." He sounded pleased to find his opinion seconded.

She laughed again. "You are shameless, you know. Does Helena really wish to see me or did you simply wish to meddle?"

"Oh, meddle, of course. She is enjoying herself immensely this night."

"You are incorrigible. For your punishment you may bespeak our carriage for half an hour's time. I don't want her to get too tired." Augusta left him and looked about for a last card game.

Before she had taken three steps, Sophronia bore down on her, then glanced longingly back the way she had come. Augusta looked also and saw Captain Vincent Trent's sturdy, imposing figure, impressive in his scarlet regimentals, laughing with several other officers. It seemed hard to believe he might be involved in something unsavory. He seemed so carefree.

And Sophronia . . . there could be no doubt the girl was fast developing a tendre for him, and Augusta felt very sure it was not returned.

As she watched, Vincent Trent turned toward the doorway and the laughter faded from his eyes. Perry entered, looked about, caught sight of Trent, and hurried away. Now why—? Her thought was broken off, for Trent spotted her and a frown showed clearly in the creased lines of his brow.

He strode up to them and bowed to first her, then Sophronia. A slight, teasing smile just touched his lips—as if he had pinned it on for their benefit, Augusta thought.

"Miss Lansdon, I have been looking for you. Do you not think we should go in search of refreshment?"

A rosy glow colored Sophie's pale cheeks. She murmured something to Augusta which she did not hear, and strolled away on the captain's arm, apparently oblivious to anything but him.

Augusta watched their departure in no little concern. Very little of the lover appeared in Captain Trent's manner. He was using Sophronia, of that she was certain. But for what? The girl's tender and inexperienced heart was going to be hurt.

She wished Edward MacKennoch might have been there to see for himself how Vincent Trent behaved toward Sophronia. For that matter, she wished Edward MacKennoch might be there just so she could enjoy his company. Because she did enjoy it. That thought still seemed new to her—and infinitely delightful.

Perry strode up to her and Augusta brought her attention back to her surroundings with a sigh. She wanted to indulge in romantic dreams, not be drawn into other people's problems.

"Where's m'sister?" Perry looked around, his manner disgruntled.

"She went with Cpatain Trent to find punch just a moment ago."

Perry frowned, seemed to consider, then went in search of her. Augusta saw them a few minutes later, standing together, his head bent toward hers in earnest conversation. They made a pretty couple, so alike in coloring. But their expressions were far from the polite social masks normally worn by members of the ton at parties.

Perry spoke forcefully for a moment, and Sophie nodded, though obviously not pleased. She cast a swift, anxious glance over her shoulder to where Vincent Trent watched them. Even from where she stood, Augusta could see the wistfulness mixed with fear in the girl's expression.

What did Perry say to her that distressed her so? Merciful heavens, she was beginning to see mysteries everywhere! Her imagination was truly running away with her. It must be.

Yet try as she might, she could not shake the sudden conviction that they had all become inextricably involved in something very dangerous.

Chapter 9

Augusta set forth on an early shopping expedition with Lizzy the following morning, determined to banish her lingering uneasiness. Her romantic nature made too much of all this! The sale of military secrets and the murder of Captain Montclyff had no direct bearing on her. That left only Perry's gaming problems and Sophronia's growing tendre for someone who obviously used her for his own mysterious purposes. Neither were her problems—though anything that so closely affected her friends could not but touch her.

Still, her feeling that they all tread a dangerous path continued. It was foolish, all part of her silly daydreaming fantasies, yet she could not shake the eerie sensation.

They returned to the house with Augusta feeling no better. Willis opened the door for them, sent a footman running for their packages, and relieved the ladies of their pelisses.

"Lord Wentworth and Lieutenant Kettering have called, Miss Augusta," the butler informed her. "They are in the Gold Saloon."

Lizzie rolled her eyes. "Not another play! I warn you, Gussie," she added darkly, "no false whiskers!"

Augusta hushed her and shoved her toward the stairs. She herself made her way to the spacious apartment, from which deep voices could be heard. She opened the door and stopped, catching her breath in admiration as she saw Edward MacKennoch, tall and elegant, standing by the mantel.

He appeared perfectly at home in the luxury of the ducal household. He belonged there, she thought—and not as a mere secretary. Something tugged at her memory, something about his being the second son of an impoverished earl. She'd have to ask Lizzie. Her enterprising sister always knew everything.

"Now, there's a profession for a man," Lord Wentworth declared. "Always involved in what's going on, getting to take part in momentous events. I tell you, I'd choose no other career than the Diplomatic Service."

Major MacKennoch inclined his head, but made no comment.

"The service needs bright new talent, Major." Lord Wentworth nodded vigorously. "Just because your military career is over doesn't mean it's the end of the world. Injuries don't matter a whit in our work. You think about it."

Augusta stared at the major, dismayed to see the spark of interest that animated his countenance. He'd do more than think about it. The realization troubled her. A man like Major Edward MacKennoch would not remain long as secretary to another. Once his battle fatigue faded and his wounds healed, he would need more: excitement, purpose, to be involved in great events. Her heart twisted uncomfortably within her.

Jack Kettering's laugh broke across her thoughts. "The military is an excellent career, is it not, Major? I would like to have seen a bunch of diplomats storming Salamanca!"

"But that's the point, Kettering!" Wentworth turned on him, the light of battle in his own eyes. "Had our service been permitted to deal with the issue, there would have been no need for fighting! But no, the country doesn't realize what we could accomplish if given the opportunity. They would rather worship the daring of a bunch of scarlet coats than listen to the talk that could have saved thousands of lives."

"You must admit, the army did a reasonable job of dealing with Bonaparte." The major's tone held mild amusement.

"Phah!" Wentworth shook his head. "A wild, reckless bunch, too ready to shoot without thinking! If Napoleon were to return to France, and the matter were left to the diplomats, you'd see a very swift and peaceful solution. *Then* the country would see what we are worth."

"Lord Wellington—" Kettering began, but Wentworth waved his hand in a deprecating gesture.

"I have no opinion of this Wellington. Can't see why everyone thinks so much of him."

Kettering cast a glance across at Major MacKennoch and

they exchanged a look of appreciative understanding. "There are many good officers," Kettering pointed out. "Captain Vincent Trent appears to be quite needlewitted."

"Power-happy, just like the rest of them." Wentworth glared at him. "Basking in the glory of his role of mystery-solver. But have we seen anything come of his investigations? Nor are we likely to. The army will defend its own in this disgraceful affair."

Major MacKennoch, a slight smile just touching his firm lips, glanced up and saw Augusta. His eyes lit with a sudden warmth that left her breathless. For one moment, she forgot the presence of the other two men in the room.

Then Lieutenant Kettering sprang to his feet and hurried over to take her hand. With a sweeping gesture, he raised her fingers to his lips. "You find us awaiting you."

"I'm sorry I didn't return home earlier." She tried to free herself, but Kettering retained his hold and drew her into the room. Edward MacKennoch stiffened, excused himself, and strode toward the door with barely a limp.

Could that have been a spark of jealousy on his part? But no, Major MacKennoch was a loner. It was more likely disappointment to find that she still flirted when he had begun to think her not so foolish. The reflection was depressing. She wanted nothing to interfere with their newly burgeoning friendship.

"You have to admit, Kettering, you haven't found the army a profitable career." Lord Wentworth returned to the argument at hand.

Kettering laughed easily. "As long as one has expectations from another source, one does well enough. It is certainly honorable and exciting. And romantic—unlike the dull folderol of diplomatic life. Do you not think so?" He appealed to Augusta.

She managed a smile. "We have certainly heard its praises sung a great deal of late." She considered. "And yes, it does seem a dashing life to follow the drum. And—I am sorry to say, Lord Wentworth"—she threw him an apologetic glance—"it does seem more exhilarating than the quiet, boring one of diplomacy with its endless talking and formal affairs."

Lord Wentworth glowered but Kettering chuckled. "Spoken with true spirit!"

A soft click sounded behind her, indicating the shutting of

the door. Major MacKennoch had only just left, Augusta realized with a sinking heart. She wished very much she had not just praised the life he had been forced to leave.

Lord Wentworth drew out the script he had promised and her attention was perforce diverted. Much to her surprise, this play bore every hope of success. She read it through and for once her first inclination was not to grab a pen and begin a reckless and massive rewrite.

"Well?" Lord Wentworth pressed her for her opinion.

"A delightful farce." She laid it down. "Do you think we can gather everyone here tomorrow afternoon for a first reading?"

Kettering, tugging at one end of his luxuriant black mustache, regarded her with warmth. "Will you again take the role of heroine?"

"I suppose I must. Miss Lansdon has been adamant about taking only small parts."

He nodded. "Then I shall press for the part of our hero."

The gentlemen took their leave and Augusta retired to her chamber with the script. In the second reading she began to spot flaws and in a very short time, she had recourse to pen and ink as several possible changes occurred to her. She settled comfortably before her writing desk and went to work with Odysseus, the large gray and white cat, dozing peacefully in her lap.

She kept at this occupation off and on during the day as new ideas occurred to her. She had just returned to it once more in the late afternoon when Willis knocked on her door with the information that Lieutenant Lansdon and Miss Lansdon awaited her below. She finished her sentence, then jotted down a note about the next change she intended to make.

As she joined her friends, she noted that both still appeared unhappy. Her own spirits sank, but she did her best to disguise this fact and strode forward with a determined smile on her lips.

Perry, who stared pensively into the fire, started guiltily when she greeted him. He muttered a response, then returned his gaze to the hearth.

"We came to see if you would care to ride in the Park with us." Sophronia cast her brother an uneasy glance, then turned back to Augusta.

Augusta couldn't turn down such a beseeching look. "Let

me just change into my habit. Will you not come up with me?"

But to her surprise, Sophronia refused. She could have sworn the girl wished to speak with her in private. With a mental shrug, she sent for Cuthbert to be brought around, then ran lightly up the stairs.

She came back down less than a quarter hour later. Perry was just finishing a glass of Madeira, which he set down in a nonchalant manner as she entered the room.

"Tolerable," he pronounced. "Very tolerable indeed." His manner, if not his expression, mimicked the connoisseur. He met Augusta's searching scrutiny and looked immediately away.

Sophronia also, Augusta noted, did not seem anxious to look her in the eye. That did it. She hadn't wanted to force any confidences, but something was clearly amiss, and more than the girl could handle. While Perry stared irresolutely into the fire, she drew his sister aside.

"What were you doing with Lord Roderick's pistols?" she whispered, coming straight to the point.

The color faded from Sophronia's face. Before she could speak, Perry joined them, his manner for once protective of his sister.

Augusta addressed him instead. "Why was Sophronia pawning Lord Roderick's pistols?"

Flustered, Perry said, "I borrowed them from Roddy after the play, when we got back to our billet. But now he claims they were stolen."

"Why?" Augusta regarded him in consternation.

He shrugged. "Oh, we were about half sprung, I'd say. Doesn't help to clarify the situation one bit."

"Redeem them and give them back." Augusta's tone held no sympathy.

"Can't." Perry hung his head, his expression one of abject misery.

"How serious is it?"

He grimaced. "Pretty bad."

"All right. I'll get them back with what's left of my allowance. I won't have you two getting any deeper into trouble."

"No, you cannot!" Sophronia protested, shocked.

"No," Perry agreed, though not without considerable

119

regret. "Can't break the shins of one of Sophie's friends."

This utterance was wholly unintelligible to Augusta, but she gathered her offer had been refused.

In the silence of deep thought, they made their way to the park. They had barely completed a half circuit when Captain Vincent Trent rode toward them. He turned his mount so that he fell in beside Sophronia. She greeted him with a cold nod and tried to slow her horse to drop back beside Augusta. But Perry had already taken that place, so Sophronia was forced to remain where she was.

Augusta watched this faulty maneuver in dismay. Her friend might try to rebuff the captain, but she could see that the girl suffered, torn between her growing tendre and an unexplained fear of the man—a fear that seemed to have come on after Sophie's conversation with Perry last night. Augusta's heart went out to her.

"What have I done to offend you?" Vincent Trent kept his voice soft, but the words carried clearly back to Augusta.

"You are always watching people. I don't like the way you stare at my brother as though you suspect him of something dreadful." Sophronia, never one for subterfuge, blurted out what was on her mind.

Captain Trent laughed gently. "I am very sorry. I fear it has become a habit—and a deplorable one at that. I shall strive, for your sake, to keep it under better control." He smiled down at the girl with devastating effect. He said something more, but his voice dropped and Augusta could no longer hear.

Sophronia obviously succumbed. She flushed becomingly and gazed up at him with a look of such adoration in her eyes that Augusta longed to shake her. The girl was too trusting and open for her own good.

They continued in this manner for some time, with the captain obviously flirting to good effect with his victim, and Augusta glowering at the back of his head, knowing she had not the right to interfere. Nothing could convince her he did not have an ulterior motive.

"Were you serious about that offer earlier?" Perry had ridden in silence since acknowledging Captain Trent's joining their party. Now, with a surreptitious eye on his preoccupied sister, he addressed Augusta in a low voice. "It's a bit over four hundred pounds."

"Yes." She swallowed hard. It was a great deal of money. The prospect of spending so much to redeem those pistols might not please her, but for Sophronia's sake she was willing to do it.

He let out a sigh of relief. "Can't say I like borrowing money from females, but the thing is, I've got to get those guns back to Roddy before he starts asking too many ticklish questions and kicking up a dust."

"Will you be free tomorrow?" she asked.

He nodded. "I'm on the morning duty roster this week, so I can get away by two."

"Then I'll give you the money at the rehearsal. Can you—" She broke off, all thoughts of the play and even Perry's problems fading from her mind.

Edward MacKennoch rode toward them, a graceful figure on horseback, swaying easily with his mount's playful tricks. His wounded knee barely seemed to trouble him at all in the saddle. He looked up, smiled, and his eyes met hers over the heads of the others.

Augusta forced herself to resume breathing. There could be no denying the attraction that almost crackled in the air between them. And she didn't want to deny it in the least.

The major joined them, exchanged greetings with the party, then moved his horse neatly into position beside Augusta. Perry obligingly dropped back, content now that his immediate difficulties were well on the way to being solved. Augusta made no protest over this change in escort.

Major MacKennoch checked his eager horse's pace, and Augusta cast him a searching look. His piercing regard rested on Trent's back, much as hers had done only minutes before. The furrows in his brow deepened.

"Major," she whispered.

He glanced sideways at her and the frown faded from his eyes. "Aye?"

"Perry borrowed the pistols from Lord Roderick—who doesn't remember—and had Sophronia pawn them. But he plans to return them." She made no mention of her own role in the business; she had a sinking feeling he would not approve. He would call her foolish and probably several other choice names—and he'd be right. But she couldn't let Sophronia worry when it was within her power to help.

"I suppose ye asked outright?" He sounded resigned, but the warmth lurked in his eyes. He, too, kept his voice low.

She looked up at him from under her lashes, her smile teasing. "It seemed easiest."

"How can anyone of so romantic a disposition approach something so directly?"

"You are perhaps forgetting I am related to Lizzie."

He chuckled, and a delightful flush washed over her, leaving her happy and content. Without a doubt, Edward MacKennoch's presence made this the most enjoyable afternoon she had yet spent in the park this season. Riding in companionable silence at his side would be far more satisfying than listening to any of her suitors' entreaties of love.

That thought struck her as absurdly funny.

She did not have the opportunity to turn her attention to the problem of Lord Roderick's pistols until late the following morning. Then, she diligently scraped together every penny she could find, but the result was not satisfactory. She still lacked more than half of the four hundred pounds she needed.

She sank down onto her bed, her chin resting in her cupped hands as she considered. She had a pair of sapphire earrings that should make up the difference. They were the only real jewels she possessed, for Helena had been very strict in allowing her to wear nothing but pearls. But she had saved and saved from the generous clothing allowance and pin money provided her by Halliford, and bought them secretly, waiting for the moment when Helena would relent. Since no one knew she possessed them, they would never be missed—except by herself.

A search of her trinket box unearthed the earrings and she regarded them with loving eyes, then with a pang stuffed them hurriedly into her reticule before she could change her mind. She couldn't allow her selfishness to cause Perry to get into further trouble. She would redeem them at the quarter day, no matter what economies she would be forced to endure for the remainder of the season.

She looked at the ormolu clock that stood on the mantel; their afternoon rehearsal would not begin for another two hours. She could send for Perry, of course, but her knowledge of that gentleman's erratic behavior gave her pause. If she handed so much money to him, in bills, he would be more like to seek an increase in the sum with the dice box than to use it for its intended purpose. He would sink himself deeper into trouble, and this time she wouldn't be able to help.

No, the most reasonable course would be to redeem the pistols herself. The idea was reprehensible, but a little thrill of excitement raced through her. It would be an adventure, and as such, irresistible to her.

Sending for the carriage was clearly ineligible unless she wanted news of her peculiar errand to reach her sister's ears. She waited until the front hall was clear, then slipped outside and hurried down the street. At a safe distance from Halliford House, she summoned a hackney and gave the name of the street in which she had seen Sophronia pawn the pistols. The jarvey regarded her from under lowered brows, shrugged his shoulders with all the air of one who has long ceased to wonder about the queer starts of the Quality, and told her to get in.

The neighborhood in which she presently found herself was every bit as unsavory as she remembered. Buttoning her pelisse so that it covered most of her sprigged muslin gown, she stepped down from the carriage and requested the driver to wait for her. Mustering her forces, she crossed the street to the shop.

She had never before entered a pawnbroker's, and the array of goods fascinated her. One might purchase almost anything here, she realized in awe. She dragged her gaze from a display of watches and snuffboxes and approached the elderly shop-keeper. Trying very hard not to be intimidated by his sharp, assessing glance that took in every detail of her appearance, she stated her business. She had come prepared to bargain, but when she at last left with the pistols in the cherry wood case tucked safely under her arm, she was certain she had gotten the worst of the deal.

That knowledge irritated her, but she was new at this sort of thing, which the proprietor of that little shop most assuredly was not. Had she been practical, she should have gotten a gentleman to help her, though she could just imagine Major MacKennoch's response if she breathed a word of this errand to him. No, it had been more fun to do it alone.

She walked quickly across the street, back to the sanctuary of her waiting hackney, only to be brought to a dead halt three paces away. Her name was called in a deep, masculine voice, and she spun about, the perfect picture of guilt, she was sure.

"Miss Carstairs?" Captain Vincent Trent strode up to her, frowning. "What are you doing in this district? This is not the place for a lady."

Augusta managed a confident smile. "It is not really so very bad. There was something I had to take care of." She bestowed a dismissive smile on him and turned away at once, but he followed her to the hackney. There was not one single chance he had failed to observe the cherry wood case she carried. With a fatalistic sigh, she allowed him to hand her into the carriage.

Captain Trent gave the jarvey the direction of Halliford House and the vehicle moved forward. Augusta sank resignedly into a corner. Intrigue did not appear to be her strong point. On her very first attempt at a secret errand, she had been caught out.

Anger filled her, directed at Perry for the trouble he'd caused her. But being furious with him didn't change the situation any. Captain Trent still had seen her in a potentially discreditable situation—and with Lord Roderick's pistols. She sighed, gave a mental shrug, and returned her mind to the question of what to do with them next.

On inspiration, she called to the jarvey and requested that he instead take her to the Lansdon house. As they pulled up in Half Moon Street, Sophronia, accompanied by her maid, came down the front steps. Augusta hailed her, then jumped lightly to the paving. She paid off her jarvey with the few coins she had remaining to her.

"Augusta?" Sophronia hurried across.

"Take these." Augusta handed her friend the box.

Sophronia stared at it for a moment, ordered the wide-eyed abigail not to just stand there, and hauled the girl back inside the house, where no one would witness such a shocking display of emotion. The butler admitted them, and Sophronia averted her face, hurrying past into the front drawing room. Once inside, Augusta dismissed the maid and closed the door, then burst into tears.

Sophronia dried her eyes. "I cannot thank you enough! But oh, you shouldn't have done it, Augusta."

"Possibly." Augusta stripped off her gloves. "But if Perry were caught, he would be accused of stealing. You must see that these are returned safely."

124

"Oh, I shall!" Sophronia declared wholeheartedly. "But Perry will not be able to join us this afternoon after all. His regiment, I suppose. He has had so few duties of late, I had almost forgotten his obligations." She looked down at the box she clutched. "What—what should I do with them?"

On Augusta's suggestion, they tucked the case under the pillows of Sophronia's bed. This taken care of, they set forth together in the Lansdon carriage for Halliford House and the rehearsal of the new play.

Augusta did not see Perry again until that evening, at a musical soiree given by Lady Glasden, which she attended in the company of Sophronia and Mrs. Lansdon. Perry still wore a haunted expression, and a whole new set of worries assailed Augusta. Had he not gotten the pistols yet? But Sophronia had not so much as mentioned them. And surely, if Perry had been caught returning them, he would not be here tonight but under guard at his regimental stockade.

Several ladies whispered to each other as they saw her, Augusta noted, and she forced back her anger. Gossips! Had they nothing better to talk about? Surely they must have exhausted the topic of Captain Montclyff's death and his pursuit of her and whether or not there could be any connection.

She should be glad her usual court still held back from her, though, she told herself. That made private conversation at a party a little easier. And she wanted to speak to someone without being overheard.

At the first opportunity, she strolled up to Perry. "How sorry we were you could not attend today's rehearsal." She flashed him a brilliant smile. "It is really quite the most delightful little play this time, not at all like the last one."

He attempted a shaky half-smile and cast an uneasy glance about the crowded room to assure himself he wouldn't be overheard. "Did you manage to—to do what we talked about?"

So he didn't have them yet. No wonder he looked as if disaster hung over his head like the sword of Damocles. "I went one step further," she assured him. "Have you not spoken with your sister?"

He looked skeptical. "Not for the past ten minutes."

Augusta's brow clouded. "But did she not tell you that the— the problem is well in hand? In her room, in fact?"

"No!" Perry stared at her blankly. "You mean you actually—?" He flushed. "She didn't say a word about it!"

It was Augusta's turn to stare. "I wonder why she didn't tell you? Perhaps—" She broke off as a laugh sounded unnaturally loud near them. She turned to see Lord Roderick standing with another officer. No trace of his recent nervousness remained. He acted, in fact, as if he had not a care in the world.

Perry and Augusta exchanged a perplexed glance and as one went in search of his sister. They found her with the dowager Lady Eddington and, after exchanging polite greetings with that lady, detached Sophronia.

She smiled brightly at them both. "It is a delightful evening, is it not?"

Perry ground his teeth audibly.

Augusta glanced about quickly, then drew Sophronia toward a settee placed in an alcove, where they could be private. "What did you do with the pistols?"

"Oh, it was the most marvelous chance. I gave them to Lieutenant Kettering."

"You what?" Her brother almost yelped.

Augusta hushed him. "Why?" she demanded, equally as startled as Perry.

"Oh, he is the nicest man. He saw that I was worried during the rehearsal this afternoon and asked if there were any way he could serve me. And that's when the wonderful idea occurred to me. I told him the truth about those dreadful pistols and he understood how it was at once, for he knows how very fuddled Roddy becomes whenever he is in his cups. He promised to restore the silly things for me so that Perry never need be involved in the least. And knowing you"—she rounded on her brother, who was making strangled noises—"he would be much more capable of doing the job discreetly."

Perry swallowed, and with a visible effort got himself under control. "You might have told me." He sounded more than a little aggrieved.

"Well, I haven't had the opportunity, have I?" Sophronia turned her indignant gaze on him. "It's not as if you live with Mamma and me, or even visit us much. And when we spoke before, we were in the midst of the most shocking crowd. Would you have liked me to blurt it all out in front of everybody?"

Augusta let out a deep sigh. "At least the matter is settled, for Roddy certainly looks happy enough."

Perry, though, she realized, did not. One worry might have been removed, but others apparently remained. She eyed him askance. "*Doesn't* this settle everything?"

"Of course it does." He spoke too brightly.

"The truth, Perry, if you please. Or don't you trust us to help you?" Augusta fixed him with a stern eye.

He looked down. "Of course I trust you," he muttered. "Lord, what choice have I had?" He gave a shaky laugh.

"Then if you want our help over anything else, you'd best—er—'open your budget'—as my brother Adrian would say. There *is* something else wrong, isn't there?"

Perry bit his lip, then nodded reluctantly.

"What?"

The face he turned to her was pale, haunted as if by a fear too great to bear.

"Perry?" Sophronia regarded him in concern. "You had best tell us the worst. What else have you done?"

"Nothing!" For a moment he rallied. "You make it sound as if I were forever in some scrape!"

"Aren't you?" demanded his loving sister.

The fight went out of him, much like a sail when the wind shifted direction. He drew a deep, shaky breath and nodded. "This time I seem to be. I—I'm being blackmailed."

"Blackmailed?"

Augusta hushed Sophronia's squeak. "Not so loud. This isn't the sort of thing we want to get around. Now, do sit down and tell us, Perry. Who is blackmailing you and why? Did someone see you taking Lord Roderick's pistols?"

"Worse." He gasped the word, then raised eyes filled with fear. "It—it's for Geoffrey Montclyff's murder."

Chapter 10

"For—" Augusta broke off, shocked. "Perry, you cannot mean . . ."

He sank his head into his hands. "I—I've no idea who's behind it. I just found a note in my coat pocket one morning."

"Perry, you—you didn't . . ." Sophronia's voice broke on a sob.

He shook his head, though Augusta doubted he'd paid any attention to his sister's interruption. "I thought it must be Roddy, at first, playing some paltry jest. But it wasn't."

Augusta glanced around to assure herself they did not attract any undue attention. As far as she could see, no one paid them any heed. She turned back to Perry. "*Why* does someone think he *can* blackmail you? What did you have to do with Monty's death?"

"I—that duel . . . It was with me." The last words came out as an anguished gasp.

Horror gripped Augusta, but she kept a firm hold on her reaction. She glanced around again and realized that Perry's last outburst caused several people to look in their direction. "Let's find Mrs. Lansdon and all return to your house."

"But—" Sophronia started to protest, but Augusta silenced her.

"Your mother will not think it in the least odd if I accompany you, and she will only be delighted by Perry's presence."

"But what are we to tell her?" Sophronia looked about, helpless.

Augusta bit her lip, then inspiration struck. "That we have

gotten an idea for the new play and want to try it out."

Just as Augusta hoped, Mrs. Lansdon laughed indulgently at their seeming enthusiasm when they approached her and obliged them by sending for her carriage. Perry sat stiffly on the facing seat beside Augusta, trying to maintain a semblance of calm, and Augusta hoped they could escape from Mrs. Lansdon's presence before he cracked under the strain.

As soon as they reached the house, fortunately, Mrs. Lansdon drifted off to check on her younger children. Sophronia led Augusta and Perry into a small drawing room. Perry collapsed on the sofa and sank his head back into his hands.

"You've done very well." Augusta took the chair opposite, encouraging him. "Now, tell us what happened."

Perry shook his head. "Not the sort of thing to be troubling females about. Can't think what made me mention it."

"The fact that no one should face this sort of thing alone," Augusta informed him firmly. "And we're the only people you dare tell at the moment."

Sophronia dropped to her knees beside her brother. "Please, Perry. Maybe, between the three of us, we can figure out who's blackmailing you and—and do something about it."

Perry nodded, wearing the expression of one desperate enough to clutch at straws. "I can't remember the evening all that clearly," he began, holding his voice steady with an obvious effort. "We—Roddy and I—were both in our cups, of course."

"Of course," Augusta murmured in agreement, but fortunately he didn't appear to hear.

"It was all over some slight Montclyff claimed. Can't remember what. Something about pushing past him in a doorway or some such nonsense. He claimed it was an insult to a senior officer."

"Then *he* challenged *you?*" Augusta pressed the point, wanting there to be no doubt.

He nodded. "Roddy was there, so I called on him to be my second. He was foxed enough to offer me his lucky pistols." Perry looked up, his face a mask of misery. "We had the choice of weapons, you know."

"Couldn't you have refused?" Sophronia looked puzzled. "It all sounds so silly."

Perry stared at her, shocked at such a ridiculous suggestion. "Refuse a challenge? And from someone with Monty's reputation?" He turned back to Augusta with all the air of addressing his remarks to someone more sensible. "Anyway, he was in the devil's own temper, said there was no need to wait, that he'd round up a doctor and a second and meet us at Paddington Green in two hours' time. Almost dawn, you see."

"So the whole thing took place in one night." Augusta frowned. "Is—is that usual?"

Perry shook his head. "Dashed irregular. But when we protested, he just laughed—you know that way he had, that left you feeling like a worm. Said I was afraid to meet him and would try to back out of it. Nothing I could do but agree to meet him at once." Perry slouched down lower in his chair.

Augusta looked frantically about, but in a household inhabited solely by females, no decanters of wine stood at hand. "Sophronia, can you send for some—some Madeira or something?"

Her friend rang the bell. When the butler entered a few minutes later, Perry stood by the hearth, staring down into the flames. Sophronia gave the order for wine and lemonade, and the butler withdrew. Perry remained where he was until the servitor returned with a tray bearing not only the two decanters but also a plate of rout cakes.

As soon as the man closed the door behind himself, Perry dropped his brave pose and turned back into the room, his expression haggard. He almost pounced on the wine, poured a glass, and drained it. He filled another and returned to his seat on the sofa.

"What happened then?" Augusta pursued.

"We got to the green first. Montclyff arrived only a few minutes later, but he didn't bring a second, only a doctor."

Augusta sat up straighter. "Who was he? The officers said they couldn't locate the man."

Perry shook his head. "No idea what his name was. Never laid eyes on him before, nor since. But Monty acted like I'd insulted him all over again when I objected. Said the doctor would act for him, and Roddy talked with him for a few minutes, then said it was all right." Perry had recourse to his wine. "Dashed irregular. If I'd been a little less fuddled, daresay I would have refused to have anything more to do with it."

"But you were still a trifle above par?" Augusta prodded as he relapsed into silence.

Perry nodded, apparently noticing nothing amiss with her use of that phrase. "Monty started snapping at us, saying he had an appointment in half an hour's time and he wanted to get the thing over with. That made me mad, I can tell you. Not that he had any need to worry, I suppose—or so I thought." He looked up, then down again quickly. "Never been what you would call a crack shot."

"But it was most unkind of him, under the circumstances, to refer to it." Augusta soothed him. With care, she brought him back to his narrative. "And then?"

"Roddy and the doctor paced out the field, checked the pistols, and Roddy dropped the handkerchief. I—well, I was pretty scared. Monty's been out at least four times, and there was a rumor he'd killed his man once, while his regiment was in Holland." He swallowed another mouthful of wine, which seemed to steady him. "When I fired, I didn't delope, but I didn't aim to hit either. I heard Monty's shot and stiffened up, wondering where he'd gotten me. Took a minute for me to realize I was all right. Then I saw that Monty was lying on the ground, and there was this great red patch spreading on his coat . . ."

He sank his head into his hands, shivering, and Sophronia barely caught his glass before the contents could spill over his pantaloons. His voice sounded muffled as he continued. "Then—then the doctor ran over to him and—and said he was dead." He raised horrified eyes. "I—never so shocked in my life! I had no idea what to do. I—I went to him and there was blood everywhere . . ."

He drew a deep, steadying breath and went on shakily. "The—the doctor said not to worry, he'd take care of everything, and told Roddy to take me home. I just stood there staring at Monty, thinking the whole thing was impossible. I—I've never done more than culp a wafer, and only once at that." He looked at his empty hands, saw his glass in his sister's clasp, and reclaimed it.

"Did you leave, like he told you to?" Augusta asked.

"Did I—oh, yes." He shivered. "There was so *much* blood. Lord, it made me feel queasy. Roddy gathered things up and drove us back to our billet. Told me not to say anything about what happened. Monty getting killed sobered us. Roddy'd gotten a lot of blood on his hands and everything else, and asked if I'd try to wash it out of the case lining while he returned and talked to this doctor. But when he got back to Paddington Green, the man was gone. Monty was just lying there, his curricle standing where he'd left it."

"What did Roddy do?"

Perry looked up at Augusta, surprised. "Left, of course. What could he do? Duels aren't exactly legal, you know. I—I'd have to leave the country!"

"But surely—" Sophronia, pale and trembling, stared at her brother.

"Dash it all, Sophie, we couldn't tell *anyone*. Duels are conducted according to the strictest rules, and ours broke every one of them." Perry shook his head. "We just kept silent."

"Until someone put a note in your coat saying he knew you shot Monty?" Augusta didn't like the way any of it sounded.

Perry's grip tightened on the stem of the glass. "When I find out who it is . . ." His voice trailed off, leaving the threat unfinished.

"What do you intend to do, fight another duel with him?" Augusta stood and walked restlessly about the room. "There is only one thing to be done."

"What's that?" He looked up at her, suspicious.

"Make a clean breast of it."

"What?" Perry rallied. "Touched in your upper works, that's what you are. If you think—"

She cut him off. "It's the only way to clear you, Perry. Consider."

"But he's right, Augusta." Sophronia, who had fallen silent, now broke in. "If the whole duel was as irregular as he says, who would believe him?"

Augusta drew a deep breath and let it out slowly, her mind racing. "The whole thing sounds like a setup for murder. A forced quarrel, the—"

"No, no one forced Monty." Perry set her straight. "He wanted a fight."

"Oh." Augusta stared at him, momentarily stymied. "All right, then it was a lucky chance for someone. You must have been overheard. Or perhaps, if Monty were already angry and looking for a quarrel, then someone might have deliberately driven him to that point. Knowing his temper, it was quite likely he'd force a quarrel on someone."

Perry nodded, slowly. "You mean someone wanted him in a duel, deliberately provoked him—but that would mean it was someone whom Monty couldn't call out." He hesitated, racking his already strained memory. "No, it was *me* Monty was after. I'd swear to that."

Well, there went that theory, Augusta reflected. Or did it? She looked at Perry through narrowed eyes. A callow youth, totally inexperienced and a notoriously poor shot. The perfect victim. A chill ran through her. Or the perfect pawn. If someone wanted Monty dead—no, this all got too confusing. If someone ordered Monty to murder Perry, that would explain the peculiar circumstances of the duel. But that same someone actually wanted Monty dead—with Perry looking like the guilty party.

She spun around. "Perry, was there anything strange about the second shot—the one Monty fired?"

He was silent a moment. "It echoed," he said at last. "Almost as if it came from behind me. But it was probably just my nerves."

"I don't think so." Augusta strode up and stopped just in front of him. "Monty's pistol hadn't been fired. Didn't Roddy notice when he put the guns away? I think someone wanted Monty dead and arranged it so you would take the blame. And when you fired, so did he, from behind you, only with more accuracy. Were there bushes around?"

Perry nodded, mute.

"I told you Monty had two wounds, didn't I? One just grazed his arm. I think that was your shot. The murderer counted on you missing."

Perry stared at her, hope easing the tenseness of his expression. "What do you think I should do?"

"I don't know. Nothing, for the moment. I want to think. I may know someone we can trust to help. Will you come to the rehearsal tomorrow? We'll talk again then."

She took her leave and the Lansdon carriage returned her to Cavendish Square. The forced quarrel, Monty's insistence on holding the meeting less than two hours later, his not bringing a second but only a doctor no one could identify—the whole thing sounded like a planned murder—but of Perry, not

Monty. And someone else must have been behind it, staging this carefully so that it would be Monty who died instead.

Augusta shivered. *Why?* Had Monty been involved in something? Like a plan to sell military secrets to Bonaparte's supporters? She had to talk to Edward MacKennoch. At once.

The carriage set her down before Halliford House. Thanking the driver, she hurried up the steps and through the door which Willis held open for her. She made her way directly to the book room, where she could see a flickering light from beneath the door. Without even stopping to knock, she entered, only to be brought up short one step into the room.

". . . your assignment," an elderly gentleman said. He broke off and turned his stern-featured face to glare at the intruder.

Augusta cast a startled look over the distinguished figure seated in the chair opposite Major MacKennoch. She recognized at a glance the significance of the Prince's buttons and the yellow lining of the visitor's coat; she had met one of the Prince Regent's aides-de-camp before. Her eyes widened and she looked from him to Major MacKennoch, who sat behind Halliford's great desk.

"I—I beg your pardon. I wished to consult you, Major, but it—it can wait." She started to draw back.

"This is the young lady who overheard that interesting conversation, sir." Major MacKennoch stood up and came around to join her.

The man rose also. "Just remember what I said, MacKennoch. We'll find you another position so you can continue your work in secrecy. No, I'll be going, now." He nodded briefly to Augusta and allowed the major to escort him out.

Augusta sank into his vacated chair. Why did an ADC to the Regent visit Halliford's secretary—and talk about some secret assignment?

She asked that question minutes later, when the major returned to the book room. He hesitated, then resumed his seat behind the desk.

"I am working on something for Lord Bathurst."

"Bathurst?" She stared at him, her eyes wide. "Then—you are not really Halliford's secretary at all, are you?"

"Only in part," he admitted. "The position allows me to go places and talk to people—supposedly for His Grace's affairs."

"Then—" She broke off, not certain what she wanted to say.

Here was romance, indeed. A secret assignment for the Secretary of War ... Undoubtedly it involved daring and cunning, perhaps even danger and creeping about in the dead of night to spy on traitors ...

"The sale of military secrets!" Blood rushed to her cheeks as the realization dawned on her. "You—you're investigating it! Aren't you?"

He nodded. "But I will thank ye not to mention that fact to anyone."

"No. No, of course not." She knew—always had known—there was a great deal hidden within Major MacKennoch. But she had never dreamed he was in reality a special investigator for the government. An investigator ... Her heart clenched painfully.

"Now, about what did ye wish to consult me?"

"I—" She broke off. She couldn't tell him about Perry! Not now. He wasn't the protector—the friend—she had thought him. He worked for the government, for those who would prosecute Perry, who would welcome the information she could provide to further facilitate her friend's destruction.

She stared at Major MacKennoch in horror, her hopes plummeting. He hadn't exactly lied to her, but it amounted to the same thing. He had *used* her, listened to everything she had to say, enjoyed her confidences, without ever revealing the truth. He had led her on, encouraging her to trust him.

And she *had* trusted him—but not anymore. Had it all been for this purpose—so that she would betray Perry when in fact she sought to help him?

She had come so close to it! But Perry had nothing to do with the sale of military secrets—did he? Even if that *might* be the reason Captain Montclyff had been murdered? She couldn't be certain—of anything, at the moment—and for that reason, until she had time to think, she would not play into Major MacKennoch's hands.

Tears stung her eyes, but she kept them back. She felt cheated, betrayed. She rose abruptly. "It was nothing. Good night, Major. I'm sorry to have bothered you."

"What is the matter, Miss Carstairs?"

His voice was so gentle, inviting confidences, soothing her. She wouldn't fall into that trap. Why, if he were such a friend, had he not told her of his secret work before?

"Why do you not wear your kilt?" she demanded, more to divert his mind than for any other reason. "It would seem you are still involved in military affairs."

His lips tightened, then relaxed. "Nay. I have sold out of my regiment. Now, what troubles ye?"

"Nothing." She turned away, then looked back over her shoulder. "Your visitor said something about finding you another position. Are you leaving us?"

His clear blue eyes studied her, and for a moment she thought she glimpsed a touch of sadness in their depths.

"Ye had better speak with Her Grace." He escorted her to the door, then closed it firmly behind her.

She made her way slowly up the stairs, feeling adrift on a troubled sea. She hadn't realized how much she had counted on Major MacKennoch. How could he have deceived her so dreadfully—though he probably did not see it in that light. He served his country. What did the heart of one foolish, hopeless romantic matter?

She thrust back the pain that filled her, that made it almost impossible to think. She still had Perry's problem with which to deal. Helping him gave her something constructive on which to concentrate.

Who else could she tell? Halliford, of course—if he were in town. But he wasn't. She forced herself to consider. Lord Roderick was clearly useless. But Lord Wentworth—no, it would only confirm his low opinion of the wild young officers and he would undoubtedly want to make an example of this whole shocking incident. No matter how callow—and foxed—Perry might have been, to have actually gone through with the duel under such peculiar conditions had been dreadfully wrong. He had played perfectly into the murderer's hands.

Frederick Ashfield she dismissed out of hand. But what about Jack Kettering? He might only be a lieutenant, but she felt certain he would take her fears seriously, perhaps know whom to approach on a higher level. But it probably would be best if she presented the story to him without any names until she felt certain Perry would not simply be arrested and the investigation abandoned.

At the second floor, she made her way to the duchess's bedchamber to see how she went on. To her amazement, Helena, in tears, sat in a wing-back chair before the fire.

136

Penelope and Demetrius crowded on her lap and she hugged the warm, purring bodies tightly.

Lizzie looked up from where she knelt at her sister's side and her expression betrayed her relief.

"What happened?" Augusta hurried forward.

"Halliford," Lizzie said simply.

Helena located her handkerchief and used it. "It—it's nothing," she managed to get out between ragged breaths. "I—I'm being stupidly missish."

Lizzie patted Helena's hand. "Halliford sent a messenger saying he's been detained at the Castle and won't be able to join us for some time yet."

"I just want to go *home*," Helena explained.

"Of course you do, dearest." Augusta sank down to the floor on her other side. "You're having the most dreadful time."

Helena sniffed. "I'm not usually such a—a watering pot."

"Considering how ill you've been, you're doing amazingly well. Now, take a deep breath. Do you think you would care for some warm wine?"

A gentle rap sounded at the door and it opened almost at once. Edward MacKennoch hesitated on the threshold. "Is Her Grace—"

Augusta looked up, and the pain of his betrayal swept over her. She looked quickly away. He wasn't there to help.

His concerned gaze rested on her for a moment, then he turned to the duchess. "His Grace has requested that I send some papers to him at the Castle. But if ye wish to go, there is no reason why I should not make the arrangements."

"Oh, if you would!" Helena exclaimed, relieved.

"Are you well enough?" Augusta's concern for Helena temporarily ousted her own unhappiness.

"Oh, yes! It would be so much better than staying here. That is—" She broke off, her expression one of consternation. "Oh, Gussie, and just as the Season is beginning. How dreadfully selfish of me to—"

Augusta managed a convincing laugh. "How dreadfully selfish of *me* if I were to demand you stay in town. Now, if I wish to remain and go racketing about society, I have only to call on our dear aunt and uncle to chaperone me. You may be quite certain they would be delighted to take me in."

Helena's eyes kindled. "Gussie, how *could* you suggest it,

even in jest! Halliford's sister-in-law—"

Augusta giggled, this time in all sincerity. "Just so, dearest. It would be like the three weeks you spent in London, with Aunt Maria inviting all her acquaintances to meet a friend of a duke's. No, to tell the truth, I think I would rather go back to Yorkshire, myself. The Season is entertaining for a while, but it becomes a bore quickly." That, at least, was the truth. "If you like, we can always come back for the Little Season in the fall."

"Are you sure you don't mind?" Helena regarded her anxiously.

"Of course she is sure!" Lizzie stood up and shook out her hopelessly wrinkled skirts. "Such a bother about going to dull parties where there is never enough to eat and nothing really *fun* to do! There will be far more to occupy us in the country in the spring. Perhaps we can help with the lambing." She seemed much taken with the idea.

"Then with Your Grace's permission?" Edward waited for her approval. "I will make the arrangements at once. When would ye care to depart?"

"Is tomorrow too soon? No, I suppose it is. The beginning of next week, then?" With that settled, Major MacKennoch left the room.

After seeing her sister safely to bed, Augusta went to her own room, lost in troubled thought. This was not a good time for her to leave town. The investigation into Monty's death still hung over her, and Perry's affairs appeared more perilous than ever. Yet Major MacKennoch made no objection. Probably, he would be glad to have her out of the way.

And what of her plays? They *must* be continued—they did too much good to be abandoned, just because she must leave town. She would turn them over to Lord Wentworth, she decided.

At the rehearsal the following afternoon, she made her announcement. The news that she would shortly return to Yorkshire was greeted with flattering dismay by all. But to her relief, when she expressed her concern that the plays be continued, Lord Wentworth agreed with her.

He patted her hand in an avuncular manner. "Well now, my dear. Can't say as it will be the same without you. But we'll carry on your good work." He then canceled the rehearsal, saying he would need time to locate another place in which to present the plays, and took his leave.

Jack Kettering cast an urgent, entreating glance at Augusta, which she ignored. Lord Roderick took him casually by the arm, as usual not noticing anything amiss, and suggested they return to their regiments together. Kettering acquiesced, though somewhat ungraciously.

Only Perry and Sophronia remained. The girl's carefully cultivated calm evaporated in an instant, and she sprang to her feet. "Have you thought of anything to help Perry?"

Augusta shook her head. "I had hoped to speak to Lieutenant Kettering, without mentioning any names of course, but there was no opportunity today."

"No!" Perry exploded. A night's sleep apparently had restored his shattered equilibrium, for he no longer looked as distraught. "I don't want this talked about. Damn it, I—" He broke off as Willis appeared in the doorway.

"Captain Trent has called, Miss Augusta." The butler stepped back to allow that gentleman to enter.

Augusta stiffened. Perry started, as if caught out in some guilty act and Sophronia looked away at once. Perry made their excuses and, gripping his sister firmly by the arm, led her from the room.

Captain Trent watched them depart, a slight frown creasing his brow, then he came a few steps into the saloon and paused. "Is there not a rehearsal today? I had thought to take part."

Was this a ploy to put her off her guard? Augusta eyed him uncertainly. "It has been temporarily called off. My sister is unwell and wishes to retire to the country at once. And that will mean closing Halliford House for the remainder of the Season."

"I see." He almost drawled the words. "I am sorry for Her Grace. And for you. How unpleasant to be forced to leave town just as the Season begins. And you must abandon your plays as well."

Augusta faced him squarely. "Did you really come for the rehearsal? You did not attend the previous ones."

"My duties merely have been getting in the way." He smiled suddenly. "I do have some official business as well," he admitted.

"Then perhaps I should send for Major MacKennoch."

"There is no need," he began, but she pulled the bell rope

139

with enough force to bring Willis running.

Augusta seated herself on the sofa and waited, refusing to take part in any but the most casual talk until Major MacKennoch could join them. As long as he maintained the fiction of being Halliford's secretary, he might as well perform that job and protect her.

When the door opened again a few minutes later, Augusta looked up to see his solid, capable figure framed on the threshold. A wave of relief vied with her sense of injury, and to her consternation, it won out. The major might have hurt her, but his presence still made her feel more secure.

Major MacKennoch addressed himself immediately to their visitor, unconsciously taking control of the situation. "How may we help ye, Captain?"

"Such ceremony." Trent shook his head, mocking. He did not appear pleased.

Augusta found herself glad a measure of animosity existed between the two men; they obviously did not work on the two investigations together. Did that mean Monty's murder and the sale of military secrets were not connected? She found that thought a relief. Perhaps Major MacKennoch had no interest in Perry's affairs, after all—perhaps he had not tried to use her, as she'd feared. She wished she could be certain.

The major seated himself in a chair opposite Augusta. The slightest smile just touched his lips.

Vincent Trent cleared his throat. "I merely thought Miss Carstairs could tell me a few things about Captain Montclyff. Perhaps who his friends were?"

Augusta frowned. "But surely you are in a better position than I to know that. I knew him only through my plays."

"That had been what? Just over a month? And he offered for you after so short a time?"

"Gentlemen have been known to make offers after briefer acquaintances," the major pointed out.

Captain Trent inclined his head in acknowledgment. "Did he seem to know any of the members of your little troupe better than others?"

Augusta considered. "The officers, of course—Lieutenant Kettering, Lieutenant Lansdon, and Lieutenant Lord Roderick Ingersoll."

"And why do you think he took part in your performances?

A desire to help the war orphans?"

Augusta started to smile, then instead stared blankly at Captain Trent. "That doesn't seem likely, does it? He was not a man to put himself out for others. I—I hadn't really thought of it before." She could hardly say she suspected him of taking part for the sole purpose of courting her—or rather, her dowry.

Vincent Trent looked at her narrowly, then allowed it to pass. "Can you tell me anything about him? Anything he might have mentioned during breaks in your rehearsals?"

Again, she shook her head. "I don't even know if he had any family. He never spoke about other interests."

"And what did you think of the evil gossip he spread about you the day before he died?"

"The—" Augusta broke off and stared at him, speechless.

"This is the first we've heard of it." Edward MacKennoch spoke smoothly. He caught Augusta's eye, warning her to silence. but she paid him no heed.

"What a—a dreadful thing to say! I have seen people whispering, of course, but no one has said a word about anything *evil*." Indignant, she looked from Captain Trent to Major MacKennoch, then back. An uncomfortable certainty took root in her mind. She was under official suspicion—but of what? Inducing someone to murder Captain Montclyff for her? Perry, perhaps? Or did Captain Trent try his hardest to make her look guilty, perhaps to protect himself?

"And what gossip have ye heard?" the major asked.

"Some very interesting—and highly unkind—comments. Quite untrue, I make no doubt." Trent kept his steady gaze fixed on Augusta's flushed countenance.

"Ye had better make no doubt." A touch of steel underlay the major's words. "Considering she had just rejected his offer, and considering his rather unpleasant temperament, I don't think too much attention should be paid to what he might have said."

Trent smiled, though Augusta did not find it pleasant. "Of course not. But protecting—or avenging—Miss Carstairs's honor, you must admit, suggests a very possible motive for a staged duel." He rose. "I will not detain you any longer. I am certain I shall see you before you leave town, Miss Carstairs. Major MacKennoch." With a nod, much as if he dismissed them, he took his leave.

Chapter 11

The following morning Augusta decided to devote to scribbling notes of apology, crying off from the various engagements to which they had pledged themselves. She had barely begun when Sophronia burst unceremoniously in on her and plopped down on a chair, her hands clasped in her lap. She raised a woebegone face to her friend.

"Whatever has happened?" Augusta thrust her pen and paper aside.

"It is Perry."

"He—he hasn't—"

"His regiment has been posted to Brussels. And without warning!"

Augusta stared at her, torn between dismay at Perry's imminent departure and relief that it was nothing worse. "When does he leave?"

"He already has! This morning."

"But the investigation—"

Sophronia shook her head. "I don't know."

"And his blackmailer! Will Perry be out of his reach?"

"I don't *know!*" Large tears formed in the girl's eyes. "Whatever shall we do?"

Augusta leaned back in her chair, thoughtful. "This might be for the best," she said at last. "As part of the Army of Occupation, there will be countless reviews and parades, and probably always something for him to do. He will be kept busy."

And out of trouble, she added to herself. Barring a full confession to the authorities, which did seem an almost suicidal course, this might be the best thing possible. By the time his regiment returned, the investigation might well be abandoned. In Brussels . . .

A chill swept through her. Those overheard words about a regiment being posted to Brussels, making it easy to steal and sell military secrets . . . could that regiment have been Perry's? And could he be involved?

No, the whole idea was preposterous. It had to be! Perry hadn't the nerve for that sort of perilous undertaking.

"What should I do?" Sophronia cried, reclaiming Augusta's attention. She sniffed. "Now I suppose your plays must be canceled after all! Lord Roderick will be gone also." She let out an unhappy sigh. "Oh, I do wish you were not to leave town, my dearest Augusta. The Season won't be any fun without you. I will miss you quite dreadfully!"

"And I, you." Augusta clasped the girl's hand, moved.

Sophronia managed a tremulous smile. "I do not enjoy the Season in the least, without your company. I know it is my duty, for the sake of the younger girls, to make an excellent match. But I don't *take!* If it weren't for my friendship with you, I daresay I'd be ignored completely."

Augusta stared at her, aghast. "What a—a plumper!"

Sophronia sniffed again and sought in her reticule for a wispy handkerchief. "Mamma might as well return us to the country, too, and save the money for Julia's comeout next year. It will be too humiliating to remain in London once you are gone, and never be invited anywhere."

"That is all nonsense, and so you know. You are just feeling low because Perry has been sent away. Here, let me ring for refreshments." She did so as she spoke, then returned to her friend's side. "You will feel more the thing directly."

Sophronia nodded, but patently remained unconvinced. Augusta turned the conversation neatly to a card party they would attend that evening, and who they would be likely to meet, until Willis arrived with a tray of tea and cakes.

When Sophronia at last rose to take her leave, she had recovered much of her composure, and her voice quavered only slightly as she said, "I don't suppose we'll be seeing much of Captain Trent, now that Perry and Roddy are gone."

"Oh, no, Sophie, I am certain—" Augusta broke off, seeing the unhappiness in the other girl's face. It would not be kind to

143

encourage her to hope, especially when she had set her heart on a man who might be a traitor and who most certainly watched her brother with calculating eyes.

The next few days flew by in a chaos of packing, refusing invitations, and sending more notes of regret. Lord Wentworth called to announce that he, too, had been posted to Brussels. He offered profuse apologies for not being able to carry on with her cause.

"You could always begin them again there," she suggested, only half teasing. "I do so hate to see the project abandoned when we were doing so much good."

He considered. "Perhaps I might try, once I'm settled. It is a pity the duchess's delicate condition prevents you from crossing the Channel. Without you to portray the heroine, our poor efforts could not meet with nearly the success they have here in London."

Augusta smiled. "Do what you can. There are so many who have suffered so terribly because of the long war."

Renewing his promise that he would not let her and her cause down, Lord Wentworth took his leave.

With a wistful sigh, Augusta watched him depart. It would be such a delightful adventure to visit the Continent, even spend the season in Brussels. There would be so many dashing officers, so much gaiety. And to be in a foreign country, one which Napoleon's troops had occupied not so long before . . .

She stifled her burgeoning daydream and instead prepared for their removal to staid Yorkshire. Romance, it seemed, was once more denied her. In an attempt to relieve Helena of as much responsibility as possible, she set about directing the servants and taking over any number of chores.

In this, she was ably, though somewhat unexpectedly, aided by Lizzie. The servants liked her, Augusta realized suddenly as she watched her forthright sister come to terms with a recalcitrant carter who refused to carry the too-heavy crate consigned to his care. Five minutes of Lizzie's companionship had the man smiling, and within another two, he summoned help and the crate was transferred to his wagon.

But if it hadn't been for Major MacKennoch's quiet efficiency, Augusta freely admitted they would never have gotten ready. He seemed to be everywhere in the house, yet never intrusive. Things miraculously were accomplished, tempers magically soothed. Throughout it all, he remained friendly, capable—and aloof.

Gratitude struggled with the remnants of her anger. *Had* she overreacted to the discovery he worked secretly for Lord Bathurst? She watched him covertly as he moved about the house, wishing she dared trust him. He was so rigid, though, expecting perfection of himself—and everyone else. He would take a dim view of Perry's involvement in the duel, even without the unorthodox circumstances. No, if she told him, he would undoubtedly feel obligated to report the whole to Captain Trent, and then Perry wouldn't stand a chance of being believed.

She slipped out of the room where he directed the boxing of the silver Helena did not want left in London. She couldn't trust him to help, only to do what was "right"—as he saw it. He wasn't, in this case, an ally. So why must her unruly heart flutter at the sound of his voice? Why should she wonder what it would be like to be held in those strong arms? It was nothing but a youthful folly, and she would grow out of it. She had to.

By the day before their scheduled departure, Augusta was frantic. Helena, not content to lie quietly as her physician ordered, roamed the house, her eyes haunted, trying to assume duties she maintained were hers despite her ill health. At least three times a day, she apologized to Augusta for taking her away from London during the Season, and nothing her exasperated sister could say would convince the duchess that Augusta would not pine, away from the entertainments of town.

At last, they merely awaited the baggage fourgon, which Willis had already summoned. Their trunks could be loaded then and taken away, leaving them with only the things they would need for their own journey into Yorkshire.

When Willis sought her out in her chamber, where she oversaw the packing of the portmanteau that would accompany her, she greeted his entrance with relief. But he had not come to announce the arrival of the fourgon, as she had hoped. Visitors were below, he pronounced.

With an exclamation of vexation, Augusta stood up from where she knelt beside an open bandbox and shook out her skirts.

"Mrs. Lansdon and Miss Sophronia, Miss Augusta," Willis explained.

She thanked him, then made her unenthusiastic way downstairs to where they awaited her in the Gold Saloon. She loved Sophronia dearly, but just at the moment she found the prospect of dealing with the girl's unhappiness somewhat daunting.

But it was a face wreathed in smiles that welcomed her. Sophronia ran lightly across the room and embraced her, her hazel eyes sparkling with unaccustomed animation. "Oh, Augusta, the most wonderful thing! We are to go to Brussels!"

Augusta stifled a sensation of envy and looked across to Mrs. Lansdon. "Good afternoon, dear ma'am. Is it true? How wonderful for you! You can be near Perry."

Mrs. Lansdon nodded. "I do not think I would have thought of it myself, for to tell truth, the idea of going abroad, without a man to arrange everything for one, is rather a frightening prospect. But a great many of our acquaintances have already gone since that monster Napoleon is safely exiled. And now my dear cousin, whom I did not even know was in Brussels, has written that they are giving up their house there to stay in Italy this spring, and has asked if I would like to use it. It seems the most perfect opportunity."

"I vow, London will be dreadfully thin of company this year, the way everyone has been flocking across the Channel!" Sophronia added, her excitement uncontainable. "I shall see Perry within the week!"

Mrs. Lansdon smiled fondly on her eldest daughter. "So many officers, gathered in that one place," she murmured.

Augusta caught that complacent smile. So many officers. What better place to find a husband for a rather plain but very sweet girl than in the Army of Occupation? That probably motivated more matchmaking mammas to make the journey to Brussels than the prospect of visiting the Continent once more after so many long years of war.

"Dearest Augusta!" Sophronia hugged her arm. "Will you not come with us?"

Augusta stared at her in blank astonishment, then turned to Mrs. Lansdon.

That woman smiled. "It would be the greatest favor to me

imaginable, my dear Miss Carstairs. For you must know I am leaving the younger girls with my sister, and poor Sophronia will find herself very much alone in a strange city. We mean to entertain, of course, but to have the company of her closest friend would make everything so much more enjoyable."

"I—" Augusta broke off, her mind whirling. She wanted to go, but it would mean leaving Helena—and Lizzie. But it would also relieve Helena's mind of any worry for her sake. And perhaps, however unlikely it might seem, she might even meet a gentleman capable of replacing Major Edward MacKennoch in her wayward heart.

The door opened behind her and Helena, pale but smiling and determined, entered the room. She came forward and greeted Mrs. Lansdon, who inquired solicitously after her health.

"Your Grace!" Sophronia interrupted, too excited to be still.

Mrs. Lansdon hushed her, then repeated their request for Augusta's company.

The duchess's worried brow cleared. "Then you will not have to forgo your season after all! Oh, Gussie, it—"

Augusta took her hand. "If you are quite certain you do not want me with you?"

"Of course not. It is the most delightful scheme. You know I want you to enjoy yourself. Do not give a thought to me. I have been thinking, and have hit upon the—the nackiest notion, as Adrian would say. I shall beg Richard and Chloe and their dear baby girl to bear me company at the Castle."

Augusta nodded, relieved. She could think of no better companion for Helena than Lord Richard's wife, the gentle Chloe. She and Helena had been friends almost from the moment they met. Her own departure for Brussels would be all for the best, Augusta assured herself.

The arrangements were settled upon with amazing rapidity. When Helena and Lizzie departed for Yorkshire the following morning, they would convey Augusta to the Lansdon house. It would be as simple as that. Within two days, she would be on her way to the Continent.

As soon as Sophronia and Mrs. Lansdon took their leave, Augusta went in search of Major MacKennoch to tell him of the new plan. He needed to be informed at once so her luggage

147

could be redirected. Yet her steps dragged in the hall.

The door to the study stood slightly ajar, so she pushed it further. Major MacKennoch sat behind the massive mahogany desk, a sheaf of papers clutched in his hand. But his eyes stared unseeingly at the opposite wall, a hint of sadness lurking in their depths. One finger traced absently the line of scar that sliced through his cheek. His expression, in repose, betrayed pain, both mental and physical.

Augusta's heart went out to him. She started forward impulsively, then stopped herself. Major Edward MacKennoch was not a man to appreciate being caught in an unguarded moment. His reserve—and his pride, she realized in a flash of insight—would never forgive this intrusion.

Silently, she withdrew and pulled the door until it was almost closed. Then she knocked briskly and entered on his call. The change in him was dramatic. Gone was the wistful air, the vulnerability. The Major MacKennoch she faced now bristled with the efficiency she had come to know.

He glanced quickly at the papers he held, then set them down. "What may I do for ye?"

"Mrs. Lansdon has asked me to accompany them to Brussels. My sister thinks it would be a good idea."

Only the slightest flicker showed in his eyes; he controlled it at once. He stood, then bent over to shuffle the papers that lay before him without looking at her. "I will have your baggage sent to Half Moon Street at once."

"Yes. It's fortunate, is it not, that the fourgon has not yet arrived." She shifted from one slippered foot to the other, nervous for absolutely no reason she could discover.

"Very fortunate." The merest suggestion of a frown formed in his brow. "Are ye quite sure the duchess does not want ye with her?"

Augusta came forward and sank into the chair opposite the desk. "You can have no idea how lowering it is. She practically ordered me to go. Apparently, she does not find me the least bit necessary. She will have Lord and Lady Richard to bear her company, you see."

His own lips twitched in reluctant response to her smile. "Have all Mrs. Lansdon's arrangements been made?"

"It seems so. We are to depart in two days. I'll stay in Half Moon Street until then. But I have no idea when they mean to return. I only hope it is before Helena is confined."

Her voice must have betrayed her worry, for he came around the desk to stand beside her. "I'm sure she will be all right. And ye will be so busy ye probably won't have a moment to think of—her."

"I suppose that is for the best." She raised her face to look up at him.

"But ye are still worried?" He leaned back so that he half sat against the newly cleared surface.

She nodded. "What about the inquiry into Captain Montclyff's death?"

His expression hardened. "They cannot make ye stay in London. Several of the officers who have been under investigation have already been sent to the Low Countries."

"With my luck the inquiry will merely resume over there. Do you know if Captain Trent's regiment has been posted to Brussels, by any chance?"

That brought an honest smile to his lips. "Nay. He is still here. Do not worry yourself about the matter. They will undoubtedly find Captain Montclyff's mysterious murderer among his gaming acquaintances."

She looked down, studying her hands. *Should* she, for the sake of his investigation, betray Perry and tell the major the truth? But no useful purpose would be served; she would only cause harm. Perry knew nothing that would enlighten the situation and his career would be ruined for his reprehensible part in the affair.

"Miss Carstairs?" Major MacKennoch spoke gently. "I won't permit them to hound ye. Ye may be sure of that."

She looked up and sudden, inexplicable tears misted her vision. Never could she have imagined that steely blue eyes could look so warm, so gentle. "You—you are very kind."

He straightened up and his impenetrable mask descended once more. "I am only doing my job."

"Your job," she repeated. "But that is to protect the interests of the government, not me."

"Is there a difference?" His eyes narrowed.

"Of course not." There it was again—he the inquisitor, she suspected of knowing more than she admitted, perhaps of shielding the guilty party. She stood and held out her hand to him. "I wish you well."

"And I, ye." He took it in a firm clasp.

His warm, strong fingers closed about hers, and a tantalizing thrill raced up her arm. If only—but she was off to Brussels, and he to continue his secret assignment. Their paths remained on divergent courses.

She started toward the door, then turned back. "Major MacKennoch?"

"Aye?"

"Will you not put on your kilt before I leave?"

He regarded her for a long moment through eyes that betrayed a fleeting sadness. "Nay, lass. I will not wear my uniform."

She went out, but as the door closed behind her, his soft words reached her.

"Not even for ye."

Chapter 12

Augusta sank down on the edge of her bed, exhausted. They had been in Brussels nearly three weeks, and it seemed as if they had been busy every moment. Never, not even in London, had she encountered so many people bent on enjoying themselves so fully. The years of war had taken their toll, and Brussels celebrated with abandon.

But so far, her own search for romantic diversion had proved fruitless. With so many officers resplendent in their scarlet regimentals or so dashing in the gold-laced blue coat of the Hussars, why did none of them capture her heart? The will was certainly there, on her part. She *wanted* to fall in love with some eligible gentleman. But of all those who paid her court, not one earned a place in her regard.

She sighed and fell back among the soft pillows on her bed. This was her second season. She had met Bucks, Blades, Corinthians, Goers, Tulips, any number of men possessed of fortune, and every title from marquis through the lowest baronetcy. But she could discover in herself not the least desire to marry any one of them.

Had Helena's happiness with her fairy-tale duke spoiled her already romantic turn of mind? But then why did Edward MacKennoch, a retired major, an impoverished second son, capture her wayward heart? He could be austere and forbidding and his eyes could be as cold as steel—or as warm and gentle as a summer sky.

A knock sounded on her door, dispelling her wistful memory, and she sat up and managed to school her face into a smile. Sophronia entered, her eyes sparkling.

151

"You will never guess who has called! Oh, do come, Augusta. It is Lord Wentworth!"

"Lord Wentworth!" She jumped up. "How delightful. I thought he had been sent on to Vienna permanently!"

They hurried downstairs together and found him in the front saloon, engaging Mrs. Lansdon in conversation. He rose at once at their entry and possessed himself of Augusta's hand.

"Well, my dear, so you came to Brussels after all. Splendid, splendid. I thought you settled in Yorkshire."

Augusta seated herself. "What? And permit my plays to be abandoned? Now that you are back, we must begin work tomorrow. I have been unable to find a new director, you must know. It will be such a relief to have something to do again! All this racketing about lacks *purpose*. I didn't realize how much I enjoyed helping a worthy cause."

"Now all we need is another actor or two," Sophronia announced, pleased. "That should not be too hard. Perry and Lord Roderick can recruit someone from their regiment, perhaps even their captain. He was one of our staunchest supporters before."

Lord Wentworth beamed at them. "Have you found a place to hold your little productions?"

Augusta shook her head. "We have concentrated on finding enough people willing to take part, so far."

"Why not hold them here?" Mrs. Lansdon looked from one to the other. "We have those large drawing rooms on the first floor that can be opened. This may not be as splendid as Halliford House, but it should serve."

"Indeed it shall, ma'am. I am very grateful." Augusta clasped her hostess's hands.

"Well then, that's settled." Lord Wentworth nodded his approval. "Shall we resume our last effort? If we work hard, we could get it ready to present by next week."

While secretly doubting their ability to perfect a play in quite so short a time, Augusta agreed. Lord Wentworth took his leave, and she saw him to the door. The plays wouldn't be the same without Lizzie's caustic comments, or even Jack Kettering's presence, but at least they would provide her with a sense of accomplishing something worthwhile—and they should help keep her mind from dwelling on a certain solid, fair, and unattainable Scotsman.

Augusta and Sophronia, accompanied by the latter's abigail, set forth at once to visit the shops to see what might be found to replace the props left behind in London. Most items they needed could be borrowed, they knew, but both ladies agreed that one never knew what treasures might be discovered if only one looked. They returned in the late afternoon, tired but satisfied. They had purchased nothing for the play, but Sophronia had found a night cap of frothy lace for her mamma she could not resist.

As they strolled back through the park to their rented house on the Rue Ducale, they saw an officer just descending the front steps. He looked up and Augusta stared in amazement.

"It is Lieutenant Kettering!" Sophronia cried, pleased. "Augusta, we have our hero for the production!" She hurried forward.

Augusta followed more slowly. He certainly looked a figure of romance in his scarlet coat, with his curling black hair and those luxuriant mustachios. It was only a pity she could not cast him in the role of her hero in real life.

Firmly, she thrust the intrusive thought of Major MacKennoch from her mind. He was in London, pursuing his investigation, separated from her by more than the many miles that stretched between them.

Lieutenant Kettering greeted Sophronia, then Augusta. "My regiment only arrived yesterday," he declared. "And you see me on your doorstep the moment I could get free."

"Not free for much longer," Augusta warned him. "We plan to resume our plays at once. May I count on your support?"

Kettering laughed and offered an arm to each lady to escort them up their steps. "How can I resist? I assume Lord Wentworth can get me special leave from my duties if necessary."

Sophronia took off her shawl in the hall, and Kettering turned to Augusta. "Now you see why I let you depart London with no word of protest. I was only too glad you would come."

She looked up, a slight frown creasing her brow. "Did you know your regiment would be sent here?"

"I couldn't be certain, but it seemed very likely. Ours generally accompanies the Tenth Foot, and when they were posted here, it seemed only a matter of time before we followed. Had we not, I would have been forced to take drastic

153

measures to reach your side."

She recoiled slightly from the flattery. As if he sensed this, he bowed to them and took his leave, bent, he declared, on visiting Lord Wentworth upon the instant and begging him to intervene with his commanding officer.

Augusta scheduled the first rehearsal for the following evening. It seemed odd to have so many of their original players gathered in a different house and so very far from London, but Augusta found it comforting. Perry, Lord Roderick, Kettering, Lord Wentworth, Sophronia, herself—only Captain Vincent Trent was missing from the cast they had assembled that last day at Halliford House, and Augusta did not miss him in the least. Together, they set to work eliminating his role from the script.

"It's no good," Lord Wentworth announced at last. "We have to find a new actor. Can any of you think of an officer capable of helping out with our cause?"

They were still engrossed in this seemingly hopeless task when the butler announced the arrival of Mr. Frederick Ashfield. That gentleman took two steps over the threshold, then stopped, his blue eyes lighting in amusement as he found himself the cynosure of six earnest gazes. He raised the quizzing glass that hung about his neck and returned the stare with unruffled calm. "Have I—er—come at an inopportune moment?"

"That you haven't!" Lord Wentworth asserted.

"For yourself, you have," Perry warned him.

Only Augusta, of the assembled company, did not greet his arrival with delight. "What are you doing here?" she demanded, with complete disregard for politeness.

"But visiting the Continent, as do you." His mobile eyebrows rose. "What did you expect?"

"That Halliford or Helena sent you to check up on me. I had no idea you meant to come to Brussels."

He laughed softly. "My poor Augusta. But really, the town was becoming dreadfully thin of company, with everyone coming here. And once I had arrived, how could I possibly resist the temptation of calling upon Mrs. Lansdon?"

"Well, you should have resisted for your own good." Perry lounged back in his chair. "What do you think? Will he make a villain?"

Augusta stared at the tall, rakish figure, her eyes narrowing, an unpleasant suspicion dawning in her mind. Frederick Ashfield, a villain? But it wasn't a role in any play that sprang to her mind at the moment. His arrival in Brussels suddenly seemed just a little too coincidental. Could it have been his voice she didn't recognize that night in the Lansdons' conservatory?

"Now, wait a minute." Mr. Ashfield drew back, sounding justifiably appalled. "You aren't trying to get *me* to join your troupe, are you?"

"But of course!" Lord Wentworth, his expression all jovial goodwill, waved him grandly toward a chair. "Do take a seat. We have the most wonderful part for you."

Lord Roderick handed over a script, and with only a token protest, Ashfield took it and glanced through the pages. "No, really!" he exclaimed, halfway through the third sheet. "You can't actually, any of you, expect me to say *that!*"

Augusta peered over his shoulder and sighed. "I *told* you it needed some rewriting, Lord Wentworth."

"Here, let me have it." Kettering took the script back and reached for the quill and ink that stood conveniently at hand. "No one can say that speech. It's all one sentence!" He went to work, crossing out words, stopping to think, then scribbling in even more unsuitable ones.

Wentworth shook his head. "We must give the play in only four days' time. We must keep it simple."

"In *what?*" Ashfield turned to Augusta, appalled. "What have I let you talk me into?"

"I don't believe I did any of the talking," she responded coolly. "But you will be helping the war orphans. Now do, I beg of you, pay attention. Lord Wentworth is quite right. We have not received a single invitation for this Thursday evening, so it will be the perfect time to introduce Brussels to our little plays."

"You cannot let us down, Ashfield!" Lord Roderick regarded him with his vacuous, cajoling smile.

Kettering handed the script back to Lord Wentworth. "Shall we read the scene through?"

They did, and Wentworth pronounced himself satisfied. They read through the entire play once, then called a halt for the night.

The following afternoon, which everyone but Perry had free from duties, was spent in rehearsals. Each line was discussed, changed, then returned to almost its original form. When the others finally departed, Augusta picked up their copy of the script and leafed through the pages.

She was thankful for the play. When she was busy working on it, her thoughts did not dwell quite as often on Major MacKennoch. Distance and time should have dulled his image in her mind. But instead, whenever she closed her eyes as she did now, his masterful figure appeared to her. Nor had he the decency to be cold and forbidding in her imagination, as she had seen him at first. Instead, his vulnerability, his fleeting smiles, that unexpected warmth which sprang so suddenly to his eyes, haunted her. And invariably, he wore his kilt, adding that finale panache. Moments like this tried a lady's well-bred vocabulary.

She turned to Sophie. "Let us study our lines outside. I need a breath of fresh air."

Mrs. Lansdon accompanied them to the Parc de Bruxelles, which stood between the Rue Royale and the Rue Ducale. They strolled down the broad, tree-lined promenade to the pond where swans glided peacefully across the still water. Mrs. Lansdon settled on a bench and drew out the stocking she was knitting for her youngest daughter, and Augusta and Sophronia seated themselves near her, each taking a few pages of the script.

Augusta found it hard to concentrate in the peaceful surroundings. They inspired dreams, not study. She got up and wandered to the edge of the water, where she gazed off down a walkway amid the shrubs. Officers in a wide variety of uniforms walked in small groups, or escorted ladies amid the gardens. Children laughed and played games on the expanses of scythed lawns.

And a tall, fair, solidly built gentleman limped slightly as he crossed the path and disappeared into the bushes on the other side.

Augusta stared in disbelief at the spot where he had vanished. Edward MacKennoch? In Brussels? She couldn't have been mistaken! She would recognize him anywhere, no matter how brief the glimpse.

She cast a quick look at her companions, both of whom

remained absorbed with their work. They wouldn't miss her. She hurried down the path until she reached the place she had last seen the gentleman. A narrow path led between flowering shrubs to a small pavilion. Unhesitatingly, she followed it.

Two men stood inside, conversing in low tones. Something about their rigid stances made her uneasy, and she moved out of their line of sight, through an opening in the shrubbery and behind a tree. She stifled a nervous, delighted giggle. Almost, she might be spying on them! If she crept closer, she could probably even hear what they said. But this was no romantic adventure, she recalled with a measure of regret. She merely meant to take a closer look at that one gentleman to discover whether or not he really was Major MacKennoch.

One man, a Belgian private by his uniform, emerged from the pavilion and strode off quickly away from her. Then the other man came out and Augusta's doubts fled. Major MacKennoch straightened his coat, then started toward her.

She waited until he came almost abreast, then stepped out into the path. "Major? What are you doing here?"

Surprise, followed by a touch of ruefulness, just flickered across his face. He drew a deep breath and let it out in a sigh. "I might have known," he muttered.

"Might you?" His lack of pleasure in seeing her stung.

"What the devil do ye think ye are at, spying on me, Miss Carstairs? Playing your romantic games?"

She gasped, hurt by his attack. "I wasn't! I thought I saw you, so I followed. That is all." Her chin jutted out in injured pride. "Why should I want to spy on you?"

A disturbingly attractive smile just curved his lips. "Nay, Miss Carstairs. Ye startled me. I should have known if I tried to pay a secret visit to this city, I would encounter ye."

Her eyes rounded. "Secret? Have—have I ruined all?"

A deep chuckle escaped him. "Nay. But ye haven't seen me, do ye understand?"

She nodded. "Your assignment—is it dreadfully dangerous?"

"I am sorry to disappoint ye, but it is not. I do not wish my work to be known, though, so it will be best if no one is aware I am here. I will thank ye not to mention seeing me."

She sighed, only half teasing. "It is not likely I could say anything that would do you harm. I hardly know anyone

157

involved in selling military secrets, do I?"

He returned no answer. His steady gaze rested on her.

Augusta's smile faded. Her fingers, which still rested on the tree, clutched at the bark. "*Do* I?"

"It would be best if ye mention seeing me to no one."

His serious tone disturbed her. "You didn't answer my question."

"Nay, Miss Carstairs. I did not. I am not certain of the answer."

Was that the truth? Or did he suspect one of her friends—Perry, perhaps? What would he think if he knew of Perry's involvement in the duel? She felt ill at the thought. Perry might well face the choice of being hanged as a murderer or shot as a traitor.

She turned away. "I will not keep you, Major. You must be anxious to be about your business."

"Miss Carstairs." His voice sounded troubled.

She hesitated, then looked back. "Yes?"

"Why do ye regard me as an enemy since ye found out about my work? Ye have nothing to hide, have ye?"

She bristled. "Of course I haven't! And I don't regard you as an enemy. I—I just felt at first as if you had used me to spy on my friends."

The fine crease in his brow deepened. "That is something I would never do. Ye may be sure I perform my job in a straightforward manner."

Her lips quirked in a sad smile. "Yes, like you do now, visiting Brussels in secrecy. You really should be wearing your kilt, Major. You may have sold out, but you are still an officer. Good-bye. I wish you every success."

She strode off quickly before she revealed the chaos of conflicting emotions he created in her. He suspected that she hid something from him. Or was it more than that? She couldn't rid herself of that uneasy feeling. It made no sense, though! He knew she wasn't involved in any treasonable activity—didn't he?

Or had she merely become too suspicious herself? Edward MacKennoch seemed so sincere, so eminently worthy of her trust. She longed to lay the whole dreadful mess at his feet and see him take charge of Perry's problems. But she simply didn't dare.

158

She shook her head, then looked about. She had wandered some distance. She switched to another path and made her way back to where Mrs. Lansdon and Sophronia awaited her. She must not let on that anything had just occurred. She might not betray Perry to the major, but neither would she betray Major MacKennoch to anyone else.

Mrs. Lansdon, aside from exclaiming in fun that she had quite begun to believe her charge to be lost, accepted Augusta's explanation of feeling in need of a walk. Sophronia, who had been repeating her lines to herself with an intensity that defied interruption, had not even realized that Augusta had drifted off. Mrs. Lansdon stowed away her knitting in her basket and they returned to the house to dress for Lord and Lady Eversley's dinner party.

Determinedly, Augusta forced herself not to think about Major MacKennoch. That only made her regret not being able to pour out the whole tale to him. Still, she would give a great deal to know what in particular had brought him to Brussels. She had heard no hint from the officers she knew that anything was amiss. Perhaps she would learn something tonight.

By the time they arrived at the Eversleys', their house in the Rue Royal was comfortably filled. Augusta released her wrap into the hands of a waiting footman and looked into the drawing room where the guests assembled. She knew everyone, she saw at a glance. It should be a pleasant evening. She would try to make it an informative one as well.

But the officers with whom she spoke revealed—or knew—nothing. Only partly relieved, she sought Sophronia amid the crowd. She still could not be easy, even though she learned nothing to confirm her fears. Major MacKennoch did not visit Brussles in secret for a lark. She only wished she could learn something that might help him—and that would not implicate Perry Lansdon.

Sophronia welcomed her back to her side with relief. "I vow, there are so many people here, yet no one I can really *talk* to."

Augusta managed a slight smile. "I know what you mean. Or will Lord Roderick do for you? I see he has just arrived."

Sophronia looked up, relieved, as her brother's friend hesitated in the doorway. He glanced around, saw them, and made a direct line to their side.

"How glad I am to—" Sophronia broke off. Her gaze had

159

been caught by an all too familiar figure. Her expression brightened for a moment, then crumpled in dismay. "What is Captain Trent doing here? I thought he was in London!"

"Captain Trent?" Augusta looked up, startled and not in the least bit pleased. What, indeed? Pursuing his suspects—as she'd jokingly predicted? How long had he been in Brussels? And perhaps more interesting, did his arrival have anything to do with Major MacKennoch's mysterious visit?

Captain Trent paused just over the threshold as Roderick had done only a minute before, and his gaze swept the room. He, too, saw Sophronia and Augusta. A broad smile replaced the slight frown that had marred his classically handsome brow and he strode up to them with all the air of one expecting a warm welcome.

"How fortunate to encounter you so soon." He took Augusta's hand, then turned his engaging smile on Sophronia.

A flicker of longing just touched the girl's features as he raised her fingers to his lips for a lingering kiss. Her eyes opened wider and she looked up into his laughing face. A visible tremble shook her.

"When did you arrive?" Augusta mastered her voice, keeping it calm and as disinterested as she could manage.

"Only yesterday. My regiment has just been posted here."

Could she glean information from him? It was worth a try. Augusta's delicate eyebrows rose. "A considerable number of regiments, of late. Do we ask why?"

"Oh, just keeping us on our toes." Captain Trent laughed.

It sounded forced to Augusta's suspicious ears. No, she didn't trust him. His manner toward Sophronia appeared just a shade too calculated. He was using her to keep a watch on someone. But who? Perry—or herself? And did his arrival have anything to do with the major's? Was it Vincent Trent whom Edward MacKennoch watched, and possibly followed?

The questions jostled each other in Augusta's mind. She shivered and glanced at Roddy, who bore a distinct resemblance to a cornered fox. Avoiding the captain's eye, Lord Roderick glanced around, then muttered an inarticulate excuse and bolted as if he were about to go to earth.

Augusta stifled her frustration. There would be no help from that quarter. Since he, in part, had helped create this dreadful mess by acting as Perry's second and permitting him to go

160

through with that shocking duel, the least he might do would be to help keep the wolf—or hound—at bay. But with Roddy, that was hoping for the impossible.

"May I beg the pleasure of your company for a ride tomorrow morning?" Captain Trent turned to Sophronia with the assurance of one who did not doubt the acceptance of his suggestion. "I find my duties are somewhat light at present, and I have discovered the most promising lane, just beyond the walls. And you, Miss Carstairs? Perhaps Lieutenant Lansdon might make us a foursome."

"I—I don't believe my brother will be free to join us." Sophronia looked up into Vincent Trent's face, then threw a frightened glance at Augusta. "Perhaps Lieutenant Kettering? I know he is coming later in the morning for a rehearsal."

Captain Trent frowned, but he agreed to the suggestion. So he wanted Perry along, too, did he? Augusta would do her best to keep that young gentleman out of his way. But the prospect of spending the morning on a pleasure expedition in Jack Kettering's company did not overly excite her either. She wished Sophronia had suggested Frederick Ashfield instead, for she could use a good dose of his caustic tongue. If only Captain Trent had not arrived in Brussels! His presence made her uneasier.

And more than that. The now familiar, unpleasant chill gripped her again. His regiment posted to Brussels. Those overheard remarks about selling military secrets returned to haunt her with a vengeance. Captain Trent, who might have been the person receiving orders to steal information, who "pulled strings" to be put in charge of a murder investigation, whose regiment now turned up in Brussels, as had been predicted by those terrible overheard words... Her conviction grew that Major MacKennoch was following him.

Lord Wentworth entered and Augusta grasped the excuse to get away from the captain. She sprang to her feet, excused herself, and hurried over to join him. Perhaps he had learned something new.

As she neared, Lord Wentworth turned and saw her. His easy smile brightened his jovial countenance and he took her hand with a sweeping bow.

"What, not exhausted from our rehearsal today? But no need to be in a pucker, my dear. The performance will go very well, you'll see. Very well indeed."

She knew a sensation of relief. He was someone who kept up on events, who would not be influenced by wild rumors. Surely, if something were amiss, he would know—and warn them.

"It isn't that. I *am* worried, but—" She broke off, uncertain how to express her concern without betraying Major MacKennoch's secret visit to Brussels.

Wentworth patted her hand in an avuncular manner. "Afraid Lord Roderick will forget his lines again? Well, that's a forgone conclusion, my dear. but his heart is in the right place."

Augusta shook her head. "It's nothing to do with the plays. It's the military."

He laughed, a comfortable, reassuring sound. "They're enough to worry anyone, my dear, especially a diplomat. A lot of useless, panic-mad children playing battle games. Have the officers been frightening you with their loose talk? That's all it is, you know. Just talk. If they can't have a battle, they must concoct other things to worry about, such as another war or espionage or some such nonsense. Never anything in it, of course, but it gives them something to do that makes them feel important."

She smiled in relief. She knew she could count on him for a dose of good sense. "With so many troops being posted to Brussels, I confess I began to fear that something dreadful might be happening."

He shook his head. "Games, my dear. Take the word of an old diplomat who has seen a great deal of service. The military is always manufacturing crises that require troop movement to keep their soldiers from getting bored and into trouble."

He excused himself, bent on making his way over to speak to his hostess. Frederick Ashfield stood at that lady's side, apparently having just put in a belated appearance. Lady Eversley laughed up into his elegant, smiling face, called him a shameless palaverer, and turned to Lord Wentworth.

Augusta noted the exchange with a touch of wonder. Frederick Ashfield's reputation as a rake seemed to have been well earned. But his carefully calculated compliments and teasing looks left her unmoved. Her taste ran to more reserved men.

162

The butler entered, announced that dinner was served, and Augusta looked about for the young officer who was to be her partner. He found her at once, and launched instantly into an attempt to impress her by relating a long and very boring tale of his heroism in the Peninsula. Resigning herself to a dull meal, she took his arm and accompanied him from the room.

While he rattled merrily on, her thoughts drifted. In her mind, if not in reality, Major MacKennoch sat at her side, relating *his* adventures. How she would love to listen to his deep voice telling her anything. She missed discussing things, even arguing, with him. But an insurmountable barrier had been erected between them, and would remain there until she was no longer classed as a suspected accomplice in a murder investigation.

Somehow, she had to clear Perry—and herself—of involvement in the matter. And soon.

The door into the dining room burst unceremoniously open, breaking off her thoughts. A footman half fell against the door jamb, panting for breath. The butler turned an outraged countenance on him and Lord Eversley raised his quizzing glass to better observe the man.

"Ex—excuse me, m'lord," the footman gasped. "Bonaparte!"

Several of the ladies gasped and one eager lieutenant sprang to his feet as if expecting to see the monster himself enter the room.

"What about him?" Lord Eversley demanded, testy.

The footman drew a ragged breath. "He—he has left Elba. They're spreading the word in the street, m'lord. He's marching toward Paris and gathering an army as he goes."

Chapter 13

Dead silence greeted the footman's dire announcement, then a chorus of exclamations broke out. Augusta barely heard the babble of shocked voices. Napoleon, on the loose again, roaming the Continent, collecting an army . . . She stared at the breathless, excited footman in horror. The dreadful war would begin all over again. She swallowed, trying to still the sudden pounding of her heart.

"So our fears are all a pack of nonsense, are they?" Captain Trent turned grimly to Lord Wentworth. An odd note of satisfaction lurked in his voice. "If it isn't just like you diplomats to think you could control any situation. This time you haven't!"

Augusta's gaze flew to him in surprise. He didn't sound the least bit startled or even alarmed. Almost, he might have known this news already! But that was impossible.

Or was it? A flicker of renewed fear raced through her. Had he heard the news earlier and been sworn to secrecy—or had he been instrumental in aiding Napoleon's plans?

"We shall control it." Lord Wentworth, alone of the assembled company, appeared calm. "You may be sure he will be intercepted and dealt with long before he reaches Paris."

"Yes, if Wellington is in command," Lord Roderick declared hotly.

Wentworth inclined his head. "We saw the bumbling efforts of the military for the past ten and more years. Now, with luck, the diplomats will be in charge of the proceedings and we will settle this problem of Napoleon. There is no need for panic, I assure you." He directed this last to the assembled company.

"We are certainly in no danger here in Brussels."

"No, that we are not," Captain Trent agreed. "We have seen to it that this city, at least, is secure for our allies." He smiled at his hostess, then turned to his host. "There is indeed nothing to fear."

Lord Eversley met his steady gaze and nodded. "Then I suggest we resume our meal."

"That is all well and good," Frederick Ashfield declared. "But you cannot deny there are certain people who are only too glad that Napoleon is once again on the move."

Augusta stared at him in dismay. Captain Trent threw him a quelling look, which he did not appear to notice.

"One hears rumors that certain military documents have turned up missing." Ashfield drawled the words. His expression, as usual, was sardonic, as if he meant to play the role of devil's advocate and would enjoy every moment of it.

Silence answered him. After a moment, Captain Trent nodded. "Yes, there is always a problem with that sort of thing, and now you may see the result! It was this that enabled Napoleon to gather support to leave Elba. And now that he is on the move, the problem will increase again."

Several other officers at the table murmured agreement.

Major MacKennoch's assignment. Augusta's heart gave an erratic beat. With Napoleon free, more intelligence concerning the Allied Forces would be needed, and the major's job would become more difficult—and more dangerous.

"Shoddy business, you know, letting secrets be stolen. So very careless." Ashfield shook his head.

"And who knows how much more is passed about by word of mouth." Lord Wentworth, who had fallen silent while he watched Ashfield intently, spoke up suddenly. He turned to Captain Trent. "I've heard rumors, but I'd been told it was all a hum. Really, if there's any truth in this shocking matter, I do feel the Diplomatic Service might have been alerted. Now it must be left to us to sort out this muddle."

"And to the army." Trent's tone took on a touch of steel.

Frederick Ashfield leaned back in his chair, a slight smile just touching his lips. "Really, it doesn't seem possible this sort of thing can go on unhindered. Have you made no progress at all in discovering the methods used to pass the information to—er—the buyers?"

"We have, indeed." Captain Trent shifted to look down the table at him. "But each time we uncover the method by which the secrets are passed, the culprits devise a new and more cunning arrangement of signals and meeting places."

Did he speak as a frustrated investigator—or a triumphant traitor? Augusta wished she could be certain. Would he help Major MacKennoch—or did the major pursue him?

"We can only suppose a new method must have come into existence within the past month," corroborated another officer.

Lieutenant Kettering, sitting across the table from Augusta, tugged at a newly trimmed end of his impressive mustache. "We should tighten down access to stretegic information."

"This is hardly a matter for dinner conversation," Trent said abruptly. "Tell me—" he turned back to his host—"is it true that the Prince of Orange has really refused Marchamp's invitation to dinner?"

The conversation slipped safely back into the latest on dits, and Augusta realized the matter of military secrets was not for open discussion. On the whole, she was amazed they had said as much as they had. But the entire company had been badly shaken by the news of Napoleon.

She shivered. The talk had also let her know how very important Major MacKennoch's assignment really was. She stared down at the tartlet that rested on her plate without seeing it. Was she right to withhold even the little bit of imformation she had from him? But Montclyff's death had no bearing on this issue. By revealing Perry's disreputable part in that, she would accomplish nothing except the ruination of his career—if not his life.

Lady Eversley rose, and Augusta realized the meal had concluded. Along with the other ladies present, she followed their hostess to an elegant drawing room. The eldest of the Eversley girls seated herself at the pianoforte and embarked on a beautiful old Scottish ballad.

Augusta forced herself to abandon her disturbing thoughts and listen. The description of the purple heather and gray-blue lochs of the highlands brought Edward MacKennoch irresistibly to her mind. She could picture him dressed once again in the dark blue and green tartan kilt of the 42nd Highland Regiment, marching into battle to the inspiring sound of the drums and pipes, brave and determined. A shiver raced through her. How she longed to see him like that. For that matter, she simply longed to see him.

She closed her eyes. If only he would come through the door and smile, just for her, with warmth in his piercing blue eyes. He would seat himself beside her and they would talk, not about mysteries or murders, but about themselves. She would tease him and he would laugh, perhaps that warm chuckle, and . . .

The song ended, and with a sigh, Augusta returned to reality. The ladies attempted to initiate polite conversation, but inevitably the discussion turned to Napoleon's return to France and what the Duke of Wellington would do about it. That great man was far away, though, attending the Congress in Vienna, and no one knew what might be on his mind.

The gentlemen, Augusta guessed shrewdly, must be discussing the same thing. They took an unconscionable amount of time over their wine and snuff, and more than an hour passed before they finally joined the ladies in the drawing room.

Two footmen arranged card tables. Augusta rose from her seat beside Lady Eversley and went to intercept Lord Wentworth, her purpose a relaxing game of piquet.

No more was said that night about Napoleon. But Augusta, retiring at last to her bed, could not be easy. Had Major MacKennoch known about his leaving Elba? Was that why he had come to Brussels? Or had he simply come in pursuit of a suspect, one who had just arrived on the Continent—like Captain Vincent Trent?

For that matter, she reminded herself, trying to be fair, Lieutenant Kettering had only just arrived also. And Lord Wentworth and Frederick Ashfield. Or any number of other men.

The question still remained with her the following morning when she made her way down to the breakfast parlor. Mrs. Lansdon, as was her invariable custom, partook of her breakfast in bed when she awoke—which was usually quite late. Sophronia was not likely to rise before nine. That left Augusta in sole possession of the sunny room.

But not for long. The butler entered and announced that a gentleman awaited her in the morning room. Curious, and not a little apprehensive, she went at once, only to draw up short at sight of Major MacKennoch. She closed the door behind her and went to greet him.

"Major? I thought you didn't want anyone to know you were here."

"I don't. Which, I'm afraid, is why I did not give my name to the butler."

She gestured for him to take a seat, which he declined. She settled on the sofa, her unease growing. "Why did you risk coming?"

He looked down on her, his cool blue eyes as impenetrable as ever. "I must return to London this morning. I think ye should come with me."

"Why?"

"Ye must have heard the news of Napoleon. I would see ye away from Brussels."

She caught her breath, then released it slowly. "But that—surely that could not be done in secret. You would reveal your presence here!"

"Aye." He waved that aside.

Warmth flooded through her. He was concerned about her! How she had longed for that. It would be wonderful to travel with him. Would it be a mad flight across foreign territory in the dark of night?

She squashed the romantic image this conjured up. She could not let him risk compromising his assignment just for her sake. But oh! she was glad he had offered.

She shook her head firmly. "I won't go. No, please, Major. I am grateful. But we will be perfectly safe here, and I will not permit you to jeopardize your work. If—if there is indeed any danger, you may be sure Mrs. Lansdon will return to England at once. There is no need to concern yourself for me."

A rueful smile just touched his lips. "I wish I did not have to go back."

She rose and went to him, impulsively holding out her hands. He took them in a firm clasp and color crept to her face. He released her abruptly.

She studied the second button of his waistcoat. "Your work is too important." She risked a glance at his somber face and looked hurriedly back down. "You had best leave now, before Sophie comes down and sees you. Then you might be quite certain all of Brussels would know of your visit."

He smiled slightly. "Do your best to stay out of trouble, Miss Carstairs."

She was having enough trouble at this moment staying out of his arms. But they didn't open for her—he didn't even give any sign that he wanted her there. He probably only offered to take her to safety for Halliford's sake.

She saw him to the door. As he started down the steps, she called softly to him. "Major."

He looked back. "Aye?"

"Will you not wear your kilt to travel in?"

"Nay, lass."

This time, she thought, his smile did not seem as sad. Wrapped in thoughts of him, she went back into the house. Perhaps his unhappy memories had begun to fade. If he completed this assignment to his satisfaction, would he once again don his kilt? How she would love to see him march toward her, filled with pride, once again in his uniform.

Sophronia joined her sooner than Augusta had expected. She had barely finished her tea when her friend burst into the breakfast parlor, already dressed in her bishop's blue habit. They were pledged to ride with Captain Trent and Lieutenant Kettering, her friend reminded her.

Less than half an hour later, the foursome rode through the streets. A great deal of activity met their searching eyes. Napoleon might be a very great distance away, but the soldiers of the Allied Forces intended to be ready. Augusta wondered if Major MacKennoch had already departed the city—and if London was, in fact, still his goal.

They rode outside the northern town walls, along the Allee Verte, as far as a bridge that led over a canal. The Laeken road stretched beyond, leading to the tiny village where Lieutenant Kettering informed them he was quartered with his regiment. Augusta sat back in her saddle, breathing deeply of the crisp air.

"Napoleon will never reach Paris, will he?" She asked the question that had occupied her mind. Only silence answered her. She turned and looked at Kettering. "Will he?"

The lieutenant glanced at Captain Trent. "I shouldn't think so. I don't imagine Wellington will remain in Vienna now."

"Do you think he will join the army here?" Sophronia

looked hopeful. "I would so love to actually see him."

Captain Trent smiled at her enthusiasm. "We shall have to wait and see. I don't think you need be in the least bit worried, though, at the present."

Augusta turned her mount and urged it into a gentle canter back toward the town. "At the present," Captain Trent had said. But what about after that? Throughout the Peninsular campaign, Wellington had never faced Napoleon himself, only his field marshals. Would that change now—and if so, what would be the outcome?

Desperate for some respite from her troubled thoughts, she sought refuge upon her return to the house on the Rue Ducale in going over the play. They had to give it in two days' time and she could not yet be satisfied with the wording.

Less than a half hour later, though, she was interrupted when the door to the drawing room opened a crack and Perry peered in around the jamb. Apparently relieved to find her alone, he thrust the door wide and sauntered inside in a manner so casual that it instantly alerted Augusta to trouble. Beneath his arm he gripped something wrapped in cloth. Augusta looked at it and knew a deep sense of foreboding.

"Alone?" he asked unnecessarily.

"As you see. Good morning, Perry."

He looked around the room as if fearful that someone might be hiding in a corner, just out of his sight. Assured on that score, he sank down onto the very edge of the chair opposite her. His haggard features betrayed him even before he spoke. "Need you to do me a favor, Augusta."

"What is that?" She gestured toward the box, but she had the sinking sensation she already knew.

"I just borrowed them." He straightened in an attempt to look less cowed and defensive, but it failed miserably.

"Perry—"

He looked up, his expression stricken. "You've *got* to help me, Augusta. I need you to pawn them for me."

"I can't! No, Perry, listen. I have no idea how to go about it here in Brussels. In England it would be difficult enough. But here it would be impossible!"

"I'll tell you how to do the trick. Thing is, can't do it myself."

"Why not?"

He flushed. "I don't dare be seen with them," he muttered.

"I don't suppose you bothered to tell Lord Roderick you've 'borrowed' his pistols—again?"

Perry's flush deepened. "Course not," he mumbled.

"Perry, why not? He's your friend! How can you serve him such a backhanded turn?"

Perry shook his head. "Look, just you pawn them for me, all right? I'll have the money to redeem them in three days. Roddy will never know they're missing—and if he does, I'll tell him the truth. I don't want him to worry about it if possible, that's all. Just need the blunt to tide me over for a bit."

"Why?" She kept her expression stern.

"I—I'm still being blackmailed."

"Still. So your blackmailer is now in Brussels, too." She drew a deep breath. "But I can't get you the money, Perry. I wish I could help. You know I would if it were possible."

He bit his lower lip. "God, what a mess I've gotten into!"

He sounded so young, so pathetic, Augusta's heart went out to him. He was, after all, not yet twenty, no more than a callow youth, and one who had been without the benefit of a father's guidance since a very young age. No wonder he was spoiled. A good dose of military discipline might be the making of him. Unless, of course, he was courtmartialed for theft or hanged for murder. Or even shot for treason. She thrust those thoughts aside.

"How else can I get the money?" he asked, rather as if he expected her to provide the solution.

"For what?"

They both looked up to see Sophronia standing in the doorway, a frown marring her plain features.

"Perry, what trouble have you gotten into this time?"

"A fine thing to go accusing a fellow!" he blustered. "No need for you to kick up a dust, you know. I need to pay that da—that blackmailer. I'll be getting money—just not soon enough."

This last he asserted with such conviction as to silence his sister. But Augusta directed a sharp glance at him. He omitted to mention from where this mysterious money would arrive. And that thought left her cold.

"Will you do it for me?" Perry turned on Augusta. His tone was beseeching, and an underlying quaver betrayed his desperation.

"I cannot." She shook her head, though not without regret.

He rose unsteadily.

"What will you do?" She regarded him with no little concern.

He shook his head. "I—I'll think of something. Not your affair, after all. Shouldn't have come to you." He started for the door.

"Perry!" Augusta stopped him. "You cannot go on like this. If—if we cannot tell anyone in authority, perhaps we can think of some way of unmasking your blackmailer and stopping him."

He nodded, but his mind was obviously still occupied with obtaining the necessary money. He let himself out, leaving Augusta and Sophronia to stare after him in concern.

"He said he'd be getting money. Did he say from where?" Sophronia turned to look at her friend.

Augusta shook her head. From where, indeed? He seemed so positive there would be no trouble about it. How could he be so certain?

Oh, how she wished she could have told the whole to Major MacKennoch! He undoubtedly would have known what to do. But she couldn't rid herself of the conviction that he suspected someone she knew—probably a member of her acting troupe—of being involved in the sale of military secrets. Would he think Perry's dual had been over that? That Perry murdered Captain Montclyff because that gentleman discovered Perry's traitorous activity?

But Perry couldn't be involved in anything like that—could he? A chill gripped her. Perry was wild to a fault; he had once said, in an unguarded moment, that they had no idea to what lengths he might be driven. . . . The thought was too horrible. Perry might be foolish, but he would never betray his country!

One part of her mind, though, refused to be quieted. Would Perry see obtaining military secrets in that grim light? Or would it all be a game to him—a profitable game? For Sophronia's sake, she hoped with all her heart it would not be true.

Sophronia settled in a corner with her embroidery and Augusta tried to return her attention to the play. It wasn't easy. She could not ignore Perry's woes, and to make matters worse, the changes on the play this time were terrible.

Over and over, she read the hero's lines, and with each repetition they sounded worse. How could anyone be expected to say such complete rubbish? The lines didn't even make sense! Had someone omitted a few words, or—

She stared at the sheets she held as horror flooded through her. Possibilities whirled in her mind, terrible and frightening. So many changes, so pointless, so often at the last minute. What a perfect situation for someone who wished to take advantage of it for unscrupulous purposes!

Her heart felt as if it beat in her throat. A new method of passing secrets, adopted within the last month. Wasn't that what an officer had said at the Eversleys' dinner last night? And these changes were far more ridiculous than any that had been made while they were still in London. Could someone be altering the lines of the play this time for a different reason— to form a code?

But that would mean that someone she knew—and worked closely with—was involved in the sale of military secrets! No, that thought was nonsense. It had to be! It only occurred to her because of seeing Major MacKennoch, because his assignment was so very much on her mind.

And possibly because it was the truth.

Chapter 14

Augusta leaned back in her chair, feeling ill. Major MacKennoch suspected one of her troupe of being a traitor, she felt almost certain. But had he guessed about the plays? Fury welled within her that someone—someone she knew and trusted!—could have turned her worthwhile cause into a treasonous undertaking!

Who could do such a dreadful thing? Surely not Perry! She laid down the pages and hugged herself, feeling cold, angry, and betrayed.

She had to think reasonably. The new method of passing information had not been in use for long, it was believed. That meant it could be a newcomer to their productions. Captain Vincent Trent had joined them quite recently. And so had Frederick Ashfield.

No, it couldn't be Frederick Ashfield. He was a friend of Halliford's. And they had practically forced him to help out with the plays.

But the duke, with his connections in Whitehall, would be an ideal acquaintance for a traitor. And Ashfield had been around from the first, watching the productions, seeing the chaos that existed. His arrival in Brussels had been perfectly timed. Even if they hadn't convinced him to take part in the performances, he could still have rewritten lines of the script—and no one else would be likely to guess whose hand had been at work.

And what about Captain Trent? Why had he joined their play production? Had he wanted to be in close contact with the suspects in Captain Montclyff's murder—or had he needed a new method to pass the military secrets he stole?

She shook her head in dismay as the truth dawned on her. If she were to list possible culprits, she would have to add every one of the others as well. They were all so accustomed to making changes that no one questioned last-minute alterations. They all expected them, in fact. Any one of her friends could conceivably be guilty.

She shivered. Her plays were perfect for that terrible purpose. Anyone could attend the performance, hear the message, and there need be no direct contact between the principals. If only she had never started them up again here in Brussels! She was responsible—a traitor herself, for providing the means!

She forced back that thought. She couldn't believe it. This was all supposition—and pretty ridiculous at that. She fabricated the whole thing out of her childish romantic fantasies, as Edward MacKennoch had once so unkindly told her. That reminded her of how much she missed his solid presence and she sank deeper into her dejection.

Not even the successful production of their play two days later eased her growing concern. She looked at the players with new—and mistrustful—eyes. Frederick appeared too suave and cynical—the perfect traitor in her eyes. Lord Wentworth was too jovial, even when they stumbled over their lines and drew laughter from their audience at the wrong moments. Perry seemed grim and nervous and Lord Roderick cast uneasy glances at everybody. Even Jack Kettering seemed jumpy and on edge, as if waiting for something to happen.

And Captain Vincent Trent was there, always watching— and more often than not, it was she upon whom his eyes rested with that considering, calculating gleam in their depths.

When the performance ended, Augusta stayed to mingle with the guests. If her fears were correct, if somehow they had just passed information to a French collaborator, *who was it?* But no one betrayed any sign of evil purpose. Finally, when the last of the guests took his leave, Augusta retired to her room, where she succumbed to exhaustion and slept.

She awakened considerably refreshed, and with her agitated nerves much soothed. In the clear morning light that streamed through her bedroom window, her fears of the last few days faded. She now attributed them to jitteriness over the production and the unchecked progress of Napoleon toward Paris.

Why on earth should she suspect that someone in her acting troupe might be involved in treason? Just because Major MacKennoch dominated her thoughts, and just because she had once overheard a questionable conversation, did not mean that her life had suddenly become filled with the villains and murderers that populated the melodramas they performed.

Yes, she had heard some talk of selling military secrets. And yes, Captain Montclyff had been murdered. But that did not mean the events were related or that anything but the merest chance connected her with either.

She needed to relax, to give her thoughts a less stressful direction. She set about this with a vengeance. Brussels' shops held a wealth of fabrics and lace that had been virtually unobtainable except at extravagant prices in England since the beginning of the war.

Accompanied by Sophronia and Mrs. Lansdon, Augusta searched the stores for presents for Helena and Lizzie. She still possessed the awe of such a pastime known only by those raised in abject poverty. The size of the allowance forwarded to her by Halliford astonished her, and so far she had spent very little of it. Now, she proceeded to rectify that.

The result of one of these shopping expeditions was a half apron of blond lace, which she intended to wear over a ball gown of white silk. When she came down the stairs dressed in this creation a week later, she was greeted by an admiring gasp from Sophronia, which filled her with a confidence she had been sadly lacking of late.

They dined alone, for Perry did not put in an appearance. His mother placed little faith in his showing up but Sophronia was not pleased by this desertion on the part of her brother. An invitation from the Duchess of Richmond was not to be treated lightly.

They arrived at the house taken by the duke and duchess off the Rue de la Blanchiserie to find the rooms crowded by notables from all of the allied armies. Augusta heard any number of great names announced, but only a few could she identify in the sea of illustrious faces that surrounded her. She drifted to the chairs placed along one wall, feeling overwhelmed by the important guests.

Sophronia followed. "Where can Perry be? I have not seen him yet," she whispered.

Augusta made a shrewd guess that a dicing box or deck of cards lay behind Perry's absence, but did not express that thought. On the whole, though, it was better than wondering if he might be obtaining—or passing on—military secrets.

Lieutenant Kettering strode up to her, bowed deeply, and solicited her hand for the first dance. He indulged in lighthearted banter whenever the movements of the minuet brought them together, and by the time the music ended, Augusta found herself much restored to her usual good humor.

It evaporated almost at once. As he returned her to Mrs. Lansdon's side, she saw Captain Vincent Trent seated next to that lady, engaging her in conversation. Both watched Sophronia approaching with Lord Roderick.

Augusta's heart sank. There could be no mistaking the predatory gleam in Mrs. Lansdon's eyes as they strayed to the captain. Nor could Augusta blame her. Captain Trent, at first glance, was everything a mother might want for her daughter. But not if he were guilty of murder or treason.

Why must he continue to make a pretense of courting Sophronia? To stay near Perry—and perhaps herself? That was certainly his best course if he hoped to make Perry appear the guilty party.

Sophronia looked toward her mother and saw Captain Trent. A delicate flush touched her cheeks and a shy smile lit her eyes. Lord Roderick gave him a short nod of acknowledgment, cast a quick, agitated glance about, and abruptly took his leave. Almost, Augusta thought darkly, one might suspect him of not wanting to remain in Captain Trent's company. On the whole, she didn't blame him.

The captain stood at once. "Would you care for some refreshment, Miss Lansdon? Kettering, will you join me?" The two officers went in search of punch.

Sophronia let out a deep sigh. "He—he truly is the gentleman, is he not?" Her mother beamed at her, but Sophronia's eyes remained on Augusta's worried face, seeking approval from her friend.

"Yes," Augusta agreed, and wished she could put more emphasis into the word. But she doubted his motives.

Sophronia sighed and sank down into a chair. "I know I am

quite—quite commonplace in appearance and far too retiring in disposition. But surely *some* gentleman must not mind those drawbacks?"

Augusta squeezed her hand. "A gentleman must be blind indeed not to be aware of your sweet disposition."

Sophronia threw her a grateful smile, then her gaze sought out the refreshment table where the two men waited their turn. Sophronia, it appeared, had begun to cherish hopes about Vincent Trent that overshadowed her uneasiness of his interest in Perry. Augusta wished she knew what to say to her friend. She mustn't let on about her own unsubstantiated suspicions of his guilt!

"Here is Perry at last!" Sophronia sprang to her feet, eager to welcome her brother.

He strode quickly up to them, paying no heed whatsoever to the crowd that filled the ballroom. His one purpose, it appeared, was to reach his mother and sister.

"Where have you been, you disobliging boy?" his fond mamma demanded.

"Waiting for someone." Perry dutifully kissed her cheek. "Augusta, are you free for the next dance?"

"It's taken, I'm afraid."

He frowned. "Then take a stroll with me." Without waiting for her consent, he grabbed her hand and thrust it unceremoniously through the crook of his arm.

Augusta stifled her irritation and looked him over. "Has something happened, Perry?"

"What?" He started, then shook his head. "No, what makes you ask?"

She glanced around to make sure no one could hear them. "I haven't had a chance to speak to you alone. Did you pay your—friend?"

He snorted at this description of his blackmailer. "Lord, yes. What choice did I have?"

"I wish there was something we could do! Isn't there anyone who could help?"

"No one I'd dare tell!" He shook his head. "Lord, I—I'd be ruined."

"There must be someone."

He fixed her with a stern eye. "Now, don't you go getting any ideas, Augusta. Promise me you won't say a word

178

to anybody."

"But Perry—"

"Promise me!"

She drew a ragged breath, then nodded.

He gave a shaky laugh. "I—I'll be all right."

She regarded him uncertainly. "Have you redeemed Lord Roderick's pistols?"

He shook his head. "He won't report them missing. Don't think he even knows I borrowed 'em." He gestured to where Roddy, quite untroubled, led a dainty little brunette into a set that was forming. Roddy saw them and waved merrily as if he hadn't a care in the world.

"What of the money you were so certain you'd get?"

He tried a nonchalant smile, but it slipped awry. "It didn't work out. I'll get it tonight, though."

It was too much for Augusta. "From where? Please, Perry, tell me the truth."

He cast a quick glance about, much as she had done a minute before, as if he was afraid someone might be listening. "Just keep that—that dashed Captain Trent away from me. And from Sophie also. Damme if I know why he sticks so close to her. Can't stand the fellow forever breathing down my neck."

The music started and he took her hand abruptly and joined the nearest set, ignoring the prior claims of her partner. Augusta went with him, though she knew a deep sense of foreboding. Perry was involved in something, but it couldn't be the sale of military secrets! The potential scandal of such a situation made her shudder. Inevitably, she would be drawn into it.

The evening did not improve. Shortly after she escaped Perry, she spotted him with Sophronia and saw the liveliness fade from the girl's manner, leaving her drooping and dejected. Captain Trent stood not far away, watching with such a satisfied gleam in his eyes that Augusta feared the young couple played into his dangerous hands. And then Jack Kettering claimed her for a waltz with the sole intention of whispering unwanted endearments into her captive ears.

Long before it was time to go down to supper, Augusta suffered from an extreme headache. Escaping her current partner, she returned to where Mrs. Lansdon sat at the side of the room and asked if they might return home. That lady, after

179

noting depressingly that neither Captain Trent nor any other potential suitor hovered over her daughter, agreed. There could be little point in remaining.

While they awaited the arrival of the carriage in the entry hall, Sophronia's restless fingers shredded her fine lawn handkerchief. The look she directed at Augusta as they entered the vehicle spoke volumes; but the confined space of the interior provided no opportunity for private speech. As soon as they retired to their rooms, Augusta guessed shrewdly, she would receive a visit from an overburdened soul. She tried to smile reassuringly, but knew it to be a feeble attempt.

They pulled up before the house and a footman hurried out to let down the steps and assist his mistress and the two young ladies from the vehicle. Lights burned brightly in the front drawing room windows, providing a homey welcome. Wishing she could postpone the impending interview with Sophronia until at least the morning, when she might be less exhausted, Augusta followed Mrs. Lansdon into the front hall. One glance at the butler's expression warned her, though, that the evening was not yet over.

He bowed slightly and took Mrs. Lansdon's wrap. "There are visitors, madam."

Mrs. Lansdon looked puzzled and Sophronia's eyes opened wide in alarm. "Who—?" The girl threw a frightened glance at Augusta.

"A Major MacKennoch, madam."

Augusta's heart soared. He was here! She took an impulsive step forward, only to stop short. He *was* here—and openly, this time. Did that mean there was no longer any need for secrecy with his assignment? Did he, in fact, come to confirm her worst fears, perhaps arrest one of her friends?

The door to the saloon opened and he stepped out into the hall, a slight smile just touching his firm lips. It didn't seem possible for any gentleman to appear so solid, so distinguished, so perfectly assured. She wanted to cry in relief, to throw herself into his strong arms, to find sanctuary from her worries in his calm good sense.

And she couldn't do any of that—and not just because he would be revolted by such an unwarranted display of emotion. Until she knew what had brought him, what he had learned—and what he suspected—she didn't dare reveal her own concerns. He would laugh at her if she were wrong. And if she were right . . . she didn't want to contemplate the possibility.

His eyes rested on her and his smile faded. The warm light disappeared from his clear blue eyes to be replaced by questioning concern. A sensation of pure longing swept through Augusta, which she stifled with difficulty. She knew herself floundering, but he turned from her almost at once, allowing her to recover her composure.

He bowed to Mrs. Lansdon and Sophronia, and his bad leg did not mar the elegance of his movement.

"I must apologize for the lateness of my visit, but I have a charge to hand over into your keeping."

A wave of fear swept over Augusta. What could he mean? But a reassuring twinkle accompanied his words. Her heart reacted in an extremely erratic manner.

He moved back into the room and Mrs. Lansdon followed, with Augusta and Sophronia close behind. Near the fire, slumped in a large, wing-back chair and with her feet propped on a table, slept Lizzie. Augusta stared at her beloved sister, then turned to the major, an impulsive thank-you on her lips.

He smiled. "Ye do not think for a moment she would remain behind once she knew I was bound for Brussels, do ye?"

She clasped his hand and his warm fingers returned the pressure. Gratitude faded under the influence of a stronger, more demanding emotion. Their gazes met and held, and Augusta forgot to breathe. "I—"

Her words were cut off by the entrance of the housekeeper, a motherly British woman who smiled indulgently on the sleeping Lizzie. "Excuse me, ma'am." She addressed herself to Mrs. Lansdon. "I have taken the liberty of having a room prepared for Miss."

"Thank you." Mrs. Lansdon beamed on Augusta. "How delightful that your sister could come. We shall be only too happy to have her with us."

Augusta released the major's hand abruptly. She succumbed to an unconscious spell of his weaving, and that she could not allow. Who knew what she might be betrayed into telling him when under the influence of his smile. Perry's secrets weighed heavily upon her. She had promised her silence—and she would keep her word. She crossed to Lizzie and shook her sister's shoulder, rousing her.

181

Lizzie yawned, stretched, and focused her bleary eyes. "Hi, Gussie," she mumbled. "Lord, what late hours you keep."

A tremulous laugh escaped Augusta. "To bed with you." She assisted Lizzie to her feet, then looked back at Edward MacKennoch. "I'll only be a few minutes, Major." She led her sleepy sister from the room.

As soon as the housekeeper left them alone in the newly prepared Blue Room, Augusta hugged her sister with unbounded enthusiasm. "Whatever has brought you to Brussels?"

"You." Lizzie yawned again. Her maid left off the unpacking to come to her assistance, but Augusta gestured her back to it and herself began to unfasten her sister's gown.

"Was Helena worried about me?"

Lizzie helped lift the muslin folds over her head. "Frantic. Edward is to arrange for our immediate return to England."

Augusta blinked at her sister's casual reference to the major, but let it pass. "There is nothing to fear, or so everyone tells us. And you may be sure, with so many troops present, we're in the safest possible place."

Lizzie nodded sleepily. "That's what *I* thought, but you know Nell. Nothing would do for her but to send someone after you. And who was I to resist a chance to see Brussels?" An impish grin accompanied the last.

"I cannot believe she let you come."

"Oh, I'm to persuade you to return home. Which I will, of course—in a few weeks."

Augusta smiled. "Get into bed. You can tell me all about everyone in the morning."

The abigail came forward with a night dress. Lizzie barely shed her chemise and donned the proffered garment before tumbling into bed and sleep.

Augusta waited only to drop a light kiss on her sister's forehead, then made her way downstairs. The prospect of seeing Edward MacKennoch—of being able to talk to him—set her heart skipping a beat. But she would have to keep a guard on her tongue, lest she blurt out her fears for Perry.

To her mingled relief and disappointment, he was not in the saloon below. The major had already left, the butler told her, then returned to his locking up. Resolutely, Augusta turned from the bolted front door and made her way back upstairs.

Hadn't he realized how much she longed for just a few minutes of his company? Apparently, he did not feel the same need for hers.

But when she went down to breakfast the following morning, she was greeted by the welcome tidings that Major MacKennoch had called and awaited her in the morning room. Ordering her nerves not to overreact, Augusta went to him at once.

He leaned negligently against the mantel, staring down into the fire that crackled merrily in the hearth. Augusta hesitated on the threshold, her gaze resting on his solid, muscled figure. He looked up and her heart stopped, then beat rapidly. The fiery redness of the scar across his cheek was less noticeable, that peculiar quirking of his lip less pronounced. How she had missed him!

He came toward her, his limp almost nonexistent. "Forgive me for calling so early. I have come to see how Lizzie goes on."

Lizzie? Her sister must certainly have established excellent relations with the very proper major for him to refer to her in that casual manner. Knowing Lizzie, that didn't surprise her. But she did experience a pang of jealousy; it was an intimacy she could not share. "She is asleep still. Nothing short of an earth tremor is likely to awaken her."

The major smiled at that. "I have also come to convey the message entrusted to me."

"Yes. Lizzie said something about it last night." She regarded him uncertainly. She suspected he came for another reason as well, but she would let him bring up that subject.

"Her Grace is very anxious for you to return home as soon as it may be arranged."

"Pray, do not pressure me to leave Brussels just now." She saw his expression alter, and wished she had not phrased it just like that.

"Why?"

"I don't want to abandon my plays." That was the truth, at least, and it didn't involve Perry or his blackmailer. "Our last production earned more for our cause than did any of the ones in London."

He made no comment, but his thoughtful gaze rested on her.

Should she tell him of her unfounded suspicions, that a traitor might lurk in the midst of her troupe, utilizing her plays

183

for his own dastardly purpose? Here, in Major MacKennoch's calm presence, the idea seemed foolish, as if she were afraid of shadows. It sounded too much like one of the plots for the melodramas they performed.

"We—we are here at the scene of such stirring events also," she finished lamely. "I wish very much to remain."

"I don't suppose I can count on Lizzie to fulfill her office of convincer." A wry note crept into his voice.

"Yes, you can. She promised she would try—in a few weeks."

A deep, appreciative chuckle escaped him. "I *thought* she was set upon some lark. She wouldn't confess to me."

Augusta looked down at the flames that licked their way along the logs. "Have—how is your investigation progressing?" She glanced up at him and found him studying her face, his expression serious.

"I have a few ideas. And do ye?"

She felt color tinge her cheeks. "Oh, yes. I certainly have those. But they seem so absurd."

He nodded. "Perhaps I will ask ye again in a week. It would be interesting to see if we suspect the same things." Amusement suddenly glinted in eyes that had been clouded a moment before. "Ye must excuse me now. My current cover is as a very junior member of the Diplomatic Service and I must report to Lord Wentworth within the half hour."

Lord Wentworth? Did the major suspect him of involvement with the sale of military secrets? She swallowed hard. "He—he will be so pleased you have sided with the diplomats. And do not be surprised if he tries to convince you to join in my plays."

"Good God! I must thank you for the warning."

"You could always become defiant and put back on your uniform," she suggested, forcing a teasing light into her eyes.

He shook his head. "Nay, lass. I've sold out. I will not wear a kilt."

He took his leave of her. She saw him to the door, then made her thoughtful way to the breakfast parlor. Edward MacKennoch created utter chaos within her, but it was such a pleasant, fluttery sensation, she could not be sorry. She only wished she could tell him everything.

Sophronia was in the room before her, nibbling on a piece of

184

toast. A cup of untouched tea sat on the table. She looked up, but the smile she managed was rather wan. "Mamma is no end pleased to have Lizzie to stay with us."

"That is very kind of her. He—Major MacKennoch—brought her over for the sole purpose of accompanying me back to England."

"Oh, Augusta, you're not going to—" Sophronia dropped the finger of toast into her full cup, but ignored it in the face of this crisis.

"No." Augusta reached over and pulled out the soggy bread. "You don't really think Lizzie would agree to go straight home without seeing Brussels, do you? We are both staying."

"I am so glad." Sophronia looked relieved, but still not happy.

Augusta poured a cup of tea for herself and sat down beside her friend. They hadn't had their talk last night, after all. "What's worrying you?"

Tears formed in Sophronia's eyes. "It's Perry. He is having the most dreadful time getting the money to pay his blackmailer. And now he has received another demand."

Augusta set down her cup in its saucer with a sharp clink, sloshing out some of the scalding liquid. "He didn't tell me that. What is he to do now?"

"He—he'll be all right, for a bit."

Augusta regarded her friend in suspicion. "Why?"

Sophronia looked down, unable to meet that stern expression. "I—I gave him my pearls to sell."

"Oh, Sophie!" Augusta stared at her, momentarily nonplussed.

"Well, what else could I do?" Defiant, she glared at Augusta.

"I don't know." Augusta sighed. "At least now I know where he planned to get the money. We've got to do something about this."

"Do you think we could? Just because Perry took part in that terrible duel does not mean he is the murderer!"

"We *must* clear him," Augusta asserted. And then, perhaps, she could turn the whole matter over to Major MacKennoch.

Suddenly, achingly, she wished she had not promised Perry she would be silent. But she couldn't have told the major about the duel anyway, not until they had some proof that Perry

185

not committed murder. At the moment, their best course appeared to be discovering—and putting out of commission—the blackmailer.

Their first chance to talk to Perry was that afternoon, but he came in company with Jack Kettering. A rehearsal, Augusta realized in dismay. She had forgotten they were to begin work on their new play that day.

The others, except for Roddy, arrived hard on the heels of the first two. Despite their missing member, they went to work reading it through. Augusta watched each of them, trying to gauge their reactions. Did one of them try to locate places in which to insert stolen military information for transmission to Napoleon?

"This opening scene is ridiculous!" Captain Trent protested after glancing over the first few pages.

"Of course it is. But that's the hallmark of our productions." Perry leafed through to the next scene, then frowned himself. "But I must say, I don't like the setting. Can we not alter it from London to Brussels, under the circumstances?"

"No, really!" Jack Kettering looked up, appalled. "There's a whole section here taking place in a forest, of all places. How on earth do you expect me to arrange the scenery for that?"

"What does it matter?" Augusta looked from one to the other, trying to hide her unpleasant suspicions. "No one expects a polished performance. The officers who come only want to laugh and enjoy themselves."

"We have our reputations to consider," Lord Wentworth asserted with mock hauteur. A smile lurked in his eyes.

"We must make the production as good as we can," Sophronia asserted.

"Must we?" Frederick Ashfield, who stood reading over Sophronia's and Lizzie's shoulders, looked up. "We are making it sound as if it is all that matters. It is nothing but a short piece, all in good fun."

Augusta turned away. Why did she have to suspect everybody? Would Sophie betray her country to protect her brother? Could Captain Trent be the blackmailer? Or Jack Kettering—or Lord Wentworth—or even the absent Roddy? And she couldn't forget Frederick Ashfield, though treason seemed more in his line than blackmail, which in her mind seemed such a cowardly crime.

"You are quite right." Wentworth laughed. "We are making a great deal over nothing. We haven't even settled yet who is to take which role."

They began to divide up the parts, which involved much lively and good-natured argument. They were still at it twenty minutes later, with Ashfield and Kettering amicably squabbling over who should take the role of hero, when they were disturbed.

Lord Roderick stormed in, his eyes blazing. He cast a quick glance about the room and settled on Perry. "Have you seen them?"

Perry, who sat staring blindly into the fire, started and looked up. "What?"

"My pistols! They're missing. If I don't get them back—" Roddy broke off, but the desperation in his voice finished his sentence for him.

Perry and Roddy stared at one another. The color drained from Perry's face.

"What have you done with them?" Roddy demanded, on the verge of panic.

"Me? What makes you think *I* have them?" Perry sounded as indignant as if he hadn't actually taken them. "Of all the ramshackle things to be accusing your friends of! As if I'd do any such thing!"

Augusta sat back in her chair, a slight frown creasing her brow. Why was Roddy so desperate? His concern seemed out of all proportion. The unique pistols must be valuable, of course, but not so much as to warrant this. Nor could it be the bloodstained case; after so long a time, there could be nothing to link it to Montclyff's murder.

"Are they heirlooms?" she asked.

Roddy spun about to look at her, his expression haunted. "No! What makes you ask that? Of course they're not. Just fond of them, that's all. I—I'd best keep looking for them." With that, he strode out of the room. A door closing in the distance announced his abrupt exit from the house.

"What a pack of nonsense," Lizzie said, disgusted.

Ashfield laughed, but Vincent Trent stared at the closed door, his expression thoughtful. Slowly, his eyes strayed about the gathered players, resting first on Perry, then on Sophronia, and finally on Augusta. He nodded to himself.

Augusta shivered and looked away from him. What, exactly, was Vincent Trent's interest in the pistols? And what made them so important to Roddy? The only time she had ever seen Roddy look so forlorn before was at a party at Halliford House, when his brother, the reclusive duke of Taversham, had caught him a trifle top-heavy. Augusta still remembered the rare trimming the tyrannical duke had given his stripling brother, with no regard for who else had been listening.

The next few days brought no answers to her questions concerning the dueling pistols. Rehearsals took up a great deal of their time, for she was anxious to present their play. Between studying the constant minor changes in the script and taking her part in the almost giddy round of entertainments to be found in Brussels, Augusta had barely a moment to herself.

Yet she did not see Major MacKennoch, and that one fact kept a damper on her spirits. What did he learn? She should be glad, though, he did not haunt their rehearsals. Surely, that must mean her suspicions concerning the plays were ungrounded after all!

But as she sat reading a particularly pointless change in her lines one morning, the butler entered to announce the arrival of Major Edward MacKennoch. Augusta looked up, her heart giving an excited double beat.

He strode into the room, and the steadiness of the gaze he turned on her caused her color to deepen. She extended her hand tentatively and the firmness of his clasp sent a shiver through her. She moved away at once, nervous. "We have seen nothing of you since your arrival."

"I have been somewhat busy."

Not daring to meet the eyes she knew would miss nothing, she looked down. Her gaze fell on the script she had dropped on his entrance. "You find me hard at work on the next play. Will you come to see it?"

"I wouldn't miss it."

The grave note in his voice increased her uneasiness. Deep lines formed in his brow, she noted, as if from worry. "What makes you sound so serious?"

"Do I?" He smiled, and the impression of great cares vanished. He strolled over to the mantel, stared down into the fire for a moment, then turned back to her, his old impenetrable mask of calm once more in place.

Augusta tensed. She returned to her seat on the sofa.

"Ye may not welcome me after all," he said. "I've come to ask ye a few questions. Do ye mind?"

"Of course not." She eyed him uncertainly. "What about?"

"A topic of which ye are not too fond, I'm afraid. Captain Montclyff."

Augusta stiffened. "Why?"

He seated himself in the chair facing her. "Certain evidence turned up among Captain Montclyff's papers that indicate he may have been involved in stealing various documents. Just in the daily routine of his service, he had access to confidential material."

"Then you believe his death is connected with that?" She stared at him, aghast.

"I seem to remember ye suggesting the possibility yourself." A smile just touched his voice.

"Yes, but I—I wasn't serious! Good heavens, the next thing you'll be telling me is that—" She broke off, horrified by what she had been about to say. The rest of her joking comment, as she remembered it, was that Captain Montclyff probably had been killed by the ruby-mounted pistols.

"Just so." He looked down at his hands, then regarded her through dispassionate eyes that betrayed nothing. "Unless I am very much mistaken, ye have something to tell me."

Chapter 15

How much did Major MacKennoch know? Augusta forced down her panic and schooled her expression into a semblance of innocence. "What is there that I could possibly tell you?"

"It doesn't have to be this way." The major took a step toward her, then stopped. "Come, ye used to trust me. What makes everything different now?"

She closed the uncertainty away in her heart. "I was never a suspect in the sale of military secrets before—was I? Only for knowing something of Captain Montclyff's murder."

The briefest trace of emotion flickered across his face, as if he, too, recognized and accepted a barrier between them. When he spoke, his voice was cool, expressionless, purely official. "And do ye?"

Pain wrenched within her, but she hid it. "Has Captain Trent convinced you that I pulled the trigger?"

He shook his head. "When did Captain Montclyff first join your performances . . . Miss Carstairs?"

He hesitated before speaking her name, as if he felt the added formality necessary. Or had he been tempted to use her Christian name, as she longed to use his? She thrust the thought from her mind. It didn't matter. As long as she remained under suspicion of anything, there could be no closeness between them.

"He was one of the last to join my troupe. I am not certain, but I believe him to have been an acquaintance of Lord Roderick's." Suddenly, she decided to push it further, to see if she could discover what he suspected. "Why do you ask? Surely you don't believe we are all involved in selling military secrets, do you? Or do you think the plays are merely a—a pretense to disguise our real objective?"

He permitted himself to smile, though it did not reach his eyes. "Nay, Miss Carstairs."

Hope welled in her. Did that mean her own suspicions about the plays were false? If only she could be certain!

Major MacKennoch returned to the mantel, where he stood staring down into the fire. When he spoke again, his tone sounded less like the inquisitor he had become and more like the confidante she remembered. "That was fresh blood I found in the case containing Lieutenant Lord Roderick Ingersoll's dueling pistols, though someone had tried to wash it away." He looked across at her. "And ye must admit, Lieutenant Lansdon and Lord Roderick have been behaving in a somewhat unusual manner ever since Captain Montclyff's murder."

Augusta's restless fingers formed creases in her muslin skirts. "It—it unsettled us all."

He regarded her with a certain measure of speculation. "Is there not something ye would care to tell me?"

"No!" She steadied herself. "No," she repeated more calmly. "What could there be?"

A frown—of disappointment?—just touched his features. He returned to stand in front of her, stopping only a foot away. "Ye were used to trust me," he repeated.

She could not meet his gaze. "Can you honestly say you would be here, talking with me, if I were *not* a suspect in your investigation?" He remained silent, and she looked up, challenging him to answer. "You can't deny that I am, can you?"

"There are certain official questions as to the extent of your involvement," he admitted.

She didn't know whether to feel triumphant at drawing that admission from him, or furious at his words. She compromised by ending the interview. She came to her feet, only to find herself all too near her adversary. She stared into the shoulder of his coat. He had a very broad shoulder, she noted. No Buckram wadding had been sewn in to give him added inches.

He did not move back to allow her room, and his nearness sent a shiver of longing through her. If she moved barely inches closer, she could lay her head against that inviting shoulder. Her forehead would tuck neatly under his chin, and

191

it would be so very comforting if his strong arm wrapped around her, holding her tightly against him, proving he did not think she was a traitor or an accessory to murder.

She drew a shaky breath. "Ex-excuse me, Major? I—I am somewhat busy this morning." She kept her gaze from his face.

He stepped back, sketched a quick bow, and took his leave. The door closed firmly behind him, and Augusta, her knees too weak to support her, sank back onto the sofa.

He had almost guessed the truth about the pistols—only he would not be likely to believe that Perry's role in the dreadful affair had been foolish rather than murderous. Until they knew who Perry's blackmailer was, and had discovered some clue as to the identity of the real murderer, she dared not confess the truth to Major MacKennoch, no matter how much she wanted to.

The next few weeks loomed ahead of her, bleak and empty without the prospect of the major's friendship.

Somehow, the days passed. She scheduled a date for the next performance, sent out announcements, and everywhere they went, someone asked about the play. Augusta busied herself with rehearsals, encouraged everyone with whom she was acquainted to make generous donations in exchange for tickets, and planned the refreshments for afterward. By throwing herself wholeheartedly into these pursuits, she found some measure of relief from her unhappy thoughts.

The performance seemed to be an event anticipated with great eagerness, and Augusta wished she could feel the same. Polite Society delighted in her productions and contributed handsomely to her fund. But a shadow now hung over them, as far as Augusta was concerned.

Theirs was not the only entertainment offered. Every day seemed crammed with visits, picnics in the beechwood forest south of town, and military revues in nearby villages. Each evening offered balls, card parties, theater visits, and concerts. It was as if the entire population of Brussels sought to escape its fears in an almost hysterical round of activity; for with each passing day, Napoleon marched closer to Paris.

The French king removed with his court to Ghent, and that cowardly retreat sent a ripple of alarm through the city. Entertainments continued as ever, but talk veered constantly to Wellington's continued presence at the Congress in Vienna.

The more nervous of the ladies expressed the wish that he would join the troops gathered about Brussels. Rumors abounded, but despite the alarm, no increase in military activity occurred.

Augusta sought relief from the unsettled atmosphere in studying her lines, and discovered they had been rewritten once more. She searched the alterations for some hidden message, but could discover nothing that made sense. She couldn't even determine whose hand had been at work this time.

Too tired to solve the problem, Augusta threw the script aside and decided to go shopping. She had not yet taken Lizzie to a certain little establishment that dealt in perfumes, soaps, and scented lotions and sachets. Knowing Lizzie, of course, she would rather visit a saddlery, but Augusta felt like a brisk walk through the park. Perhaps they could feed the swans on the pond by the pavilion on their way back. That should provide her with a break from her mysteries.

Lizzie, with only a little coaxing, agreed to accompany her. Sophronia, who had picked up Augusta's abandoned copy of the play, declined the invitation. The two sisters therefore set out for the shop with the intention of purchasing a new scent for Helena.

Lizzie could not long be fascinated by a store that smelled so shockingly, as she put it. Leaving Augusta to complete her purchase, she wandered along the street, gazing into windows. Augusta found her three doors down, studying the French and Dutch titles of books.

"Are you ready?"

Lizzie checked her reticule. "I have brought three rolls. Do you think that will be enough for the swans?"

"I am sure it will be." Augusta started forward. "Do you not even care what I found for Helena and Chloe?"

"Don't remind me of Chloe!" Lizzie declared.

Augusta stared at her, startled. "But—you *like* Chloe."

"Of coures I do. But really, listening to those two talking about *babies!*" She said the word with loathing. "Honestly, it was enough to drive anyone from the Castle. She's expecting another one, you know."

"No, is she?" Augusta laughed. "Do you not remember Richard being convinced he would never have children just

193

because he lost his leg? And now a second! Oh, how happy they must be."

Lizzie shook her head. "What is there to get so excited over? All babies do is cry and want to be fed."

"Just think how much fun it will be to teach them to ride and pick berries when they are older," Augusta advised.

Lizzie considered a moment, then brightened. Apparently, she would enjoy being an aunt—in a few years.

They passed a jeweler's, and Augusta paused to look inside. Her sacrificed sapphire earrings still rankled. If the shop had been empty, she would have gone inside, for she couldn't quite see into the glass display cases set about the small room.

A scarlet-coated officer, who leaned over one of the cases, straightened up. Augusta caught a glimpse of a gleaming sapphire set in heavy gold that flashed on his hand. He held it aloft so that the stone caught the sunlight. Repressing a wistful sigh, Augusta started to walk on.

"I'll take it," she heard the officer say clearly. At the sound of that familiar voice, she stopped dead. Perry Lansdon? Without a second's thought, she entered the shop.

He swung around at the sound of approach, and she would have found the expression of guilt on his face hilarious if she hadn't been so bewildered. "Perry?" she asked, not quite believing that her impoverished friend was in the process of purchasing an extremely expensive ring.

"Oh, hello, Augusta." He kept his tone nonchalant. After the first shock of being caught, he seemed to recover remarkably well. He handed over a wad of bills to the jeweler, then fitted the ring onto his hand. "Rather pretty, isn't it?"

Augusta glanced at Lizzie, who was inspecting snuffboxes. Satisfied that her sister would be occupied for a moment, she grabbed Perry's arm and drew him aside. "Perry, where did you get the money? Have you been lying to us about being blackmailed?"

He glared at her, honestly injured. "Take the ready from you under false pretenses? No, really, Augusta! That's insulting!"

"Then where did you get so much money? Sophie told me she had to give you her pearls."

"Now, don't you get into the fidgets. Just had a very lucrative winning streak, thanks to a certain pair of pistols. They seem to have gotten their luck back. I'm beforehand with

194

the world for a change, and I must say, it's a nice feeling. I've got Sophie's pearls in my pocket, and I'm on my way to give 'em back to her right now. And as for you—" He broke off and drew the handful of bills back out of his pocket. "Four hundred and twenty pounds, wasn't it?" He handed her the money.

She stared at it, blankly, then tucked it away in her reticule before anyone could see it. "Perry, are you sure—?"

"I'll be all right for a bit. And I'm working up a little plan for—for someone—next time I get one of his notes." He patted her arm clumsily and moved past her toward the door. He stopped short with an audible intake of breath. "Oh, my God—"

Augusta spun around. Just outside, watching them with extreme interest, stood Captain Vincent Trent. At his side stood Major MacKennoch.

Blood rushed to Augusta's cheeks, then receded. leaving her shivering. "Lizzie, let us go," she shot over her shoulder. She swept out of the shop with her sister at her heels.

As they passed the major, Lizzie stopped to greet him. Augusta bit her lip, then managed a bright, if false, smile. "Good morning, Major."

He nodded. "Miss Carstairs." His expression held no accusation, merely inviting confidences and explanations.

Augusta didn't succumb to the temptation. What had just transpired between Perry and herself was none of his business—she hoped! "You must excuse us. We have an urgent appointment with some swans in the park." Taking Lizzie firmly by the arm, she led her protesting sister off.

Much to her mingled relief and regret, the next two days passed without Edward MacKennoch seeking her out to demand an explanation of the money Perry had given her. Had he assumed the worst, that he had paid her for passing information? But if that were the case, why had the major or Captain Trent not appeared to arrest her? By the morning of the third day, she began to breath more easily, though part of her wanted to summon the major and make a full confession.

On the afternoon of the fourth day, as she strolled through the park with Lizzie and Sophronia, she caught a glimpse of the major talking to two men she didn't recognize. But she did notice their blue frock coats and sashes, indicating their positions as Wellington's aides-de-camp. Sudden uneasiness made her long to run and hide. The only shelter of which she could think, though, was the major's arms, and that haven was not for her.

"Does that mean Wellington will be coming soon?" Sophronia also noticed the significance of Edward MacKennoch's companions. "Has the major told you anything?"

Augusta shook her head. "I—I haven't seen him for days. I have no idea what is happening. Perhaps someone will know something at the Lathrops' dinner party tonight."

Nothing new was to be learned there, though. Napoleon was in Paris, that much was agreed upon. Some thought he had ordered his army toward Belgium. Others claimed he remained where he was, solidifying his power. Augusta found the talk distressing.

Two days later, however, all thoughts of Napoleon were banished from her mind by a more pressing—and far more immediate—disaster. Their play would be given that night.

The Lansdon household bustled thoughout the day with the final preparations for the performance—finding chairs, refreshments, setting the stage, and generally creating such an air of chaos that Mrs. Lansdon retired to her bedchamber with a pastille and burnt feathers and requested, in tragic accents, that her daughter and Augusta handle the whole.

Augusta, who had hoped to go over the script with the nervous Sophronia one more time, set it regretfully aside and turned her attention to convincing the footman to visit every one of their acquaintances in the hopes of borrowing more chairs, and stopping the underhouse-maid from having hysterics.

Somehow, by seven o'clock when the troupe gathered, everything was in readiness. Lord Wentworth demanded that they go through one scene that gave them problems. Augusta fetched their copy of the script and gave it to Sophronia, then stood up with Perry and Frederick Ashfield to go through it.

After a few minutes, Lord Wentworth stopped her. "That should have been 'an hour past dawn,' not 'an hour before.'"

"Are you certain?" Augusta closed her eyes in an effort of memory. "I thought I had learned that line."

"You had." Sophronia looked up from the pages. "That's the way it reads here."

Lord Wentworth frowned. "Has someone been reworking

my copy again?" Only denials met his accusing gaze. He sighed. "An old version, then."

"It makes more sense the way you have it now. I think you should change it, Miss Carstairs." Trent caught and held her gaze.

He did, did he? Was this change part of a secret code? Excitement and fear jostled within her. But would Trent reveal his hand like this, so openly? He would know she suspected him, of course—or his dreadful use of her plays. She ought to tell Edward. . . .

An idea occurred to her. She'd test her suspicion, first. She'd go along with the change now, but make a "mistake" during the performance and read the old line instead. That way, no information would be passed to the enemy and she could see for herself, from Trent's reaction, whether or not he was guilty. *Then,* when she had something tangible, she would tell Major MacKennoch.

A thrill of nerves danced along her skin. Forcing herself not to betray it, she managed a convincing shrug of indifference. "As you wish. Lord Wentworth?"

He nodded. "Read it the way I have it here. Can you remember that? 'Past dawn,' not 'before.'"

Augusta nodded, tried it again, and the scene resumed. At last they separated to put on their costumes. Augusta hurried back down so she could obtain one last look at the lines before the performance began.

Jack Kettering was there ahead of her, she noted in dismay, also checking his lines. He looked up from the copy as she entered, then laid it down, a gleam lighting his eyes.

"Are you ready?" She moved past him quickly to take the script, but he caught her wrist and drew her toward him. "Please, Lieutenant. I need to go over it again."

"Do you know?"—he smiled at her—"I could almost wish you had not decided to give any more plays."

"If it weren't for our cause, I would, too." She kept her voice light. "I vow, I dread tonight."

"I only dread the crowds that surround you and make it impossible to see you alone."

She cast a frantic glance at the mantel clock; she couldn't expect any of the others to come down for at least a quarter of an hour. Her heart sank. "I am glad to be so busy."

"Enough of this." He raised her fingers to his lips. "I cannot go on this way any longer, seeing you only when we are involved in one of these ridiculous plays. Augusta, my love, marry me at once!"

She tried to pull back, but he possessed himself of her other hand as well. "No, Lieutenant Kettering, please!" With difficulty, she kept him from drawing her into his arms. "This is highly improper, and so you know."

He released her abruptly and ran an agitated hand through his carefully arranged black locks. "I ought to approach Halliford first. But my fortune is not yet secured. The duke would think me unworthy of you. I know I am—now—but I swear to you I will prove myself."

She stepped back, torn by the anguish in his voice, yet unable to return his regard. "Please, Jack—"

He possessed himself of her hand once more. "Forgive me, Augusta. It was my love for you, and my knowledge that I am not advancing rapidly enough to impress His Grace, that drove me to suggest so shocking an idea."

"It wouldn't do," she said with feeling.

"No," he agreed, though without much conviction.

She pulled free and looked frantically about. "Where—oh, there is the play. I need to go over that scene."

He walked away from her and seated himself by the fire in their small, backstage area. Augusta buried herself in the script. Normally, the sheer melodrama of his words would have had her giggling. But not in this case; he had spoken in all sincerity.

She looked surreptitiously across at him, wondering what went on in his mind. He sat hunched over, hands clasped between his knees, gazing into the flames. Her heart went out to him—but not her love. His attachment to her was very real, she could not doubt it, but she could not face the prospect of becoming his wife. Resolutely, she turned to the one problem with which she could deal and concentrated on her lines.

This play was not as good as the last one, Major MacKennoch reflected. He sat at the back of the audience, arms folded, with Lizzie and Mrs. Lansdon at his side. Augusta carried off her role with surprising grace, though. Even

Frederick Ashfield gave a creditable performance—which was more than he could say for any of the others. Captain Vincent Trent, in particular, should have been glad he had pursued the military rather than the stage as his career. His performance was laughable—or would be, if the major were in the least mood for laughing.

Lizzie, beside him, knew no such problems. From the moment the curtain was dragged back, which had almost brought down the scenery, she had been giggling and murmuring snide comments to him. At least she enjoyed herself. And now, at last, the ordeal neared its end.

Surprisingly, Augusta stumbled over her lines. The major frowned; that was the first time he could remember her making a mistake. Lord Wentworth, barely visible holding the script behind the curtain, prompted her. She went on.

Major MacKennoch's brow lowered. He remembered that line. There had been some nonsense about changing it at the one rehearsal he attended. It had been better the previous way, the way Augusta had just spoken it. Why had it been changed? It only confused everyone.

His eyes narrowed and he stared very hard at the players. It was ridiculous to change that line—unless there was a damn good reason for doing it. Unconsciously, his shoulders straightened and he leaned forward, his mind racing. The idea that occurred to him was preposterous, there was not—at the moment—one single shred of evidence to support such a conclusion. Yet he was as certain of it as he had ever been of anything.

These plays, which were presented at such frequent intervals, were the device for passing the military secrets to the enemy.

The details eluded him, but he would discover them if it was the last thing he did. He leaned back, watching each of the players as they gathered on the stage for their final bows. One of them was a traitor. But who?

And if information was being passed, that meant someone in the audience, someone whom the actor dared not approach in the normal course of events, received it. His piercing gaze moved slowly about the crowded drawing room. Not much to his surprise, he didn't see any suspicious characters who might have been taking rapid notes. The receiver could be anyone.

And whatever was being passed must be simple—perhaps a meeting place, perhaps a single fact or a key to a code.

He joined in the applause, then rose and wandered among the other members of the audience. Would a meeting take place here, where the players could mingle freely, exchanging polite words with the numerous visitors? Almost anything could be said in the course of a two-minute conversation. He would do better to concentrate on discovering the traitor in the acting troupe.

And he wanted to speak with Augusta. She dealt with them on a daily basis; she had come up against the problem of those rewritten lines. He looked about and spotted her as she entered the room, dressed now in a deceptively simple evening gown of amaranthus-colored gauze. Part of his mind approved her appearance while the rest contemplated her ability—and willingness—to help.

He strode up to her, waited while she received the congratulations of her numerous acquaintances, and caught her eye. Color flooded her cheeks and she looked away, only to turn back to him as if she couldn't help herself. Now, what the devil made her look like that? As if he had caught her out in some guilty activity . . .

That incident in the jewelry shop, he remembered suddenly. He hadn't seen her since. A slight frown creased his brow. Now that he thought of it, he wouldn't mind hearing her explanation—or at least the story Lieutenant Peregrine Lansdon must have given her to induce her to help him in one of his cork-brained schemes. Decidedly, this interview with Miss Carstairs should not be delayed.

He touched her arm. "Could ye spare me a few moments?"

She managed a shaky smile. "Officially or unofficially?"

"Officially. Is there a room where we won't be disturbed?"

"Can this not wait? If you hadn't noticed, we are holding a reception."

"One which the guests are required to pay handsomely to attend." She said nothing, so he prompted her. "Now, Miss Carstairs?"

With a quavering sigh, she led him out of the room and down the hall to a small, unused chamber at the back of the house. He held the door for her and ushered her inside. She seated herself in a large wing-back chair that had been too large to

200

move into the drawing room. "What may I do for you?"

He caught the coldness in her voice and was surprised that it bothered him. He strode over to the empty hearth, then turned back to face her. "I have a theory I wish to discuss."

"Indeed?" She eyed him in frigid disdain.

"Ye may relax that pose, Miss Carstairs. The play is over." Even to himself, he sounded stiff.

She paled visibly. "What do you mean?"

He crossed over and stopped just in front of her. Without wasting any words, he informed her how he suspected the plays were being used.

She blinked her eyes. "Dear God. I hoped I was wrong."

He blinked. "Ye knew?" Despite his effort, he could not quite keep an accusing note out of his voice.

"I couldn't be certain." She sounded defensive. "Would you want to believe such a terrible thing about a project for which you were responsible?"

"Nay, I would not!" He spoke with feeling.

She stared at her hands. "I—I am so glad to be able to tell you about it! If you knew how I have worried! You see, the possibility of the plays being used occurred to me shortly after you left Brussels before. Had you been here then, I would have told you. But the more I thought about it, the more ridiculous it seemed. I tried to convince myself it was just another of my silly romantic fantasies. I still cannot believe it to be true."

"Why not?" He made it a simple question.

"Because that would mean that one of us was guilty! And—"

"And what?" he prodded.

"I would be party to it." She finished in a very small voice.

"Not intentionally, though." He prevented himself from reaching out to touch her pale cheek.

She shook her head. "But who would believe it? The plays were my idea. Even here in Brussels. *I* am the one who wanted to start them up again." She raised troubled eyes to him. "Do you not see. Even though I didn't know about it, I provided the means for the—the traitor—to pass on the information." Sudden horror filled her expressive eyes. She rose to her feet, distressed. "Is that what you've suspected me of all along. You thought *me* a traitor?"

"Nay." He kept his voice calm, soothing. "I think ye the best person to help me."

"Oh, how dreadful of someone to use such a good cause for such a terrible purpose! What are we to do?"

The idea that came to his mind, of gathering her into his arms and kissing her, was clearly ineligible. He moved away a few steps to avoid temptation. "We are dealing with a limited number of suspects. Now we must begin eliminating them."

"Sophronia, then. Surely, you cannot think her involved. Can you?" she demanded as he remained silent.

"Not intentionally, no. Her involvement might be quite innocent."

Augusta bit her lip and resumed her seat.

"And that brings me to another question. Why did Lieutenant Lansdon give ye a large sum of money the other morning?" He waited, wondering why her answer seemed so important to him.

A wry smile just touched her lips. "I wondered when you'd get around to asking me about it. It was really quite simple. He—he had a number of gaming debts he couldn't pay. I loaned him the money."

"When was this?"

"Some time ago. We were still in London."

"And ye had that great a sum by ye?"

Her eyes flashed. "You *do* still suspect me!"

"Nay, I do not." His calm tone appeared to soothe her.

"Actually, I didn't," she admitted. "I sold a piece of jewelry—nothing that mattered. I knew he would pay me back when he could. When I saw him the other day, he said he'd had a run of phenomenal luck."

"Or something," the major murmured, then hoped Augusta hadn't heard. She was loyal, she would defend her friends. But he could not be satisfied with that explanation of how Lieutenant Lansdon came into so much money.

"You really do think the information is being passed in the altered lines?" she asked suddenly, as if still trying to deny the probability.

He allowed her to change the subject. "It seems reasonable. The words being continually changed assures that no one is suspicious when something is altered at the last minute."

She drew a shaky breath and nodded, as if he confirmed her own thoughts. "How do we begin discovering the truth?"

He shook his head. "*If* we are right, this could be no more than the first or second time this method has been used. Do ye have a copy of the last play?"

"Yes. It's in my room. I'll get it."

She sprang to her feet and hurried out. He waited, and in a few minutes she returned with the copiously annotated script. Edward took the top few sheets and sat down on the arm of the chair. Augusta hesitated a moment, then perched on the edge of the seat, peering over his arm.

"Can ye remember which the last changes were?" he asked.

But try as they might, they could see no pattern to the rewriting. Everyone's hand appeared scribbling between the lines. Augusta's own perfect copperplate cropped up with alarming regularity. They pored over the sheets for more than two hours, finding nothing but a mish-mash of altered and re-altered lines.

A frustrated sigh escaped him. "The only charge on which I could convict any of ye is literary murder."

That caused her to smile. "You would have no trouble of that. I had forgotten how terrible that one was." She stifled a yawn. "How I wish we knew what we were looking for—and if in fact we are right. This might be nothing but a waste of time. And oh! how I hope it is."

He shook his head and tossed the much-handled script onto a table. Standing up with care, he stretched his aching back. She rose also and yawned once more.

He looked down at her, his expression gentle. "My poor Miss Carstairs, what a night ye have been having. First the play, and now this."

"Yes. It's like having to give that last one over again."

A deep chuckle escaped him. "Accept my apologies. I wouldn't have subjected ye to such an ordeal for anything." He gazed down at her and the smile died from his eyes to be replaced by a frown. "And speaking of ordeals, I believe ye have done enough. Get out of this sordid business. Go back to England."

She shook her head. "I cannot desert them. These are *my* plays. To run would make me look guilty—or worse, as if I believed all of *them* to be guilty. I am involved, however unknowingly, and I intend to help uncover the traitor."

"Loyal," he murmured, his tone a caress. The next instant, he recovered. "Foolhardy, but loyal."

Chapter 16

Augusta went up to bed, exhausted but happy for the first time in a very long while. What a relief to hand the worst of her worries over to Edward MacKennoch. And he didn't think her guilty.

Or did he? That brought her to a halt. Determinedly, she forced back the terrible suspicion that he might deceive her to further his investigation. He might be a dedicated officer, but he was straightforward, honest—and unyieldingly rigid in principle.

But if he continued to smile down at her with those lights dancing in his eyes, she couldn't find it in herself to protest, whatever he did. He turned her blood to fire, sending it coursing through her veins; he turned her bones to water and made her muscles quiver in response.

He also turned her thoughts into the most ridiculous, romantic nonsense she had ever encountered! At this rate, she could take to writing plays herself! Still, it was with a pleasantly dreamy frame of mind she sought her bed.

Would he return in the morning to talk over his ideas with her once more, she wondered? She hoped he would.

She was doomed to disappointment. Not so much as a brief message did she receive from the exasperating major. Apparently, she had served her purpose and he would now pursue his work on his own. In frustration, she called for horses to be brought around and rode out with Lizzie beneath the lime trees that bordered the Allee Verte. Surely, Major MacKennoch would come on the morrow to report his progress.

He didn't, and Augusta found herself fretting, trying to remember something that might be of help, that might justify her sending for him to come to her.

On the third morning after the performance, Captain Vincent Trent called, and encountered the ladies outside their door as they returned from feeding the swans in the park. He bowed low over their hands, retaining Sophronia's a moment longer than necessary. Augusta saw an odd gleam light his brown eyes and a slight crease form in his brow as he stared down into Sophie's plain, sweet face.

He drew his gaze away and turned to Augusta. "The plays have been such a success that several of the officers in my regiment got together and created this for our use." He held out a stiff folder which contained about forty close written sheets. "I read it over, and it's really not bad."

Augusta took it, pleased that her hands didn't tremble. A play, and very possibly written by Vincent Trent himself. Was it designed for the sole purpose of passing on military secrets? Her heart skipped a beat in excited anticipation.

She cast a sideways glance at his watchful eyes and experienced a sinking sensation. He tried to gauge her reaction—what should it be? She forced a smile to her lips. "How very—enterprising of them. Please give them my thanks."

"When can we schedule the first rehearsal?"

Augusta shook her head, feeling momentarily on safe ground. "I have no idea. I believe Lord Wentworth has gone to the French court at Ghent. He will be our director again, if he agrees."

She was more concerned with showing the play to Major MacKennoch, but she didn't say that aloud. She hugged the script to her. At last, she might hold a real clue. She could hardly wait to see the major's face. She flushed softly, realizing that that would be true even if she had nothing to show him.

"What fun this will be." Sophronia spoke up brightly. "Perhaps we could look it over now?" She raised hopeful eyes to the captain's watchful face.

An emotion Augusta couldn't identify flickered in his eyes, gone in an instant. "I must leave. Duties, I fear. Until later." He strode off down the street, leaving Sophronia and Augusta to stare after him.

What had that emotion been? Remorse? Did he perhaps have the decency to regret involving Sophronia in his evil schemes? Or if he were innocent, did he regret using her to spy on and entrap her brother? Augusta wished fervently she knew the truth.

A shaky sigh broke from Sophie as she entered the house. "Shall we go over the play?" she suggested.

They spent the next two hours reading it, but try as hard as she might, Augusta could find no hidden messages within the lines. It was more serious than was their wont to produce, but with a few appropriate changes—and the lack of acting ability on the part of their troupe—Augusta saw no reason why it would not be a success.

By that evening, she had decided not to send for the major. Aside from its being a most indiscreet thing for a lady to do, she wanted to punish him a little. If he didn't bother to inform her of what went on, why should she go to any effort to alert him to clues? If he were so good at solving the problems on his own, he didn't need her help. And if he had been keeping an eye on Vincent Trent, as he undoubtedly should have been, he would have known what just occurred and put in an appearance on their doorstep as soon as the captain left.

In this defiant state of mind, Augusta dressed for a ball that evening. It seemed odd to concern herself with her appearance when treasonable activities took place in her very house. But she could not betray her suspicions and fears; she had to continue as if nothing were amiss.

Sophronia came downstairs in a delicate pink gauze half robe over a white silk underskirt, looking uncommonly pretty. Augusta, in the blond lace over blush-colored satin, thought she had never seen her friend appear to better advantage. She had a shrewd suspicion they would see Captain Trent this night.

To her surprise, she saw no sign of him in the comfortably crowded rooms. She kept a surreptitious eye out as she promised dances to the eager officers who surrounded her. One waltz she held open, on the hope of luring the captain, if he arrived, into discussing the play.

Perry, who had done his duty in escorting his mamma and her charges to the ball, spotted Frederick Ashfield and excused himself to join him. The two disappeared in the direction of the card room. Augusta looked after them, surprised, for she had not thought them friends.

Lord Roderick joined her, but did not request a dance. Instead, he stood in silent reverie, his expression disconsolate.

"What on earth is the matter, Roddy?" Augusta spoke softly, not wanting to draw attention to them.

He grimaced. "My pistols," he said shortly.

"They're not missing *again!*" She regarded him in dismay.

He nodded. "Can't understand it! Word must've gotten out that they're lucky, and now they keep disappearing. I've *got* to get them back."

"Why worry so?" She tried to keep her voice casual. "They're bound to turn up—they always do. Surely they'll be returned as soon as whoever has them finishes his gaming spree. Then you can hide them in a safer place."

He opened his mouth, changed his mind about whatever he had intended to say, and shook his head. "You don't understand."

"Perhaps not, but you know I'd help if I could."

He met her serious gaze and a bleak smile just touched his lips. "Thank you. But you can't. No one can." He walked abruptly away.

Augusta drew a deep breath. She might not know why Roddy was so worried about the pistols, but she had a fairly good idea where they might be. That, at least, she could settle for him. At the first opportunity she intended to have a very brief but pointed conversation with Lieutenant Peregrine Lansdon.

But the music began and her partner claimed her for the country dance. Not until this ended could she escape. She looked about and spotted her quarry coming out of the card room, and with a hurried word of excuse to her partner, she slipped away and cornered Perry before he could disappear in the crowd.

"Well?" He eyed her with a mixture of unease and defiance as she drew him aside.

"Where are Roddy's pistols *this* time?"

He laughed. "Lord, has he missed them already? Never fear, they'll be back at his bedside by morning."

"*Why*, Perry?"

Her question had nothing to do with their return, and he knew it. "Just came up unexpectedly short. I'm getting some more money tonight, though, so all's right and tight. Now, don't you keep worrying about me."

"How can I help it, Perry? Where are you getting the money?"

He shrugged. "There are ways."

He spoke in tones of such provocative mystery that she longed to box his ears. "Perry . . ."

He shook his head, suddenly sobered. "When a fellow is desperate, it's amazing what he can mangage to do."

"As long as it doesn't include the sale of military secrets," she said softly.

"Good God, what sort of rum touch do you think I am?" His voice rose in anger.

She hushed him. "I don't mean knowingly. Are you being paid to do something, such as deliver papers? Even something that has a reasonable explanation?"

He appeared revolted by the idea. "Of course not. Do you take me for some ingenuous pawn? I only fuzz the cards a little. Nothing to make a fuss over. Besides, I'm not the only one enjoying unaccustomed wealth. What about your friend Jack Kettering?"

"What about him? He has an allowance from his aunt."

Perry gave a short laugh. "Only when he wins it. Lord, what a fool you must be to believe him rich. Is that why you've been on the catch for him?"

"I am hardly 'on the catch,' as you so vulgarly phrase it, for anybody. It is quite the opposite." She spoke through clenched teeth, but his words gave her pause. Could the Halliford fortune be behind Kettering's paying her such ardent court? No, his sentiments were real; she had been around enough to know the difference. Her dowry, though, might have prompted him to lie, to importune her to elope with him.

"You're being offensive, Lansdon."

She spun about and saw Vincent Trent standing behind them, a smile on his lips that robbed his words of force. Edward MacKennoch stood at his side. Hot color flushed Augusta's cheeks. "I did not expect to see you this evening, Major."

"I came with Trent."

She regarded the two men uneasily. Why did Edward MacKennoch cultivate that acquaintance? To work with him—or to entrap him? She opened her mouth, the question

208

trembling on her lips, but Jack Kettering strolled up, effectively preventing her from uttering unwise words.

Trent eyed the newcomer with speculative interest. "You must know that the most shocking things are being said about you, Kettering."

Perry cast a darkling look at the captain, turned on his heel, and stalked off.

Kettering, affronted, paid him no heed. "What is being said?" he demanded.

"There is a vicious rumor that your income springs from the gaming tables."

The lieutenant appeared to struggle with himself, then met Augusta's worried eyes. His own held only apology. "I have supplemented it that way." He spoke to her, not Trent. "At the moment, I have a meager income. But my aunt has sponsored my military career and has promised that if I make a marriage of which she approves, she will settle a substantial sum on me. And luckily for me," he added, his smile warming, "my affections have lighted upon a lady who could not help but win anyone's approval."

Augusta looked down, discomfitted by his assertion, but also relieved. She might not love him, but she did not want him to be guilty of treason.

Kettering hesitated. "Excuse me. I—I wish to speak with Mr. Ashfield." Without another word, he left to join the other man.

Vincent Trent caught the major's eye, winked, and strolled off.

Augusta stared after him. Why had Trent brought the subject up to Jack Kettering? To warn him? Could they be working together? And what was the tie between Trent and Major MacKennoch?

"What prompted that little interchange with Lansdon?" The major offered her his arm.

She took it, and a rueful smile just touched her lips, replacing her confusion for the moment. "I might have known you'd be there to overhear me making a muddle of things. I was trying to find out what he'd been doing. Lord Roderick's pistols are missing again. I just asked Perry about them."

He shook his head. "Cramming your fences, Miss Carstairs. A young colt needs a light hand."

"So I discovered. Halliford will tell you I was never very good with young, resty horses."

That brought a genuine smile to his lips. "Handling anyone is an acquired talent."

"You seem to be expert at it. Did you really come with Captain Trent?"

He nodded. "I find him quite interesting company."

"I can imagine," she muttered. "Has he told you about the play he brought to me?"

"He has." His bright, blue eyes lit with amusement. "You can have no idea how much I am looking forward to its performance."

Try as she might, she could get no more information out of him. Irritated, she flounced off with her next partner. If Edward MacKennoch thought she would bestow her saved waltz on him, he was very much mistaken. Recklessly, she promised it to her current partner, who was prompty reduced to a stammering incoherence of delight.

She spent the remainder of the ball trying to decide which annoyed her more—the fact that Edward MacKennoch did not tell her what he had been about for the last few days, or the fact that throughout the course of the very long evening, he did not try to claim her for a single dance. He took the floor with no one, of course, because of his leg, but he might at least have asked her to sit one out with him. She was not, she decided, in a forgiving mood.

In fact, if he approached her now, she would truthfully be able to tell him she had no more dances left. Then she would proceed to have so much fun—without him, of course—that he would see how infinitely unimportant he was to her. He would be brought to the realization that without her company, the evening was sadly flat.

Unfortunately, her vindictive fantasy worked on the wrong person. Without *his* company, *her* evening fell flat.

Her disconsolate mood hung on after they returned home and lingered even into the morning. She rose early, sent for horses, and, accompanied by Lizzie, sought diversion in a brisk canter outside the city walls.

The rest of the day passed in preparations for a dinner party they would give that night. As the majority of the guests were involved with the plays, she decided to use the occasion to rally

210

them all into agreeing to Captain Trent's offering. Changing from her habit into a simple round gown, she set about arranging flowers in the numerous vases.

The party proved to be every bit as casual as Augusta anticipated. Lord Wentworth appeared even more jovial than usual over the captain's play, and the two stood in one corner of the saloon before dinner, arguing amicably over whether or not to make any major changes. Perry, Sophie, and Lord Roderick mingled with the other guests, though they all contributed their share of comments.

Major MacKennoch, Augusta noted, fitted the picture of the perfect diplomat. He circulated about the room, exchanging pleasant words with everyone, expanding his acquaintances. Augusta might be certain he possessed an ulterior motive, but no one else would ever suspect. He was brilliant at this profession; when he finished his assignment for Lord Bathurst, he ought to seriously consider diplomacy as a new career.

Lizzie, who had joined the party by the simple expedient of waving aside her sister's halfhearted protests that she was not yet properly out, pounced on Frederick Ashfield the moment that gentleman put in a belated appearance. "Now I will have someone to talk to! Tell me, do you mean to go through with another of Gussie's ridiculous plays? I never thought you one to enjoy making a cake of yourself."

"I did not!" Ashfield regarded her in mock indignation, obviously amused by her outspokenness.

"Of course he didn't." Augusta joined them. She didn't want him to withdraw—she needed all the players to take part again. How else could she determine which of them was guilty?

Kettering strolled over to join them and, to Augusta's surprise, engaged Lizzie in conversation. The next moment, she realized his intent and could only smile at his naiveté. His purpose was to charm her sister. Augusta watched in no little amusement his vain attempts, for Lizzie was patently revolted by his cultivated charm and compliments.

"How can you tolerate such a cockle-brained nodcock?" Lizzie demanded as he finally walked off, defeated.

"You are a shocking hoyden," Mr. Ashfield informed her, hard-pressed not to laugh. "What would Helena say if she heard you talk like that?"

"She has any number of times." Lizzie waved his comment aside as being of totally no importance.

Dinner was announced, and as Augusta was seated, she watched Ashfield and Lizzie covertly, wondering about the easy terms on which they stood. *Could* he be the traitor? Lizzie considered him a "right 'un," though. Her sister wasn't usually wrong in her reading of a person's nature, and she never showed any hesitation whatsoever in making her opinions clear to all concerned. Her inexplicable liking for Frederick Ashfield might be an indication. Augusta sighed. She certainly shared Lizzie's opinion that Jack Kettering was not for her.

Somehow, the meal passed, with talk fluctuating between the next play and the rumors—unfounded, the officers assured them—of Napoleon marching toward Brussels.

"Thank heaven Wellington has arrived at last," Mrs. Lansdon exclaimed.

Lord Wentworth snorted. "I can't see where the fellow will do much good. I suppose it makes you happy just being situated so close to his headquarters."

Mrs. Lansdon shook her head and laughed. "Though to be sure," she told the ladies after they withdrew to allow the gentlemen to converse over their wine and snuff, "to know that he is just along the other side of the park in the Rue Royale cannot but be a comfort to me."

Lord Wentworth, serving in the role of host to the gentlemen, brought them in shortly. Card tables were set up, and Mrs. Lansdon, Sophronia, and Augusta busied themselves arranging partners.

Neatly, Augusta placed Jack Kettering with Lizzie, Lady Eversley, and Miss Eversley for a hand of loo, thus avoiding having to play with him herself. What she would really enjoy would be playing piquet with Major MacKennoch. But Ashfield invited him to join in a hand.

Augusta, partnering Lord Wentworth in a game of whist, kept an eye on the major's game. What did he make of Ashfield? she wondered. They were quite different types, the one so calm and taciturn, the other so rakish and cynical. She could not be entirely at ease with that gentleman's friendship with her sister. Still, Halliford considered him a friend, and she had a high opinion of her brother-in-law's good sense.

As their various games ended and they changed tables, Augusta glimpsed Lord Roderick slipping surreptitiously out of the room. Without a second thought, Augusta excused herself and set off in pursuit. What was he up to? she wondered.

He paused in the hall to look about, and Augusta ducked into an empty drawing room so he wouldn't see her. He took the stairs two at a time. Augusta waited until he reached the first landing, then started slowly up after him.

When she reached the second floor, she couldn't see him anywhere. A slight frown just creased her brow—and then she noted that the door to Sophronia's room stood open. Augusta regarded it, perplexed, then crept down the corridor, doing her best imitation of a heroine in pursuit of a suspect. She slipped into her own chamber, pulled the door mostly closed, and waited.

Less than ten seconds later, Lord Roderick emerged from Sophronia's room with such an expression of relief that it was almost ludicrous. He clutched the cherrywood pistol case under his arm. Augusta stared after him, too surprised to move. *Where* had the pistols come from? Sophie's room? Why? And how had they gotten there? They floated about far too freely for her taste. Suppose they fell into the hands of Perry's blackmailer?

Or had they? The thought took root. Lord Roderick was one of the very few people who knew the truth about the duel, and she knew his brother Taversham kept him on a tight allowance. Could Roddy be blackmailing his friend? That might explain his almost irrational concern over those horrid guns.

As she watched, he descended the staircase, crossed the hall, and had the footman let him out. Slowly, Augusta returned to the drawing room, where apparently only Edward MacKennoch had noticed her absence. He stared hard at her as she re-entered, and she gave him a look indicating that she wished to speak to him. He excused himself from his game and strolled over to join her.

He ushered her into a connecting drawing room, leaving the door ajar. They settled on a sofa on the far side where they could hold a low-voiced conversation without being heard or seen.

"Has something occurred?" he asked as soon as she

213

was seated.

"Those pistols have cropped up again." She related the most recent incident in the unconventional travels of the guns. His brow snapped down and she quaked internally at the anger that flashed in his brilliant blue eyes.

"Have ye no more sense than to follow him? Ye are forever throwing yourself full fling into things ye don't understand."

She stiffened, irritatingly aware he was right, which only added fuel to her flaring temper. "Someone must keep track of those ridiculous pistols."

"Do ye enjoy exposing yourself to danger?"

"You are making a great deal out of nothing! It was only Roddy, for heaven's sake, not someone dangerous."

"And how do ye know Roddy *isn't* dangerous? Ye have absolutely no more sense than a newborn kitten!"

His sparkling eyes and animated features did wild things to her pulse rate. She vented her rampant confusion into anger. "I have at least enough sense to know I have nothing to fear from Lord Roderick!"

"And what about the other members of the troupe? Do ye find them equally innocuous?"

"I prefer to see the good side of people. They tend to live up to it."

He drew an exasperated breath. "You're like to get yourself into serious trouble."

"How can I, with you and Captain Trent watching every move I make?" Her own eyes flashed.

"We weren't watching ye tonight when ye chased after Lord Roderick."

"It would be the most shocking piece of impertinence imaginable if you did, in my own home!" With difficulty she kept her voice from rising.

"Didn't ye realize it was a potentially dangerous situation? I'd rather ye were just a bit afraid."

"You'd know if I were. *I* don't hide behind a mask of stupid indifference."

That stung him, she saw. Before she had time to recover, to make the apology that sprang to her lips, he dragged her ruthlessly into his arms. His mouth pressed firmly down on hers, not in anger, but with an evocative pressure that turned her bones to water and left her clinging to him, lost in a welter

214

of desire she barely understood. He released her slowly, his lips claiming hers once more with a feathery touch, then he set her aside.

"Is that enough emotion for ye?" His voice shook slightly. With a visible effort, he recovered his equilibrium. His calm mask returned, but it could not disguise the fire that glowed in his eyes. He touched her cheek in a gentle caress.

She covered his fingers with her own, pressing them against the hollow of her cheek. For once, words failed her.

"Ye are too vulnerable, too innocent." His gaze held hers and she found it impossible to breath.

She shook her head, fighting the urge to throw herself back into his arms and experience his glorious strength once more. For perhaps the first time in her romantic life, she had to be as logical and pragmatic as Lizzie and fight down her longing.

"I—I am eighteen, not a child," she managed.

"But ye've led a very sheltered life."

He moved back, and she felt him closing her out once more. "That does not make me helpless. I will not be excluded from this problem. Perhaps I should be the one to don the kilt."

"I have no need to wear my uniform. And I will not be hampered by worrying about ye." Instead of making it a joke, as she had hoped, he seemed to become his old impenetrable, infuriating self again.

"I can help!" She dreaded his withdrawal into his closed shell, now that he had unbent so far.

It was too late. He moved away, as if he sought to put distance between them. His narrowed eyes rested on her face, their expression masked. "All right, if ye really want to assist me?"

"I do!" She leaned eagerly toward him.

"Then ye can begin by telling me everything ye know about Lord Roderick's pistols."

She had fallen into a trap. Augusta's heart turned over, then plummeted into her stomach.

Chapter 17

For one long, horrible minute, Augusta stared at Major MacKennoch. She couldn't betray Perry! But the knowledge of the duel's true nature, so far hidden from the major, might provide the missing piece that would help him sort out the rest of the puzzle. Was it more important to protect Sophronia's brother or to uncover a traitor and murderer? And Perry hadn't actually killed Monty. . . .

She looked up into Edward MacKennoch's eyes and read there an unexpected compassion for her dilemma. He smiled at her in understanding and she was lost. She lowered her gaze, knowing full well she had succumbed to the carefully woven spell of a superb diplomat.

"You—you have probably guessed at least part of the story. Roddy's pistols *were* used in the duel with Captain Montclyff. Perry fought him. But *Monty* forced the quarrel on Perry and made those peculiar arrangements himself!" Briefly, she told him the tale as she had heard it from Perry. "Perry and Roddy merely fell into the trap," she finished.

"Trap," Major MacKennoch repeated softly. He stared at her, unseeing, as his keen brain sorted ideas, his progress reflected in the changing shadows of his eyes. "So you think Montclyff had been ordered to pick that quarrel?"

Augusta nodded, relieved that he seemed to accept what she said. "I think he'd been told to—to do away with Perry for some reason. Perry was really the ideal choice for Monty's killer, under the circumstances. He is a notoriously poor shot. No one who had ever seen him with a gun would expect any bullets he fired to so much as graze anything—or anyone—he aimed at. With Perry as the opponent, Monty should have been found with only one wound, and it would have been thought an unparalleled event on Perry's part."

"And our villain would have been rid of Monty, for whatever reason." He fell silent, thinking once more.

Augusta sank back, exhausted, yet unable to drag her eyes from his dynamic expression. Edward MacKennoch was alive, vividly so, and the vibrancy of his presence wreaked havoc on her. Energy radiated from him, enveloping her, making her so fully aware of him that he filled her thoughts and senses.

"Do ye have any idea who might have been behind it?" He looked up suddenly, his face once more that impenetrable mask.

"I believe Perry's story." She hesitated, but he didn't disagree. "It—it *might* have been Lord Roderick. He brought Monty into the plays, they are his pistols, and he has been so very desperate to keep them safe ever since."

"And so incredibly adept at losing them." Unexpectedly, his eyes twinkled.

"Roddy was the only second at the duel," Augusta pursued, trying to ignore her reaction to those sparkling glints in the crystal blue depths. "Aside from the doctor that no one can locate."

"That doctor is a mystery." The major leaned forward, clasping his hands between his knees as he frowned, his gaze resting on her softly flushed face. "Lord Roderick could conceivably have fired the second shot—but only if that doctor were in on the scheme."

"Or the doctor could have fired, if Roddy were in on it. The shot had to come from *behind* Perry, not off to one side. Oh, if only we could find that man!"

"I don't think we can count on it. We cannot even be sure he really was a doctor, under the circumstances." He shot her the look she dreaded. "And we only have Lansdon's word that the doctor existed."

Her throat went dry. "Do you think he made it up? But that would mean—"

"It's a possibility that has to be considered. The whole situation is really too smoky by half, you know. If his story is true, they both must have been badly foxed not to be sobered by the prospect of a duel. Or they could have contrived

217

together to murder Captain Montclyff."

"But *why?* Neither has a reason for wanting him dead!"

The major's expression softened once more at her distress. "Unless it was to protect their involvement in the selling of military secrets. Both of those two young gentlemen game and lose far too much for their meager pay."

She drew a shaky breath. "Perry says he fuzzes the cards—but you heard that. And do not forget there are other suspects. What of Captain Trent?"

Edward smiled suddenly. "And while we are at it, don't forget Kettering, Ashfield, and Wentworth. Money is always a powerful inducement. It has turned loyal men into traitors before."

"That ought to clear Lord Wentworth of suspicion, at least. I don't believe I have ever met a man so passionately devoted to his country."

"It could be an act."

She swallowed. "It—Oh, how dreadful of you to make me suspicious of everyone! Very well, then, but I had not thought him a good enough actor."

"Is that why he directs?" If anything, the major looked amused.

"Yes." Her eyes opened wide. "He also has no control over what is actually said during the performance! Only the actors do. That could be why no one reacted when I changed a few words in the last play. The information must be passed in the—the traitor's own lines, not someone else's!"

Edward nodded slowly. "That would make sense. Our 'traitor' certainly couldn't count on any of your troupe remembering their speeches with any accuracy." He leaned forward, a gleam in his eyes that sent her pulses racing. "What of your actors, then?"

She hesitated. "Lieutenant Kettering is not wealthy. I don't know about Captain Trent. And Frederick Ashfield—he is very expensive, but I have no idea whether he has money or not." She looked up at the major, somber. "It could be any one of them. As you say, money is a strong motivator."

"Ye forgot to mention yourself and Miss Lansdon among the suspects, my dear."

The last words held so much warmth, she could not take offense. He invited her to share the joke he found in the difficulty of their task. She smiled in response.

He rose. "We've been in here much too long." He held out his hands.

Tentatively, she took them and he drew her to her feet. She gazed up into his eyes, which still held a lingering smile, and breathing ceased to be important. Without breaking their gaze, he raised first one of her hands, then the other, to his lips. It was the first time he had ever done that, she noted, bemused. He took his leave of her and she stayed where she was, staring after him, loath to break the spell that lingered from his presence.

When she at last followed him into the other drawing room, she found the rest of the party had already broken up. She wandered into the hall and up the stairs, barely feeling the floor. She floated, as if she had had too much wine with dinner. But she knew that the explanation was far more complex, far more exciting and far more wonderful. Something within her seemed to sing.

It was not until she climbed into her warmed bed that she realized the major had deliberately avoided answering her direct question concerning Captain Trent.

That troubling thought remained with her throughout a shopping expedition the ladies undertook the following morning. Sophronia needed a new pair of evening gloves, but once these were purchased, they wandered from shop to shop, browsing, with Mrs. Lansdon exclaiming over the various treasures discovered amid the soaps and perfumes, the delightful array of books, and the beautiful laces.

Augusta, restless, walked ahead with Lizzie, drawing farther and farther from the other two. *Why* hadn't the major answered her? Did he suspect something about Vincent Trent he didn't want her to know—about which he didn't want to alarm her?

They drew abreast of the jewelry shop where Perry had purchased his ring, and suddenly a new question sprang to her mind. She stopped abruptly, staring unseeingly at the window, the image of Perry inside with the sapphire gleaming on his finger vivid in her memory. She could not recall seeing him wear that ring since. Did he sell it back to pay his blackmailer?

As she stood there, lost in thought, waiting for Mrs. Lansdon and Sophronia to catch up to her and Lizzie, two men came out of the shop. She barely noticed them.

"What a pleasant surprise." Captain Trent bowed to her.

Augusta started, then managed a polite greeting. But the next moment she saw only the solid, distinguished figure that stood framed in the doorway behind him. The light that brightened Edward MacKennoch's clear blue eyes as they rested on her brought warm color to her cheeks and a more rapid beat to her pulse.

Lizzie stared from her to the major, her eyes wide with sudden mirth. Abruptly, she turned away, her shoulders shaking. Augusta ignored her, though her heart sank. Lizzie was far too perceptive. Sophronia and Mrs. Lansdon hurried forward, and in the ensuing exchange of greetings Lizzie recovered her countenance.

Vincent Trent greeted them, and disclaimed any chance of his attending a rehearsal that afternoon. "It will be more difficult in future to schedule them. Military duties have been stepped up, I fear."

"Does this mean there will be war soon?" Mrs. Lansdon regarded him in real fear.

Major MacKennoch shook his head. "Merely drills and parades. Each of the allied troops hopes to impress the others. It's time-consuming, nothing more."

"There is certainly no need for alarm." Captain Trent's brilliant smile flashed.

Augusta thought it false. Did he, in fact, want war? It didn't seem possible that anyone could.

Mrs. Lansdon beamed on him. "If *you* say we are safe, then, of course, we must be reassured."

"Of course we must," Augusta muttered to herself.

Sophronia, who had been smiling shyly at the captain, overheard and cast her friend a sharp, bewildered glance. She seemed on the verge of asking a question, then subsided.

"Will ye be attending the Stapletons' card party this evening?" The major stepped neatly into the momentary gap.

"We will," Mrs. Lansdon assured him. "Such delightful people. I vow, I quite look forward to it."

"Then so shall we, all the more." Trent bowed to them, and the gentlemen took their leave.

Lizzie linked her arm through Augusta's and hurried forward, pulling her sister ahead of Sophronia and Mrs.

Lansdon, who followed more slowly. As soon as they were out of earshot, Lizzie collapsed in a fit of giggles.

"Edward, of all men!" she gasped. "Edward is the most *un*romantic man possible!" She took one look at Augusta's indignant face and went off into whoops of laughter.

"I have not the least notion what you are talking about," Augusta informed her coldly.

"Oh, haven't you?" Lizzie's voice still quavered. "You're in love with him!"

Augusta's flush deepened. "Pray, do not be absurd. With Major MacKennoch? You cannot possibly believe for one moment he could consider me a suitable wife."

"That's the cream of the jest!" Lizzie assured her blithely. "You wouldn't be in the least suitable!"

Augusta came to an abrupt halt, seeking words with which to express her sentiments concerning this utterance, but fortunately they failed her. While she still sought to convince her sister that she did no more than admire Major MacKennoch, as anyone must, Sophronia caught up with them.

"Oh, do hush, Lizzie," Sophie exclaimed with uncharacteristic urgency, cutting across the girl's teasing. "Augusta, why are you being so cool toward Vi—Captain Trent? Has he done something to offend you? I—I thought, once before, that you avoided him. Why?"

Augusta knew a momentary panic. Should she tell Sophronia of her suspicions? That she believed Major MacKennoch to be keeping a close eye on that gentleman? She would more likely alienate the girl than do any good. Frantically, she sought for a plausible excuse, and found it readily at hand. "It—it is just the odious way he persists in including me among his suspects in Monty's murder."

"You? Involved in Monty's death? But that's ridiculous!" Sophronia cast an indignant glance back in the direction in which Captain Trent and the major had disappeared. "And so you may be certain I shall tell him when next we meet."

Far from stilling Sophronia's concern, though, this answer raised many more questions in the girl's mind. She refrained from further comment until they returned to the house. There, she followed Augusta to her room and proceeded to pelt her with demands to know what Captain Trent had questioned her about, what he must have heard to make him suspect she might be involved, and what Augusta had said to him. She ended with an impassioned tirade against the disagreeable, jealous cats who delighted in the opportunity of spreading vicious and untrue gossip.

Augusta was deeply touched by her friend's loyalty, but by the time they had partaken of a light nuncheon, she found it difficult to contemplate an afternoon spent in listening to more of the girl's questions. Eventually, if Sophronia persisted, Augusta might betray the tie between Monty's murder and the sale of military secrets—and Captain Trent's possible role in both. And that she did not want to do.

Inspired by necessity, Augusta begged Mrs. Lansdon to order out the carriage for a drive through the countryside, an activity sure to divert Sophronia's mind. Less than an hour later, the barouche, with Lizzie and Augusta riding alongside, passed through the Namur Gate, through the suburbs, and on to the Boise des Soignes, a delightful wood of beech trees through which the road to the village of Waterloo passed.

Her problems, almost forgotten in the warmth of the mid-April sunshine, returned that evening at the card party as she observed the subtle byplays between Vincent Trent and Major MacKennoch. She could not trust Captain Trent, and it appeared that the major felt the same. Trent's presence in Brussels, his being placed in charge of the murder investigation, his being outside that conservatory door after what she'd heard . . . There might well be an innocent explanation for all of it, but she could not rid herself of suspicion.

The questions still haunted her as she retired to bed in the early hours of the morning. Sleep, she knew, was far from coming. She dismissed her maid and curled up among her pillows with a copy of *Patronage* by Maria Edgeworth, which she had purchased the day before.

A light tap sounded on her door and Sophronia entered at once, without waiting for an answer. Her dressing gown, a filmy cloud of nakara-colored muslin, was her only garment, and she shivered in the cool air. She disposed herself on the end of Augusta's bed, tucking her chilled feet beneath her, and Augusta obligingly handed her a shawl.

"You must tell me the truth!" Sophronia wrapped the warm wool about herself and hugged it tightly. "Why did you watch Captain Trent all evening?"

222

Augusta closed the book and laid it aside. "Did I?"

"You *know* you did. Has—has Major MacKennoch told you anything? Please, Augusta, I *must* know!"

Augusta gazed at the tense, distressed face, and knew she had to say something. But not the truth. Or *should* she warn her, give her the merest hint that the captain might be playing an underhanded game? Sophronia's tender heart grew more deeply involved every day.

Augusta stared down at her hands, which she twisted in the bedclothes. "It—it is probably nothing but the most absurd coincidence. Just my foolish romantic disposition, as Lizzie will assure you."

"What is?"

Augusta drew a deep breath, stalling. "It is all nonsense, I am persuaded."

"Tell me!" The force of her own words appeared to startle the gentle Sophronia.

The door opened and both young ladies jumped. Lizzie stuck in her head. "I saw your candle was still lit. What's going on?" She took a bite out of the apple she carried.

"Lizzie, what on earth are you doing up? Have you been down to the kitchens?" Augusta fixed her sister with a reproving eye.

Lizzie sauntered over and plopped down on the bed beside Sophronia. "Why not? I was hungry. And don't tell me I should have rung for my maid, for I could find myself something to eat much more easily."

Augusta sighed. "Go to bed, Lizzie."

She shook her head. "Not till you tell me what's bothering you. Both of you," she added, eyeing Sophronia's pale face and tragic expression with disfavor. "You've been walking around looking like Atlas, with the weight of the world on your shoulders."

"There is a certain drawback to having a brother devoted to a classical education," Augusta informed Sophronia. "Lizzie comes out with the most ridiculous comments." She directed a pointed glare at her sister.

Lizzie sat placidly munching her apple, refusing to budge. Augusta sighed in resignation; now she had little choice. Sophronia, she could have fobbed off with some fanciful story. Lizzie was too sharp and knew her too well.

With a mental shrug, she embarked on the tale of what she had overheard in the conservatory of the Lansdon townhouse in London, including Vincent Trent's presence in the hall immediately afterward. She looked up when she finished, and detected an odd gleam in Sophronia's determined eyes. "It—it is all so coincidental," she finished.

"Of course it is," Lizzie declared in disgust. "Lord, what a fuss you two are making over the merest *chance!*"

Augusta nodded, unhappy, wishing the story had been left untold. "Lizzie is right. Even his listening like that before he was put in charge of the murder can probably be explained. Perhaps he was already looking into the problem of the sale of military secrets. Investigating something like that could make one look very suspicious."

"I knew it!" Sophronia exclaimed. "I knew there was something behind your distrust of Captain Trent! But it cannot be true. I—I simply cannot believe he would do such a thing. He *must* be just helping Major MacKennoch to investigate." For a moment, she appeared on the verge of dissolving into tears. "It cannot be true," she whispered, but her voice lacked its earlier conviction.

"Oh, Sophie, I—I'm so sorry! I should never have said anything, when it is all nothing but the merest speculation." She threw a furious look at Lizzie, who just rolled her eyes.

Sophronia shook her head, fighting back her emotions, and Augusta could tell that the suspicions had taken hold. "I—I had begun to wonder, too. I knew of Major MacKennoch's work from something Lord Wentworth said, and although I am not as quick-witted as you, I could not help but see the connection. But Augusta—" Unshed tears glittered on her stubby lashes and an almost fanatic light shone in her eyes. "It makes not one whit of difference to me. I—I would give up anything for Captain Trent's sake, and love him even if he were a traitor."

Lizzie hooted. "You're both talking yourselves into some Cheltenham tragedy! Captain Trent is a regular right 'un. He'd never have anything to do with such nonsense."

Sophronia drew a deep, shaky breath. "Well, if he *is*, we will extricate him," she decided.

"We will do nothing at all," Augusta told her firmly. "Only think how foolish we would look when it all turns out to be a hum."

"I just said that," Lizzie pointed out, but the other two ignored her.

"Now, go to bed and think no more about it," Augusta ordered. "Or since I know you will, concentrate instead on how best we might help discover the truth."

In the morning, though, Augusta found that her words had not been taken to heart. Sophronia greeted her at the breakfast table with the information that she had formed the intention of telling Captain Trent of Augusta's suspicions. This way, she assured her appalled listener, the captain might be frightened into abandoning any traitorous thoughts he might cherish.

Augusta's heart, which had already felt near bottom, sank even further. It took the better part of the meal for Augusta to convince Sophronia of the ineligibility of such a scheme, but at last she succeeded.

She had barely breathed a sigh of heartfelt relief when the butler entered to announce that Lord Wentworth awaited them. Augusta gulped down her last sip of tea, cast an appraising glance at Sophronia to make sure her friend disguised her distress sufficiently, and they went down to him.

They found him seated in their usual rehearsal room, leafing through the new play, a frown on his normally jovial countenance. He looked up, then rose to his feet on their entrance, but his smile of greeting lacked its usual spontaneity. "Glad you could spare me a moment." He waited until they had seated themselves, then sank back into his own chair.

"What may we do for you?" Augusta leaned forward impulsively, concerned by his unusual solemnity.

He shook his head. "Tell me I'm making a great deal out of nothing, I hope."

A sense of foreboding settled in Augusta's stomach. She exchanged an uneasy glance with Sophie. "In what way?"

"These plays." He waved the script he held. "Have you noticed anything odd about the productions of late?"

Sophronia gaped at him, but Augusta managed a blank look. "Do you mean besides their—their lack of professionalism?" she asked.

He awarded this sally a smile that only served to emphasize his uneasiness. "So many changes, so much fuss over something that is all for fun. Is it just me, or has that bothered you?"

225

Augusta hesitated. "It doesn't seem anything more than just each one of us wanting a turn at the rewriting. I admit I've done more than my share. But it all seems perfectly normal, considering how many different people are involved. Has something in particular happened to cause you concern?"

He looked down at the script. "It was just something Captain Trent said to me at the Stapletons' card party last night. He wanted to know how I was coming with reading the play." He frowned. "I think it was the manner in which he requested that I *not* rewrite a certain scene that bothered me."

"He asked that you *not* change a scene?" Sophronia looked up, her expression a picture of dismay.

"Yes. And as you well know, it has been our troupe's habit to point out the lines we *want* altered and ignore the ones that can be left alone. No, something about his whole manner got me to thinking. And I don't like not knowing answers. The worrisome thing is, I don't know what I'm suspicious *of.*"

Chapter 18

By the time Lord Wentworth took his leave, he was only partially reassured by Augusta's blithe comments about the meddling natures of the various members of their acting troupe. Augusta, though, felt more certain than ever that her plays were being used by a traitor. And at the moment, Captain Trent appeared the likeliest suspect.

While she and Sophronia still sat where they were, lost in silent thought, Perry arrived at the house, his uniform covered in dust from the ride to Brussels. The young man paced about his mother's elegant drawing room, distracted, unable to sit still. He stopped by the fire, adjusted the clock on the mantel, then turned back to face Augusta and his sister, who watched him in no little concern.

"Wellington is having the devil of a time with the Allied troops. He seems to be unifying them at last, though." He launched into speech as if eager to be saying anything.

Augusta leaned back in the overstuffed chair, her eyes partly closed. "It was to be hoped he could."

Perry nodded, off already on a tangent. "The best of our troops are in America still, you know. They're coming back, of course, but it takes time." He gathered enthusiasm for this new theme. "The rumor is they're mustering everyone they can and sending them over here."

"It will be war again, will it not?" With difficulty Augusta kept her voice level.

"Oh, it's not definite yet, of course, but it's bound to be." Perry sounded eager. "Whatever Wentworth may say to the contrary, I don't see Boney backing down. Do you? When I rode into town just now, I saw a great deal of activity in the Rue Royale." He gestured in the direction of the two houses that comprised the British headquarters. "Wellington's not satisfied with the preparations that have been made. Not at all satisfied. I hear he has written to Bathurst to complain."

"How do you know?" asked Augusta.

He threw her a scornful glance. "Common knowledge."

"Yet all His Grace seems to do is hold balls!" Sophronia seemed to feel that disproved her brother's words.

"Enjoys 'em," Perry asserted with all the authority of being on friendly terms with an officer who had served briefly in the Peninsula with the Iron Duke.

Sophie shivered and cast an uneasy glance toward the window. "Are we in danger?"

Perry snorted. "Not with the duke in charge. The Belgian troops are gathered at Nivelles to guard the Charleroi road, you know. You may be sure the French won't be able to approach *that* way."

"There are other roads from France," Augusta murmured.

"Oh, there are always rumors that Boney is on his way. But so far, there's nothing to 'em."

He fell silent, and Augusta made a shrewd guess that he racked his brain for something else to discuss. She had had enough of beating about the bush, and forestalled him before he could hit upon a new topic. "What did you *really* come to talk about, Perry?"

He looked up, met her gaze, and something that might almost have been a sheepish expression flickered across his face. "How did you know?"

"You forget. I have a brother. What is it?"

Perry drew a deep breath. "I received another blackmail note last night."

"Oh, Perry, no!" Sophronia regarded him in dismay.

"Where is it?" Augusta sat forward, alert.

"Here." He handed a crumpled piece of paper across to her. The words, printed in tiny blocked letters, left little to doubt. "Leave five hundred pounds between the cushions of the settee in the Lutridges' Blue Drawing Room by 9:30 tomorrow night."

Augusta frowned as she read the brief message through once more. "Whoever wrote this knows that you have been invited

228

to the Lutridges' musical soiree."

"That could make it almost anybody." Perry didn't seem overly daunted at the prospect. "I haven't made any secret about it."

She folded the sheet and absently tapped it with the tip of one delicate finger. "Yes, but your blackmailer must be one of the guests."

"That doesn't narrow it down much." He sounded skeptical, but Augusta thought she caught an almost eager note lurking beneath. "All the world goes to the Lutridges' parties."

"He's right." Sophronia sighed.

With the distinct suspicion she was being led neatly into a trap, Augusta pursued her line of reasoning. "If the money is to be left where anyone might stumble across it, whoever it is must intend to pick it up tonight, before it is discovered by accident or the Lutridges' servants turn out the room in the morning."

Perry grinned, his eyes gleaming with suppressed excitement. "That's what I thought, too. How'd you like to help with a little plan I concocted?"

Augusta regarded him with disfavor. A three-year acquaintance with him had not left her with an overly favorable opinion of his plans. "What did you have in mind?"

"Just watching, I swear it. I don't want to accost the fellow, just find out who he is. Once I know that, I can decide how to deal with him." He kept his tone light, but a grim note crept into his voice.

Augusta considered and a slow smile crossed her face. "I believe I would very much enjoy helping with this." And so would Major MacKennoch—though she didn't feel it necessary to mention that to Perry.

"Oh, Augusta, will you really?" Sophie raised wide, half-frightened eyes to her. "I think it is of all things the bravest! I should like to catch this—this villain!"

Perry's plan, much to Augusta's amazement, was simplicity itself. Perry would deposit the packet of money as instructed, then leave the vicinity of the Blue Drawing Room. Sophronia and Augusta would take turns standing guard, selecting positions where they could see the door into that room at all times. One of them would find out who entered to retrieve the package.

229

After begging them not to let him down, Perry took his leave. He had to report to his commanding officer for the afternoon, he said, but riding back to his billet would be no problem; he needed to change his dress before the evening anyway. He departed in a far more cheerful frame of mind than when he had come.

Shortly after nine o'clock that night, Sophronia, Mrs. Lansdon, and Augusta arrived at the Lutridges'. They greeted their hostess, then Augusta moved forward through the rooms, Sophronia at her side. Her usual court gathered about her, and for once she did not try to discourage them. If she appeared to be involved with her admirers, the blackmailer might not suspect that she really kept an eye on the Blue Drawing Room.

She and Sophie found it with little difficulty. The designated room stood near the front of the house, next door to a saloon laid out for cards. Only the Blue Drawing Room was not thrown open for the evening. Its door remained closed. Satisfied, they strolled down the hall, away from it, and returned to Mrs. Lansdon's side. Augusta could see the door from where she stood.

A few minutes later, Vincent Trent and Edward MacKennoch arrived together. They paused to exchange greetings with acquaintances, then moved on only to be stopped by someone else. They came steadily closer to where Augusta and Sophronia stood with Mrs. Lansdon. She would not be able to speak to the major, though, Augusta realized with dismay; too many people stood about them.

Trent and Major MacKennoch reached the outer rim of her court. The major stood half a head taller than the other man, she noted. He made a magnificent figure, so tall, so strong, with that easy assurance and quiet reserve of manner that filled her with confidence and longing. . . . She lost the thread of a tale told to her by an ardent young officer, and tried to pick it up once again. She smiled at him, more brilliantly than she had intended, but Edward MacKennoch filled her thoughts to the exclusion of all else.

A slight stir beside her caused her to turn, and to her surprise the major stood there, having neatly displaced the nearest of her court. She could not but be pleased by this piece of presumption, but she threw a challenging glance at him, only to encounter an expression of calm innocence. A smile lurked in his eyes as they rested on her, and her heart beat with disconcerting force.

"How delightful it is to see you." Mrs. Lansdon, who stood next to Sophronia, greeted Captain Trent warmly. "As you see, I do not stand upon formality with you any longer, for I consider you quite one of our little family here."

Trent smiled and sketched her a bow. "I am honored." He cast a teasing glance at Sophronia and the girl looked hurriedly away in pretty confusion.

A commotion occurred at the door and the guests parted to allow two footmen to wheel in a harp. They pushed it through to the connecting drawing room, where chairs were arranged in neat rows. Captain Trent offered one arm to Mrs. Lansdon and the other to Sophronia, and the major obligingly followed with Augusta as the guests trailed after the harp. They found seats near the back, and much to her pleasure, Augusta found herself sitting between Major MacKennoch and Mrs. Lansdon.

But no opportunity presented itself for private speech. And even worse, she realized, the other long chamber stretched between this one and the Blue Drawing Room so that she could not see the door. She frowned, wondering how to correct this problem.

A rather pretty young lady took her position at the pianoforte and her plainer sister seated herself at the harp. Augusta settled back, barely listening in spite of the fact she normally enjoyed such an evening very much. She made some quick calculations. It would be long after nine-thirty before the first interval would be called. She must make an excuse to escape, then figure out how to keep an unobtrusive watch on the Blue Drawing Room.

As soon as the sisters finished their performance, and the polite applause that filled the room faded, Augusta excused herself. Major MacKennoch rose to his feet, concern clouding his eyes.

"Are ye all right?" He bent over her, murmuring the words in her ear.

"I'm just feeling a trifle faint from the heat in here," she lied for Mrs. Lansdon's benefit.

"Let me help ye." He offered her his arm and led her through the other drawing room, away from the packed chamber.

Augusta paused in the hall, frowning at the door she had to watch. It didn't seem likely anyone would yet seek entrance there; it still lacked a few minutes before nine-thirty.

"In here, I believe."

Augusta looked up, startled, and found that the major guided her to a long, narrow saloon in which refreshments had been laid out. Two footmen were engaged in filling punch bowls, and Edward procured a glass from them, which he handed to her.

"Thank you." She took a sip, then drew him back out into the hall. She could see nothing from within there, either. The blackmailer had selected his room well. "Are you familiar with this house?" she asked softly.

"A little." His brow furrowed. "Why?"

Quickly, Augusta explained. "Perry doesn't know I'm telling you," she finished. She peeked up at his face, and her heart turned over at the warm approval in his eyes.

"Good girl," he said softly, his fingers tightening on hers. "Now, if we—" He broke off.

The door next to the card room opened a crack, and a sandy-brown head peeped out. Apparently reassured, Perry strolled into the hall, waved in a nonchalant manner to Augusta and the major, then wandered into the drawing room from which the sad strains of "Barbara Ellen" drifted.

"The money has been left," the major murmured.

"Now what?" she whispered back.

Absently, his hand caressed her arm, sending thrills through her that made it almost impossible to concentrate.

"Now we also return to the music—but we will be very polite, I believe, and stand near the door so as not to disturb anyone."

She let him escort her inside, pleased with the instant comprehension and capability of her chosen assistant. She did not really expect anyone to try to retrieve the money before the interval, when guests might be expected to be wandering about the house, so she did not feel any anxiety when they saw no one.

But the interval, she realized quickly, created new problems. People wandered freely from room to room, not restricting themselves to the hall, the card room, or the saloon in which the refreshments had been laid out. And they moved, constantly, rarely standing in one place for more than a minute or two unless they held cards in their hands. Reluctantly, Augusta turned over her post to Sophronia and drifted away so as not to be too obviously watching that one door.

The major, who talked with several officers, strolled casually back to her. "Does this not seem an odd manner in which to pass money to someone?" He kept his voice low, murmuring the words under the pretense of handing her another drink.

"It seems like an excellent one to me—or at least it would if people went in and out of there."

He nodded. "I think I will. In fact—" He broke off.

Vincent Trent, accompanied by Lord Roderick, emerged from the card room, opened the door into the Blue Drawing Room, and went in. Edward and Augusta exchanged surprised glances and hurried down the hall. Through the open door, they glimpsed Trent dragging a round occasional table into the center of the small chamber. Roddy pulled a blue upholstered chair up to one side, then set a branch of candles near by.

"No room next door?" The major lounged casually against the jamb.

Trent looked up and shook his head. "Too noisy. I prefer silence when I play piquet."

Augusta drew back, keeping out of sight. Could the blackmailer be one of them—or even both? But if not, no one else would make a try for the money as long as these two occupied the room. She moved away, leaving the major to converse with Trent and Roddy.

Jack Kettering stood on the other side of the hall, deep in conversation with another officer. At sight of her, he excused himself and hurried over, his expression so intense that Augusta almost turned and ran. He could hardly importune her here, though. She squared her shoulders, managed a smile that betrayed nothing more than friendship, and went to greet him.

He took her hand and raised her fingers to his lips. "You look concerned," he murmured.

"It is just all these rumors we keep hearing. It seems that every day someone thinks Napoleon has started forth. Have you heard anything new?"

Kettering shook his head. "There is nothing definite. But

233

still I cannot like you to be in Brussels. It would be best if you returned to England."

"Whatever for? Napoleon will never win through to Brussels!"

A lopsided smile just touched his lips. "I cannot bear the thought of you in danger. Forgive me, I know I speak out of turn, but it is my ardent desire for you to grant me the right to concern myself with your welfare."

She shook her head. "It is very kind of you to be worried, but there is no need."

"Let me take you away." He clasped her hand, but she withdrew it.

"You cannot leave here yourself," she pointed out.

"I could take you to a village nearby, somewhere that the French would never find you—but where I will have you near." His voice dropped to a hushed, passionate whisper. "I want only to be with you."

Augusta took a step backward, unnerved. "I—I would never do anything in such a clandestine manner. We are quite safe here."

She hurried away, disturbed by his words, by his whole manner. Suddenly, she wanted Edward MacKennoch. She made her way quickly back to the hall, but the major was nowhere to be seen. The extent of her disappointment surprised her. Fighting off a ridiculous surge of loneliness, she went in search of Mrs. Lansdon in the card room. For perhaps the first time in her life, she wished for chaperonage, for that lady's inconsequent but soothing chatter.

As soon as she entered, she spotted the major seated in a corner near a flickering fireplace, playing piquet with Perry. Edward's face, which she saw in profile, appeared a perfect mask, giving nothing away. Perry, she noted in dismay, once again wore that haunted, harried expression, as if everything was slipping beyond his control. Several scraps of paper lay on the table in front of Edward.

Lord Lutridge entered behind Augusta and announced that they would now resume in the music room. Most of the players rose, with the notable exception of Ashfield and his partner Lord Eversley, a fanatic card enthusiast. Perry started to rise but Edward stopped him with a word that Augusta couldn't catch. Perry subsided and returned his attention to the cards.

Mrs. Lansdon came to her feet and saw Augusta. "Ah, there you are, my dear. Shall we go back in?"

Through the door to the Blue Drawing Room, Augusta glimpsed Vincent Trent and Lord Roderick, still at play. Sophronia stood near the back of the next room where she could watch the chamber. Satisfied, Augusta accompanied Mrs. Lansdon and remained at that lady's side throughout the remainder of the performances.

Whenever Mrs. Lansdon applied to her for her opinion, she made appropriate comments on the musicians and singers. The rest of the time, her thoughts focused on what might be happening in the Blue Drawing Room. She applauded politely as an officer with a pleasing tenor finished "The Knight and the Shepherd's Daughter" and realized she hadn't heard a single note.

When at last the final performance ended, the guests made their way either to find refreshments or to seek amusement once more in the card room. Augusta stood in relief, assured herself that Mrs. Lansdon wanted nothing but a game of loo with her particular friends, and accompanied her to find them. Fortunately, Lady Eversley had already claimed a table for the ladies in the crowded card room.

In their corner, Major MacKennoch and Perry still played. Only now, Augusta noted in amazement, a very large pile of vowels rested on the table before Edward. Perry had been losing heavily—and she would not have expected a man of Edward's character to take such disgraceful advantage of a young man who had not yet attained his majority.

She started forward with the fixed intention of informing him of this. But too many guests blocked her way as they arranged their own tables, and she had to content herself with peering over their shoulders. As she watched, thus held at bay, the major swept the haphazard pile of vowels together and patted them into a semineat pile.

Perry rose unsteadily to his feet, muttering something unintelligible. Augusta stared at Edward MacKennoch, wondering what he had been about. And what would Perry do now to get up the money he would need to redeem those dreadful vowels? Augusta pushed past Lord Wentworth, murmured an apology, and headed for the table.

Edward stood, strolled over to the hearth, and consigned the stack to the flames. "Never play with a more accomplished fuzzer," he advised Perry in lowered tones. "The wolf becomes the sheep with amazing rapidity."

Perry made a strangled sound and turned abruptly away. He made his way into the hall as quickly as he could. Edward, his smiling gaze resting on his departing opponent, caught sight of Augusta staring at him in bewilderment. He raised a haughty eyebrow.

"What—" she began, and to her further amazement, a dull flush crept into his cheeks. Without saying a word, he offered her his arm and led her from the crowded room.

They retired to the refreshment table and armed themselves with glasses of punch. Resolutely, Augusta led him to a settee in a far corner and sat down. "Tell me!" she ordered.

He grinned unexpectedly, causing a transformation of his features that for a moment totally disrupted her thinking abilities. "Ye have caught me out, I see."

"But—did you really—?" The idea of the very proper Edward not playing fairly at cards dumbfounded her.

"To my lasting shame, I am adept at most forms of cheating."

She blinked. "You're . . ." Her voice trailed off.

"My elder brother is a somewhat enterprising gentleman, I fear. He took charge of my education in such matters." Rueful laughter glinted in eyes that had been solemn for too many years.

"But *why?*"

"I thought to test young Lansdon's abilities and found him extremely capable at his game—but not quite up to my brother's standards."

"Did—did your brother 'fuzz' cards regularly?" She regarded him in awe.

He nodded, but his grimace could not quite conceal his inner amusement. Augusta found the play of emotions on his normally expressionless countenance fascinating in the extreme.

"I fear he did. He brought my father about when he nearly lost the estate."

"And did you learn anything from this—or were you just keeping your hand in practice?"

"Ye will never let me live down my discreditable secret,

236

will ye?" he sighed. "Yes, I did learn something. Lansdon is good enough to have obtained his unexpected funds from the gaming table instead of from the sale of military secrets."

Augusta let out a deep breath. "You—you mean he may be—" She broke off, aghast to realize that, in spite of her loyalty to the Lansdon family, part of her had still suspected him. Her relief found expression in a brilliant smile.

The laughter vanished from Edward's eyes. He still gazed down at her, but now he seemed to search for something that eluded him in her face. Abruptly, he rose. "Shall we mingle with the others? I believe ye intended to watch a certain chamber this night."

"Sophronia is on duty. But we will go if you wish." She preceded him from the room, only to stop short just through the doorway. Perry and Roddy stood in the hall, whispering urgently to one another. Perry nodded and they separated almost at once, heading in different directions.

Roddy, who came toward them, looked up and for one moment appeared on the verge of panic when he saw them. With a visible effort, he gathered himself together, gave them an almost cheery wave, and ducked into the card room.

"What if this whole blackmail payment was nothing but a setup?" Augusta asked softly, not bothering to turn around, too confused to consider her words.

"Do ye think Lansdon and Lord Roderick might be in this together?" Edward's voice sounded just behind her. "The murder of Montclyff, perhaps?"

His warm breath stirred the soft hairs behind her right ear, and she couldn't be certain whether it was that or his words that made it difficult for her to breathe. "It—it's impossible," she managed to say.

"Is it? Montclyff might well have caught them in a fleecing scheme and threatened to expose them."

Augusta spun about to face him, her heart sinking. That would be a real motive. . . .

"It would." A grim note sounded in his voice as he agreed with her.

She realized she had spoken aloud. "And the blackmail money?" She didn't want to hear his answer, but it came anyway.

"Possibly nothing more than a ruse to obtain funds from his

sister to cover his gaming debts."

She shook her head, rejecting that idea. "If he cheats to win—"

Edward held up a hand, stopping her. "He has to lose occasionally. And sometimes it is almost impossible to fuzz the cards without being caught."

"What should we do?" Even to herself, her voice sounded hollow.

"I want ye to stop playing investigator, right now. No, don't argue with me. There are too many peculiar circumstances, too many possible suspects. I can't guarantee to keep ye safe if ye continue to involve yourself. And Halliford would personally murder me if anything happened to ye."

She flushed. "I am not a child. There is no need to protect me."

"Not a child," he agreed. A lopsided smile touched his lips. "A delicate China doll. I would never forgive myself if ye were broken." He left her without another word.

But she wasn't a China doll either, she longed to shout after him. She was a person—a woman. The longing that stirred deep within her left her shaken.

She turned away, wanting solitude. No, if she were honest, she wanted Edward's arms about her. The sensations this thought created brought warm color to her cheeks and an unfamiliar tingling sensation coursed through her body. Confused, she started toward the Blue Drawing Room, where she had a chance of semisolitude.

Ahead of her, Sophronia came out of the card room, from which vantage point she had been keeping watch. Augusta quickened her pace, but was not in time to catch her friend. The girl ducked into the Blue Drawing Room. Augusta followed, wondering if something had occurred in there. Had the card players gone? Or the blackmail money . . .

She almost ran the last few yards. But in the doorway she stopped short and drew back, concealing herself from view. The room was not empty. Sophronia rushed forward and threw herself straight into Vincent Trent's arms, raising her face for his kiss.

Chapter 19

Augusta leaned against the wall, shocked. How long had that been going on? But Sophronia could not be involved in any illicit game of Trent's contriving—she would never be party to setting up her brother for a murder charge. No, Augusta would swear the girl was being used. A cold, sinking sensation settled in her stomach. What lies had Trent told her to protect himself?

"I know what you're involved in." From outside the mostly closed door, Augusta could hear Sophronia's muffled words.

"It won't be for much longer." Trent's soothing voice reassured her. "Soon everything will be all right and we won't have anything to worry about any longer."

Sophronia's low tones answered, but Augusta couldn't make out her words. It *could* mean that he would solve the mysteries. But it could also mean his nefarious business was almost completed.

Augusta walked away, knowing this meeting must, of necessity, be short and not wanting to be there when they came out. Sophronia obviously believed that Vincent Trent loved her as desperately as she loved him. Augusta suspected the opposite, and wished very much that she did not.

She did not again encounter Sophronia until the guests began to depart. In the intervening time, she would swear that almost every person present entered the Blue Drawing Room at least once. She might have known that no plan of Perry's would work.

While they awaited their carriage, she saw Major MacKennoch slip into that chamber one last time. He came out, caught her eye, and gave a slight shake of his head.

She joined him. "What do you mean? Is it still there?"

He matched her hushed tones. "No. I mean the money is no longer between the seat cushions where Lansdon placed it."

"But who took it?" Or had Perry really put it there as he claimed? She didn't dare voice that thought, but it haunted her throughout the night.

Another problem also disturbed her. She would have given a great deal to know how deep the involvement went between Vincent Trent and Sophronia. But Sophronia, for a change, did not seem prone to confidences.

She was able to observe the two together again the next evening, when Trent arrived for their scheduled rehearsal. When the butler announced him, Sophronia flushed delicately and turned away, busying herself with leafing through one of the two copies of the script. Trent, Augusta noted in unpleasant suspicion, betrayed no such sign of lovesickness.

Jack Kettering, whose copy of the play Sophronia unceremoniously appropriated, objected, though teasingly. "You had all morning to study your lines. It's my turn!"

"It will take her longer than that," Perry put in, in true brotherly fashion.

Lord Roderick, standing at the window, stared out toward the park across the broad street. "Are we going to argue this evening or rehearse the scenes?"

Lord Wentworth turned a disapproving eye on him. "Starting with this one, we are not going to need to spend as much time about our plays." He glanced at Augusta. "We are going to settle a few things here and now, so there will be fewer changes at the last minute."

"Hallelujah!" Frederick Ashfield, lounging on the sofa beside Lizzie, flashed his blinding smile.

Lord Wentworth directed a chilly glare at him. "You are not even taking a role this time."

"I'm your self-appointed critic. Along with my assistant here." He acknowledged Lizzie.

"Yes, if there's one thing Lizzie can do, it's criticize," Augusta agreed at once.

"To the play." Wentworth regarded them with a ferocity belied by the twinkle in his eyes.

"You can begin by changing the setting." Captain Trent

240

folded his arms. "Under the circumstances, with rumors of Napoleon's approach running rampant, I don't think having a play about the Peninsular campaign is a good idea."

"Wellington won." Lord Roderick looked back into the room. "Let's leave it as it is."

Augusta shivered. "Since it must be about war, can we not place it in a time far removed from the present? No one wants to think about Napoleon right now."

"I quite agree," Lord Wentworth nodded. "Shall we make it one of medieval history? Miss Carstairs, Miss Lansdon, you would both look delightful in peaked caps."

Augusta shook her head. "It relies heavily on Spain, does it not? Perhaps we should make it Elizabethan with the Spanish Armada."

"Not earlier?" Kettering regarded her with humorous eyes. "I, for one, have always wanted to play Robin Hood."

Perry shrugged. "You may have any setting you please, as long as you alter my character so he's not so bacon-brained."

Lord Wentworth promised, then ordered Trent, Lord Roderick, and Sophronia to read through a scene. Augusta sat back beside Ashfield and Lizzie, lost in thought. Could setting be the clue instead of the lines? With all her heart, she wished Edward MacKennoch might be there. Any one of the players could be the guilty party!

She glanced up and caught Captain Trent watching her through narrowed eyes. She shivered and looked away. Had Sophronia revealed to him her suspicions? With a pang of regret, she knew she could no longer trust her dear friend. Love created blindness and new, sometimes treacherous, loyalties.

They had just begun reading through Augusta's main scene when Edward MacKennoch entered the saloon where they gathered. He caught her eye, smiled, and her heart soared. He took a seat toward the back of the room.

Lord Wentworth nodded to him. "You're welcome to watch, just don't disrupt things," he said tersely. "Miss Carstairs? I am waiting."

Thus rebuked, she returned her attention to her speech. Just knowing he was there made her feel better. She must tell him of the strength of the connection between Trent and Sophronia.

On Wentworth's insistence, they read through the entire

241

play from beginning to end. As they neared the final scene, Mrs. Lansdon entered. She seated herself on the sofa beside the major, smiled her welcome, and settled back to watch.

"You will all stay to tea, will you not?" She directed her inquiry to Lord Wentworth as soon as he called a halt.

"We will be honored." He picked up both copies of the play and set them neatly on a side table.

Mrs. Lansdon rang the bell, and almost immediately the butler wheeled in the tea cart. He placed it before his mistress, and she began to pour out. "Sugar, my lord?"

Major MacKennoch rose. "Miss Carstairs, might I have a word with ye? Pray excuse us, Mrs. Lansdon. There are a few questions I must ask her concerning my investigation."

"Of course. Augusta, my love, you may take the major to the Rose Study."

"Certainly, ma'am." Augusta excused herself to the others and joined the major where he waited at the door for her.

He held it open. "The Rose Study?" he murmured as they went out into the hall.

She smiled. "That's the euphemistic name we have given that little room where we spoke before—on the night of the play. Do you remember it?"

Walking ahead of him, she led the way to the table at the foot of the stairs, where an oil lamp burned low. She lit one of the candles waiting there, and carried it to the back room. This now bore a less deserted appearance, for the chairs and settees, which had been used for the audience, had been returned. It made an inviting little study.

As soon as the major closed the door, she turned to face him. "You are looking uncommonly grave. Has something happened?"

"I want ye to cry off from the play."

"Why?" Her brow clouded.

He smiled slightly. "Can ye never simply do as ye are asked?"

She considered, then shook her head. "I'm sorry, but there it is. I need reasons. Why?"

"Because, my dear Miss Carstairs, ye are under official investigation in the sale of military secrets."

She gasped. "But—"

He took the hands she unconsciously extended toward him. "Because the plays were your idea. Ye have been the driving

242

force behind them. By rights, I should not have told ye." He sounded rueful, but not repentant.

Her hands clasped his warmly. "Thank you for telling me. Oh, how I wish I had never begun them!"

"Do ye understand why ye must withdraw from them?"

She shook her head. "How can I? I *do* understand why I should—but I cannot. Would it not look suspicious to our villain—whoever he may be—if I suddenly stopped?"

The pressure of his hands increased. "Even though I have told him it is nonsense, I fear Captain Trent is more than half convinced of your guilt. His theory is that ye ordered young Lansdon to murder Montclyff because he discovered the true purpose behind your plays."

Augusta opened her mouth, but words failed her. At last, she managed, "And *I* think *he* murdered Monty because Monty discovered what *he* was up to."

"Do ye?"

She raised her indignant gaze to his face, and the urgency of their discussion faded from her mind. How could anyone's eyes be so very blue? And how could she have ever thought them expressionless? They contained vast amounts of warmth, concern, and humor.

Before she could sink into their mesmerizing depths, she looked away, focusing instead on the scar that sliced across his cheek. Hesitant, uncertain, she drew a hand free and raised a finger to that reddened line. He stiffened, then stood rigidly as she traced the clean saber slice. Her breath came more quickly, as did his. It fanned her cheek, gentle, tantalizing, filling her with sensations she could not identify.

She made no effort to try. All that mattered was that they stand there indefinitely, united by that strange magic that shimmered between them. He held her spellbound, himself enraptured as well, neither wanting to break free. Slowly, she raised her face for the kiss for which she longed. He moved closer, as if drawn by a force he had no desire to resist. His breath brushed her lips as his mouth hovered less than an inch from hers.

Abruptly, he stepped back. "I—" He broke off, swallowed, and with an effort pulled his calm mask back into position. Only his clouded eyes betrayed the emotions that raged within, hidden from the rest of the world. "I'd better return to the others. There are a few questions I need to ask Trent." He looked down at her hand, which he still clasped tightly in his, and raised her fingers tentatively to his lips.

Disappointed, Augusta drew a shaky breath, and realized it was the first she had taken in a very long while. "Edward?"

He hesitated. "Yes?"

"Will you not wear your kilt for me?"

His tension broke and he smiled. "I am no longer with my regiment. Good night—Augusta." He left the room.

A slight smile parted her lips as she stared at the closed door. It was now their joke, something they shared that the rest of the world would not understand. And he had come to enjoy it, too. She hugged it to her, silly perhaps, but a source of secret happiness.

A contented sigh escaped her. She had no desire to face the others—not at the moment, not with Edward's lingering presence wrapping about her like a caressing shawl. And they would probably never miss her. She relit her candle, extinguished the branch on the table and left the room.

No one was in the hall, so she crossed quickly and hurried up the stairs. At the second landing, she heard a muffled noise coming from down the corridor. She hesitated, a smothered exclamation reached her, and without a second thought she strode resolutely in that direction. The only room in use along there was the one Perry occupied on his infrequent stays at the house.

Another muffled cry emitted from within and she rapped firmly on the door. Only scuffling sounds answered her and she thrust the door wide, but drew up short. Perry, his face livid, struggled with an equally enraged Roderick. Each clutched one of the ruby-mounted pistols, which they waved about with complete disregard for safety. Roderick cried out, Perry lunged, and his elbow landed firmly in Roddy's midriff.

Roddy's gun went off with a resounding explosion. The bullet whizzed past Perry's ear, missing him by a bare inch, and embedded itself in the wall. Acrid smoke filled the room. Augusta gasped, saw the other gun wavering in Perry's suddenly slackened hold, and she dove in after it. Perry jerked back, his hand clenched, and his gun fired. The bullet shot over Augusta's shoulder, shattered a vase, and buried itself in the door jamb. Augusta fell back, trembling from reaction, and stared in shock at Perry's horror-filled countenance.

"A falling-out among thieves?" Vincent Trent stood in the doorway, inches away from the bullethole, surveying the signs of the recent struggle and the three people in the room. Augusta tried to steady herself, but failed miserably.

Booted footsteps pounded unevenly down the hall and the next moment Trent was thrust aside as Edward burst into the room, Kettering at his heels. The briefest glance took in the tumbled chair, the smoking pistols in each of the young officers' hands, and Augusta's shattered expression.

"Take everyone downstairs," the major ordered Kettering. "It's naught but horseplay."

He waited until the lieutenant had left the room to face the others who crowded in the hall, then closed the door on them. He turned back to the two shame-faced combatants.

"Just what the devil do ye mean by this nonsense? Have ye no more sense than to engage in this sort of ramshackle behavior in your own mother's household?" In his best major's voice, Edward proceeded to ring a peal over their heads. He continued for a good five minutes without stopping or repeating himself. Augusta barely took it in, but from the chastened miens of the two young gentlemen, it would seem to be to good effect.

Lord Roderick, standing stiffly at attention, cast a furious look at Perry, whose posture mimicked his. "He stole my pistols, sir."

Perry shot back an equally angry glare. "That's no reason to fire at me."

"I didn't! I—"

"Enough!" Major MacKennoch silenced them. "What in blazes do ye mean by having those things loaded?"

Roddy shuffled his feet. "We—we meant to experiment—but not in here."

"Ye will report to your commanding officer in the morning and give him the full details of this disgraceful affair." He held their gazes for a long moment, then nodded. "You're dismissed."

Perry, his features rigid, turned on his heel and marched out of the room. Roderick, ashen, gathered up the pistols, replaced them in the cherry wood case, and left without looking at anyone.

Augusta regarded Edward in a combination of wonder and respect. "Will they really report to their commander in the morning?"

"They will." The grim note remained in Edward's voice. He turned to her. "What are ye doing here?"

"I heard the fight. I—I walked in just as Roddy's gun went off. It was an accident, you know. They were struggling the way boys do, but holding the pistols the whole time. They shouldn't have been loaded!" she added with feeling.

"Nay, that they shouldn't." His expression relaxed.

"Do you know," Trent said, straightening up from where he had been leaning against the door jamb, "I don't think I would have cared to be one of your lieutenants."

Edward smiled suddenly. "That ye might not have."

"Do you believe me now?" Trent held his gaze.

The major regarded him with that impenetrable expression and returned no answer.

Trent shrugged. "If you will excuse me? I shall go downstairs and assure Mrs. Lansdon and Miss Lansdon that no lasting harm has been done." He withdrew and shut the door behind himself.

Edward turned his thoughtful regard on Augusta. "I should like another word with ye, Miss Carstairs."

"Yes?" She tried to keep it light.

The marshal light rekindled in his eyes. "What the devil do ye mean by walking in on a fight?"

She tried to smile, but it was a feeble attempt. "They were only arguing—and struggling just a little. They both have shocking tempers, but there would never be any serious fight between them. Neither intended in the least to fire."

"In the future, ye will not do anything so foolhardy."

She ignored him. Certain aspects of the last few minutes began to dawn on her as she calmed down. "How did Captain Trent get up here so much before you? I thought you had gone to talk with him."

"I had, but he wasn't there."

She shivered and folded her arms, hugging herself as if to ward off a chill breeze. "I don't like any of this. I—" She broke off.

"Ye what?"

She turned away, not meeting his piercing eye. "I just

246

wonder how much truth there is to Perry's blackmail story, that is all."

"So do I."

"And what of Captain Trent?" She tried to direct his suspicions in another direction, but it didn't seem to work. She could get nothing more out of Edward. At last she bid him a somewhat stilted good night and made her way to her own room.

The more she thought about it as she stared unseeing into her mirror, the guiltier Perry seemed. Everything involving him that happened since Montclyff's murder could well be no more than a smoke screen, designed to confuse. If that were so, he had succeeded very well.

Abandoning this fruitless line of thought for the night, she rang for her maid, then began getting ready for bed. When her abigail left her, she did not climb between sheets, but instead sank into a chair by her window. Blindly, she gazed out into the dark starlit night.

She must have fallen asleep, for shortly before dawn, odd noises awakened her. She stretched, stiff, and looked out. Pale moonlight flooded the park across the street. The noises still reached her, but she could see no one.

She rose, crossed to her other tiny window in the corner, and looked down. It took her a moment, for deep shadows engulfed the side of the house, but a dim form took shape before her peering eyes. Someone was in the little garden beside the house, digging by the meager light of the moon.

Augusta made a quick calculation as to which room on the ground floor would look out on that particular spot, then rekindled her candle from the low-burning oil lamp beside her bed and hurried downstairs. The dining room, not surprisingly, stood empty. She crossed to the curtained windows, extinguished her candle, then pulled back a corner of the heavy drapes.

Perry, clear even in the meager light, stamped on the ground with his booted foot, dusted off his hands, and walked off around the house, carrying a shovel. Augusta stared at the trampled ground in bewilderment. In a minute Perry reappeared, stamped on the spot once more for good measure, then let himself out by the side gate.

Augusta did not waste a second. As soon as she was sure he

was out of sight, she ran lightly down the hall. Ignoring her bare feet and the chill of the predawn air, she slipped out the back door to the shallow yard. A small tool shed stood on the far side of the vegetable garden, and she made her way to it, walking with care. Just inside she found the shovel.

She located Perry's digging place with ease, for the disturbed earth gave him clearly away. Half terrified of what she might find, she went to work with the shovel. By the time she had gone almost a foot down, her nerves neared the breaking point. But one more spade full produced results. A dull thud reached her as she struck something solid.

She let out a ragged breath in relief, and her fanciful fear that a body might have been hidden there evaporated. Something hard she could deal with. She cleared off a little more dirt, then set the shovel aside and went to work with her hands. Smooth wood met her questing fingers, and a few minutes later she drew the cherry wood pistol case from its grave.

Somehow, she should have guessed. Of all things she could have found buried in a mysterious manner, these pistols should have leapt to her mind as the likeliest candidates. She held the case for a long mement, considering, then came to a decision. It would be safer inside. Ever neat, she refilled the hole, then returned the shovel to the shed. With the pistol case firmly in her hands, she let herself back into the house and bolted the door.

She relit her candle once more and hurried up to her room. With trembling hands, she set the case down on her dressing table. Her fingers were caked with damp earth, she realized. She washed off the dirt in the water remaining in her basin, then returned to the cherry wood box. Steeling her nerve, she opened the lid.

The pistols lay inside, undamaged. Frowning, she touched them, wondering what had caused Perry's peculiar actions. They appeared perfectly normal. She lifted them out, testing their weight, but gained little information from that. They were both the same, but whether loaded or unloaded she couldn't tell.

Perplexed, she replaced them and ran a finger along the deep crimson stains of the red velvet lining. It felt damp. She drew her hand back and studied it by the flickering candlelight.

Fresh blood. *Again*.

Chapter 20

Augusta stared at her reddened finger in revulsion. Fresh blood, her bemused mind repeated. *Whose?* And how had it gotten there? Her heart plummeted and for one terrible moment she felt squeamishly ill.

She leaned back in her chair, weak with reaction. What had Perry done? This was no simple case of hiding the pistols with the intention of returning for them later. He had *buried* them— probably hoping they would never be found. *What had he done?*

But then logic took over, fortunately for her nerves. If he wanted the pistols to disappear completely, it would have been far more reasonable to take them deep into the woods, find a secluded grove, and dispose of them. He was billeted several miles from Brussels! There should have been any number of likely locations between there and his mother's house. He could even have thrown the horrid things into the sheet of water in the park where the swans swam. His burying them here could only mean he intended to return for them— eventually—but wanted them unreachable until then.

She stared at the loathsome guns, shaking her head, and knew it to be a singularly futile action. What was this all about? "Why can't you tell me?" she demanded of them, but they remained unhelpfully silent.

The first thing to be done, she decided, would be to hide the pistols. Then as soon as it was light, before the servants were astir, she would return to the garden to make certain she had covered the traces of her digging. It would never do to have Perry know the guns were no longer there.

After subjecting her room to a thorough scrutiny, she

located a hiding place that was not likely to be discovered accidentally by a maid. As quietly as she could, she placed a chair beside her bed and climbed up on it. If she stood on her tiptoes, she could just reach the upper rim of the frame from which her bed curtains hung.

The amount of dust she encountered assured her that no housemaid would invade this stronghold. Satisfied, Augusta thrust the case back as far as she could, then twitched the hanging ruffle back into place. She scrambled down, replaced the chair, then surveyed her handiwork. At least by the dim light of the growing dawn, the hiding place could not be detected.

A quick survey of the side herb garden from the dining room window proved equally satisfactory. Perry had selected a place mostly covered by bushy sage. The freshly turned earth appeared to be no more than cultivation. With luck, it would pass unnoticed.

Now, that only left her with the problem of *why* Perry had buried them in the first place. Definitely, Edward would want to know of this turn of events.

But she did not see him that day, and the waiting did nothing to soothe her agitation. He might, of course, turn up at their rehearsal that evening, though she couldn't be certain. Firmly, she resisted the temptation to check that the pistols remained safely in her room and instead applied herself to drilling Sophronia on her lines.

The members of their troupe were not scheduled to arrive until eight o'clock, but nearly a half hour before then, Augusta positioned herself on a sofa where she could see each person as he entered the saloon door. They began to wander in shortly after the hour, and as each one greeted her, carefree and uninjured, her shattered nerves began to mend. In the back of her mind, she had honestly believed that Perry had shot—perhaps killed—one of them. His blackmailer, perhaps—if such a person existed. She could only hope this proved the innocence of her friends—and of Perry.

That young gentleman, to her utter amazement, strolled in with Roddy, the two once more obviously on their usual good terms. And neither, Augusta noted in growing astonishment, seemed any more on edge than usual. Perry's step, in fact, seemed almost jaunty, and he waved a casual hello to her.

Roddy did the same. Neither showed the least constraint, considering that their last encounter in this house had involved pistols going off.

Augusta shook her head, bewildered. Burying pistols in the predawn hours might almost have been the norm for Perry. Was it only she who found such an activity to be unusual?

Edward arrived in company with Captain Trent, and her relief at seeing the major left her shattered once more. At last, after the others left, she could tell him of this latest turn of events. She could hardly wait to be free of the pistols.

He met her strained gaze and his brow furrowed in concern. He went to her at once and sat down at her side. "Has something occurred?" he asked softly.

"It has. But apparently it is nothing desperate. I shall tell you later."

"Or now. I do not like to see ye so worried." He rose and offered her his arm. She hesitated a moment, then allowed him to lead her into the next drawing room. He waited until she took a seat. "Now," he began in a low voice. "Tell me what is troubling ye."

"Wait here." She hurried up to her bedchamber and, with a bit of balancing, retrieved the pistol case. She returned to the room where Edward waited and handed it over to him.

"Where did ye get this?" His voice sounded sharp despite his lowered tone. She told him of her nocturnal adventure, and he swore softly under his breath. He opened the case, cast only the most cursory glance at the pistols, and shut it again.

"The bloodstain is fresh! It was quite wet still this morning," she protested.

He opened the box once more, but did not test. "Does it appear so?" He didn't sound overly interested. "It must merely have been dampened. Lansdon probably tried to wash out the old stains once more. Don't be concerned over it."

She stared at him in mingled dismay and relief. "Do you mean I've been that worried over *nothing*?"

He chuckled softly, and Augusta decided any amount of worry would have been worth it to hear that sound from him.

"My poor—Miss Carstairs." He caught himself. "Did ye have your bloodthirsty heart set on another murder?"

She shook her head, but his teasing words brought a smile to her lips. "I was so *afraid!* I thought Perry might have

251

discovered his blackmailer and shot him."

Edward's lips maintained their smile, though his eyes took on a frown. "Ye have nothing to worry about," he repeated. His voice took on an almost grim edge. "I am keeping a watch on that young gentleman."

"You weren't last night," she pointed out.

His lips twitched in self-derision. "I was—somewhat otherwise occupied. But he will not get into serious trouble, that I promise ye."

"I am glad." She eyed him with suspicion. "*Why* are you watching him?"

Edward studied the case and brushed traces of clinging dirt from the hasps and locks. "Either he is responsible for a great deal of what is happening, or someone wants to make him appear that way. Having him watched may prove his innocence."

Or his guilt, but Augusta followed his lead and did not mention that possibility. She, also, gazed at the cherry wood case. "What should I do with those?"

"Leave them with me for the moment. And ye had better join the rehearsal," he added as Lord Wentworth's raised voice reached them, ordering the scene on which they would begin work.

Augusta nodded, though she wished he would say more. At least those dreadful pistols would no longer be in her room.

The rehearsal proceeded with fewer problems than usual, and they ended early. Sophronia, loath to end the evening, suggested they celebrate by indulging in a hand of cards.

Lizzie loudly endorsed the idea, for she normally was excluded from such "grown-up" events as card parties. She had developed a penchant for piquet, thanks to Mr. Ashfield's company Augusta was sure. Without waiting to secure her sister's permission, Lizzie rang for the tables to be set up and calmly took her place at one.

Somehow, though Augusta tried to avoid it, she found herself seated with Jack Kettering at a table slightly apart from the others. Her mind must have been wandering, she thought in disgust, to have permitted this to happen. And she knew just where her errant thoughts had been.

She glanced over to where Edward sat at a whist table with Sophronia, Captain Trent, and Lord Wentworth. Perry and

Roddy played against each other, as did Lizzie and Ashfield. Mrs. Lansdon, engaged in knotting a fringe on a shawl in a comfortable armchair in the corner, beamed approval on them all.

Edward looked up, caught her watching him, and smiled at her. His expression seemed somewhat strained, though, she thought. And he had been unusually subdued during the rehearsal, even more so than could be accounted for by his habitual reserve. An almost irrisistible urge assailed her to kiss away the tiny lines that marked his forehead.

"Your attention is far from me tonight." Lieutenant Kettering leaned across toward her, his tone one of mild complaint.

She glanced back. "Of course not. I am just somewhat tired. I never realized how much work we have been putting in on these plays."

"Is that all?" Kettering regarded her closely. "You look preoccupied."

"I was just wondering if I will ever be able to retire to my chamber before one o'clock in the morning." At least that had the ring of honesty about it. But her answer did not appear to please him.

"You have been avoiding me."

"No. Please, Jack, let us not argue tonight."

"Arguing is the last thing I have on my mind." He reached across the table, covering her hand with his. "I want you to marry me."

His words were so soft, no one else could possibly hear, yet her cheeks burned as if he had shouted. "No, please, Jack—"

"Listen to me! My marriage is all it would take for my aunt to triple my allowance. She is bound to love you as I do myself."

Augusta drew an unsteady breath. "It will not do. Pray, say no more."

"You are trifling with me." He kept his voice low with an effort. His eyes burned; a stray lock of black hair hung over his forehead, giving him an almost wild look.

"I—I find I do not think of marriage. I am deeply aware of the honor you do me in offering, Jack, but—"

His grip on her hand tightened, cutting off her formal words of refusal. "Do not say it! You loved me once, I would swear you did. I will win you back." His fiery eyes held hers for a

253

moment longer, then he released her, leaned back, and picked up his cards.

With hands that trembled, she sorted through her own cards, called her point, and tried to force the unpleasant incident from her mind. She wished he hadn't pressed her, that she had never encouraged him, that things had never reached such a pass between them. But wishful thinking never did any good.

They played three more games, and to her relief Lieutenant Kettering behaved with propriety. Still, it was with profound relief that she saw Captain Trent rise from his game. She stood at once, eager to escape Kettering's brooding stares, and offered the captain her place. He took it, and Augusta looked quickly about for Edward.

She hadn't seen him for some time, she realized, surprised. Nor was he in the room now. Her spirits sank. He must have succumbed to the weariness that had afflicted him earlier and gone home. She wished he could have at least said good night.

If he was not present, she could find little inducement to remain either. Whispering her apologies to Mrs. Lansdon, and blaming the headache, she slipped out of the room. The last was true, at least. Her head had begun to throb abominably. An early night would do her a world of good.

She made her way upstairs and entered her room, only to stop dead just over the threshold. Edward stood by her dressing table, bare from the waist up, the golden blond hair scattered across his firm stomach glistening damply. Augusta caught her breath, her heart pounding erratically. She had encountered her brother Adrian in this state of disarray, of course, but this—Edward—was different.

She swallowed and averted her eyes from him with difficulty. Her unsettled gaze found his coat and shirt, which he had cast across the bed, but that only served to remind her of the broad, bare shoulders, the muscles clearly delineated even beneath the curling hair. . . . She started to back out of the room, but he stopped her.

"I could use your help." His voice sounded stiff, as if he detested the idea of asking anyone for assistance.

The pain she saw in his face drove all other thoughts from her mind. "Edward!"

This time, a more comprehensive glance took in something

besides his chest, which still wreaked havoc within her; this time she saw the jagged gouge that tore across his lower ribs and the basin of reddish water cradled in the stand. Instinctively, she shut the door and locked it behind her.

"What happened?" She went to him, fought down the chaotic sensations that filled her at sight of him like this, and concentrated on the wound that seeped blood onto the cloth he held.

"I find I cannot bandage this alone."

She nodded and forced herself to regard his injury with a detached efficiency. "Where did you get the strips of lint?" He had even located basilicum powder.

"Brought it with me." His words sounded clipped. "I was afraid this would happen. Sorry to use your room."

"You obviously had to change that bandage somewhere. No, here, let me take those." While she tied two of the lint strips together, he made a pad from a third and held it in place.

"Pull them tight," he ordered, and gritted his teeth as she complied. When she finished, he drew a shaky breath. "Thank you." He picked up the handful of blood-soaked cloths.

The old pad, she realized. "What happened?" she demanded for a second time.

Edward finished his methodical collection of every trace of his presence in her room. At last, only the bloodied water remained. He opened her small corner window, then threw it outside to the herb garden below. He turned back to her and managed a shaky grin. "You'll have to help me into my shirt."

"Not until you tell me what happened."

He had the grace to look sheepish, an unexpectedly endearing expression which tugged at her heart. "I was watching young Lansdon last night."

Augusta's eyes widened in horror, but he held up a hand, stopping her outcry. "I had the dubious honor of seeing him leave Lord Roderick's quarters, carrying those pistols." His expression grew grimmer.

"I—I assume he did not mean to go gaming?" Her voice sounded tight even to herself.

"No." Edward shook his head. "He did attend a card party, though. At least, he waited outside a certain billet near Brussels until Captain Trent came out. Then, I fear, we got into a little scuffle when he took aim. But I really couldn't let him shoot Trent."

"Shoot . . ." Augusta sank onto the edge of the bed, ill with shock. "Do you mean—"

Edward grasped her hand in a sustaining clasp. "He assured me he didn't mean to do more than scare him, but knowing Lansdon's reputation as a terrible shot, it seemed more than likely he would have accidentally hit Trent. And then there would have been the devil to pay, and nothing I could do for him. Fortunately, no one heard that blasted pistol go off—at least, no one came to investigate. I didn't want to alarm ye, as I obviously have now, which is why I lied before."

"The fresh blood in the case—"

"Mine. I bled like a stuck pig," he said bluntly.

"But in the case?" She asked the question that had been troubling her.

He grinned, albeit a trifle crookedly. "Lansdon was rather upset. I didn't realize at first how deep the graze was, and I'm afraid I cleaned the pistols and put them away before I realized I was adding to the stain."

"And—and what was Perry doing?" Augusta demanded.

"Mostly moaning. He thought I was going to turn him in for attempted murder. It took me the better part of half an hour to get him to listen to reason. He swore he'd return the pistols, and by that time I was feeling the wound a bit, so I let him go."

"Of all the infamous, *stupid*—!" She broke off, satisfying herself with glaring in indignation at Edward. "He should have seen you to a doctor after what he did! Oh, I wish you had just let him shoot Captain Trent instead!"

That brought an unsteady laugh from him, which set his broad shoulders shaking. Augusta hastily averted her eyes, located his shirt, and smoothed it out.

"Trent would not have been as forgiving," Edward said as she helped him ease his arms into the fine muslin sleeves.

"Why did he take Roddy's pistols?" she asked suddenly. "Surely he has his own."

"He said he was going to fire over Trent's head, then leave the gun for him to find—and wonder about."

"Of all the foolish starts! Can you arrange for Perry to get a hefty dose of discipline?" Unable to resist temptation, she allowed the tip of one finger to just trace the line of his shoulder blade as she eased the shirt up toward his neck. She

256

turned away while he fastened it and tucked it into his breeches.

"Ye may turn around now." Gentle amusement sounded in his voice.

She did so, to find him holding his rumpled cravat. "It's not going to be easy retying that."

"Ye forget. I'm an old campaigner." Deftly, he wrapped the cloth about his neck and refolded the creases until he achieved an admirable imitation of his earlier style. "Now the coat, if ye please?"

She eased it over his arms. Even though it fit to perfection, it was cut loose enough so that she had little trouble. She smoothed the cloth across his back, loving the feel of the superfine, and of the firm muscle beneath her palm.

He turned around and took her trembling hands between his own. "Thank ye, my dear. Ye have saved me from a great deal of awkwardness."

She stared at their joined hands, too nervous to look into his face as she longed to. "Why are you being so kind to Perry? He deserves more than the rake-down you gave him."

"Most assuredly." She could hear the smile in his voice. "But that would hardly win his confidence, and at the moment, preventing any more secrets from being passed to the French is of far more importance than disciplining a hey-go-mad colt unbroken to bridle."

She looked up at that, and warm color flooded her cheeks at the gentle expression she encountered in his eyes.

"Is—is that all you think him?"

"It's possible. A few years of hard campaigning may be the making of him, unless he gets himself into more serious trouble before he has the chance."

"He may get it all too soon, if the rumors are true."

His grip on her hands tightened. "There well may be fighting," he agreed.

She nodded, unable to look away from his clear, compassionate eyes. Here was a man who had known the horrors of war, and had been both strengthened and gentled by them. Her heart turned over with the recognition of love, pure and unreserved, that flooded through her. She didn't worship him as a hero; she knew his faults and idiosyncrasies, and they were all part of this wonderful, capable man. She wouldn't have him

257

any different.

Except . . . "When will you wear your kilt for me?"

A slow, sad smile touched his lips. "I am no longer with my regiment."

He released her hands with a caress. "We had better go downstairs." He cast a quick glance about her room to assure himself that he had removed all traces of his presence, then collected the small bundle containing the soiled lint. Augusta opened the door, peeped into the hall, and let them both out. There was no one to know he had spent the last half hour in her chamber.

"Your reputation is safe," he murmured. She smiled up at him as they started down the hall. "Do ye really wish young Lansdon had shot Trent?"

"Better him than you," she said softly. She looked away in a futile attempt to hide her deepened blush.

"Murderous wench," he murmured.

She shook her head. "Not in the least." If he looked at her like that once more, she would risk everything and beg him to kiss her. For the first time, that thought didn't fill her with mortification. Only chaotic longing.

A sudden smile that did little for her composure lit his eyes. "Do not worry. I will not permit Trent to arrest ye for murder."

"Will you arrest him for treason?"

He took her hands between his. "I will find your villain, lass, never ye fear."

"*Is* it Captain Trent?"

He shook his head. "Nay, I canna be certain, and even if I were, I would still have to prove it. There is more than one suspect, ye know. He's a clever one, our traitor. He'll not be easily uncovered."

The burr in his voice became more pronounced, and she decided she liked it. He released her and allowed her to precede him down the staircase. As they reached the lower hall, laughing voices could be heard coming from the drawing room.

She hung back. "It—it will appear somewhat singular if we go in together."

He nodded. Suddenly, a gleam lit his entire countenance. "Would ye care to learn more of the pistols?"

"Yes! Of course. But how?"

258

"I left them in that Rose Study of yours. Wait about five minutes, then bring the box in here."

She nodded, took the blood-soaked pad from him to throw away, and hurried down the hall.

That gave him a few minutes to set the atmosphere in the drawing room. His plan only half formed, he pushed the door open and went in. Mrs. Lansdon sat on the sofa with the tea cart before her. The others were gathered about in a casual circle, at their ease. That pleased him.

Captain Trent looked up and raised a quizzical eyebrow. "I had thought you left us."

"There were one or two things I needed to consider—in peace." Edward smiled easily, held Trent's eye for a moment, then turned to Lord Wentworth. "I understand that ye have been concerned over the plays. Perhaps, with all the upset over Napoleon and the increased duties for the officers, it would be best if ye staged no more after this one."

Wentworth regarded him gravely. "It has crossed my mind. Only my concern for Miss Carstairs's cause, and the eagerness of the people who have delighted in our humble presentations, have kept us going with them."

Perry stared at the major, his eyes narrowed. "Do you think we should stop, sir?"

Edward forced back his smile at Perry's newfound respect for him. The lad might well shape up to admiration with some much needed discipline and a bit of seasoning—provided he had not already committed any heinous crime.

"My dear boy, you never should have begun!" Frederick Ashfield declared, amused.

"Oh, no." Lizzie shook her head. "I've enjoyed the laugh."

"Surely there is no danger!" Mrs. Lansdon protested. "Do you mean that the officers will shortly be going into battle?" She looked toward her son in alarm.

"Nay, not that. Merely that it will be more difficult for them to obtain leave from their regiments for rehearsals."

"I say we keep on with them." Trent folded his arms across his chest and thrust out his chin in a stubborn manner.

"You see Mrs. Lansdon's reaction," Jack Kettering said. "If we stop, we will have all of Brussels convinced we are on the verge of war."

"And we are not—are we?" Sophronia gazed trustingly up

259

into Trent's face.

"No, we are not." He smiled down at her.

Edward, pleased with the response so far, looked to the one member of the troupe who had remained silent. "Lord Roderick? How would ye vote? To continue or stop?"

"Oh, whatever the others decide." He glanced toward Perry, read no clue there, and shrugged. "Continue, I suppose. They're great fun. Gives a fellow something to do."

The door opened and Edward knew from Lord Roderick's expression that Augusta had entered. The blood drained from the young man's face, leaving him pale and wide-eyed.

"Where—how—?" Roddy broke off, staring in shock at the pistol case.

Perry started, and his gaze flew to Edward, who smiled grimly. Trent raised his eyebrows, watching the others with interest. Edward turned around, smiled at Augusta, and held out his hands. She went to him and handed over the cherry wood case.

"Good girl," he said softly.

She turned quickly away and sat down by Lizzie. Her sister stared hard at her, then returned her attention to Edward.

He looked about the assembled company, then held out the box to Lord Roderick. "I believe these are yours."

The young man stood at once and grasped the box. Edward did not release it. Roddy looked up into his face, an expression of dismay on his own. "What—?"

"I think it is time we had a few answers." Edward allowed him to take the case. "Why does it worry ye so when they are out of your possession?"

Roderick flushed. "That—that's none of your concern."

"At this time, I fear it is. Do not worry. I believe I can vouchsafe that not one word of what ye say will go beyond this room. But your pistols, however innocent, were involved in Captain Montclyff's death." He ignored Mrs. Lansdon's gasp. "A few answers are now necessary. Why are ye so concerned about the guns?"

Roddy drew a shaky breath, darted a frightened glance at Perry, but found no help from his friend. He stared hard at the cherry wood case. "They—they're not mine. They're my brother Taversham's."

Edward frowned. "That doesn't seem sufficient somehow,

for your concern."

A hollow laugh escaped Roddy. "You ain't acquainted with Taversham, are you? Cold fish of a fellow," He shivered. "We've never been close, you know. Almost twenty years between us. He has the devil's own temper."

"I gather you stand somewhat in awe of the duke," Edward said dryly. He glanced at Perry for confirmation.

"Frightful man," that young gentleman agreed cheerfully. "He'd have Roddy's hide if he knew he'd borrowed them, even though he has no use for them himself. And if he so much as guessed his pistols had been involved in such scandalous doings, Roddy'd be done for."

"He'd cut off my allowance and see me sent to India," Roddy concurred resentfully.

"Buck up, my boy, he knows you have them." Wentworth nodded as Roddy gaped at him.

"He—" Roddy broke off and sat down abruptly. He bore a distinct resemblance to one who momentarily expected to be struck down by a thunderclap.

"He asked me to keep an eye on them over here."

"He *knows* I took them?" Roddy repeated. "He—he never said a word to me. I don't understand this! Not like the old tartar at all. He nearly suffered a palsy stroke when I borrowed 'em once before."

"That was before you enlisted. When I saw him, he said he hoped they'd be lucky enough to protect you."

Roddy shook his head, dumbfounded. "If that don't beat the Dutch! I've been putting myself in a quake over—over nothing, like a stupid looby!"

"Exactly like one," murmured Ashfield, who had been sitting in silence.

"I didn't think Taversham was overly plump in the pocket." Trent leaned back in his chair. "Those pistols must have cost him a pretty penny. How much are they worth?"

"A fortune," Roddy breathed.

"Devil a bit." Wentworth shook his head. "The stones are paste."

Roddy's jaw dropped. "Paste?"

"Taversham told me himself, a long time ago."

"But—" It all seemed to much for Roddy to comprehend. "He—he always told me they were *real!*"

Wentworth shook his head. "He didn't want you treating them as toys. Lord, he has quite a fondness for them. They kept him out of any number of duels in his heyday. Meetings were more common when we were your age, you know. A pair of pistols rumored to be lucky stood a fellow in good stead." He shook his head, reminiscent.

"When were the stones changed?" The major sat down on the edge of a chair. "Do ye know, Wentworth?"

Lord Wentworth shook his head. "Before Taversham bought them, I'd say. He got the pistols from a pawnbroker thinking the rubies were genuine. He put them up the spout himself once or twice before a sharp moneylender spotted them as fake."

Perry picked up one of the pistols from the case and subjected the paste stone to a careful scrutiny. "There goes their pawning value, if this ever gets out."

The major met Augusta's frowning gaze. "And there goes a very promising line of inquiry," he murmured.

Chapter 21

Augusta looked from Lord Roderick to Lord Wentworth, then to Major MacKennoch, feeling vaguely as if the ground had fallen away from beneath her feet. She had been so certain those ruby-mounted dueling pistols would prove an important link with the sale of military secrets. Instead, they led nowhere.

Or did they? The guns *had* been used in the duel. If Perry told the truth, someone besides Roddy and himself had known that fact before Edward revealed it this night. Had anyone betrayed that knowledge—and revealed himself to Edward's keen eye?

Perry turned to Lord Wentworth, effectively interrupting her racing thoughts. "Have you known Taversham long?"

"A good number of years. We were at Eton together."

"Then why is he so hard on Roddy?"

"How would you feel if you, at your age, with your somewhat wild tendencies, were left *in locus parentis* to an infant brother?"

Perry looked appropriately revolted.

"Taversham wasn't ready either," Wentworth said dryly.

Lord Roderick shook his head again. I—I think I'd better write to him tonight." He got up unsteadily. "Are—are you through, sir?" He looked to the major. Edward nodded, and Roddy took back the guns. With a last, bewildered shake of his head, he left.

Roddy's departure signaled the end of the party. The others took their leave also, and in a very little while only the ladies remained.

Augusta drew an unsteady breath. She might understand Roddy and his desperation over his pistols a little more, but the evening had not answered enough questions, as far as she was concerned. What, exactly, had Edward learned? He had revealed no clue concerning his thoughts as he'd studied each person seated in that circle. Yet she felt certain he had been pleased with the outcome. She would give a great deal to know why.

How typical of him to leave without telling her! Inwardly, she fumed. At least Roddy had benefited. She had few doubts that young gentleman was well on his way to being reconciled with the elder brother he feared.

Edward did not put in an appearance the following day. She longed to see him—just to demand a few answers from him, of course. But the whole next week slipped by and still he did not come. The night scheduled for their next play drew steadily closer. Augusta vacillated between dejection at not being able to speak with him and irritation that he should ignore her so completely.

What should she do about the performance? Did one of the members of her troupe plan to pass information to the enemy? It could be done so easily, just a seeming mistake in reading the lines while on stage. They all stumbled over the words. How could she determine which errors were intentional?

She continued in this frantic state of mind for five more days. The last traces of April chill gave way to warm May sunshine, and the night of the performance arrived. Edward showed up—she caught a glimpse of him in the audience—but he did not remain to talk to her after the play. Her heart sank and her temper flared. If military secrets had been delivered to the French, it had gone undetected by her.

Why did he not tell her what to do? She couldn't allow this to continue, to keep on providing a traitor with the ready means to pass on his information. But neither could she discontinue the productions, for that would betray their suspicions. The traitor would merely find a new method—as he had done several times before—and they would have to start all over.

Augusta tried to conceal her growing fears in a dizzy round of parties, but everywhere she went, the talk centered on Napoleon. The British in Brussels appeared to live on the verge of panic. Rumors raced through dinner parties, purporting the worst, yet were never substantiated. If French troop movement was reported one night, the following day it would be discovered that the Belgians had spotted the Prussians on maneuvers, or some other such nonsense. The officers laughed, albeit uneasily, and discussed the next party and the latest gossip.

Augusta's search of the bookstore produced an English play suitable for her productions, and her troupe began work on it at once. She tried to dig up an enthusiasm to match theirs, but couldn't. She hadn't spoken with Edward in almost three weeks, she realized. No wonder she felt so depressed.

When she suddenly came face to face with him at a card party several nights later, it stunned her, for she had all but given up hope of seeing him. As she gazed up at him, her pulse racing erratically, warmth replaced his polite social mask. He clasped the impulsive hand she extended and raised it to his lips. His lurking smile spread to his eyes, which caressed her.

"You—you're here," she stammered, then realized how unutterably foolish that must have sounded. She felt hot color race to her cheeks and she lowered her gaze from his beloved face.

"Yes, I am back." His voice was gentle. "I have been in Ghent this age."

"Ghent?" She looked up, startled. "I—I had no idea."

"Neither did I, at first. I rode over for what I thought would be a day, or two at the most. I never thought I would be gone so long from—Brussels."

His eyes held hers, and she felt herself sinking beneath their tender spell. "Why to Ghent?" she asked. A card party was hardly the place to stand lost to the world, gazing at a man.

"I wanted some background information, and found more to learn than I expected."

"In Ghent?" She gave him a quizzical smile, which faded as she sensed his slight withdrawal. Suddenly, she knew he'd lied about where he had been. "Of course, Ghent would be the very place, considering what it is you are investigating. You did not, I suppose, in reality ride in the opposite direction?"

"I *suppose* it would be impossible to ask that ye keep your speculations to yourself?" He smiled affably, but a note of command colored his words.

"No, it would not. I can hold my tongue." He had answered her question and that surprised her. She caught his eye, discovered a twinkle, and added, "At least until I may speak with you alone."

"Oh, by then I'll have concocted a more believable story, I assure ye. Unless I am much mistaken, there is a piquet table vacant over there. Would ye care to try your hand?"

"For what stakes?" She accepted his arm.

"Oh, pennies on the point. Or has Lansdon made no demands on your purse of late?"

"Unkind." She took her seat. "I have no idea what you said to him that night, but he has been a pattern card of all the virtues ever since, I promise you."

Edward chuckled. "He is like to break under the strain."

Augusta shook her head and watched him cut the cards and shuffle. "You should hear him speak of you. It would quite set you up in your own conceit." She shot a quick look around, assured herself that no one paid them any heed, and leaned forward. "Was there really anything you could learn on the road to France?" she whispered.

"Incorrigible," he murmured. "I tried to follow a messenger, but we lost him."

Augusta's eyes widened and she subsided into silence as he dealt the cards. When he finished, she picked hers up and sorted them without really paying any heed. "Have you discovered anything new?"

He shook his head. "I believe it is your discard."

She selected two cards at random, laid them at her side, and drew from the stock. Somewhat to her surprise, she found herself holding four kings, one part of a seven-card sequence.

He discarded, examined the remaining cards, and selected three. "Let us say I tested a theory and found myself only partly right."

She threw him a dazzling smile. "I declare a point of seven, and also that you can be the most exasperating gentleman of my acquaintance."

His smile broadened. "I concede both. And if your sequence is the same as your point, which I greatly fear it may be, I can see that I shall shortly be rolled up."

"Yes, penny points can be shocking, can they not? And which part were you right about?"

He shook his head. "There is a certain house that will bear watching, but no more will I tell ye."

He said the last with such finality that she subsided and they played out their hand. Not until they were well into their second did she venture another question. "Have you narrowed down your list of suspects?"

He shot her a quick smile. "I suppose the likeliest are Kettering, Lansdon, Lord Roderick, Trent, Wentworth, Ashfield, and yourself."

She made a face at him. "Kindly do not forget Sophronia. I gather that any one of us might be involved."

His expression sobered. "They could. And aye, ye will note I said 'they' and not 'ye.'"

"I'm honored."

"So ye should be." His smile returned.

They fell into a companionable silence again and both concentrated on their cards. While he shuffled once more, an idea occurred to Augusta that was too tempting to be ignored.

Edward started to deal, caught sight of her face, and halted. "What are ye plotting?"

She peeked guiltily up at him through her long lashes "Am I that obvious?"

"Ye are. Out with it, baggage."

She laughed. "Can we not set up a test on the next play? We will be giving it in just over two weeks, you must know. We could alter lines and setting and see what happens."

He shook his head. "I don't want ye involved in something like that. It would prove to anyone concerned that we are suspicious of the plays and making a definite attempt to learn the truth."

"What other choice do we have? Go on suspecting everything and everyone while military secrets continue to go astray? I would much rather see if we can prevent a battle on our doorstep."

He met her gaze and the frown melted from his eyes. "All right. We'll try it. But not yet. We'll wait until the last minute."

She did not see Edward again until three days later, when she drove out with Mrs. Lansdon, Sophie, and Lizzie to the banks of the Dender near Grammont, where Wellington intended to inspect the British Cavalry. The entire British population of Brussels appeared to have turned out for this event, along with that of Ghent as well. But the blazing heat of the day made Augusta feel ill, and she wished herself safely at home long before the great man himself arrived.

After an hour passed and nothing happened, Lizzie muttered to her that she had seen quite enough of soldiers standing about. Augusta could only agree, but she knew Sophronia and Mrs. Lansdon wished to remain, in the hopes of catching a glimpse of Perry—and Vincent Trent. Augusta sank lower in the carriage, protecting herself with a sunshade, feeling the headache coming on with a vengeance.

Lizzie suddenly poked her in the ribs with her elbow. "Look who is coming."

Augusta raised her head to see Edward, driving a curricle, maneuvering into position beside them. His eyes narrowed as they rested on Augusta's heat-flushed countenance. "Are ye feeling unwell?"

"It is just this dreadful weather." She managed a smile.

"She is forever melting with it," Lizzie said, not with disgust but as a statement of fact.

Edward nodded. "It is only like to get worse. Would ye care to return home?"

Mrs. Lansdon looked up, not quite hiding her dismay. "Of course, my dear. We cannot allow you to be made ill. We will return at once."

"There is no need." Edward smiled. "If ye should permit it, I will drive Miss Carstairs back."

"Excellent idea," Lizzie pronounced. "I will come with you."

"Are you certain?" Mrs. Lansdon regarded him with hope.

"Do you not wish to remain?" Augusta asked, not wanting to drag him away.

He shook his head. "Boring things, these reviews, especially when ye have had to take your part in them. No, I, too, find the heat oppressive. I am a Highlander, remember." He held her gaze with a challenging look.

"Without his kilt," she murmured, and he smiled.

It was a tight squeeze, for the curricle had been designed for only two passengers, but both Augusta and Lizzie were lightly built. Seated snugly between her companions, Augusta leaned back and closed her eyes, trying to block out the disabling heat.

Edward pulled his curricle out of line and maneuvered back toward the road. For nearly a quarter of an hour they drove in silence while he negotiated the heavy traffic occasioned by the military review. Free of the immediate vicinity, he urged his horse into a trot, and they moved forward quickly. Edward looked down at the top of Augusta's becoming chip straw bonnet. "Have ye informed your sister of our intentions for the next play?"

Lizzie at once looked across. "She has not. Tell me."

He did, along with their reasons, and Lizzie, gleefully, offered to help. She beguiled them the rest of the journey with a lively and not very complimentary summary of the setting and roles involved, then all three began to think up new ideas to confound their traitor. By the time they had reached the house, Augusta felt much recovered and thanked Edward warmly.

He shook his head. "It is I, I'm afraid, who have made shocking use of ye. I needed an excuse to leave the review to pursue business of my own in town this afternoon."

She tried to keep her disappointment from showing. "You mean while most people are away?"

He nodded, and retained her hand a moment after helping her to the flagway. "I will call upon ye as soon as I can."

He kept his word, though his call—and all successive ones for the next two weeks—invariably coincided with their rehearsals. These were more difficult to schedule, for with the coming of June, rumors of a French advance were confirmed. Regimental duties increased, and it was seldom all the members of the cast could be present at one time.

She saw more of him at evening parties, which he attended with increasing regularity. He mingled freely with the other guests, furthering acquaintanceships, and on more than one occasion asked her to perform introductions. He refused to discuss his investigation, but as he sat at her side at a musical soiree or engaged her in a hand of piquet, a slight frown touched his brow and a fleeting shadow clouded his normally clear blue eyes. Augusta could not rid herself of the suspicion that he found her company more useful of late than enjoyable.

At a ball two nights later, she spotted him conversing with one of the gentlemen—a leader of the ton—to whom she had introduced him at a card party. Edward looked up, saw her, and excused himself to his companion. He approached her through the milling crowd, a determined expression on his face. He greeted her, and retained her hand. "Will ye save me a waltz?"

"How unkind of you to wish me to sit it out," she protested. "I do so love to dance it."

"Then by all means we shall."

She glanced up, startled, and saw those mesmerizing lights twinkling once more in his eyes. "Is your knee—"

"Much recovered," he broke in, as usual loath to discuss this weakness. He bowed and took his leave.

She had the dubious pleasure of seeing for herself this was true when he led Lady Georgianna Lennox into a quadrille a few minutes later. From the way that young lady laughed at something he said, Augusta had little doubt she would see him at the duchess of Richmond's next ball. Major Edward MacKennoch was making remarkable headway into society.

Only for the briefest moment did she regret introducing him to Lady Georgianna. She should be glad to see him mixing so freely with so many eligible young ladies, an acquaintance with whose families could not but help a future diplomatic career. To her further annoyance, her glance kept straying in his direction, away from her own set, so that more than once she stumbled through a step she knew perfectly well.

When at last he claimed her, her normally calm temper was sadly shattered. "Why the waltz with me?" she could not help asking. "It appeared that you managed very well with the other dances."

"There was no telling but that I might have been tired by now, or strained my knee beyond endurance. I knew I could rely on ye if I needed to sit this one out."

She threw him a fulminating look. "I might have known you would have something odious to say."

His soft chuckle was her only answer as he swept her onto the floor.

The firm pressure of his hand on her back sent a rush of pleasure through her. He danced exactly as she'd dreamed he would—confident, assured, guiding her with ease. And she needed guiding. His nearness drove all rational thought from her mind.

She forced back her longing for him to wrap his arms more tightly about her. Just to break the alluring spell of his weaving, she sought something to say. "Do you not find an entire evening of dancing somewhat strenuous?"

"Of course. I shall presently discover I have pushed myself too far and be obliged to spend the rest of the evening in a chair."

"Then why not start now?" She must sound like a jealous cat, she realized, and bit her lip. The awful truth was that she *was* jealous.

He looked down, a warm, special smile in his eyes just for her. "Nay, I wouldn't miss this dance for anything."

Breathless, she threw caution to the winds. "Why?"

One eyebrow flew up in a comic expression. "It provides the perfect opportunity to converse with ye in private about the little joke we are playing on your troupe."

Unhesitatingly, she stepped down on his toes, only to discover his pumps were better protection for such activity than her satin slippers. "How clumsy of me," she muttered.

His deep chuckle sounded again. "Indeed it was. How have I made ye angry?"

"I'm not in the least angry. What did you wish to say?"

"That it is about time ye changed the scenes as we discussed. I think tomorrow evening's rehearsal would be the perfect time to try it out. Do ye not?"

She nodded. "Lizzie and I will go to work on it in the morning."

"Do not frown so. Only think, if this works, we might catch our villain."

"Perhaps that is what bothers me. I cannot wish—or even believe—any of them to be guilty of such treason."

His hand pressed gently against her back, drawing her closer. "I know. Ye are too young and innocent to be involved in such treachery."

"I am not all *that* naive," she protested.

He smiled down at her. "Are ye not? To me ye seem perfectly so."

She lowered her gaze, uncertain whether or not she had just received a compliment. What use did a man in Edward's position have for a naive young female? Better she should be worldly-wise, experienced in the realms of politics and diplomacy, instead of having spent most of her life in a village so small few people had ever heard of it. The hand that held hers pressed gently, but her pleasure had faded.

"Tomorrow evening's rehearsal," he repeated. He released her, and she realized the music had ended.

It wasn't easy to make the changes in the script the following day, but Sophronia, who stood somewhat in awe of Lizzie's determined manner, acquiesced in everything that lively young damsel suggested. Before the first of their troupe arrived that night, both copies bore identical and far-sweeping changes.

Edward and Lord Wentworth arrived together, almost half an hour after the others, having come directly from a meeting with Wellington. Neither would disclose what had been discussed, a circumstance that could not please any of the others. Edward caught Augusta's eye and she gave him an imperceptible nod. She had done her part.

"Well, well, shall we begin? Day after tomorrow, you know, day after tomorrow." Wentworth picked up one of the scripts. "Shall we go through it from the beginning?"

Ashfield leafed through the other. "What? More changes? No, really, this is too much!"

"Where?" Perry grabbed it from him and stared. "Who's been altering things? We don't have time for this!"

Lord Roderick leaned over his shoulder, read a few of the scribbled notes, and chuckled. "I *like* that. But can't we change the scene back? Thought it was better the other way."

Kettering laughed. "You have made it into a farce. No melodrama can survive these lines."

Lord Wentworth nodded. "Miss Elizabeth, I detect your hand at work."

The girl grinned, but kept her tongue, for which Augusta was grateful. She glanced across at Edward, who stood toward the back of the room, watching the troupe intently. Did his gaze rest on Vincent Trent or on Fredrick Ashfield, who stood at his side? Or could it be Kettering, who lounged in a chair right behind those two? Even Perry, standing near the sofa, might be the object of his scrutiny.

On the whole, she decided in disgust as she watched the troupe trying to memorize their new speeches, Edward probably had learned nothing. No one seemed to really care *what* they said in the play! They might very well be wrong, and the plays were completely innocent and had absolutely nothing to do with the passing of military secrets! Augusta met Edward's frowning gaze and wondered if he shared that thought. It would be embarrassing, after making such a fuss over it all—but it would also be a tremendous relief.

The players mastered the lines with surprising ease, and they faced the performance two days later with no more than their usual nerves. Augusta donned her costume early and slipped down the stairs and into their backstage area. Drawing a corner of the curtains aside, she peeped out at the audience.

An impressive array of notables and dignitaries attended; she ought to have felt flattered. The room was filled, with a number of officers standing outside in the hall looking in through the open doorway. Their audience grew with every performance. When they gave the next, they would have to borrow a larger house, one with a ballroom. Georgianna Lennox and her mother, the duchess of Richmond, were present. Perhaps they could be induced to help.

Filing that thought for later action, she returned to scanning the audience. Was one of those people more interested than the others in the play? *Could* someone sitting out there be a traitor, waiting for information? She sincerely hoped not.

The other performers joined her, they checked the stage setting and props, and Jack Kettering pulled back the curtain. Somehow, as always, they bumbled along, drawing more than their proper share of laughter. By the end of the second short act, Augusta began to relax and played it for even more fun. Ashfield, as her hero, rose admirably to the occasion so that she was hard pressed not to dissolve in giggles at his too-dramatic reading of his lines.

She held out her hands and he clasped them tightly, drawing her toward him. "Meet me at the pavilion by the water, in the dark secret times of the night," she breathed, naming a place for a clandestine meeting in the next scene.

She never heard Ashfield's answer, though fortunately for her sake it was the last line of the act. She stood transfixed, staring at his face without seeing him. The pavilion by the water. That had been a line she'd changed. Before, it had read "in the garden." But that didn't matter! Anywhere that she had said would become the next meeting place.

She would have to check the other plays, see what each of them said at the end of Act Two. Had they been setting meeting

273

places all along, so simply? The changes wouldn't matter in the least!

Edward. She had to find Edward, tell him her idea, get him to bring back the plays he had borrowed so they could go over them. Or more important—she had to tell him to keep that appointment at the pavilion!

As soon as the last act drew to a close, Augusta slipped away from the others to search out the major. But he anticipated her and met her at the drawing room door. Grasping his hands, she dragged him to the Rose Study, where they could speak in private. She barely waited until he had closed the door behind them.

"I have the answer! The meeting will take place tonight, at the pavilion near the swan pond!" Unable to contain her excitement, she clasped his hands once more.

He regarded her from behind his impenetrable mask, his features calm, emotionless. Her own enthusiasm evaporated. "Is—is something wrong? Edward, have I—" The letdown left her feeling physically ill. "Have I made a mistake—have I given away my suspicions to someone?"

He freed one hand and brushed the stray tendrils of dark hair from her stricken eyes. He looked down into her troubled face, and his mask slipped. His fingers trembled with his firm control. For one moment she saw the burning desire in his eyes, the raw need in his expression, then his mouth claimed hers. Joy, wild and unrestrained, raced through her as she melted against him.

He released her slowly, and she returned regretfully to reality. Somehow, her hands had crept to his shoulders. She left them there, reveling in the feel of the strong muscles beneath his coat. His arm about her waist felt natural, as if it belonged there, and a contentment she had never before experienced flowed through her. Vaguely, she wondered if this was what Helena experienced when Halliford kissed her. If so, it was no wonder her sister was only happy when her husband was there.

"Ye shouldn't have looked at me like that." Edward stroked her hair, pressing her head down to his shoulder.

"Did you not like it?"

An unsteady laugh shook him. "Too much. Almost, ye make me feel young again."

She snuggled closer. She liked him like this. Vulnerable, that was it. It made him less godlike, more approachable. And she wanted to approach him, very much indeed. "You are young."

"I'm thirty."

"And you are only just now learning how to laugh." She felt him tense and feared she had gone to far.

His hand stroked her hair once more. "Maybe I'm learning a few other things as well." His chin brushed the top of her head as he bent to kiss her brow. Regretfully, he put her from him. "We have a few plans to make. Will ye be missed in the drawing room?"

She shook her head. His hands held hers, and she didn't care what happened in the other room. Her entire world was centered right here, with Edward.

"Plans," he repeated. "I have a traitor to catch."

"We," she corrected at once. With an effort, she wiped the fatuous smile from her lips. "The pavilion."

He nodded. "The pavilion. It's a real possibility."

"Of course it is!" She pushed him down into the overstuffed wing-back chair, then perched on the arm at his side. He made no move to put his arm around her waist, and mentally she sighed. He was back at work.

"Do ye have any idea when?" he asked.

"The rest of the line read 'in the dark secret times of the night.'"

"That doesn't help much. Which night?"

"Now?" she suggested.

"I can't afford to take the chance that it isn't." He rose, causing her to get up also to avoid falling unceremoniously into the chair he just vacated.

"May I help?"

He took her hands and shook his head. "Nay. I have soldiers at my command. Will ye give me your promise ye will not go to the park tonight?"

She bit her lip. "How did you guess?" she asked in a very small voice.

That deep, warm chuckle sounded in his throat, wreaking havoc on her already heightened senses. "Ye see I really have come to know ye. Do I have your promise?"

She hesitated, then nodded. "Who do you expect to come?"

she could not help asking.

"I have my ideas, but nothing certain. I'd rather not say."

"Why? Is it Perry? Do you think I would give it away?"

"Goose." He murmured the word. "Nay, I think ye might laugh at me. And to be honest, I hope ye have cause."

Ashfield? Did that mean Frederick Ashfield? After all, Edward knew him to be a friend of Halliford's. Or Kettering? Or Lord Wentworth—or Captain Trent? Or even Roddy? That *would* make her laugh—though not for long. The suspects were endless!

"What will you do?" Suddenly, she became aware that he still held her hands. She had no desire whatsoever to pull them free.

"There is a certain house not too far from here, and nay, I will not tell ye which one. I have no faith in your being able to resist the temptation to have a peak at it. I have already put a watch on the place, but I think I will make sure there is someone there at all times. And now I must go." He raised first her one hand, then the other, to his lips. "Sleep well," he murmured.

She caught the twinkle in his eye and stuck her tongue out at him in a most unladylike manner. He knew perfectly well she would lie awake, staring out her window toward the park, wondering what occurred—and whom he might catch.

"Will you wear your kilt?" she asked suddenly.

"Vixen," he murmured. "I have no need to wear a uniform."

Chapter 22

Sometime during the night, Augusta must have drifted off to sleep, for a pounding on her door awakened her at last. Heavy-eyed, she dragged herself up in bed. Before she could call, the door flung wide and Lizzie bounced in.

"Are you all right, Gussie?"

She nodded, yawning at the same time. "What time is it?"

"It's gone on nine-thirty! I made certain you were at death's door. You never stay abed."

Augusta yawned again and sank back against the pillows. "I had trouble getting to sleep."

Lizzie nodded wisely. "Can't say I blame you. I'd have a guilty conscience, too, if I'd appeared in that play."

Augusta fixed her sister with a pointed stare. "What are you doing up so bright and early?"

"Oh, Edward has called to take us for a drive."

That brought Augusta up with a start. "Has he? How long has he been here?"

Lizzie shook her head. "Oh, he left nearly a quarter of an hour ago. I told him you were too tired."

"You—you didn't!" Augusta stared at her, dismayed. "Oh, Lizzie, you—you wretch!"

Lizzie grinned. "No, I didn't. But lord, you should see your face, Gussie! You're in love with him, devil a doubt!"

"You watch your language, or Helena will send you to a polite ladies seminary in—in Bath!"

Lizzie's only response to this dire threat was an evil chuckle. She jumped off the bed. "He said he'd be by for us at eleven o'clock. Did I mention it was to be an *al fresco* luncheon?"

She watched as Augusta scrambled out from between the covers. "If you don't want Edward to get bored kicking his heels, you'd best make haste," she added, and ducked out the door, inches ahead of the pillow Augusta threw after her.

Still seething at her self-betrayal in response to her sister's teasing, Augusta made her way downstairs a half hour later, considerably out of temper. Both Sophronia and Lizzie occupied the breakfast parlor. Sophie greeted her with a subdued, bleary-eyed "good morning," not yet recovered from the late night. Lizzie grinned in complete lack of repentance and advised her sister to have a strong cup of tea.

A pile of untouched letters lay by her plate, and absently, Augusta leafed through these. She stopped suddenly. "Lizzie, didn't you check our morning's post?"

Lizzie shook her head. "Should I have?"

"Here's a letter from Halliford—and another from Helena—and one from Chloe!" She did some rapid mental arithmetic, cried out in excitement, and tore open Halliford's, which she knew would be the briefest and most informative. Lizzie pounced on Helena's.

"It's a boy—Viscount Grenville!" Augusta scanned the sheet, eager for word. "He says they're both doing well, and we're not to worry."

"Gervase Augustan Valerian Chatham," Lizzie pronounced in disgust. "The poor little thing!"

Augusta laughed, tears of happiness for her sister's joy slipping unheeded down her cheeks. "He'll be Grenville until the day he succeeds to Halliford's room." She raised her teacup in a toast. "And may that be long in coming."

"How exciting!" Sophronia breathed. "The dear little baby. Oh, how wonderful for the duchess."

Lizzie made a face at her, but sobered. "Do you think he will be forever crying and—and whatever else babies do?"

Augusta nodded, seeing a chance for revenge. "Pulling and spitting up. And as his aunt, you will be able to hold him and—and help his nurse whenever she needs a rest from his screams."

For the first time in her life, Lizzie quailed.

Augusta burst out laughing. "Lord, you should see your face, Lizzie," she murmured in fair mimicry.

Lizzie stuck out her tongue. "You're holding Chloe's letter," she pointed out, philosophically accepting her sister's punishment.

Augusta broke the seal and spread out the four sheets. The next moment, she giggled. "Here, Lizzie, read this. She says Halliford was absolutely distracted and refused to leave Nell's room. He scandalized the maids, and she says afterwards he looked absolutely sick, but he stayed there the entire time, holding Nell's hands. And I must say," Augusta added after a moment's consideration, "I do think it very brave of him."

Lizzie, now engrossed in the first page, vouchsafed no reply. Chloe spared them most of the details, but Lizzie could read between the uncrossed lines. She looked a trifle ill herself. "I—perhaps it *was* best we were here in Brussels," she said as she laid the last page aside.

Augusta nodded. "Nell and Halliford deserve some time alone with little Grenville. And you may be sure Chloe and Richard will take the best of care of them all."

Sophronia rose. "I will go and tell Mamma. I know she will want to write to the duchess." She hurried out of the room.

Lizzie stared at her plate, absently selected another roll, but did not bite into it. "Do you think we should go home at once?"

Augusta met her frowning gaze. "Would you like to?"

Lizzie considered. "I'm not certain. Do you think Nell needs us?"

"Not in the least," came Augusta's honest response. "I rather think they'll enjoy our—our absence, for once. But we could go, if you'd like. We would not be the only ones returning home, with so much unrest here. And there—there is nothing to keep us in Brussels, if you wish to return."

"Isn't there?" For once, Lizzie did not tease.

Augusta bit her lip. "No." If Edward loved her, he would follow her as soon as he could. If he did not—that was something she didn't want to think about. But if he didn't, the sooner she left his vicinity, the better it would be for her.

That concern now became urgent and occupied her mind for the remainder of the morning. Not even the question of what had occurred the night before at the pavilion by the lake mattered as much to her. But she could gain no information on either subject until Edward arrived—if even then he would give anything away.

It took her almost an hour to dress for their outing, although

279

she hurried so that she could have a chance for private speech with him before the other ladies came downstairs. Still, the rival merits of a pomona green carriage gown almost outweighed those of a jonquil muslin walking dress with lace ruffles. The decision was not easy. She caught herself vacillating, and in annoyance, directed her maid to assist her into the green, which was the first gown that came to hand. She descended the stairs at last, trying not to run.

Sophronia and Mrs. Lansdon were in the front saloon ahead of her, engaging Edward in conversation. He stood as she entered, and the slightest shake of his head told her his watch had been to no avail. Her spirits sank, but not by much. They couldn't possibly, when he was there. And the whimsical thought that she detected an answering smile in his eyes, meant only for her, sent a warm glow flowing through her.

"Mrs. Lansdon has told me of the birth of the Viscount Grenville. May I offer my congratulations?"

"We are so happy, you can have no idea." She took his hand.

His smile faded, and his eyes rested on her with an unfathomable expression lurking in their depths. With all her heart, she wished he were not so perfect a diplomat. She would give anything to be able to read the thoughts that went on behind that polite mask.

Lizzie bounded into the room, wearing her Devonshire brown habit. Instead of her normal riding shako, her fingers crushed the satin ribands of the chip straw bonnet that dangled down her back. "Are we ready?" she demanded.

"What?" Augusta rallied, and indicated the hat. "You, making allowances for the sun? Where do we go?" She turned to Edward, attempting to recapture his attention, but he remained elusive. He tried to hide something from her—or, the terrible thought struck her, he had withdrawn again.

Mrs. Lansdon answered. "Major MacKennoch has suggested an expedition to the Boise des Soignes. Captain Trent and Mr. Ashfield are pledged to join us. Is that not the most delightful scheme?"

"It is, indeed." She managed a bright smile, but secretly was not pleased. There would be little opportunity for private conversation with Edward when so many other people were about.

To her surprise, that one obstacle did not stand in her way. Either Edward had planned this outing before he closed once more into himself, or he still wished to speak with her. When they made their way outside to the waiting barouche, she found Edward's curricle drawn up on the other side of the street with a groom holding his pair's heads. Lizzie's horse waited restlessly by the carriage. Frederick Ashfield rode up, mounted on a gray hack, and assured Augusta he would escort the lively Lizzie and keep her from getting into trouble. Mrs. Lansdon and Sophronia took the barouche, piled high with hampers, which left Augusta to ride in the curricle with Edward.

"Very neat maneuvering," she murmured as he handed her up to the seat.

"I hoped ye would not be disappointed." He climbed up beside her, dismissed the lad who had held the horses while he was inside, and they set forth in the lead.

Lizzie, Augusta noted, already had launched into some lively and undoubtedly ridiculous argument with Ashfield. She would not be joining them for some time. This was the perfect opportunity. "Tell me what happened last night."

"Nothing." He shook his head. "I posted men at strategic spots. No one could have approached that water without our being aware of it."

"So it was the wrong night." She chewed her lower lip.

"We might have been working with only one of the clues. If your guess was correct, then the place was given at the end of the second act. Can ye remember if any information might have been provided at the end of the first or third acts? Such as a time or a person?"

She closed her eyes in concentration. "*Four days hence,*" she said slowly, as a sudden, vivid memory struck her. She turned to him, eager. "It was my line, at the end of the last act, setting the time for the wedding!"

"Your lines," he repeated. "What did ye say at the end of the first act?" For once, he, too, sounded excited.

Her eagerness evaporated. "*You are no stranger to my arms,*" she quoted. "That doesn't help much."

"Aye, it does." He threw her a grin. "We know that whoever will pass the information is no stranger, probably the usual person. We at least remove him from their plans."

She nodded, feeling better. "And we know *when*—or at least, I hope we do."

Edward did some quick calculations. "Not tomorrow, nor the next day, but the night after. June fifteenth. Ye may be certain we will be waiting."

She was silent a moment. "That is the night of the Duchess of Richmond's ball, is it not? I wonder if that is by design or chance. And I wonder who will keep that appointment."

He threw her a measuring glance. "Ye may be sure I will *tell* ye, on the morning of the sixteenth."

She blinked innocent eyes up at him. "Do you actually think I would try to be present?"

"I do." His voice held a grim note. "And that, lass, I will not allow."

She subsided, but she was not one to give up—though there was no need to tell Edward that. Surely, since it was she who had uncovered the code, it would be only fair for her to be in on the capture.

She shivered in anticipated excitement. It would be dark, lit only by the moon and stars. Two cloaked and masked figures would creep through the park from opposite directions, casting furtive glances over their shoulders. There would be the hurried meeting and passing of information, but before they could escape, Edward, in the full splendor of his uniform kilt, accompanied by his men, would surround them, and . . . A slight frown knit her brow. This scenario positively cried out for a sword fight. A serviceable pistol would be too tame an ending, but far more likely.

She sighed. As much as she would like to envision it, it would be impossible for Edward to spring a trap if his men came marching in to bagpipes and drums. Her ridiculous, fanciful imagination. She looked up at Edward and discovered that he paid her no heed. From the careful blankness of his expression, she assumed he made plans. What was a romantic lady to do?

Around them, the scattered trees thickened, closing them in. The dry, musty smells of the forest filled the air and insects buzzed loudly about them. Lizzie and Ashfield left the road to ride through a shaded grove. Augusta longed for that freedom.

"When will ye be returning to England?" he asked abruptly.

"I—I am not certain. Soon, I suppose. We want to see Helena and the baby."

"Naturally." His voice held a harsh note, discernible only by one who knew him—or perhaps loved him. "I am surprised ye are not leaving this day."

She shook her head. "There is some unfinished business here." She bit her tongue to keep from saying more.

"Ye have not yet begun another play." He kept his eyes straight ahead.

"You know what I meant. If—if we do not capture—"

"*I,*" he broke in. "And my men."

"If *we,*" she repeated with emphasis, "do not capture anyone, we may need another play."

He glared at her. "Are adventure and daring deeds all ye can think of lass?" The Scottish burr came forward with a vengeance. "How bored ye would—will be, back in your London season."

Before she could answer, a lone horseman came into view, approaching from the south at an easy canter. Captain Trent, she saw. He had come from Nivelles, he declared, where the Belgian troops were quartered.

"Any news?" Mrs. Lansdon leaned eagerly forward in the carriage.

Trent shook his head. "There is movement, of course. There always is, of late. It would be best if you turned back and spent the afternoon somewhat closer to Brussels. You have come a great distance already."

"Have we?" Lizzie rode up. "What lies ahead?"

"About four miles farther and you would reach the village of Waterloo. It is in no way remarkable, I assure you."

Lizzie lost interest.

"Do you think we would not be safe if we continued?" Mrs. Lansdon clutched her reticule and sun shade as if she expected to use both as weapons against the invading French.

Trent shook his head. "There is merely routine troop movement. You would not want your picnic overrun by Belgian dragoons, would you?"

"Rather like an army of ants," Augusta murmured.

Edward did not seem to hear. He watched Captain Trent with a slight frown. Augusta knew a sinking sensation in the pit of her stomach; she recognized that look. It said, more clearly than words, that he had closed her—and everyone else—out once more. She was not a partner, merely one of the players

283

in this deadly game. The day, in spite of the brilliant sun and warm breeze, dimmed.

Nor, from her point of view, did it improve after they reached a likely site for the picnic. Edward drew Vincent Trent aside under pretense of tethering the horses, and Augusta guessed they spoke of the approaching French. War, she realized, might be only days away. Perhaps they should seize the excuse of Helena's baby to return to England.

Tension seemed to spark between the two men, and Edward moved away. Only by the set of his shoulders did he betray his unease. Trent, lacking Edward's natural reserve, showed his emotions more clearly. Abruptly, he turned from the animals and carried a hamper over to Sophronia.

Lizzie settled on the corner of the huge blanket Mrs. Lansdon, with Ashfield's help, had just spread. Captain Trent deposited the hamper in front of the girl and she dove in happily. Before he returned for another, Augusta caught the glance he directed at Ashfield and her heart almost stopped. Suspicion? Distrust? Fear? It ran rampant these days.

While Lizzie and Sophie distributed plates and covered dishes from which wafted a variety of fascinating aromas, Augusta leaned back against the base of a tree. Edward glanced toward her and she beckoned him with a slight movement of her head. He hesitated, then picked up a plate of tea cakes and carried it over to her.

"What did you learn from Captain Trent?" she whispered. She selected a thin slice of almond cake, then looked up at the major. She encountered only a calm, expressionless mask.

"Nothing of importance."

She glared at him. "Are you shutting me out?"

The briefest flicker in the depths of his eyes betrayed his surprise. "Why should I?"

"Because you have closed over again. And you aren't telling me the truth."

He rose. "Let me get ye some chicken. Your sister appears to be enjoying it." He moved away, only to return a minute later with another dish.

She regarded him in growing frustration. "You're not answering me."

"That is because there is nothing to answer." He sounded too smooth, the diplomat at work.

284

She bestowed her sweetest smile on him. "Has anyone ever told you that you are the most exasperating creature in nature?"

He considered it a moment, then nodded. "I believe ye mentioned that once before."

"And has no one else brought it to your attention?"

A slight smile just touched his lips, but it didn't reach his eyes. "I don't believe so."

"Amazing." She hesitated, then pressed on. "Will you not tell me what disturbs you?"

His brow clouded over, and for a moment she thought she saw a trace of regret. It vanished in an instant. "I cannot." He rose, offering her no further explanation, and returned the plate to the blanket. He did not bring her another.

The drive back to Brussels would have been accomplished in silence, except that Lizzie rode on one side of the curricle and Frederick Ashfield on the other. Their current argument, in which they tried to involve Edward and Augusta, centered around the likelihood of the duchess of Richmond's ball being held in three days' time.

"Going to a ball when there might be a battle at any moment is ridiculous!" Lizzie maintained.

"But why cancel it after all the preparations have been made?" Ashfield countered.

She directed a "but who cares" look at him. "Who would want to waste their time *dancing?* There are probably any number of more important things to be done."

Edward stirred from his thoughtful abstraction. "Wellington is very partial to balls."

Lizzie snorted.

"And since it is not canceled," Edward continued, "ye may be sure there is no immediate cause for alarm. Personally, I find the races at Grammont tomorrow to be of more interest."

Lizzie, disgusted by this lack of proper interest in discussing an impending battle, allowed her horse to slow. Ashfield followed suit, and the next moment their voices raised once more in friendly bickering.

Augusta cast Edward a shrewd look. She knew him fairly well, and to her, that reference to Grammont sounded suspiciously like a platitude. "Do you really intend to go to the races tomorrow?" she demanded.

"Of course. I am told that that is where most of the fashionable gentlemen will be."

"Then you are going to watch someone?"

"No one other than a horse." He kept his eyes focused just above his own pair's heads.

"Are you deliberately trying to be provoking? Tell me honestly, do you expect war?"

Edward shook his head. "We must hope not."

"I don't like being lied to."

He looked at her, surprised.

"Or is that what diplomats are best at?"

"I'm not lying to ye. There is a chance it can still be averted by a show of force."

"A very slim one, though?"

He hesitated, then nodded. "But kindly don't spread that about."

"As if I would!"

"Ye know perfectly well ye would." He spoke shortly.

"You are deliberately provoking an argument!" she accused. "I can be very discrete."

"That ye cannot. Ye possess not the least semblance of subterfuge. Your countenance is an open book for anyone to read. And when ye embark on some foolish crusade to help some poor friend, ye never consider the consequences."

She stiffened, more hurt than she cared to admit by this attack. "I had never thought loyalty to be a dishonorable trait."

"When carried to extremes, it is!"

Her throat hurt with the welling of angry tears she refused to acknowledge. "Are you quite through cataloging my faults?" She spoke through clenched teeth.

"I'm sure I have only begun." He cracked his whip, sending the horses forward into a canter.

Not a single word more passed between them on the ride home. When they reached the house, he handed her down, bade the others a curt farewell, and drove off. Augusta repressed the impulse to look after him. Instead, she marched up to her room, where she found some relief by throwing her maltreated pillow across her chamber and thinking up several ripe names she would dearly love to hurl at a particularly infuriating Scotsman.

Whether or not he actually attended the races at Grammont the following day, Augusta assured herself she had absolutely no interest. But the suspicion kept returning that he had deliberately provoked her, perhaps trying to throw her off the scent. By midday, she had convinced herself this was the case.

If so, he would not get away with it, she vowed. The meeting by the lake in the park was set for the night after tomorrow— the same evening as the ball. Perhaps she could slip away from the latter to attend the former. Her fertile brain went to work sorting out details and subterfuges. Edward claimed she had none; he would learn he was wrong.

The day of the races passed, but Edward put in no appearance to tell her what he had learned—if anything. Augusta fumed, but it did her no good. There was nothing she could do but wait.

The following morning, her thoughts were diverted by the rumor that the French had crossed the frontier. This time, Wellington himself confirmed its truth. His calm reassured everyone, and in spite of Mrs. Lansdon's fears, everything continued undisturbed in the city. No military activity alarmed them that day, though they waited—and wondered how long this calm could continue.

Lord Wentworth, calling on them shortly after noon, brought further reassurances. "It seems hopeful that the French will be held at some distance. No need to worry, none whatsoever." He patted Sophronia's hand in a fatherly manner and left with the promise of seeing them on the morrow at the duchess of Richmond's ball.

But as that day dawned, new rumors reached Brussels of a Prussian attack. Augusta's irritation with Edward grew for not coming to tell them the news. Not even Vincent Trent called, as had been his wont of late. That made Augusta even more uneasy. With the inevitable approach of the French, it seemed more than possible that their traitor would depart abruptly to join his cohorts. She could not help wondering if Captain Trent—or one of the others—would suddenly disappear.

Still, it was the contrary Edward and not the impending battle that occupied her mind. She dressed with even more care than usual the next evening. The pink satin ball gown with the apron and ruffled edgings in blond lace appeared more beautiful to her than ever. After a brief argument with her maid, she directed that lady to tie her long, curling hair into a knot at the top of her head. Four heavy, dusky ringlets hung down her back, and feathery tendrils framed her face. She wore only her pearls for ornaments, and two perfect pink roses tucked securely into the knot of her hair. *That* should make Edward look at her.

Her confidence received a boost when she made her way downstairs. Sophronia gasped in approval and Mrs. Lansdon sighed in a combination of pride and resignation for her own daughter's less breathtaking appearance. Yes, unless Edward were blind, he must appreciate the effort she made.

And Sophie, Augusta noted with pleasure, actually looked pretty this night. There was a happiness about her, which Augusta knew, unfortunately, was due to Vincent Trent. The girl almost floated outside to the waiting carriage. Sincerely, Augusta hoped she was wrong about the captain's involvement in all this trouble.

They arrived shortly at the duchess's house off the Rue de la Blanchisserie, and moved through the ballroom, greeting acquaintances. Rumors of what was occurring only miles away dominated the conversation. The numerous officers who usually attended any offered entertainment were noticeably reduced in number. Augusta felt on edge, then realized it came from the excitement that hummed about the room. Everyone appeared worried, anticipating the coming conflict.

She tried to close out the talk of war that hummed in her ears. Deliberately, she allowed her gaze to roam about the ballroom, noting the rose-trellised wallpaper, the lillies, the candles, the flowers everywhere. It was a beautiful setting— made for romance, for balmy summer breezes, soft, lilting music, and handsome, attentive gentlemen. The heat of the evening and the tension of impending war sat heavily on her, forcing her back to a reality that did not belong at such an event.

She danced with a young officer whose excitement at the prospect of facing the French forces could barely be contained. Her next partner, a more sober young man who had served both in the Peninsula and in the more recent conflict in America, did not speak much. A faraway look haunted his eyes, as of remembered pain. Augusta clasped his hand warmly as the dance ended, but she knew he would find little comfort until the inevitable battle reached its end.

As she came down a country dance, she glimpsed Edward standing to one side of the ballroom. She had no idea he had arrived. Relief filled her just at the knowledge he was near. He glanced at her, but immediately looked away, as if not wanting to be caught in the act. The suspicion that he intended to avoid her, to keep from telling her his plans for later, crossed her mind. He wuld not get away with that.

Before she could go to him, the duchess's entertainment began and out marched a number of soldiers from the 42nd Highland Regiment to the accompaniment of their pipes and drums. Excitement filled Augusta at the dramatic sight they made in their kilts and plaid stockings, with their tartans cast across their shoulders. Edward's regiment. How she would like to see him among them. . . .

And how he would like to be with them, she realized. She caught sight of his frozen expression. He stood stiffly across the floor from her, then he turned abruptly away as the soldiers began to dance to the celebratory music of their pipes. Her heart went out to him. She could just picture him in his kilt, alone in some misty moor, playing a pipe. Or perhaps with a comrade who would play for him while he danced over his sword. . . .

The Highlanders withdrew and the ball resumed. Augusta's next partner claimed her and she could not go in pursuit of Edward as she longed. Perhaps it was best; he might need a few minutes of solitude.

That thought nearly choked her. Edward, she discovered to her chagrin, appeared to have found ample diversion. He was dancing with a vivacious blonde. She turned back to her own partner, refusing to succumb to the urge to watch the major.

She did not glimpse him again until a little later, when he approached an alcove on the other side of the ballroom. He looked about, casually, then slipped inside. Now what—? The question barely formed in her mind before she spotted Captain Trent slipping toward that same alcove. With a quick glance, repetitious of Edward's, he ducked behind the curtain also.

Augusta felt a small hand grasp her elbow, and jumped.

"I *must* know what they are talking about!" Sophronia started across the floor.

Augusta knew not one moment's hesitation. With her longer

strides, she led the way. They could easily take the chairs by the curtain, pretend to talk, and listen to what went on within.

Augusta seated herself, waving her fan before her warm cheeks. The heat made an admirable excuse. When her partner tried to claim the next dance, she would merely send him for refreshments.

The deep murmur of masculine voices sounded behind her and she strained her ears.

"I cannot like it," she heard Edward say.

"Do you think I like it better?" Captain Trent's voice rose slightly. "I feel a cad whenever I am with Miss Lansdon."

"With luck, it will be over this night." Edward's Scottish burr became more pronounced.

"It had better be! I cannot say I have succeeded very well with my damnable methods." A scuffing of shoes sounded on the marble-tiled floor, as if he took a few rapid, pacing steps. "Not even dancing attendance on Miss Lansdon has been sufficient to help me get to the bottom of this mess. That should have given me the entrée to at least her brother's confidences. But I have learned nothing."

Augusta's hand shot out, instinctively stifling the cry of dismay from Sophronia. She did not dare look at the girl. Her worst fears for her sake confirmed. . . .

"Nay. It is Miss Carstairs who has won that, and we have learned what little we have because I—" Edward broke off.

Derision echoed through Trent's words. "Because you play the same damnable game with her."

"Aye." The syllable came out cold and uncompromising, a death knell to Augusta's dreams. "That I have. And I thank God it will now be over."

Chapter 23

Thank God it will now be over. The words ran through Augusta's mind. She turned away, shattered, betrayed by her foolish romantic dreams. Edward cared nothing for her, only the information and insights she provided. She had suspected that once. . . . Why had she ignored that inner warning? It must have been obvious to everyone else. Even Lizzie had pointed out how ridiculous such a match would be. But she had been too besotted—too much in love.

Tears she refused to shed misted her eyes. This explained so much: his seeming to enjoy her company only to win her trust; his curt withdrawal once she had served her purpose. Even his kisses he had used to draw information from her, to make her only too eager to share everything she learned. She thought she had pierced his armor, penetrated to the warm heart he kept buried deep within. The truth was that he didn't have one.

Sophronia touched her arm and Augusta looked down to see the girl's hazel eyes swimming with tears that slipped over her lashes. Her own pain she thrust aside.

"At—at least we know Captain Trent is not guilty of treason," she whispered.

For a moment, relief showed in Sophronia's expressive countenance, then it clouded over once more. "This—this is every bit as dishonorable, in its way. I—I have been a *pawn*, allowing him to use me just to spy on Perry!" She sprang to her feet, her chin quivering, and before Augusta could stop her, she tore back the curtain.

Edward and Captain Trent looked up, startled, from a roughly sketched map of the park they studied. Trent's brow snapped down at sight of her.

"I hate you!" She breathed the words. "Your behavior has been despicable. If I were a man, I would call you out."

"Sophie—" He thrust the paper toward Edward and took a step toward her.

"I never want to see you again." She turned on her heel and marched off.

Augusta remained where she was for one long moment, staring at Edward, memorizing the taut lines of his face, the tense jaw, the eyes that seemed brittle and icy by the flickering candlelight. She couldn't hate him, but she could hate herself for being a fool. A hopelessly romantic fool.

He said nothing, made no apologies or excuses. He just stood there, watching her. Well, what had she expected? For the ever-correct Edward to go down on his knees and beg her forgiveness? The mere idea was laughable. She turned and followed Sophronia.

The girl had stopped a few feet ahead of her, wrestling to control the emotion that threatened to overcome her. The face she raised to Augusta was a picture of misery. With an obvious effort, she mastered her expression. "I—I am sending for the carriage. Will—will you please tell Mamma?" Her eyes widened as she stared over Augusta's shoulder and she almost ran away.

"Augusta." Edward's soft voice warned her.

Slowly, giving herself time to control her own emotions, she turned to face him. "I am so glad we were of use in your investigation, Major. You can have no notion the pleasure that thought gives me."

"Augusta—" His brow snapped down and his mouth tightened.

A savage satisfaction shot through her. At least she had succeeded in irritating him, even if she had done nothing else. Small compensation when she had longed for love, but that emotion must be alien to his nature. "Excuse me, Major."

She broke free of the hand that had clasped her elbow and strode off with what dignity she could muster. She found Mrs. Lansdon seated on the far side of the ballroom with Lady Eversley, calmly discussing the gowns of every lady present. Augusta just touched Mrs. Lansdon's arm and that lady looked up at her, smiling.

"Yes, dear?"

"Sophronia has developed the headache. Would you mind terribly if we went home?"

Mrs. Lansdon, all concern, rose at once. "Excuse me, Lavinia. How dreadful for poor Sophie. Where is she, dear?" She took Augusta's arm and hurried off to find their cloaks.

As they neared the door, a stir occurred and the duke of Wellington entered. A number of couples stopped dancing, watching as several people hurried up to him. Augusta did not need to hear to know what their question would be. The answer rippled across the room.

"War, tomorrow," Augusta whispered. Her throat filled with emotion and she turned wide, stinging eyes to survey the ballroom, where the officers had deserted their partners and now stood in little knots, tense, excited. How many of them would not return?

Perry stood frozen to the floor, his partner staring up at him in horror. Across from him, Roddy met his gaze in mute understanding and camaraderie. They were so young, mere children—as were so many of the men who would march off on the morrow.

Vaguely, she was aware that the music continued, that a few couples still danced, but it seemed dreamlike, out of place now. A number of officers, who were quartered at some distance from Brussels and were anxious to rejoin their regiments before dawn, took their leave. Augusta watched them depart with a sense of loss. Captain Trent was one of them.

A strong hand pressed on her shoulder and she looked up to see Frederick Ashfield, his expression solemn. "Say the word and I will take you and Lizzie back to England."

Augusta swallowed and shook her head. "How could we? Leave, without knowing what—" She broke off, then continued. "Are you planning on running?"

"No." His eyes remained on the departing officers. "Do you know?" He sounded odd, almost whimsical. "At a moment like this, I could almost wish I had embraced a military career."

"It would not be your style in the least," Augusta informed him, trying to rally her spirits. "Could you see yourself in a black neckcloth? Or perhaps the blue frock coat and sash of an aide-de-camp?"

"Very true." He shook his head in mock sorrow, but it did not hide the envious light that flickered in his eyes. "You are quite right, as always, my dear Augusta. I must find my amusements elsewhere." His hand tightened momentarily, then he released her and strode off in search of the duchess of Richmond to take his leave.

How typically male, Augusta thought. Frederick Ashfield was one of the few men in the room who would not face battle and possible death on the morrow, and he regretted it! She turned, saw Jack Kettering striding toward her, and her heart lifted. If he had to go to war, she was glad of the opportunity of seeing him once more.

Impulsively, she reached out and he clasped her hands, then drew her into the waltz that continued. It felt odd to be dancing, but she matched his steps. "I didn't know you were here. I looked for you earlier."

"Did you, my beautiful Augusta? I was delayed, and arrived only a few minutes before Wellington."

She looked up and saw the agony of his expression. Her fingers tightened about his.

"It is war," he said abruptly. "I—I never thought it would come to this. Wentworth was so certain the diplomats could control Napoleon."

"Take care." She couldn't keep from saying the words.

His eyes burned into hers. He stopped, but still held her, gazing down into her face. "Marry me when I come back. Give me that hope to live for."

She opened her mouth, but couldn't bring herself to send him into battle with her refusal haunting him. "We—we'll talk about it when you return." At least she could promise that with all sincerity.

He drew her fingers to his lips, then pressed an ardent kiss into the palm of her gloved hand. He turned and left her without another word.

Shaken, she went in search of Sophronia and Mrs. Lansdon, and found them with Perry and Roddy. Sophie's tears streamed freely down her cheeks. The expressions of both young men were sober, though excitement kindled unexpected animation in Roddy's face.

"We had best be off," Perry said shortly. He kissed his mamma, then his sister, then turned and held out his hand to Augusta.

She took it and knew the sick fear that it might be for the last time. She bade him farewell, then Roddy also, and the two friends strode out. To meet their fate, she thought, and somehow that phrase did not seem in the least bit trite. This battle might well be the making of both of them—if they lived.

She turned away, encountered Sophronia's and Mrs. Lansdon's bleak unhappiness and fear, and knew she would have her hands filled comforting them to the best of her ability. She could only hope the battle would be short, and Perry—and the others—would ride home safely the following night.

At least the man she loved would not face this danger. Augusta looked about, but she could see no sign of Edward. With a sense of shock, she remembered the meeting in the park that night. Would anyone bother to keep it? she wondered. What point could there be, with the French troops already poised to engage in battle.

"Let us stay," Sophronia declared, wiping her eyes. She was not the only young lady in the room resorting to her handkerchief. "I want to hear everything I can."

Mrs. Lansdon sank down onto a chair. "What—what does Lord Wellington say?"

"I have heard very little," Augusta replied, her eyes seeking out the great man. "He seems calm. Perhaps it will all be no great thing. The officers are being sent to so many different places, they don't seem to be concentrating in any one area. Surely that must be a good sign."

The dancing continued, and Augusta was claimed by a serious-faced officer who uttered no more than two words to her. She welcomed the end of that dance with relief. Sophronia, she noted, fared better, partnered by an eager young Hussar who appeared to welcome the morrow as a splendid adventure. Augusta could only hope he would not say anything to distress the girl.

Apparently, he did not, for when they presently went down to supper, Sophie managed a smile and whispered to Augusta that perhaps there would not be so very much fighting after all. "It will be a display of force," she informed Augusta with all the authority of one green lieutenant's hopes. "Perry and—and the others should be quite safe."

But a dispatch, reported to Wellington by the Prince of Orange a few minutes later, shattered those hopes. Charleroi had fallen that morning, there had been several skirmishes, and the French advanced steadily.

"We won't be able to hold Napoleon at Quatre-Bras." Augusta's last partner, seated at her side, spoke softly.

"Is—was—that the intention?"

He glanced down at her and nodded. "There is nothing to fear. Wellington will redirect troops to meet him somewhere else." But to Augusta, the words sounded like mere platitudes, and her foreboding grew.

Wellington's departure, shortly after the supper, signaled the end of the ball. Outside, bugles sounded, summoning men from their lodgings, and the drums beat steadily. Soldiers filled the streets, their coats partially buttoned, their knapsacks and muskets in their hands as they ran to find their regiments.

The carriages leaving the ball slowed, giving way before this urgent mustering. Augusta shivered, wondering how she could ever have thought the military to be a romantic career. The sight was moving, exhilarating—but what would it be like on the battlefield tomorrow?

They were put down before their house, but they did not go inside. Augusta walked forward, toward the corner, and watched as the first tracings of dawn touched the chaos of the city. Wagons were loaded and regiments formed, then began their long procession along the Rue de Namur toward the gate. Abruptly, Augusta turned and went inside, trying to block this from her mind.

She found no relief in sleep. She lay awake, listening to the unmistakable sounds of an army setting off to war. Wagon wheels jostled over the cobbled paving, booted feet tramped steadily to the cadence of the drums, the shod hooves of the horses stamped nervously, then moved forward. The bugles still sounded, then faded beneath the stirring bravado of bagpipes. The Highlanders gathered, perhaps the same ones who had danced at the ball, playing their pipes once more—but for a very different reason. . . . She rolled over and buried her face in her pillow, wishing war could have remained remote and unreal to her.

She must have dozed off, for a slight clicking sound, followed by the protesting creak of her door, brought her fully awake. Her eyes flew open as a hand clamped over her mouth. Terrified, she tried to bite it, but it was too well placed.

"Quiet." Edward's voice hissed the word and she stopped

struggling. He waited a moment until she nodded, then he released her.

"What are you doing here?" she demanded, anger replacing her terror of the moment before.

"I need ye to do something for me."

Her indignation swelled. "You have the nerve to come to my bedchamber and demand my assistance? At least you have the decency not to pretend to make love to me this time!"

"I don't have time for an argument." He hissed the words. "Keep this for me. The man who was to take it has already left with his regiment." He thrust a key into her hand. "Keep it on ye. I—or someone else—may have need of it if we are to capture our traitor."

She accepted it, reluctant. "Why can't you keep it yourself?"

"Because I may not be here when it's needed."

She ground her teeth at this half-answer. "What happened at the meeting?"

"It wasn't kept."

A smile of disdain just curved her lip. "How could it, with the soldiers all over the streets?"

He shook his head. "It wasn't kept earlier either."

She struggled to a sitting position and pulled the coverlet to her neck. "What did you expect? With war so close, they probably had no need to pass their information."

His jaw tightened. "We still have a traitor to capture."

"*You* do. You made it clear what type of help you want from me." She snapped the words. "You've given me your key, now I will thank you to get out of my room."

He looked down at her, his face a blur in the meager light of dawn. "There is unfinished business between ye and me."

She stiffened. "There is no need to continue with this ridiculous pretense, I assure you. I will not complain to Halliford of the tactics you employed to gain your information, if that is your fear."

"It is not." His voice sounded tight.

She bit her lip to stop its trembling, glad of the semidarkness that hid her flushed cheeks. "There is no need to apologize either. I served to help your investigation, you served to divert my boredom. I believe we are even." She tilted her head back to gaze up at him, defiant.

297

"Boredom." He drew a deep breath and let it out slowly. "Was that really all it was for ye? Ye cannot imagine my relief, madam, to hear ye confirm that ye were not the foolish innocent ye seemed. But since your heart was not engaged, there has been no harm done." He sketched her a bow and strode toward the door.

"Edward!" She tried to stop him, but her only answer was the soft shutting of the door behind him. He was gone.

She sank back on the pillows. If her heart had not been engaged, he said. But it had been—it still was—and perhaps his had been as well. There was something still for them to settle—if he gave her that chance.

Sleep refused to return. Light seeped into her room, and too restless to remain still, she rose and dressed. She went to the window to look out onto emptiness where there had been so much activity only a short time before. Silence engulfed the city. The sheer lifelessness of the scene below filled her with a sense of dread rather than the relief she should have felt.

Sophronia, heavy-eyed and pale, joined her in the breakfast parlor barely an hour later, followed almost at once by Lizzie.

Lizzie went to the window and stared out. "It's *too* quiet."

"Did you hear—?" Augusta rose to join her.

Lizzie nodded. "It's being said there will probably be no action today."

"Where did you hear that?" Sophronia, not familiar with Lizzie's penchant for discovering information, looked at her in surprise.

"From the baker, who heard it from some gentlemen who watched Wellington ride out." She fell silent for a minute, watching as a carriage drew up in the street before the neighboring house. "People are leaving Brussels and returning to England."

"We—we are staying." Sophie's voice trembled.

"Of course we are." Lizzie sounded disgusted. "And we are going to help get ready for the arrival of any wounded."

Augusta turned from the window, smiling in spite of her heavy heart. "I suppose you even know where we should go and what we should bring."

"Well, of course." Lizzie regarded her in surprise. "And that reminds me. I must see your mamma, Sophie." She swooped down on the plate of rolls, selected two, and strode

298

back out of the room.

The remainder of the day passed in a whirl of activity, for they joined the other ladies of the city in preparing bandages and gathering medicines. Lord Wentworth found them in the early afternoon, piling pillows and blankets to be taken to the tents that would be erected at the Namur and Louvain gates for the care of the wounded.

"What is happening?" Augusta demanded, eager for any word.

He relieved her of her load, and she picked up another pile. "There is no word yet. I thought I would ride out toward Waterloo and see if I can learn anything."

"Oh, would you? We should be so glad to hear!"

By three o'clock, the distant rumble of cannon reached them. Augusta stopped her shredding of lint and turned to stare out the window, torn by the ominous sound. The battle had begun.

Nor was she the only one to long for information. Few of the gentlemen remaining in the city could resist trying to discover what occurred, and a number of them set forth, only to return in the early evening with conflicting reports. The sheer lack of definite knowledge wore at Augusta's nerves.

Lord Wentworth, along with the grim-faced Frederick Ashfield, joined them for dinner. Ashfield, too, had been one of those to ride out. The soldiers with whom he had spoken had given him a very different account from that given by the ones Lord Wentworth had interviewed, but it was no more encouraging. Once more, he suggested the ladies depart Brussels.

"It cannot be that bad!" Mrs. Lansdon protested, torn between protecting the girls and remaining as near to her only son as possible.

"Where is Edward?" Lizzie asked suddenly. "I thought he'd be here this evening. Has he gone to learn more, too?"

Augusta's jaw clenched. His key, which she had threaded on a long chain about her neck, felt cold against her skin where it rested. "We haven't seen him since the ball."

"Didn't you know?" Lord Wentworth turned to her in surprise. "He has rejoined his regiment."

The blood drained from Augusta's cheeks, leaving her face cold and damp. "His—his regiment? You mean to fight?"

Ashfield nodded. "I saw him briefly at Waterloo."

"What-what did he do there?" Augusta demanded.

"Rode on," Ashfield said. "He said he was for Quatre-Bras."

Augusta lowered her eyes to her plate. That must have been what he wanted to tell her, the business that lay between them. And she had angered him instead, making him think she didn't care. Tears stung her eyes. She couldn't bear the thought of him riding once more into battle! He had seen enough of war. For once, the thought of him again in his kilt did not bring her pleasure.

Cannon rumbled on into the night, growing less distinct as the hours passed, finally fading. Still, Augusta could not seek her bed. She sat up in the drawing room, waiting with Lizzie, Sophie, and Mrs. Lansdon.

Ashfield and Wentworth, who had gone out to collect news, returned with the first word of casualties. Lord Roderick, Wentworth said, had taken a ball in the shoulder and had been removed fron the action. There was no word of Perry, though Sophronia and Mrs. Lansdon cried out in alarm. Nor of Captain Trent—nor Edward. At last, knowing there would be work to do on the morrow, they separated and made their way to their chambers.

Exhaustion overcame Augusta's troubled thoughts and she slept, only to be awakened a few short hours later by Lizzie calling her to come down. The sun still rested low in the sky, for it was only six, but panic had broken out in the streets. A troop of Belgian Cavalry rode in, Lizzie reported. Everyone cried that the British were in retreat with the French following rapidly.

But the alarm died down, soon discovered to be nothing more than another unfounded rumor. Augusta set to work with the others tearing bed linen into strips for bandages, and somehow the morning passed.

About noon, Lord Wentworth called at the house, his face grave. He glanced at Augusta, then drew Mrs. Lansdon aside. "It has gone ill with the Highland Regiment, I fear."

Augusta, craning to catch his murmured words, felt her heart stop, then resume with a painful jerk. Her scissors fell from her nerveless fingers and she hurried over to him. "What—what have you heard? Please, tell me."

He hesitated, then took her hand gently between his own. "I

am sorry, my dear. They say their losses have been terrible."

"And—and Edward—Major MacKennoch?"

He shook his head. "It is probably no nore than a rumor. You know how little accurate information we have received."

"*What have you heard?*"

The pressure of his hands increased. "He is dead."

Chapter 24

Augusta's knees deserted her and she sank into a chair. "Dead?" she whispered. She felt cold, then blazing hot. Edward . . .

Something pressed against her lips. She blinked, then sipped from the glass of brandy Lord Wentworth held for her. She drew her trembling hand away from Mrs. Lansdon, who made vain attempts to chafe her wrist. "When? How?"

Lord Wentworth shook his head. "It could be nothing more than a rumor. We know so very little."

She nodded, but knew this diplomatic ploy for what it was. Edward. . . She took another sip of the brandy, then pushed it away.

Lizzie perched on the arm of her chair, her expression somber. She slipped an arm about Augusta and squeezed. Augusta stood, dislodging her sister from her precarious perch.

"We—we have blankets and bandages to get to the tents. Have—have they been erected yet?"

"Augusta—"

She shook her head, waving away Sophronia's solicitous hands. "We have work to do! If—if the Highlanders have sustained such heavy casualties, there will be any number of injured as well. We must get everything ready!" She scooped up an armload of neatly wound linen strips and ran blindly out the door, fighting back tears that would do no one any good now.

Reports continued to filter into the city throughout the day, but Augusta paid them no heed. Later, she knew, it would matter that the Prussians had been defeated, but not now. The pain of Edward's loss filled her, leaving room for nothing else.

With the arrival of the first wagon loads of wounded, her attention found a worthy direction. For some reason, the tents had not yet been erected, and the soldiers filled the streets, lying anywhere they fell or could drag themselves. Augusta and Sophronia directed anyone they could find to help carry men into their house, where Mrs. Lansdon and Lizzie awaited them with blankets, laudanum, and bandages.

Lady Eversley and Lady Lutridge joined them, as did several other ladies of their acquaintance, and they set to work at once. Augusta returned outside, carrying a pitcher of water and a glass, doing what little she could to ease the pain and misery of the men who lay in the street, exhausted, dying. She swallowed to ease the tightness in her throat. Had there been anyone to ease Edward's last hours? Looking about, seeing the suffering, she could only pray he had been killed outright.

By late afternoon the tents were at last in place at the gates, and she spent the next hour and more helping the wounded to shelter. Rain, incongruous after the blazing sun of the morning, recalled Augusta from her numbness. Lightning flashed across the sky. In minutes, she was soaked through, but she continued her work.

Why did the stark emptiness of Edward's loss not fade with the passing hours? Later, she knew, the wound to her heart would feel as raw and terrible as those she bandaged. But now she existed in a void, with a vast nothingness where her feelings ought to be. Sudden, piercing pain shot through her, only to vanish again, leaving her hollow and cold.

She drifted among the men under the cover of the tent, pouring water and brandy, changing bandages, moving compulsively to keep herself busy. Lizzie joined her, and threw a shawl about her shaking shoulders. They went on. She searched for Edward, she realized; she denied the fact he had been killed, refused to accept the truth. She ached to tell him how much she loved him.

In the dark of the late evening, Frederick Ashfield found her back in the street, oblivious to the rain that pelted down as she gave what comfort she could to the weary men who dragged themselves back into town.

"Come." He gripped her firmly by the shoulders and compelled her to accompany him. "Mrs. Lansdon sent me to find you. Lizzie and Miss Lansdon have returned already. It's time you had something to eat and a few hours' sleep."

She nodded, too exhausted and empty to do anything else, and allowed him to take her back to the house. After her maid assisted her into a warm gown and towel-dried her hair, she went back downstairs. The horrors of the day effectively killed any appetite in her, but to please her hostess and the ever-practical Lizzie, she managed to swallow a few mouthfuls. As she raised a fork, she caught sight of her knuckles, scraped on the paving stones as she'd lifted a private's head. The vivid memory of his agony tore through her like a knife.

Lord Wentworth came in while they ate, but the only news he brought was of retreat, the French advance, and tremendous casualties. The panicked desire to escape that gripped Brussels didn't touch Augusta. She left Wentworth in low-voiced conversation with Ashfield and went to bed, though she was too tired to sleep.

Instead, she lay there, refusing to acknowledge her grief, unable to give up her determined belief that Edward must live. He would come back. Somehow, he wouldn return to her. For a very long while, she watched the flashes of lightning illuminating the night sky and tried not to flinch at the rumbling thunder that sounded so much like cannon bursting upon them.

Morning came, and Augusta dragged herself from her bed and prepared to return to her work. Mrs. Lansdon, ably assisted by Lady Eversley, saw to the soldiers they had taken into their home. Lizzie and Sophronia accompanied Augusta back to one of the great tents to lend what assistance they could.

All seemed calm, for the deep rumble of the cannonading did not reach them that day. The wounded still came in with alarming and depressing regularity, despite the almost impassible roads which were blocked by carts sunk deep in the mud.

"It never ends," Sophronia sighed as she brought Augusta another stack of bandages.

Augusta nodded, fastened the lint about a Belgian private's head as she had done so often that day, and rose. Another wagon of wounded had arrived. They would need water, brandy, and whatever else she could give.

Lord Roderick, his face grim and his right arm useless in a

sling, limped among the men who lay on blankets on the ground. He assisted the doctor as that overworked gentleman hurried from one makeshift bed to the next, casting a cursory eye over the occupant's wounds and the treatment received at the battle site.

Roddy managed a smile when he saw them, but he did not waver from his job as he held a soldier's arm for the doctor to extract a bullet. Only two days before, he would have flinched and been of little help; this was not the Roddy she knew. He had aged, matured, and with a sudden pang it occurred to Augusta that none of them would ever be the same.

She turned away, trying to block out the low moans, the cries of agony, the smells of blood and festering wounds that would haunt her nightmares for years to come. Resolutely, she joined the other ladies in rendering the men as comfortable as possible. There seemed more than they could possibly help, but they had to try.

She knelt down beside an officer, half of whose face was covered in bloody bandages. He turned his feverish head on the rolled blanket that served as a pillow, and with a sense of horror, she recognized Vincent Trent. His muddied coat had been cut back, revealing the remnants of his shirt and a shoulder wrapped in dirty bandages. All animosity forgotten, she saw him only as a colleague, a friend of Edward's—of all of theirs.

Her hand trembling, she brushed the lank dark hair back from his forehead. "Captain Trent? Vincent?"

He opened bleary eyes and tried to focus on her. "Sophie?" The name was barely audible as he spoke through dry, cracked lips.

"I'll find her." Lizzie spoke from behind Augusta and hurried off.

Augusta poured him water mixed with brandy and held it to his mouth. He sipped it with care, then sank back, exhausted by this simple act.

Sophronia ran to them and dropped to her knees beside Augusta, her face filled with fear. Tears streamed down her cheeks. "Vincent?"

"Sophie?" He spoke her name more clearly. He reached out with his good hand and the girl clasped it tightly between her own. His eyes closed and his head rolled to the other side.

305

"Laudanum," Lizzie said knowledgeably, before Sophronia could panic. "They're giving it to them to ease the pain, but it makes them sleepy."

A low, soul-wrenching groan from the next man recalled Augusta to the urgency of her work. She rose. "I had better not stay."

Sophie nodded, barely noticing. A shaky sob escaped her and she nursed Captain Trent's hand to her tear-dampened cheek. "I—I can't leave him."

This penetrated the captain's fuzzed brain. He dragged his eyes open once more. "Love you," he managed to get out, though his voice was little more than a croak. Pain shuddered through him, but when he got it under control, he clasped her hand tighter. "Marry me."

Sophie appeared unaware of his slurred speech or the unorthodox circumstances of this proposal. She kissed him gently, then with a tremulous laugh, wiped her falling tears from the unbandaged portion of his face.

Lizzie rose, patently disgusted by such maudlin sentiments. "If you two are going to murmur the most revolting endearments to each other, I'm off."

Sophronia looked up, smiling mistily. "Oh, yes, Lizzie. We are running low on almost everything. Do you think you could go to a chemist's?"

The captain turned to focus on Augusta, who had just stood from tending to the man next to him. "MacKennoch," he breathed.

Augusta stiffened, then forced back her anguish at hearing his name. "I know, Captain. Lord Wentworth told me."

Trent managed to nod. "Saw him. Yesterday, I think. Sent his love. Said he'd see you soon."

Unbearable pain seared through her, then receded, leaving her emptier than ever. He must have seen Edward just before—

Tears filling her eyes, Augusta turned away. She couldn't tell him about Edward—he'd learn soon enough, and her loss was still too great to speak of it. She fled, accompanying Lizzie on her errand.

They hurried the three blocks to the chemist's shop they had frequented over the last few days, buoyed somehow by the knowledge that at least Captain Trent and Lord Roderick both lived.

"If only we could get word of Perry and Jack Kettering," Augusta exclaimed as they walked.

Lizzie nodded, unusually subdued. "I wish Edward had made it. Captain Trent didn't know about him."

Augusta fought back the tears that blocked her throat and didn't answer. Someone ran behind them, she could hear the rapid footsteps, but she didn't look until her name was called.

"Jack!" Relief at seeing him alive and unhurt flooded through her, briefly dispelling her numbness. "Your safe! What is the news?"

He gripped her hands. "The battle is turning. Wellington is still in retreat, but he will have them yet. Come, Augusta, I need you."

"Of course. But—" She glanced at Lizzie. "We were on our way to get medicines for the tent."

"Can you get them, Lizzie?" Kettering didn't release Augusta's hands. "I have an injured friend. He needs help, more than I can give him."

"Could you, Lizzie?" Augusta threw an uncertain look at her sister. She couldn't refuse. Lizzie hesitated, then nodded and started off. Kettering grasped Augusta's arm and drew her back the way he had come.

"Vincent Trent is badly injured, but here in Brussels." Augusta hurried to keep pace with him. "We'll have him transferred to the house as soon as possible. And Roddy has taken a ball in his arm, but is helping with the other wounded. Have you news of Perry?"

He shook his head. "I've seen no one." His grip tightened and he almost dragged her along.

"Where is your friend?" Augusta looked about in surprise. They turned onto a narrow side street and Kettering's pace quickened once more.

"Not much farther." He looked down at her, a queer, desperate light in his eyes. "I cannot thank you enough for your assistance."

"I only hope there is something I can do."

A soft laugh escaped him. "Believe me, my dear, you are doing a great deal."

His tone surprised her, though after the horrors he must have witnessed, it was probably only natural that he should be so on edge. He must have found time to change, for his

307

uniform, unlike the others she had seen, bore few traces of dirt.

"Here." He almost dragged her up the steps of an old house.

Under other circumstances, she would have hesitated to enter such a place, situated as it was in an unsavory quarter of town. But if there was someone inside who needed help, she couldn't permit foolish scruples to weigh with her. Kettering shoved her ahead of him into a darkened hall and closed the door, locking it behind him with an ominous click. The sound echoed, hollow, through the empty house.

Augusta looked about, noting three doors standing open. She peeped through one and saw a room devoid of furniture, then looked at Kettering in uncertainty. "Where is your friend?"

"There is no friend, my dear." He pocketed the key and took a step toward her.

Instinctively, she retreated. "What is this about?"

A stair creaked as someone stepped on it, and she almost cried out in relief as she saw Lord Wentworth descending. Kettering's brow snapped down in displeasure.

Wentworth stopped on the landing as he saw them. "What the devil are you doing?" he demanded.

"I have brought her." Kettering put his arm around Augusta's shoulders and she pulled away, startled and not in the least bit pleased.

"Damn it, man!" Wentworth, furious, came down the last steps. "What are you trying to do? Ruin all?"

"Not in the least. I'm going to marry her. Don't look so grim, she'll be silent."

"No, Jack, please." Augusta looked from one to the other, uncertain. "I have no wish—we would not suit—" She knew she was stammering, but he had taken her by surprise.

He took her chin in his hand, forcing her to look up at him. His expression held a wealth of longing, but it was the determination underlying his desire that frightened her.

"Please, Jack—" she swallowed, trying not to give in to the panic that crept over her.

"You will marry me, my love. Once I have you safely wed, you will come to enjoy it, that I promise you." His fingers stroked her cheek and she tried to pull free. "But understand this. You will not leave this house until Halliford has

308

paid handsomely."

"Ransom?" She shook her head in disbelief. "He won't."

"I think he will."

"Lord Wentworth!" Augusta, seriously alarmed, looked to the other man, confused as to why he just stood there and let Kettering threaten her.

"This is folly!" He strode up to them, hands on his hips, and glowered.

"She will do as I say, you need have no fear." Kettering faced him squarely.

Augusta looked from one to the other in growing understanding. What a complete fool she had been not to see it before! Their desperation altered them from the men she had known for the last six months, making them dangerous—or perhaps revealing them as they actually were, stripped of their polite social manners. She faced not one enemy but two, and that knowledge firmed her quavering courage.

"Why?" she asked Kettering, her voice oddly calm.

"Folly!" Wentworth glared at her.

"It isn't." Kettering's unsteady fingers tugged at a button of his uniform coat. "Napoleon will be defeated before this day is out, mark my words. And even if he *did* win, he would have no need to pay us any longer for information!"

"You won't get the money you covet from *her!*" Wentworth snorted in disdain. "You're a fool! You may wish to live out your days on the Continent, but I have no such desire now."

Kettering gave a shaky laugh. "What choice do I have? I deserted my regiment!"

Wentworth ignored him; he ran an appraising eye over Augusta. "We will have to kill her and be done with it." He regarded her with honest regret. "It's a pity, my dear, for I am really very fond of you, but you must see you cannot be permitted to give our little scheme away."

"No." Kettering grasped her wrist and pulled her to him again. "Once she is my wife, I will have the ordering of her. We'll go to Italy, where nothing she could say would do you harm."

Wentworth regarded him in disgust. "She is no biddable pea goose. If you had eyes, you would see it is not you she loves. The moment she walks out of here she will bring her precious major and that confounded captain down on us."

Augusta swallowed. "Edward is dead," she breathed.

"No, my dear. To my unending regret, that rumor proved false. But when I told you, I honestly believed it to be true."

Shock left her momentarily weak. Edward lived. . . . Then so must she. Her brain, numbed by the continuous onslaught of horrors over the past three days, began to function once more.

He must have seen the hope shine in her eyes, for he shook his head. "I am sorry, my dear. If you are imagining some dramatic rescue on his part, you might as well forget it. He will not have the opportunity."

She couldn't abandon hope. She had to see Edward, to tell him of her love. She had to stall. "Why—why did you become involved in this?" She addressed Wentworth. "How could you betray all you have worked for?"

He raised surprised eyebrows. "Because Napoleon is a genius. His defeat will be a tremendous loss to Europe. With the right diplomats at his side, he could have ruled the world and brought about a golden age unparalleled in history."

"With . . ." Her voice trailed off. With diplomats in control, he had frequently said something similar. She should have guessed how deeply he believed in that.

"In England, a diplomat is no more than a tool, too often set aside and ignored. Under Napoleon, we would have wielded real power. So you see, my dear, it *was* a question of loyalty—to my chosen profession. Napoleon promised to elevate us above these tawdry armies. We would have directed relations between countries. *We* would have ruled, at his side."

"And—and Captain Montclyff?" Did she merely prolong her agony or could she manage to escape? She glanced at Kettering, whose restless hand ran along her arm, but saw no help there. She had to formulate some plan, but none presented itself.

"Yes, Captain Montclyff. A most unsuitable cat's paw. He actually tried to demand more money from me for obtaining bits of information. Foolish of him."

The coolness of his tone left her feeling ill. "Did—did you order him to fight that duel with Perry?"

"Oh, you mustn't think it went against his will. He was only too happy to dispose of Lansdon for me. I merely told him the young fool had discovered what he was about. The rest was quite easy. I just waited for them."

"Then—it was you who blackmailed Perry."

Lord Wentworth's face hardened. "That particular bit of folly belongs at Kettering's door." He turned to regard the lieutenant, his eyes steely. "I am not pleased about that, you know, not in the least. You might well have given all away. The only wonder is that it took me so long to find out what you were up to."

Kettering shrugged, the picture of an errant schoolboy hauled on the carpet. "I wasn't like to get caught. And why should Lansdon be the only one to profit from his ability to fuzz the cards?"

Augusta looked away, repelled. It amazed her that he had managed to hide his conscienceless side—that she had never glimpsed the shallowness that lay hidden within him.

"Any more questions, my dear?" Lord Wentworth's smile lacked any trace of warmth.

"What about the doctor at that duel? Who was he?" Her desperation grew.

"What you might call an associate of mine. A gentleman of French parentage, with whom you would not be acquainted. He is no longer in England, if you are concerned."

"What—" she began, but couldn't think of anything more to ask.

He nodded. "I am pleased to have been able to satisfy your curiosity. But now, my dear, I am very sorry for the necessity. You must see how it is—I cannot permit you to live with all you now know."

From his pocket, he drew a pistol and pulled back the hammer.

Chapter 25

Augusta cast a frantic glance in both directions, but saw no line of escape. Lord Wentworth, still smiling, raised the pistol and aimed at her heart. The soft click of the hammer sounded loud in the silence that engulfed them.

"No!" Kettering, with a strangled cry, launched himself against Lord Wentworth. The man staggered back from the impact, his hand coming up to fend off his attacker, but Kettering came in with a swinging right fist to his jaw. Wentworth caught his balance, threw off Kettering, and before the lieutenant could recover, jerked up the pistol and fired. Kettering slumped to the floor, blood seeping sluggishly from a hole in his forehead.

The paralysis that gripped Augusta evaporated and she dove for the front door, but the locked handle refused to turn. She swung around, panicked, to see Wentworth throw down the empty gun and start toward her. Heedless, she ran through the nearest open door and dragged it closed behind her. Blackness engulfed her, but she gripped the knob, holding it tight, and felt it move in her hands.

A deep laugh sounded from the other side and she heard the unmistakable sound of a bolt being thrown. She stepped back, startled, and nearly tumbled down a flight of stairs as her foot encountered nothingness in the dark. She caught herself on the rickety railing and her heart sank. Of all the possible rooms she could have ducked into, she had selected a cellar!

"There is no way out," Wentworth called to her. "I fear I must leave you for a little bit, my dear. But never fear. I will be back—and soon."

312

She heard his receding footsteps, punctuated by his self-satisfied chuckles. Trembling, she sank onto the top step. She had fallen first into Jack Kettering's trap, then another of her own making. Self-disgust filled her at her gullibility, only to vanish the next moment.

Jack . . . She closed out her mental picture of his fallen body. He had not been evil, only weak, she told herself firmly. In the end, he died trying to save her. She would remember that, and it would redeem him in her heart for his treachery.

The fragments of her spirit rallied together once more and she rose. She still had to save herself. She looked about, but could make out nothing in the darkness. Her eyes would accustom themselves to it, she knew, but she might not have the time to spare.

She gripped the rail beside her and carefully descended the thirteen steps to a cold stone floor. Following the side of the stair, she groped her way back to the wall and set about exploring the confines of her prison. Four paces brought her to the corner. Two more paces and she banged her shin on a broken chair.

She picked it up, testing its weight. One of the turned wooden legs came loose in her hand. She might be able to use it as a weapon. Carrying it, she stepped around the rest of the chair's remains and continued her search.

The room couldn't be more than ten by twenty feet, she decided at last. And it boasted not so much as a single window. Except for that one chair, it was empty. She returned to the steps and sank down on the bottom one, hefting her makeshift weapon while she thought.

Lord Wentworth might, of course, simply leave her there to starve. She forced that possibility from her mind. He would come back—he had to!—and when he did, she would be ready for him.

With new resolution, she mounted the steps. The doorway could be discerned by a thin line of light that outlined the frame. The top step was actually a landing, perhaps six feet square, which was why she hadn't simply pitched headlong down the stairs when she darted inside. That gave her plenty of room to maneuver. She lifted her weapon, ready to strike over the head the first person so unwise as to enter her little prison.

After about five minutes, she lowered the chair leg, her arms aching. She didn't really need to stand like that; she would hear him approach. She remained in position, far enough from the door so that it would not hit her if he threw it wide. One end of her weapon she let rest on the step.

A weary hour passed, and doubts assailed her. Still, she did not move. She would only have one chance—she dared not risk losing it. The minutes crept slowly by and she shifted her weight. Exhaustion, kept at bay by desperation, brought an unnerving lassitude to her muscles, inch by insidious inch. She hadn't slept in days, she was so very tired. . . .

A scraping noise outside the door recalled her wandering thoughts. She stiffened. The bolt squeaked in protest as it was drawn back, and Augusta raised her chair leg. The door slid open cautiously and a stealthy figure came forward. The flooding light behind him blinded her, but she swung with all the strength she could muster.

The blow went awry, striking the man's shoulder rather than his head, but she floored him. He rolled, caught the railing to break his fall, and slid feet first down the first three steps. The railing gave way and he tumbled to the bottom.

She would need the front door key to escape. . . . She hefted her club and ran after him, her footing clear in the dim light. She turned the limp figure over, and a cry of mingled horror and consternation escaped her.

"Edward!"

He had changed from his uniform, and a bulky, bloodstained bandage, wrapped about his left thigh, showed through a tear in his pantaloons. She sank down abruptly on the ground at his side as shock left her giddy.

Wentworth had told her the truth. Edward wasn't dead—unless she had done the job herself. She reached for his neck to check his vital artery as she had done so many times with the dying men in the last few days. It beat steadily and a sob of relief broke from her.

He groaned, his eyes opened, and he pulled himself into a sitting position. With difficulty, he focused on her. "What—" He raised a hand to his throbbing shoulder and swore softly. "You hit me!"

She nodded, unable to command her voice to speak. The next moment it was impossible. He dragged her against his chest with his good arm and kissed her soundly. "Thank God

314

ye are alive," he breathed against her hair at last.

Her shoulders trembled. "I—I could say the same about you. We heard you were killed at Quatre-Bras."

She felt him shake his head. "Most of us were. The lads fought bravely." His voice held an infinite sadness, but the peace of acceptance underlay it.

He would never have forgiven himself had he not fought at the side of his comrades, she realized. She slipped her arms around him, holding him tight, sharing his grief and pride.

The creak of the door proved their only warning. Lord Wentworth stood framed by the light behind him, holding a lantern high in his left hand. In his right he held a pistol. One glance proved sufficient to alert him to what had happened.

Edward threw Augusta sideways as Wentworth fired. He rolled, landing on his feet running, and rushed the stairs, tackling Lord Wentworth about the lower legs before the man could retreat. Wentworth collapsed forward, landing on Edward's outstretched body, and the lantern flew from his hand, crashing to the floor with a shattering of glass. Oil splattered, catching fire from the lantern's flame.

The two men tumbled to the stone floor at the foot of the stairs with Edward, miraculously, twisting from beneath and coming out uppermost. Wentworth might be the elder by twenty years, but Edward's leg and shoulder hampered him. The major landed his opponent a facer, but with a mighty heave, Wentworth threw him off and closed after him.

Augusta dove for the lantern, dragged her shawl from her shoulders, and smothered the rising flame. Her hand came away beading blood from a deep scratch from the shattered glass, but she paid it no heed. In the semidarkness, she sought her discarded chair leg, then turned back to the struggling men.

Edward, momentarily on top, freed an arm from Wentworth's grasp and swung hard, connecting with the other man's jaw in a sickening thud. Wentworth collapsed.

Edward sat back, his breath ragged. He jerked free the man's cravat and used it to secure his hands, then used his own to bind Wentworth's feet. He stood, wiping blood and sweat from his bruised face.

Augusta staggered toward him, the unneeded weapon dropping from her nerveless hands. He gathered her into his arms.

For one eternal minute she clung to him, then turned her face up for the kiss she wanted so desperately.

"Really, this is hardly the place for such goings-on."

The voice from the doorway startled them. Edward's arm tightened about her, protective. She grasped the lapel of his coat as she spun about to look.

Frederick Ashfield lounged negligently against the door-jamb, helping himself to a pinch of snuff. Lizzie stood at his side, watching her sister and Edward with extreme interest by the light of the lantern she held.

Edward sighed. "Can I not even propose in peace?" he demanded.

"Certainly." Ashfield shut his box with a snap and returned it to his pocket. "But not until you have satisfied our curiosity. What, for instance, are you doing here? We heard you were dead."

"Disappointed?" An amused light glinted in Edward's tired eyes.

"Not in the least, dear boy. Quite the otherwise, in fact. Bye the bye, young Lansdon has been brought in. He's in a pretty bad way, but they think he'll pull through."

"Oh, I am glad!" Augusta exclaimed, momentarily diverted. She had been staring at Edward's rugged but dirtied profile in a bemused manner since his comment about a proposal.

"You'll never believe it, Gussie," Lizzie chimed in. "Perry actually saved Captain Trent's life! That's how he got shot, standing over his fallen body."

Edward broke in smoothly. "I might ask what you are doing here."

"Oh, I didn't trust Kettering," Lizzie said simply. "He was too clean. So I followed you."

"Lizzie!" Augusta stared at her pragmatic sister in awe. "How *very* bright of you. I—I was too upset to really notice him."

Lizzie beamed. "You haven't noticed anything since we heard Edward was killed. Actually, I thought it was pretty bright, too. But then I heard something that sounded like a shot, and a few minutes later Lord Wentworth came out, and that didn't make any sense." The girl frowned. "Neither you nor Kettering appeared, and the door was locked. So I went for help. Frederick was assisting in the tent, you know, and I knew he'd come."

Edward nodded. "Good for you."

"And your story?" Ashfield raised an inquiring brow.

A low groan sounded behind him and Edward glanced over his shoulder. "All in good time. Ashfield, will you be a good fellow and have a look outside? Just wave your arms. One of my men must be back at his station by now." He released Augusta and knelt down beside his captive.

In a very few minutes, Ashfield returned with two soldiers at his heels. They drew Wentworth to his feet, secured him more efficiently, and conferred low-voiced with Edward. Augusta averted her face, not wanting to watch as they dragged the man out under guard.

"Your story," Ashfield prompted as the front door closed with a dull thud behind them. "Unless you would like to leave here?"

"In good time. This cellar seems an admirable place for discussions. So few people to interrupt," he said pointedly.

Lizzie ignored the obvious hint. She sat down on the top step and prepared to listen. "What happened?"

Edward sighed. "Where was I?"

"You hadn't begun yet." Lizzie propped her chin on her cupped hands.

He inclined his head. "We took part in a rather nasty engagement at Quatre-Bras. We tried to regroup, but there were so few of us left—there was so little we could do." He shook his head, then forced the haunting memory from his mind. "I was grazed in the leg—it looked worse than it really was. My colonel relieved me of command and ordered me to escort our wounded to Brussels. We got here just before dawn."

His arm, which encircled Augusta's waist, tightened. "I checked wih the men I'd left watching this place, and they said a meeting took place here during the night. There was no sign of anyone by the time I got here, so I went for some clean clothes and a few hours sleep." His jaw clenched. "My men awakened me with the news that Wentworth visited the house this afternoon, but that he left."

"You knew!" Augusta accused him. "Why didn't you warn me that Wentworth was behind this?"

"I told ye ye'd laugh at my suspicions."

"Get back to your story," Lizzie ordered.

"I couldn't return to the field with this," he gestured to his leg, "so I thought I'd look the house over for myself. Unfortunately I left the key I had made to this place with someone for safekeeping. I was forced to break in."

"I didn't hear you." Augusta protested.

He directed a pained look at her. "I'm rather good at it."

Augusta found it difficult to suppress a giggle. Her shoulders quivered, betraying her amusement at the prospect of the ever-respectable Edward engaged in the act of housebreaking—and because *she* possessed the key. He threw her a suspicious glance and she forced her face into an appropriately somber expression.

"I found Kettering's body in the hall," he continued after sternly holding her gaze for a moment. "After we'd checked the rest of the house, I made the mistake of allowing my assistants to take him away, thus leaving me alone. I hadn't expected to find anything in a bolted cellar." A grim smile just touched his lips. "I came in completely unprepared—another error, I admit—and faced a very worthy opponent. Miss Carstairs, ye swing a very nasty—what was it?"

"A chair leg."

"Good thinking." Lizzie approved of her sister's resourcefulness.

Warm color flooded Augusta's cheeks and she stammered an apology.

Edward smiled and drew her firmly against his side. "It is a matter I intend to discuss with ye. At considerable length." He dropped a kiss lightly on the top of her hair.

Augusta gazed up at him, a welter of emotions and sensations she barely recognized filling her. Breathing became extraneous, if not impossible because of the pounding of her heart.

"Oh, no!" Lizzie shook her head. "This is all I can take. I absolutely cannot support the sight of any more lovers this afternoon."

Ashfield smiled. "I find myself in complete agreement with you. Perhaps we should leave this besotted pair to continue alone."

"Quite right," Edward agreed. "Take yourselves off. We'll

318

manage much better without ye."

Ashfield took Lizzie's arm and led her toward the hall. "I will tell Mrs. Lansdon you will escort Augusta back shortly," he called over his shoulder.

The two departed, and silence filled the cellar for a long, pregnant moment. Augusta drew a shaky breath, breaking the spell. She gazed up into Edward's smiling face.

"Did—did you mean what you said?"

"About proposing?" He didn't pretend to misunderstand. "I had better, or ye will be deeply shocked by the manner in which I intend to kiss ye."

"But I am hopelessly unsuitable!" she protested. "You said so yourself!"

"And I am hopelessly ineligible, which is much worse." He grinned. "But I have no intention of letting that stop me. Halliford," he added as his lips brushed hers, "would be quite justified in calling me out if I did let it." He drew her even closer and she raised her face eagerly to his.

"My hopeless romantic," he murmured when he could speak again. "A staid Scotsman will be a sad trial to ye."

"You are exactly what I want." She pulled his head back to hers. His response left her incapable of speech—or even conscious thought—for several blissful minutes.

He released her at last. "Ashfield was quite right." His voice held a tremor of laughter. "This place may be private, but it is in every other way most unsuitable. My soul *must* be lacking in romance, to make ye an offer in such surroundings."

She shook her head, which rested comfortably against his shoulder. "It is quite delightful. I shall remember it fondly."

He chuckled. "My poor darling, ye are a hopeless case indeed."

"So I thought you knew. Are—are you quite certain you will not regret this?"

His smile slipped awry. "I tried to tell myself I would." He gazed down into her eyes and his slow smile returned, lighting his whole face. "The diplomats of Europe will be at your feet, and ye will add life and joy to even the most boring function."

She sighed in pure contentment. "My most *unromantic* lover," she whispered. She pulled back and looked up at him.

"What a husband I shall have! Adept at fuzzing cards and housebreaking."

"I knew ye wouldn't let me live that down." He sounded resigned.

"Perhaps I had better reconsider this." She touched his lips with her finger and he kissed it. "I will marry you on one condition."

"And that is?" Suspicion sounded rife in his voice.

"That you wear your kilt for our wedding."

His lip quivered but he straightened up in mock affront. "Madam, as a major of the 42nd Highland Regiment—"

"Retired," she thrust in.

"Retired," he agreed, his Scottish burr heavier with every word. "I wouldna' be wed in anything else."